BY THE SEA

Henry Gee

ReAnimus Press

Breathing Life into Great Books

ReAnimus Press
1100 Johnson Road #16-143
Golden, CO 80402
www.ReAnimus.com

Cover photograph copyright by Henry Gee

ISBN-13: 978-1500247942

First ReAnimus Press print edition: June, 2014

10 9 8 7 6 5 4 3 2 1

For Karl and Rinoko: A Wedding Present

Other books by Henry Gee:

Siege of Stars: Book One of The Sigil Trilogy
Scourge of Stars: Book Two of The Sigil Trilogy
Rage of Stars: Book Three of The Sigil Trilogy
The Science of Middle-earth

The Accidental Species
Jacob's Ladder
In Search of Deep Time
Before The Backbone
A Field Guide to Dinosaurs (with Luis. V. Rey)
Futures from Nature (ed.)
Shaking the Tree (ed.)
Rise of the Dragon (ed.)

When asked why he was out walking with a lobster at the end of a blue ribbon, the poet Gerard de Nerval (1808-1855) is believed to have replied "because it does not bark, and it knows the secrets of the sea".

Part One

1: Corridor of Shadows

Under your feet, the sea surges and rips. Spume like icy razors rakes your flesh.

"It's not the way you think, really, it isn't," he insists. The water, churning and milky, is up to your waist. He is a pale swine-thing, wispy hair aping the curled waves, spray fuming overhead like spittle from a galloping horse.

But at least it is marginally warmer beneath the waves, where the wind doesn't reach. You duck down, feel the dark foam lap over your shoulders, and so your rage towards him calms. You become icy, like this wind. Like this water.

"Oh, and I suppose you know how I think, do you? As if you care?"

You look towards the beach. The crowds, dressed up against the north wind, shining anonymously towards you on this shortest of days. A winter carnival, celebrating the Solstice. It is not, though, an attentive audience. All it sees are the intrepid Solstice Sea Bathers, recalling with forced seasonal jollity, and a few column inches in the *Deringland Mercury*, an ancient rite of this coast: a rite whose provisions have been long forgotten apart from the mere fact and longevity of the celebration, that it is a contract between the pliant Land and the unforgiving Sea. But not all is mirth, and the sea drowns all in its enveloping noise.

"We've been over this so many times. I have nothing to say".

"But I have seen you together", you mock: "so many times." Your reasoning deserts you, like the shifting sand beneath your feet.

"And your point is?" he replies, Oxbridgely arrogant. "Can I not associate with whom I wish?"

"Yes!" you scream, oblivious to all but him, him, your cries like the squawks of gulls. You hate yourself for it, the shrillness, and then, quietly, chastened: "yes, Evan, of course. But not … her."

He calms too, comes closer, looks down at you. You can smell the thick grease on his skin, proof against the chill. You can see it. It makes him look like a pithed frog.

"Look…" he begins.

Under your feet, the sea surges and rips. Something brushes against your calves.

"Look, Heather, I'm sorry you feel that way. But I'm afraid there is nothing I can do about it. I'm leaving soon. I have my life to lead, and so do you."

So, you look away. You see a dozen or so Solstice Sea Bathers, greased, like you, but unlike you (so unlike!) they are all men, all in briefs or boxers or flappy trunks. But there is one, alone, a little further out to sea. A woman.

It is *her*.

She is looking your way. Inquisitive, with concern. How dare she! And he has pretended not to notice. For a split instant you swear you could kill her.

No, kill *him*.

Under your feet, the sea surges and rips. It is a rip too far, a sudden high wave towers above your head, above his head, above her head, indeed, above you all, and crashes down. Your feet leave their moorings and you are buffeted by the cold sea, helpless, beneath the waves.

You open your eyes. Yes, if only for a fraction of a second, but it feels much longer, and in that long moment you have a glimpse into water of almost infinite clarity, of a world flattened between sand and surface, stretching outward to a greater blueness.

And there are shapes out there, moving in the blue.

You regain your footing, thrust your head above the surface into the now, the new-minted coldness, and, like you all, like him, like her, you struggle to the shore. The sea tastes bitter in your mouth. Bitter, and warm.

All she can now see are her knees, flexed, together forming something like a gun-sight for the arched window beyond, its white sashes sharp against the night.

She had seen that window before. It was that painting, *American Gothic*, and now she sees the kindly and pious farmer (with the little round glasses and the pitchfork) and the even more God-fearing farmer's wife (with the pursed lips and buttoned-up collar) from that painting, now standing one either side of the window, each one a guardian to a knee at the foot of her iron-framed bed (yes, it *is* iron-framed, she knows that now, as befits a Victorian maternity wing, which this is) as she strains and strains to get this—this *thing* - out of her womb.

And then, pure release: blood pours out of her to soak the bed, but she does not care. The farmer's wife reaches down as the farmer looks benignly on and smiles. The farmer's wife comes back up, now dressed in a theater gown and thick blue rubber gloves, with a squalling infant clothed in a towel. The farmer's wife betrays no change in expression from the thin-lipped and Presbyterian, as if she is not a real person but a cardboard cut-out, or a mask.

"Oh, Alex, well *done!*" says the farmer, his eyes sparkling behind the glasses. As he bends over her he notices that he isn't as bald as she thought, but has long wisps of gray hair, and in fact he has no glasses at all. She recognizes him as the baby's father. He is her husband, not the husband of the starchy farmer's wife. But she's not married … is she? Panic. She struggles to remember his name. Is it 'Evan'? Or perhaps 'Evanston'?

The farmer looks down at what the farmer's wife is holding in her hands, now holding up for inspection.

"Oh! Alex! It's a… it's a …" The farmer, whose name might be Evan or Evanston, turns a uniform dead-flat gray and turns away.

The farmer's wife looks at her. Her expression now changes … or, rather, not so much changes, but dissolves.

"Here is your baby, Alex," she says, her voice surprisingly deep, but compressed, as if heard from the far end of a telephone. Her mouth opens. There are a lot of teeth in it. In fact, Alex thinks, if she opened that huge mouth any further it would cover her entire face.

"Here is your baby, Alex," repeats the farmer's wife in the same harsh monotone, her tongue moving behind her teeth. "Look at your baby, Alex," she insists, thrusting out a nameless object dwarfed by those same, thick, blue rubber gloves. "Just run it up the flagpole, see if anyone salutes. You've got to roll it out now, Alex. You have targets to meet. *Look* at it, Alex. It's all your fault."

She, herself, that is, Alex, is gripped by a sudden urge to look at the baby, and an equal and opposite urge *not* to look at it. The negative wins, and she feels she has been spared something horrific. Instead she looks up at the insistent face of the farmer's wife. But she has changed: the blonde bun has gone. She is a man, with slick black hair, and a business suit. But still those same thick blue rubber gloves. And those teeth. And that smile. "Look at the baby, Alex. It's all your fault."

Alex whimpers, wakes and sits up in bed. The noise batters immediately in from all sides, for a storm is blowing, rain blasting at her dormer window. She switches on her bedside light. Her arm is assailed by chill the moment she extends it from the beneath the duvet. The action seems to drive away the noise, to create a small primeval pool of security. But the bulb glows weakly through the pinkish, tasselled shade that reminds her of old ladies' knickers. It is a mockery of light, and looking up, all she can now see in its womb-glow are her knees, flexed, together forming something like a gun-sight for the arched window beyond, its white sashes sharp against the night.

She had seen that window before. It was that painting, *American Gothic*. But there are no others here. No kindly, bespectacled farmer. No starchy farmer's wife. She is quite alone, and for that she is grateful. She exhales a damp cloud into the room. As she does this, the ghostly walls and high ceilings of the Victorian hospital close in on her to make a room that is smaller but much more real. She rubs her stomach. It is not bloated and sore, but flat, or at least no more rounded than she has a right to expect for a 22-year-old woman who has never been pregnant. She sits up further, relieved, steeling herself against the night, the draughts that seep into her room through the rattling panes, shreds of nightmare scattering off her duvet like scraps of Christmas paper, torn in haste from gifts and soon forgotten.

Her room. Her room, here at the Institute.

The arched and sashed window is a dormer in the room which itself is a hived-off corner of one of the huge attics. She remembers how she cannot open the window fully, because a crumbling iron gutter, now gurgling with a load of water it cannot contain, runs right across its width, splashing greenish onto the steep pitch of the roof below.

Apart from the bed there is an office chair and a cheap deal desk piled with papers and books; and a wardrobe, over-ornate by comparison with the desk, a mahoganized excrescence of the kind found readily in cheap antique shops, because nobody really wants them. It is too large for the room. She has sometimes wondered how they got it up the steep stairs and narrow corridor. Perhaps it had always been there, grown *in situ* from the skewed walls and warped rafters of the creaking building. Accommodation for scullery-maids or junior post-doctoral fellows: the names may change, she thought, but the social position never varies.

Under the arch-pointed dormer window is a tiny kitchenette, equipment for a postdoctoral fellow where once stood a washstand for a scullion. There is a gas ring, a small and never-quite-cleanable fridge, a collapsing melamine-and-chipboard cupboard for food and crockery, and an aluminium sink. Bathroom facilities are next door, down a narrow hall.

Alex looks at her bedside clock. It is hardly two in the morning. She has no desire to go back to sleep now, for fear of blundering into *American Gothic* again, even though the details of the dream are now fading into a washed-out sepia. Even then, the storm howling outside would probably keep her awake. That, and the unplottable howling from the organ-pipe plumbing. And she can hear that drip again, from a corner of the dormer, splashing stern, rusty drops into the sink. That settles it: against such nocturnal orchestrations there can be no victory. She decides to get up instead. The thunder of water re-minds her that she needs to go to the loo, and that she is thirsty. So she swings her legs out from under the duvet and plants her feet on the threadbare rug, a comfort of home to hide the frigid linoleum floor.

Alex Beach. That's Doctor Alex Beach, yes it's 'Alex', never 'Alex-andra', because that would make 'Sandy', and, well maybe it's no surprise she swerved from the life of busy biochemistry, doctorate newly-minted, and into marine biology and this ... backwater. Per-haps if she'd never met Morrison at that conference last summer in Atlanta, she'd have stayed on the straight and narrow of biochemis-try, with its order, its measure, and its cleanliness. *Damn* Morrison for his targets and indicators and, well, being so ... persuasive. If not for Morrison, she bit her lip until a tear started, she'd never have been exiled to the Lowdley-Purslane Institute, stuck out here in north Nor-folk, practically at the ends of the Earth: literally so, being perched on the very edge of a cliff. She might even be getting on with her career, in a lab with contacts, or at least people. Damn it, and damn *him*, she might even be doing something useful.

Alex sits up, the smooth arcs of her white body pinked by the lampshade's glow, silent against the noise of the wind and rain. And then she stands, looking down at herself, and then at her reflection in the mirror on the front of the unavoidable wardrobe. Her large, round gray eyes and short, brown bob stare back at her from her pale face, inquisitorially, and stooping slightly, because of her height: Alex Beach is almost six feet tall. She grabs a sweatshirt from the end of the bed and shucks it over her head. In so doing she looks down at her legs, then her knees, and has a stomach-churning flashback to her dream, in full technicolor clarity, if only for a fraction of a second.

She sits down again.

Her dream was one of guilt, guilt at what she has let herself become. Within months she has turned from a hopeful career prospect in biochemical natural-product synthesis to a Sex Object, a brood mare, captive at this dreadful place as a focus of men's desires, as much a part of the collections as … well, as Pickled Lily.

With a rising gorge she remembers how Evanston Bland keeps looking at her breasts and her legs and making comments. That is, when Bland is not fighting off the attentions of that Heather Franks creature, who curls up in on herself in another attic room not too far away. Alex takes a deep breath as she reminds herself that she really ought to be able to handle such things by now. Her legs were always long, and her height has always put her breasts within easy male staring range. In any case, Bland will be leaving soon, or so he says, now that Morrison has taken over his job as Institute Director.

Oh God … Morrison. His ideas for rolling out new, re-synthetic natural products. His contacts at MagusPharm that led to her fellowship, buying her. Resource acquisition. Drug discovery. Secrets of the Sea. And none more Secret than at the LPI. And she, fresh from a PhD and a career for the making. Or the taking. There is nothing for it. She has made her bed, she muses, turning to straighten the duvet, and so she must lie in it. Do the work, fulfil the contract, get out, move on. She puts on her slippers and pads into the horrid, white-chipped, never-quite-cleanable bathroom.

Now dressed in jeans, Nikes, sweatshirt and flask of tea, Alex pads from her attic study-bedroom onto the varnished boards of the corridor outside. It is barely 2.19, but she is wide awake. The lonely life of a postdoctoral fellow in a team of one, at work on her own strange *cul-de-sac* of a project, has shaken her free of the companionship of lab work she'd been used to until six months before, the social norms that dictate the conventional routine of the diurnal cycle. She has decided that she will work until breakfast on those Victorian microscope slides, drawing, taking notes; grab some food from the refectory, and then return to her eyrie to ravel sleep. Despite her conscious misgivings about her situation, the work has its attractions and is beginning to draw her down like a dark undertow.

She commutes from 'home' to 'work', threading her way through the enormous shadowed building as surely as filaria through the limbs of an elephantiasiac.

First: there is the corridor under the eaves themselves, boards creaking beneath her feet in sharp, woody exclamations; rain arrowing into the slates just inches above her head as she stoops through too-low attic doors, squeezing past many other attic doors and grimed cases removed from exhibitions and long since forgotten. A ruff forever displaying before a reeve, with blown eggs. Shells of giant tortoises, each endemic to an island of which she has never heard, Antilia, Santanazes, Saya, Ymana, each one long extinct in the wild. Skeletons of fetuses in various stages of development, artfully arranged around preserved coral. The baculum or penis-bone of a walrus, as long and dense as a baseball bat and probably as effective, mounted lovingly on a carved wooden plinth (she can't help thinking of Morrison here, as what he lacks in size he makes up for in brutality). A cat with some advanced intestinal infestation, sliced through sagittally, and mounted against glass, so one can see concentric circles of cat and worm, cat and worm, compelling as patterns on polished agate. All cast woolly shadows from the sparse bulbs screwed at intervals into sconces in the walls and eaves.

At the case containing that something-or-another, mercifully unseeable by virtue of the accumulated dust, and cracks in the thick glass liberally patched with old parcel tape, she turns left, along a short corridor from whose ceiling hangs, uvulous, a brass chandelier shaped like an astrolabe; and then almost tumbles down a series of narrow, precipitous stairs.

First, they wind, as if just inside ancient stone walls, painted a bald white but peeling psoriatically in the all-penetrating damp.

Although illuminated from high, blue-stained windows during the day, the too-narrow, carpeted treads themselves remain in dense shade. She found this disconcerting when she was new, but after a while her feet learned to pilot their way on their own, so the sensation was less one of climbing or falling, but of floating through blue holes drilled deep in a reef.

The curving stair tightens into an anxious knot amid rafters and beams that jut from walls and corners like the ribs of a decomposing whale; but then, quite suddenly, the staircase straightens out: but is made narrower still, as the walls on both sides, and some of the ceilings beneath which she is forced to stoop, are festooned with bookcases. These are stuffed with volumes she is sure no-one ever sees, for none ever seem to be moved.

The books are wedged in with bookends of a most bewildering variety. African masks; preserved heads; assorted fossils; fragments of marble pediment; brass instruments of unfathomable purpose, all lenses and dials and knurled wheels. And there are things suspended in spirit whose jars she never dares brush against for fear of breaking them and disgorging the contents so that once released, they would follow the splashes of the once-suspending fluid and slop, glutinously, down the stairs before her.

Ah yes, *things*. The Institute has so many *things*, the esoteric strandline refuse of the ages, cast up from wide oceans of ignorance before our wondering eyes. Alex is as personally untidy as any other young scientist, but the Institute comes as a shock to one used to the uncluttered lines of a modern laboratory. It is the shock of diseased floridity, of almost obscene extravagance. It is like the once-respectable citizens in a Hogarth painting who have abandoned themselves to gin and whoring.

It is like an outbreak of new leprosy.

At one point on a half-landing, the left-hand wall of the stairwell vanishes entirely for a spell of no more than three or four feet, bridged by a guard rail at shin-height, giving a vertiginous view of a corridor below, hung with a once-rich but faded tapestry showing what look like scenes of dismemberment. The lower edge of the tapestry fades into the unseen gloom of the floor, whence a vast stuffed animal looms upwards. Alex has never wanted to stay long enough on this perch to learn what this animal might be, clothed as it is in a shapeless mass of black fur. All she remembers are huge, accusing eyes that seem to follow her with unblinking gaze as she bridges the catwalk above, gripping the bookshelf to her right and trying not to trip on the low rail and fall into the chasm.

Alex has searched for an entrance to this corridor at floor level, but she has never found it.

The stairway continues past this void, stuffed with bookshelves, bookends, and the books between. She knows that just part a shelf straining to hold, frustratingly, just eleven of a twelve-volume *Records of the Natural History and Antiquities of Anchester, Radnorshire*, the stair-case takes a downward lurch to the right and debouches between two vast portraits of nameless eighteenth-century worthies, nameless be-cause their heads ascend into the gloom, into a broad corridor on the ground floor of the building.

She turns left and walks in the centre of this wide corridor, throw-ing her long arms wide to left and right, glorying in its wide spaces after the contortions of the staircases. The corridor is punctuated to right and left with grand entrances. By day these are brightly lit by the cold north light. By night, brass chandeliers bearing dim, candle-style bulbs, many of which have long since expired, shed a sickly light that fails to reach the further corners of the great space.

To her left, the landward side, great square archways give access to the public galleries; each door, as she passes, giving no more than an unlit hint of the attractions within. By day, these galleries host occa-sional stray visitors, refugees from the Deringland wind and rain who have nothing better to do than to gawp at the curiosities the Lowdley-Purslane Institute has to offer; and the gaggles of excited schoolchil-dren who, steered by their teachers past Kitten Hell, gurn and giggle at Pickled Lily. Alex prefers to avoid the public galleries by day. Even more so by night, when the play of shadow and light on the exhibits is unsettling.

To her right and seaward are the rooms used by the Institute's small cadre of resident scientists; the common room and the refectory. The common room is immense, cheerless and rarely used. The furni-ture, mainly second-hand old sticks and the occasional half-sunk chesterfield, is dwarfed by height of the room, the monumental cor-nicing and plasterwork. The room is always cold: the enormous, cast-iron radiators can never adequately heat this vast north-facing space, because the huge, single-glazed windows quickly suck out such feeble warmth as they can produce. The fireplace, once so grand, is blind, boarded up during the war as an economy measure and never re-claimed. But the views over the sea through the wide windows are as magnificent as those enjoyed by a guillemot perching on the very teeth of the cliffs. She can hear the storm now, like thunder against the rocks below, almost as if she were right in it. The waves hurl sand and grit at the panes, but she can see nothing: the electric sconces burn low, and the windows are covered with thick velvet curtains which by day are deep maroon. At night, they are black as squid ink.

The refectory, in a room just as vast as the common room, has similarly good views, and such make its interior yet more dismal. It is furnished with modern tables and chairs of a quite calculating mean-ness, given the architecture (it had once been a ballroom). On one side is a counter, staffed, very grudgingly, three times a day, by reluctant part-timers serving generic overpriced snacks and tepid stodge to such scientists and members of the public desperate enough to avail themselves of its services.

At 2.27 a.m., the refectory is closed, the common-room unpopu-lated, and Alex walks the wide avenue, charting a course straight along its meridian spine. As with everywhere else in the Institute, every spare inch of wall space is crowded with specimens: this corri-dor, however, has exhibits commensurate with the scale of the spaces they inhabit.

On each side, between doors and beside and beneath windows, are more glass-and-darkwood cases, some of them huge, depicting geol-ogy, fossils, exquisite glass models of microscopic creatures of the plankton expanded to the size of footballs, each case surmounted by mounted trophy heads and antlers of the number and density to make a true stampede of beheaded carnage; there are detailed dioramas of life on land and at sea during every age of the Earth; and vast antiqui-ties. Broken columns, parts of temples raided; menacing totem poles depicting potlatches from the violent edges of Pacific prehistory, each towering toplessly into shadow; Egyptian gods seated in splendour, and gods of other cultures she cannot identify. She tries not to look too closely at one vast seated figure, carved in what looks like green-ish soapstone, of a god that looks like nothing so much as a giant toad. There is something repulsive in its curves, its lines, but what disturbs her is that she cannot quite put her finger on what it is, pre-cisely, that is so repellent.

The corridor ends in a series of broad, marble steps leading down to the mosaic-floored entrance hall, which has but one exhibit: a statue of the Institute's founder, Sir Frideric Lowdley-Purslane (1776-1845), Carrara marble on a gray granite plinth. The statue is thrown in a weirdly rotating shadow, for it is here, through the thick stained-glass of the Institute's immense front doors, that one can trace the yellow beams of the Deringland Light, just a few hundred yards along the clifftops, and slightly inland. As the beams glance in rhythm on the image of Sir Frideric, they create a kind of slow-motion strobe effect. As Alex walks past the statue, she is convinced that, seen out the corner of one eye, it moves.

Alex turns left and down a small flight of stairs that grazes Sir Frideric's plinth, and confronts a green-painted fire door marked 'Private, Staff Only'. She gets out a set of keys, unlocks the door, and arrives in a familiar world. It is 2.31 a.m., and she sighs with relief.

At no time during her ten-minute hike has she met another living person.

She has not been at the Institute quite long enough to take for granted that she can now get from attic to basement without getting lost. Her first few days were a nightmare, often literally so, as her mind would replay her mishaps in anxious dreams of hopeless mazes. The Institute is, however, nightmare incarnate, tuberculous with fractal corridors and Escherian staircases which all looked the same to Alex until she could learn the landmarks, each of which was, inevitably, something stuffed, or half-seen in a glass case; to each of which she stood in immediate debt, praying that it would not move to a different place between one journey and the next, mocking her still-fragile grasp of the building's mazy geography. In this way the landmarks became more than zoological curios, but household gods, worthy of votive offerings and prayers, silent but knowing keepers of secrets. They would watch her closely as she passed by.

2: The Night Intruder

Cellars had been drilled deep beneath the Lowdley-Purslane Institute on the landward side. The cellarage was once vast, and not all of it completely explored, for episodic landfalls and floods within the friable cliffs had made caverns of some of it, and blocked off much more.

But in the early years of the last war, as part of the scientific effort to develop radar on a stretch of a coastline teeming with Spitfires and Hurricanes, some of the cellars were reclaimed and made into the underground laboratory complex Alex now enters. Beyond the thick green fire-door she finds a wide, well-lit corridor pinioned with conduits and cabling, computers and centrifuges, and mercifully free from the cabinets that record the jackdaw obsessions of Sir Frideric. This is a part of the building to which Sir Frideric never came, and from which he is, in a sense, barred: it is the scientific part, a haven of rationality in the distended belly of Georgian excess. Only here does Alex feel content.

Doors to right and left signal the presence of laboratories. A single door at the end, marked with a variety of hazard signs, gives entrance to the spirit store, and the bulk of the collections from the Victorian survey vessel HMS *Spaniel*, some of whose specimens form the subjects of Alex's current research.

Alex turns immediately, to the first door on the left, unlocks her own laboratory, enters, and closes the door carefully behind her. This laboratory can accommodate two postdoctoral researchers in comfort, three at a squeeze; but she is the only one currently in residence, the only name on the door above two vacant spaces. How different it seems from her draughty attic room, thrust like a hangnail into the heart of the storm. Here the storm cannot be heard, replaced instead by the hum of mechanical contentment, the whirr of compressors behind freezers, the purr of hard-disk drives. Here, all is clean; all is bright; all is warm. And it is hers, solely. She perches on a stool in front of a microscope (her own microscope, which she brought here from Cambridge, bought with her own grant), as cleanly silver-gray as the worktop on which it rests.

Sitting next to the microscope is a box of slides, hardwood with brass catches, in which rest forty-eight neat rectangles of glass in two ordered rows of two dozen each, each slide in its own machined slot. Alex loves the order of it; that each slide is numbered with a printed label ('HMS *Spaniel*, 1831-1836'), and precisely recorded in fine India ink in ledgers kept in the Institute Library, with its contents, the stains used, the initials of the preparator, and the date. It gives her hope, that there can, after all, be found an island of predictability within the careless chaos of the Institute's collections.

But no science progresses by standing on the edge of chaos and looking inwards. For the objects on the slides are puzzling. Her aim is nothing less than to solve that puzzle, to venture a little way from the islet of the known and deliver answers, preferably ones that can be made into neatly publishable packages, gift-wrapped with bows round them for her patrons.

The sea that clothes more than two-thirds the Earth's surface is the least known of any part of the planet, with a biological diversity that makes a pygmy of the more celebrated rainforest. The ocean contains more different kinds of animals and plants than the rest of the world can offer, and many of these creatures are, and always have been, exclusively marine. Nothing like them ever appears on the shore, or near it.

As a result, the things we know of the sea are acquired infrequently, in half-snatches of knowledge and bolstered by much guesswork. The few facts generally known about most marine things penetrate no further into the general consciousness of Man than the dusty ends of zoology textbooks, where they remain largely unread, even by students of zoology. The wider public knows nothing of this diversity whatsoever.

And even those few scientists who know of the existence of such things, even if they had not seen them in person, might legitimately ask what is known for *certain* of most marine life, especially of creatures living at depths too great for light or scuba-divers to penetrate.

The answer is very little, because such creatures are hard to find, the subjects of enigmatic photographs taken in the harsh lights of deep-sea probes, or caught infrequently in nets by uncomprehending fishermen; or hoisted from deep-sea trawls, the results bloody and uninterpretable from explosive decompression, after having been pulled through thousands of fathoms into realms which, for them, are the edges of space. One marine biologist famously likened our knowledge of the deep to what an aerial civilization might learn of human life, were its methods to consist solely of lowering the occasional skyhook to street level, and rootling around for anything it might pick up. A trash can. A bicycle. Roadkill. Almost nothing would or could be learned of the normal course of human life, just as almost nothing is known of the residents of the deep sea.

Even today, when scientists have peered behind every tree in the remotest jungles on land, they are still startled to learn of the strandings of whales of species hitherto unknown to science. These are not small creatures, but animals the size of cars.

Who knows what other secrets the sea might contain?

To explore the secrets of the sea: that was Sir Frideric Lowdley-Purslane's avowed mission when he came to Deringland to set up the Institute that bears his name. Sir Frideric used his influence, and his wealth, to add the most interesting and remarkable examples of marine life to his already famous cabinet of curiosities. It was natural, then, for survey vessels of the early nineteenth century to deposit their collections here, for the expertise that Sir Frideric had assembled to curate and preserve such things was unequalled, anywhere in the world.

The jewel in the crown was the immense collection from the five-year Pacific voyage of HMS *Spaniel*, which included creatures never encountered before, and very seldom since. Alex Beach is here to study a tiny fraction of this remarkable collection.

But there are motivations beyond mere knowledge. For marine creatures have biochemistries that can do incredible things. That there are ascidia, for example, humble, sponge-like encrustations on rocks, that gather exotic metals such as chromium and vanadium into their skins: atom by atom, from seawater. Nobody knows how, let alone why, but they do this with an elegance and economy as yet unmatched by the energetically wasteful fires and smokes of human technology. Just as the ancients thrilled at the ability of molluscs to produce Imperial Purple that no human dyer could recreate, there are creatures of the sea that produce biologically active compounds of a subtlety and complexity that defy the efforts of the most skilled human biochemists to synthesize.

For this reason, people are attracted to the sea with less pure motives than edification alone. The sea, or some obscure organism from the depths, might yield the next new wonder-drug to relieve the rich and profligate of their high blood pressure; the poor of their malaria, their AIDS; the elderly of their cancer, their dementia, or of death itself. To these ends the sea has a diversity that can be explored, tapped, wrapped, sold.

That is why Dr Alex Beach is here.

MagusPharm, a company set up with the explicit aim of trawling the sea for new drug-discovery opportunities, has contracted her, through Morrison, to investigate a small and utterly obscure group of microscopic marine worms called carnostomids. The drug company that can exploit material of interest from these almost-unknown creatures will steal a march on the competition.

Alex knows little of her sponsors. She has heard rumors that they have built their prospects on a powerfully psychoactive substance extracted from a marine creature, identity shrouded by thickets of legality. She knows little, therefore, hardly more than a name - 'Tube-Wave'. She asked Morrison about this once, at the hotel bar at that conference in Atlanta, but he brushed it off as gossip and changed the subject.

Carnostomids are so obscure that nothing is known about even the most basic features of their anatomy beyond what is contained in short reports written by scientists immediately after the *Spaniel* expedition returned, and which, it seems, they were very keen to abandon after the most cursory sketches. All known examples of carnostomids are here, at the LPI, and no reference to carnostomids is made in even the most comprehensive zoology textbooks. What knowledge, what opportunities, might not await the researchers with the wit to study even the basics of these long-neglected animals?

So, before she can do any biochemistry, which is what she knows and loves best, Alex must investigate the basics of anatomy - something unfamiliar, a subject hardly touched since she was a schoolgirl and which she has always secretly despised as yesterday's science. She must reacquaint herself with animals as whole creatures, not fractionated preparations, looking at them as the Victorians must have done. Much to her surprise, she finds this way of working immediately fascinating and wonders why she had shunned it.

A reason soon suggests itself, however: with modern laboratory science, there is no aspect that cannot be regulated, controlled. At its basics, though, biology is no more than a journey of discovery, and one cannot know what one might run into around the next corner. Alex soon realizes that the world is immensely, perhaps unknowably vast, against which one's own self is infinitesimally small, weak and powerless.

It is this, she suspects, which is why she finds the LPI as a whole, with its air of insouciant biological abundance, quite so disconcerting. And the same reason, perhaps, why she finds her current work so unexpectedly absorbing. For is this not what science is all about, not a series of well-coiffed routines elaborating what is known, but a seat-of-pants thrill-ride into darkness? Although she is sometimes brought up short with the vertigo of the unknown, she has learned to appreciate it as a cool, refreshing wind, the kind of breeze one notices, on a sudden, blowing up from the sea, after hours of confinement in a too-hot room.

Alex pours herself a cup of tea from her thermos and sets to work, doing science at the most basic but in many ways the most informative level, that is, pure observation. Slide after slide she mounts; showing the pink-stained outlines of the tiny worms, each no more than a few tenths of a millimeter long, and which seem to have a curious discordance in structure.

Half the body, the longer, wormlike half (she has come to think of it as the 'back' half), appears to be an unstructured bag of cells. Just a bag, with no internal organs, not even anything as simple as a digestive tube with an anus at the end. There are no external features, either - no fins, no spines, nothing - just a smooth membrane to keep the cells from dispersing. A structure so simple that the lowliest grade of polyp would outpace it in structural sophistication.

The 'front' half of a carnostomid could hardly be more different: small and dense, it is intricate and complex and looks like nothing so much as a dragon-mask of the kind paraded through the streets at the Chinese New Year.

The 'head' of all carnostomids (she knows that the designation is prejudicial, but here it seems unavoidable) has a pair of prominent, pigment-rich structures (she tries hard not to think of them as 'eyes'), connected to what can only be a brain of formidable intricacy, given the general simplicity of the animal.

Most prominent, however, are the teeth. There are always thirty-two of these, arranged in two occluding, bow-shaped jaws. The teeth are compact and covered in enamel. This tissue is unmistakable under a microscope, and cross-sections reveal its crystalline structure in slide after slide.

The problem is, Alex has learned, is that enamel is only found in vertebrates, creatures with bony skulls and backbones, creatures such as fishes, and mammals, and humans. Carnostomids, however, are far too simple, and have no trace of a skull or a backbone, or indeed, any bone at all, apart from that which supports the enamel in these enigmatic teeth. Teeth which look just like human teeth, mounted in human jaws, albeit on the microscopic scale. Alex remembers one slide in particular in which a carnostomid is caught, as it were, face on. It looked like it was grinning. No, laughing.

The laughter of a death's head.

It is no wonder that the *Spaniel* scientists abandoned carnostomids almost as soon as they had seen them. Even in the years before Darwin and evolution, they were monsters, and literally so, each one an affront to common-sense. How could it be that an animal should show such simplicity and such complexity together, in the same body? The carnostomid head showed all the refinement of the vertebrate head, with its complex brain and jaws, albeit on a very small scale. Alex looks forward to preparing some of the specimens from the spirit store, to reveal signs of head- or brain-specific genes that would prove this vertebrate affinity. In the arcane world of such genetic abbreviations, *Pax*, *Otx*, *Hox*, she'd feel truly at home.

But such a result would only deepen the conundrum. For attached to the head was a back end that was as primitive as could be imagined. The delicate teeth and jaws of carnostomids gave entrance to - nothing. It was as if carnostomids were microscopic fakes, playful fusions of the front ends of tiny fishes with the simple roving larvae of sponges. Alex laughs when she thinks of this: how typical that would be of the LPI, whose most famous specimens (the ones that feature most prominently in the literature available free from the Deringland Public Library) are 'mermaids', Georgian and Victorian taxidermic sports created from fishes and monkeys, and in which Sir Frideric displayed an abiding (some might say almost pathological) interest. Just as the LPI contained the best (indeed, the only) collection of carnostomids in the world, it could also boast unrivalled exhibitions of taxidermatous mischief.

There had to be a more serious explanation, Alex wonders. Who'd want to fake thousands of carnostomids, not just the ones prepared on these slides, but the creatures suspended in alcohol which she'd sampled from the spirit store? And more to the point, why? Such careful micro-forgery would be beyond the capability of a modern microsurgeon, let alone naturalists on the cramped and lurching deck of an early nineteenth-century sailing ship.

She ratchets her thoughts back a few notches, forming a mental picture of the simple, larvae of other marine creatures. Might carnostomids not be adult animals, but the larvae of something else?

Something, perhaps, quite different?

The shock of this intuition hits her with a kick that makes her sit up. If carnostomids are larvae, that would explain something about their curious mixture of simplicity and sophistication. Perhaps the brain, the eyes, the jaws, are there simply to anchor a worm-like animal to some convenient rock, so it can metamorphose into an adult of unguessable form? It is not such a far-fetched idea: Alex has lately read about some of the tunicates, distant cousins of vertebrates, which as adults are simple, blind bags that filter seawater, but which as larvae have tiny but fully-formed heads with sense organs, tails and complex brains, but no digestive systems at all. The larvae use their senses to guide them to suitable rocks, their tails to propel them there, and having arrived, they lose these structures and develop, instead, into an adult that consists almost entirely of a digestive system, as if to compensate for its earlier deficiency.

Yes, carnostomids are the larvae of something. But what? She smiles, inwardly, ruefully: the literature of marine biology is peppered with records of creatures that could be the larvae of other creatures, but linking larva and adult is often extremely difficult. For life in the sea is often sequestered by age. Larvae of many marine creatures are often tiny, transparent and microscopic, drifting in the sunny surface waters of the ocean. Until, that is, some occult signal is given for change, when the larvae undergo startling metamorphoses to produce the adult residents of the very different world of the deeps. The efforts of early zoologists to link larvae and adults were often heroic. Alex suspects that in carnostomids she has just one part of a more complicated story. Discovering the rest might not be a trivial problem.

Alex rips her gaze from the eyepieces, sits up and stretches. It is 3.15 a.m., she has been staring at microscope slides for a solid half-hour, and it is time to refocus and pour herself another cup of tea.

She hears something strange, though, in mid-pour. The sound is nothing dramatic, and more of an absence, an interruption in the all-enveloping laboratory background hum. Holding her breath, Alex strains to hear more, and, hearing nothing, tries to categorize what she had just heard. A kind of wheezy gurgle, and then a thump, from outside the laboratory, in the corridor. Damn it, she thinks, one of the fridges in the corridor had been faulty, something wrong with the compressor. She thought it had been fixed. Even though it has nothing directly to do with her, she feels she ought to take a look. If it is the fridge she thinks it is, it contains some of Garry Williams' hydroid preparations, which would soon be ruined if they edged up towards room temperature. She helped Garry prepare them before he flew back to California for Christmas. She recalls how she allowed the grizzled Emeritus Professor to boss her around as if she were just one of his graduate-student teaching assistants back at Berkeley. But Garry has a twinkle in his eye. Oh, to be sure, he's an exploitative martinet, just like Evanston Bland. And yet so unlike, more a loveable rogue. Whenever she thinks of Garry, she can't help smiling. She likes Garry. She'll check.

So she puts down her teacup, half-drunk, on the bench next to the microscope. She slides off her stool, pads to the door, and puts her head round, into the harsh light of the empty corridor. Nothing. Just the usual whirr, not the grumble of a compressor straining on the edge of failure.

So she decides to take a better look, and as she walks over to the fridge, she is gripped by a strange premonition (*American Gothic*) that the fridge will be fine, and she will find out something ... well, something else. Her skin crawls with a sudden hot chill.

The fridge in question, the one that had malfunctioned but which is now, purportedly, fixed, hums with all the mocking, nonchalant smoothness of all well-run machines. Nothing is wrong. Alex decides to look inside the fridge, just to check (the kindly and pious farmer, the one with the little round glasses and the pitchfork) but despite premonitory terror, all Garry's vials are there, lined up in plastic-coated wire-framed racks. Just where she'd put them. Puzzled, she closes the door, and looks up, and along the corridor.

That's odd. She notices that a door at the end of the corridor, on the same side as hers but at the far end, next to the door to the spirit store, is ajar, and a light streams out. That's Evanston Bland's room. ("Oh, Alex, well done!" says the farmer, his eyes sparkling behind the glasses). Alex is no longer seized with terror alone, but an even worse combination, terror mixed with indecision. Perhaps that noise was just Dr Bland doing something or other? But what was he doing here, at this graveyard hour? Bland is never seen much before the morning coffee break at ten-thirty, and is always gone by four in the afternoon. So perhaps, she thinks, it's not Bland, but someone else, an intruder?

She wonders if she shouldn't raise the alarm on her mobile. But if whoever-it-is is Bland, she'll look silly, and if it isn't, she'll give herself away. There is nothing for it but to sidle silently along the wall to Bland's room and look in.

As she approaches Bland's office, she becomes aware of the silence. Nothing stirs from his room, no hushed voices, no play of torch beams, nothing. Perhaps whoever-it-was swept through while she was engrossed in her own work? She shudders, thinking of her vulnerability, and stops, gathering her breath, and her courage. She has now reached the hinge of the door, now the lip. (She struggles to remember his name). She peers round, and sees a pair of Oxford-brogued feet, attached to linen-trousered legs, stretched out stiffly on the floor, the rest of the body disappearing behind a desk. (Is it 'Evan'? Or perhaps 'Evanston'?)

Alex rushes into the room. (The farmer looks down at what the farmer's wife is holding in her hands.) It is Evanston Bland, lying on his back, face puffed and blotchy, mouth open, disgorging two skeins of faintly pink drool. His eyes are open, rimmed with red. So open, in fact, that his eyeballs look as if they would, if nudged, burst clear of their sockets. It is plain that he has collapsed very suddenly and hit the back of his head on the edge of a bench as he fell. As if confirming her thoughts, congealing them into viscous reality, she now sees that a bench close by has a reddened edge, and smears of blood follow him to the floor. His gray, wispy hair has a halo of blood.

("Oh! Alex! It's a... it's a ...")

Alex sits down hard on Bland's office chair and wonders what she should do. Well, call an ambulance, obviously, but ...

Alex Beach calms herself. Her first call must be to the new Director. That's Morrison. She rises and squeezes her cellphone from the tight front pocket of her jeans. She keys the number.

Morrison answers his own cellphone after just two rings. "Hello?"

Alex is taken aback at Morrison's swift answer, given the time (the clock in her phone says 03.26): "Morrison? Alex. Sorry to wake you, at home, but ..."

"No problem, Alex. I was ... er... up and about anyway. Couldn't sleep in this storm. Came up to the kitchen to fix a drink. You called just as I got here. What's up?"

Alex pictures the spacious upstairs kitchen in Morrison's nouveau-brick-and-flint barn conversion at Tribenham, a few miles inland. She can even hear what sounds like the hum of Morrison's big American-style fridge with its ice-maker.

"Well, I'm in the lab, couldn't sleep either, you know? And, well, I heard a noise, and, well, it's Evanston Bland..." Despite herself, Alex starts to break up. Staring at Bland's body, his eyes bulging from his skull as if his last sight had been of something beyond imagining, she feels her gorge rising.

"Alex, calm yourself, everything's fine, just tell me what's wrong ..." Morrison's voice, so clear, so consoling and yet so powerful, damn him, as if all you ever needed to do was tell him your problems and it would, whatever it was, be all right. Alex sits down again.

"Morrison, he's dead." Silence at the other end of the line. She can hear the ghostly crackle of static. "Morrison?"

"Yes, I'm here, Alex, and don't worry. Did you say, 'dead'?"

"Yes, he's stretched out on the floor of his lab, knocked out, eyes open, blood everywhere ... I ... what should I do?"

Morrison answered quickly. "Do nothing. I'll phone an ambulance now and get down there myself. You should go straight back upstairs, make yourself some sweet tea and go back to bed. Leave the scene exactly as it is, touch nothing, just go to bed. Got that?"

"Yes, but ..."

"But nothing, Alex. Don't worry. I'll handle it. Sure, you'll have to give some kind of statement, I guess, but just wait for me to call you, okay?"

"Yes, Morrison, but …"

"Alex, I know you're shocked, but you'll be good for nothing, half asleep, hanging around with nothing for company but a dead body. Go upstairs, now, and wait for me to call you." Morrison rings off.

Alex can't remember how she made it upstairs and into her room, but here she is, in her bed, under the duvet and yet fully clothed. Her mouth is dry, her eyes full of tears. Suddenly, she is tired, and more than tired. As her eyes close she recalls Bland when he was alive. He had been a lecherous nuisance, but the thought of him dead makes her panic, as if it had been her wishes alone that had done it. As if wishes could kill.

Look at it, Alex. It's all your fault.

3: Princess of Death

Leaning in at an awkward angle through the front passenger door of the car, rain glancing from his back and shoulders, the man bends over the child in the car seat on the rear bench.

"Are you strapped in, little one?" he smiles. The child gurgles in recognition, "Love Daddy! Love Daddy!", and waves well-padded arms and legs. The man clicks the straps home, smiles again, closes the door, shrugs his hood against the rain and moves round to the driver's side. Settling in, he starts the engine. The car, an ancient three-door hatchback painted a vivid yellow (the family calls it the 'Flying Banana') skitters into the glutinous morning traffic.

"Playgroup, here we come! Vroom! Vroom!" says the man, heart on his infant son, eyes on the bumper-to-bumper morning gridlock in the September downpour.

"Woom! Woom!" comes the excited response.

The traffic grunts slowly forward, stop-and-start, stop-and-start, seen rhythmically through each pass of the squeaking wipers. And so, fitfully, the yellow car makes its way through the side streets to a run-down high road that no amount of water can wash completely clear of the fast-food containers and the gum splodged to its sidewalks. The tiny yellow corpuscle edges along this clogged artery, slowly past the newsagent and mini-mart, the betting shop and the fried-chicken res-taurant, towards a junction with an intimidating gyratory beneath an urban freeway. The yellow cell now halts quivering, queueing for en-trance to this urban cyclone.

Frustration creeps in, dark counterpoint to the cheerful nursery banter, the well-worn tape of children's favorites on the stereo. Stuck behind a building-supplies truck full of sand, and in front of a white delivery van which has been hanging on impatiently to the yellow car's rear fender, the driver feels cramped, boxed-in, fearful. He wipes condensation from the inside of the windshield.

"Mummy doesn't have to put up with this," he murmurs, as Nellie the Elephant says goodbye to the circus. "Mummy drives a police car with a big blue light and a siren. Nee naw! Nee-naw!"

"Nee-naw! Mummy car! Mummy car!" returns the antiphon.

Mummy got up early and drove in her own car through silent streets to the Police Station, where she is a detective working with a huge team which is nonetheless never quite large enough to rein in the many-headed monster that is TubeWave, the new drug sweeping the city. But a part of her remains, willing on this little yellow bubble of joy. Mummy sits in the empty passenger seat like a ghost from the past and the future, watching, helpless, unable to answer - or to warn.

The car edges to the front of the line, to take its chance on the gyratory. Nellie the Elephant sets out on the road to Mandalay, as she always does. I hate this junction, the driver thinks, I fear it. Even now that it's controlled by lights, the moment of willing green is too fleeting within the parsimonious red for more than two or three vehicles to be admitted to the gyratory at any one time. With this little car, it's always hard to gun the engine over to the much-desired, almost-unattainable farther lane of the gyratory before it runs the risk of being stampeded by a wave of traffic surging from the right. But if you, the driver, don't take that chance, you'll be hooted by the line of traffic behind you, drivers cursing that you didn't have the guts to dare that tiny launch window, and will thus, through your pusillanimity, have condemned everyone to another two-and-a-half minutes of fuming immobility.

The lights go green, and the driver, whose name is Nicholas, floors it.

The elderly gearbox, despite this daily round, is always surprised by this sudden demand for acceleration. Lazily it selects a lower gear and prompts the engine into renewed life. Nicholas, both eyes on the far-side lane and praying that the car will reach it, at least one more time, is only vaguely aware of a sudden complete lull in the traffic, of a battered silver car running against the lights on the gyratory and zooming from right to left across his nose; of the blue and yellow flashing lights and sirens in pursuit.

The little yellow car is a mustard-seed, momentarily frozen in time on a deserted asphalt plain of infinite extent.

"Look out to the right, Nick!" Mummy screams, impotently, in the passenger seat, knowing with the omniscience of all ghosts that in the battered silver car is a runner carrying a briefcase full of TubeWave with a street value of three million pounds, and that it is being chased at high speed. "Pull up, Nick! For God's sake, brake!" She turns to the driver, eyes bulging in terror, face white, veins throbbing in her neck and temples. But as she is only a ghost from the past and the future, the driver quite naturally ignores her.

Three-tenths of a second later, Nellie the Elephant has packed her trunk and the car is almost there, front nearside wheel breasting the line that marks the desired far-side lane, when the police cruiser slams into the little yellow car at ninety miles an hour.

Mummy, disoriented, finds herself confronted in her office by a female uniformed police officer she's never seen; in a hospital with grim-faced doctors and nurses with unquenchable dark cisterns for eyes; in a crematorium with two coffins of unequal sizes; in a flat that seems too large and empty even though full of toys, all now untouchable; in another hospital where she herself is the patient; and everything, everywhere, always under grey skies which the Sun will never relieve, because the Sun has turned its back on this world.

Mummy, whose name is Detective Inspector Persephone Sheepwool, lately of the Metropolitan Police, finds herself transferred, at her own request, waking four months later in a storm streaking the windows of her neat sea-front flat in a town called Deringland where she might once have been taken on holiday as a very small child. Taken. Child. Don't go there. Listen to the wind, Percy, and the surf. The waves will wash it all away.

Sheepwool is always an early riser, and has leapt out of bed and into the shower almost before she knows she's awake. Hot jets to chase away the cold rain and the shreds of dreams.

Bordfield Court, facing the Winter Gardens and the sea on Deringland's once-fashionable West Promenade, had been a hotel in the town's Victorian heyday, but hard times had loosened its slates until a developer bought it for a song and took his time turning it into posh flats. Having fled London, Sheepwool could afford to buy one of the poshest: on the third floor, with spectacular sea views. It is a haven of bright metropolitan warmth and neatness in what seems, to her, to be a town of clustered shadows.

But Bordfield Court cannot but retain its character, which it gathers jealously to itself, a bombazined dowager hoarding funereal jet. Although a fundamentally sound structure, it had been faced in parts with soft sandstone, which has all but given up its centuried battle with the North Sea. So what might once have been finials, pseudo-palladian ornaments or even gargoyles are now polished into anonymous, abstract shapes. Where the sandstone had disappeared completely, successive owners had tried patching it with concrete, which made any surrounding sandstone wear away even more quickly: or the local Norfolk Red bricks, which, while more forgiving, started to erode in their own characteristic patterns. And so the face of Bordfield Court could be read as its autobiography, as weather-shorn as that of any fisherman pulling up his crab-boat on the beach below its high gables.

Inside her flat, Sheepwool can ignore such external manifestations. But she cannot forget them, because they intrude on her life in the form of the keening of the storm-wind, blowing conch-like across any channel in the gothic roofline; and the elevator, restored to its art-nouveau glory and unreliability. Unless laden with shopping, Sheepwool usually decides not to risk it and takes the stairs instead, heels clattering up uneven marble treads.

Now Sheepwool towels and dresses, ceaseless animation emphasizing her tall, angular frame, her cool blue eyes. She has always been restless, but these days she feels that she simply cannot stop, must fill every moment with activity, the kinesis as of a child, which catches up with it on a sudden, freezing it into the immobility of sleep while still in the midst of play. Because she knows that if she pauses, even for a moment, she would be sucked down so far and so fast that she might never find her way back up to the light.

The storm eases a little into the chill gray of an early January morning. Even as she dresses in the half-light of dawn, Sheepwool can see the white wave-crests out to sea soften and fade, leaving a sullen sea beneath a sky scrubbed clean as a fishmonger's counter. She swallows a too-hot mouthful of instant coffee, pours the remainder down the sink, swishes on her overcoat, grabs her bag and sets off for work. But weather viewed from the seclusion of an interior, even one with spectacular sea views, is deceptive. As Sheepwool opens the heavy front door of her building, pulling it towards her, the wind seizes it and pushes it brusquely into her face, needles of the blast ripping at her lapels and sleeves.

Once outside, Sheepwool turns right and clicks determinedly along the seafront towards the town, the breeze etching cold lines on her left cheek as she walks, eyes half-closed against the relentless salt. She passes boarded-up hotels, bed-and-breakfasts with forlorn signs creaking like gibbets on rusted chains, advertising vacancies. On the corner of Charles Street, a canyon between tall Victorian rooming houses that stabs southwards into the town centre, the wind takes her, blowing her along the sidewalk. Dislocated refuse clatters along around her: a loose sheet of the *Deringland Mercury* catches up with her and wraps itself around her calves which, already strained in her high heels, tighten further as she buttresses herself against the pressure. Blown and tottering for another twenty yards, she finds the protruding frontage of the Three Kings, weatherworn picnic tables chained to the frontage, sign-board straining.

She stops in the lee of the pub to draw breath, and to do something with her hair, the moisture has darkened it from dirty blonde to a near-black chestnut and pasted it crazily across her face. Each wayward strand seems to have fixed itself to her face with the tenacity of a limpet. Her skin stings as she pulls each one free, as if she were removing a band-aid. She is glad she has her hair cut fairly short, but wishes she'd sometimes be less unbendingly fashion-conscious, more acquiescent towards practicality (not to mention middle-age), and worn a headscarf. And thick trousers instead of this twin-set. And sneakers instead of heels. Ah, she smiles to herself, When I Am Old I Shall Wear Purple. She presses on.

At the mini-roundabout just after the pub, she turns south-west and climbs the gentle ascent of Cable Street, the petrol station and the supermarket providing welcome relief from the wind. Across the road and thirty yards further she attains her goal, Deringland Police Station, its heavy blue lamp hanging over the gravel yard of what must once have been a pleasant Edwardian villa, hydrangeas leafing around chafed iron railings. The Station's stone-trimmed storm-porch is a null of the weather, the air hanging completely still and without character: pausing here before entering the building and getting entangled in the routine of the working day, she finds herself unnaturally warm, the only conscious recognition of her body's efforts to stave off the remorseless chill. She's an idiot, she thinks, to be walking to work on a day like this. Especially in these heels.

Only now does she recall not having seen a single pedestrian on her walk, not even a dog-owner grimly parading his charge, whatever the weather: and very few cars, either. Only two are parked on the Station forecourt: the regular patrol car, and the highly-polished mulberry-purple Rover 75 belonging to her superior, Superintendant Ivan Methwold.

She has hardly clacked her way down the checkerboard-tiled hall and into the small office she shares with Elaine Fitch; hardly sloughed off her overcoat which, dark with moisture, almost drags her to the ground as it falls, when her desk phone rings. It is an internal call. Methwold.

"Sir?"

"Sheepwool. Saw you come in. A word?"

It was Methwold who had first welcomed Sheepwool to Deringland, as a favor to an old colleague in the Met. To her he has been nothing but kind, keeping out of her way as she finds her feet, establishes her new life. She wonders, though, whether his self-effacement has something more to it: that beneath the rotund, fifties-ish exterior there hums an engine of incredible power. It is just a feeling, though, but her feelings have always been reliable, as has her observation, that whenever Methwold walks into a room, all attention is diverted towards him, all conversation stops. He is one of those people whom one is always surprised to find is smaller than you expect.

Certainly, he is nothing special to look at. Grayish, both inside and out, he seems quite forgettable, once his quiet authority has been established: as if, once he has ordered his Universe, it can be trusted to run quite well on its own without his direct intervention.

Forgettable, that is, until you see his eyes.

Shielded beneath heavy spectacles with bottle-glass lenses and thick black frames, it is hard to see his eyes at all unless he is looking directly at you. And when that happens, one sees not the eyes of a human being but of a golden retriever of great age, wells of trust and loyalty which, it seems, have been lately betrayed; and which, helpless to express some great loss and therefore lessen it, are all the deeper and more sorrowful. Both eyes, Sheepwool notices as she sits neatly before his desk, often flicker, so briefly as if he seems ashamed of the fact, if he is aware of it at all, to the silver-framed photograph of a smiling middle-aged woman, the only object on the green-leathered desktop apart from the telephone.

"All well, I hope?"

"Perfectly well, Sir, thank you." A pause.

"Sheepwool, something's come up. Something I'd like you handle. I can let you have Fitch, if you like." He smiles. Sheepwool had been handling some routine, low-level crime. Very little worse than after-hours drinking at the Dazed Haddock. Liaison with Rammell from Customs and Excise. Far less exalted, for certain, than the kind of work she'd been used to at the Met. But for a while it was all she felt she could manage.

"My other casework…"

"… will be taken care of." Another pause. An antique clock ticks benignly on the wall behind Methwold. The many voices of the wind can be heard faintly in the background.

"Sir?"

"Ah. Yes. It's a death, sad to say. During the night. One Dr Evanston Bland. A scientist up at the Institute. Found dead, on the floor of his lab, by another scientist."

"Suspicious?"

"Don't know. Maybe, maybe not. Probably not. Elderly man, on the point of retirement. Could just be a heart attack. In any case, that's for Levy to decide." Jim Levy was the police pathologist. "But one never knows. After last night's storm, and, well, it is the Institute, after all."

"There'll be an inquest, Sir?"

"Oh, definitely. So you get up there with DS Fitch. She knows the details. Find out what's going on." Sheepwool takes that as a dismissal, orders having been issued, and is just about to rise from her seat, when something occurs to her.

"Sir, you said something about the Institute?" Methwold looks up, surprised, as if he'd expected that Sheepwool would already have departed.

"Oh? Yes, ah, the Institute. One of Deringland's more … ah … unusual attractions. Have you been there?"

"No, Sir. Not yet."

"Well, you will, with Fitch. Today, if possible. Let me know what you come across." The atmosphere comes down like a theater curtain. Sheepwool takes the hint and gathers herself to leave.

In the car, Sheepwool is left almost alone with her thoughts as Fitch, driving, chatters on. Sheepwool chides herself for being so uncharitable, that she can let Fitch's near-continuous monologue become the aural equivalent of floral wallpaper while she pieces things together in her own mind. In any case, Fitch's unceasing talk is something like having the radio on in the background. Even without listening to every word, it is a companion, a friend, even, in any case, a bulwark against the otherwise all-consuming silence. Fitch, for her part, seems to like to work for a DI who lets her own stream of consciousness become a flood, her boss interrupting only occasionally. The partnership, while clearly not made in heaven, rubs along very well.

The police car is an elderly MG Metro that huffs down the hill and into town, the same hill up which Sheepwool had toiled a few minutes earlier, although now turning right at the mini-roundabout just before the Three Kings to enter the High Street, the town's main thoroughfare, parallel to the sea. Sheepwool notices that the wind has dropped and an apologetic winter Sun has come out, casting Deringland into flat planes of wan light and smudges of charcoal shadow. Even now, only few people can be seen, as if subservient to the architecture rather than its masters. Square arches outside Woolworths conceal slouchy youths, bored at the fag-end of the Christmas holidays. The few restaurants are boarded up. The florist, the butcher, the all-for-a-pound discount store, the greengrocer, all are open, but waiting, tense.

"The Institute? Oh, yes ..." says Fitch, pulling up at a zebra crossing to allow the passage across the street of a woman, old beyond her years, bacon-red face and streaky russet hair scraped back violently into a ponytail. The woman is accompanied by a snotty toddler and some complicated kind of stroller-car-seat combo with tiny child in it, cosseted like a pearl in an oyster's mantle.

Child. Stroller. Road. Car.

Sheepwool wakes from her musing with a start, swimming alongside Fitch's chatter. Sheepwool senses that for all their apparent mindlessness, Fitch's words actually connect as if they have in fact some higher order, some end in view, like the seeming purpose of a great flock of birds about to migrate a thousand miles, for all that the consciousness of any one individual might barely count even as one dim spark.

"You were saying?"

"Yes, Ma'am, the Institute, funny old place. Went there a few times as a kid, with school. Full of glass cases and weird stuff. But we all laughed at the mermaids - especially one of them, Pickled Lily - even though she gave us all nightmares, you know? The way she looks at you… gave me the willies, I don't mind saying. Haven't been back since. She's still there, though, Pickled Lily, you'll get to see her, my own kids saw her the other day on a school trip. Couldn't get Eric - he's my little boy - to sleep for a week after. I don't think much ever changes up there. But the Institute, well, it's a bit of a landmark, really…"

"Did you say 'mermaids'?"

"Oh yes, Ma'am, loads of them. All fakes, or at least, I think so. It all started with the founder, I made sure to read up on it again soon as I heard about the death, just to remind myself, of course, but everyone here knows all about it."

Of course. The Institute slouches on a clifftop bluff at the very highest point of Deringland. It lurks in the background of every view, seen out of the corner of every eye. "Well, he was some old nutcase called Sir Freddy … ay-kay-ay Sir Frideric Lowdley-Purslane. He was some kind of surgeon in London in Georgian times. Regency. You know, Mr Darcy and all that stuff. He - that's Sir Fred, not Mr Darcy - had a big collection of curios, you know, fossils, antiques and stuff, and retired up here, kind of. He bought the big house that became the Institute, up on the cliffs, and…"

"He 'kind of' retired?"

"Yes, well, there were all sorts of stories about that, too. About how Lady Fred was an invalid who hated the big city and pined for the sea air. At least, that's the quotes 'official' story. But there were other ones, you know, about how Sir Fred had to flee London because of some kind of bad business, you know, hushed up." Fitch turns her blue eyes to Sheepwool, her slightly greasy, laugh-creased young face framed by disordered straw-blonde curls: "Secret experiments. Vivi-section. Bodysnatching." Sheepwool starts.

"You were going to tell me about the mermaids."

"Yes, sorry, Ma'am. Well, apparently, I read, it was quite the fash-ion for old Sir Fred and his surgeon pals to cut up bits of different animals and sew them together to make fake monsters, just for fun. Fred made a few of his own and collected a lot more. Cats with wings. Furry fish. Frog princes! You know, all sorts. But mermaids were his favourites, you know, the front ends of monkeys sewn to the back ends of fishes. But Pickled Lily ..." She shudders.

Past the gray, gothic mass of the church, an edifice of a hugeness out of all proportion to the town of which it is a part, the High Street narrows between older buildings that lean slightly out of true. Fitch concentrates on the road, her speech breaking up into syntactical fragments.

The car approaches a set of traffic lights and Fitch indicates left, to the eastward coast road, rather than straight ahead, up the hill, the road which would eventually take them to Norwich. As the car slows, Sheepwool looks to her left and finds herself confronted, not six feet away, with a model of what looks like a gigantic octopus. She can't be sure, given the shadows, and the double reflections on both the passenger-side window and the glass of the shop window, but the eyes follow her malevolently, and some of the plasterwork tentacles end in human hands.

She glances upwards and realizes it's just a shop display: the shop itself is called 'Secrets of the Sea' and appears to sell glass fishing-net floats, model boats, preserved starfishes and similar lobster-pottery. She wonders why she'd never noticed the shop before, especially given the extravagance of the display, but realizes that it's only fully visible from the passenger door of a car, slowing at the lights. The low-set window, giving on to a very narrow pavement in an otherwise dark street would mean that a passing pedestrian would see only glancing reflections from the plate-glass window. You could pass it on foot a thousand times and not realize it was there, unless, of course, you were looking for it.

Fitch senses her unease. "Ah yes, 'Secrets'. We've had some trouble with them. Stolen goods. Never quite managed to pin them down, though. There's a connection with the Institute, funnily enough, did you know that? There are suspicions, and only suspicions, worse luck, that some of the specimens turn up in 'Secrets' from time to time, though they've always gone before we can be sure. It's very frustrating. For my money I'd finger that Bob Honeypott."

"Honeypott?"

"Yes, Black Bob. He was in my year at school. A sly one, that one. Always on the edge of the bad crowd but too clever by half to be caught actually doing anything naughty. Believe it or not, he asked me out once! Thank goodness I said no. I had just started going out with my Jason at the time, and, well, anyway, he, that's Bob, not my Jason, works some evenings at the Dazed Haddock. It's his Mum, Ma Honeypott, now, who runs 'Secrets'. And by day he's a janitor at the Institute. So he's got the means, and the motive. We just haven't been able to finger him, that's all. And, oh yes, " Fitch selects another idea from her bird's-nest mind as she slides efficiently into second gear, eyes darting to the mirrors as she knits the wheel to turn left.

"Bob's fingers are in all sorts of pies. Gerry Rammell, you know Gerry? He's that nice man from Customs and Excise…" Sheepwool recalls seeing Fitch and one or two of the younger female staff gushing over their recent visitor, tall and well-groomed with a smooth Irish lilt. "Well, Gerry said that he thought someone's been spiking some of the spirits at the Dazed Haddock with pure alcohol, you know, like from a laboratory. He said, strictly off the record, mind, that he'd not be surprised if our Bob wasn't lifting other things from the Institute apart from the occasional seashell. Well, Gerry, he's a laugh, but sometimes I think he's kissed the blarney stone a few times too often!"

"He told me something of the sort, too."

"But sorry, Ma'am, the Institute." Fitch, realizing that she's strayed a little way from the well-measured path of the subject, swerves back on to her intended course. "Well, it's more than a Museum, as you know. It's a kind of research institute. Scientists work there. Some of them even live there. Dr Bland, though, he's the one who died, didn't, so I wonder what he was doing there in the middle of the night. You know? I don't think I could go there at night, let alone sleep there. Imagine, tucking yourself in bed at night in the same building as Pickled Lily. Anyway, there they are, working on all kinds of obscure stuff connected with marine biology…"

"'Secrets of the Sea'?"

"Yes, exactly. Who knows what they are up to? But apparently it's all in Sir Fred's 'mission statement': we all have to have those, these days, don't we? But it was the same back, then, too. Nothing new! Anyway, Sir Fred made it known that his Institute would be devoted to uncovering, hang on…" A crease interrupts Fitch's blonde brow.

"That's exactly it. I read it. Fred's statement uses those exact words, 'secrets of the sea', just like the shop. It's in all the Institute's publicity and I never noticed, all this time. How funny!"

The car thrums along the gray eastward road out of Deringland. Old and stately houses, faced in brick and flint, huddle on their right: on the left, under a lingering skein of mist, is a small municipal park extending to the cliff tops, overlooking the sea itself.

Connections form in Sheepwool's mind. What, indeed, was Bland doing at the Institute late at night, if he didn't live there?

"What more do we know of Bland? The deceased?" she asks.

"Sixty-five next birthday, March twenty-first, and due to retire, Ma'am. He was the Director of the Institute, just handing over to a new broom, a Dr Morrison. We'll meet him when we get there. Bland didn't do much research, nothing for years. Lived in a bungalow at Halberd Park, just up the hill from here. Not far from us, actually, next street, funny, I never met him, or maybe I saw him around, you know, in the local shop. No children, never met him on the school run, anyway, and never married, as far as I can find out. Cause of death? The Super thought probably natural, heart attack, but being the Institute, he said, we should go in to rule out anything unusual." Sheepwool remembers her own less-than-revealing conversation with Methwold.

"Form?"

"Dr Bland? No, Ma'am. Except ..."

"Except?"

"Well, there had been a few complaints about him over the years. Sexual harassment."

Sheepwool is silent for a spell. The park gives way to a few more houses, then, on both sides, brick-and-flint barns, and what look like fields behind wind-wracked Scots pines. The road begins to twist and to climb. Within moments, the town is behind them, and as the road winds, Sheepwool gets a good look at it. Seen like this, from above, sunk within the folds of mist-laden hills, Deringland looks like it might be charming in the summer. Children playing on the beach, making sandcastles, beachcombing with Daddy, Mummy watching them both against the sea, small silhouettes against huge foreshortened waves ... But no, in January, in the apologetic sunshine that follows a storm, it looks like a flayed carcass. Sheepwool turns her face against it.

"Who found the body?"

"Dr Morrison reported the death, Ma'am."

"Not what I meant."

"Ah, sorry, Ma'am. Bland was actually found by a scientist called Alex Beach, working late in another lab, close by."

"Alex?"

"Yes, Ma'am. Morrison didn't say so, but the only Alex Beach at the Institute is a woman. I wondered, you know, why Morrison didn't say that, or why the Super didn't tell me. Do you think there's a connection with Bland and his... er ... previous?"

Sheepwool mutters abstractedly that there might be. Why should a woman call herself Alex, she thought, if not to hide her gender in a discipline, science, probably as male-oriented as the police, in which advertising oneself as a woman might be held against you?

Just like her.

Persephone, princess of death, whom death would always follow. But in the police force, always 'Sheepwool', and to everyone else always 'Percy', once upon a time to Nick, and now even to herself. She has not yet met Alex Beach, but already she feels they have something in common. Even though she could be first in line, were a suspect required; and if Bland were making advances on her; and if this Morrison person were trying to protect her... no, wait and see. Already too many maybes, too many unknowns. Wait until we get there, Percy, she tells herself.

4: Pickled Lily

Now quite outside the town but not yet at the crest of the ridge that dominates its southern skyline and which, to an extent, determines the peculiarity of its weather, Fitch signals left. Sheepwool can see no sign of a turnoff, although she records with quiet amusement a notice advertising 'Restful Paws Luxury Cat Hotel' over five gold stars, with the subscript 'Fully Licensed'. But there it is, just past a coven of low brick-and-flint cottages half-hidden in a spinney of sepulchral trees.

The side road is steep at first, and surfaced only in scabrous patches of asphalt between scaphes of chippings. Fitch grits her teeth, slipping down into first gear and willing the car to scramble up the potholed ascent, sharps flying in all directions. The grade soon becomes less precipitous, and the lane continues upwards as a rutted track between low hedges of writhen beech which thin out and eventually vanish altogether. After a few hundred yards the lane is the only mark left on an otherwise featureless landscape, a scar across a sea of close-cropped grass which, swept into swirls by the gusting wind, extends to a horizon over which nothing can be seen but sky.

A lone mote in a vast green-gray space, the car, breeze-buffeted, reaches the top of the grade and, quite suddenly, Sheepwool can see the sea before her, welcoming and terrifying. Buildings appear to punctuate the expanse and give it scale.

The track passes, first, to the right of the Deringland Light with its keeper's cottage and walled outbuildings, its flawless whitewash exuding, to Sheepwool's eyes, nothing so much as a witless smugness, strange in view of the maritime destruction to which it is a testament.

Behind the Light, on a bluff set somewhat to the right and further along the track, on the very edge of the cliffs, is a building which Sheepwool has seen every day since her arrival in Deringland, although never at close quarters. This is their destination, The Lowdley-Purslane Institute. From a distance no more than a vague smudge of disquiet, close up it rises like a thunderhead behind the whiteness of the Light, and is quite possibly the ugliest building Sheepwool has seen in her life.

As the car slows on its final approach to the Institute's gravel forecourt, Sheepwool sees the many gables and rooflines of the over-large building, cast against the white of the sky, as a constantly shifting line. And so it is for the building more generally. The closer she gets to it, the harder it is to see as a cohesive entity. One factor never changes, and that is its loathesomeness.

The building might once have started, she supposes, as a Jacobean folly, that is, a kind of mistake, set on a headland perhaps more extensive than it is now. But where the building should have been admitted straightaway as an architectural abortion and cast down, either replaced by the elegant lines of a Georgian mansion, or removed entirely, it was, in fact, built on, compounding the error. So it is that big, rectilinear Nash-style windows were forced into its structure like the stigmata of traumatic violation.

In subsequent years, no expense was spared to make the place as hideous as possible. If any one theme could be said to dominate the raucous parliament of styles, it is Victorian Neo-Gothic, whose singularly inappropriate lines form the greater bulk of the building. Being, as it is, one of the very earliest examples of the Gothic Revival in Britain, the architects had not quite managed to achieve any particular harmony of proportion: explaining why, perhaps, the third and fourth storeys of the building, with their elaborate gables and dormers, perhaps more appropriate for one of London's larger railway stations than for a remote seaside mansion, seem shambling and unfinished; and why the stained-glass windows seem either too large or too small.

Even the Neo-Gothic parts of the building have not proven immune to later alteration and replacement, subsequent builders being always careful to leave the very worst examples, as if they were the stubbornest marks on the base of a scorched frying pan which no amount of scrubbing can erase.

But worse was to come. Plastered ineptly on to the Victorian revival of the Gothic is the Edwardian revival of the Tudor, such that in between the dark buttresses one can see exposed beams and pargetting, a juxtaposition which Sheepwool would find sad were it not quite so comic, given that much of the ornate plasterwork has pitted and fallen away, revealing the underlying structure in wide, unseemly holes.

By that period, Sheepwool realizes, the structure of the entire building was becoming compromised, not only by the ill-assortment of its component parts, but by the unsoundness of the cliffs on which it rested. For the entire building is riven with cracks, such that the supreme ugliness of the architectural additions of the later twentieth century might be excused, if only partly, by their utility: for the building now stands in part thanks to steel bonds and what must be thousands of tons of reinforced concrete. Even that shows signs of disfigurement, with the efflorescent stains of rust from corroded steels showing through, as dispiriting here as in any 1960s shopping mall.

As Fitch brings the car to a halt, Sheepwool reflects that were the building a living thing, it had died sometime in the last quarter of the nineteenth century, with any Edwardian additions analogous to embalming. In this light, subsequent alterations comprised the kinds of makeshift patch-up jobs required only to offer the appearance of soundness, concealing what is in fact an inexorable slide into putrefaction.

But as Sheepwool gets out of the car into the cool breeze and looks around at the palleted stacks of cement bags in various corners of the car park, the large piles of sand, gravel and scaffolding poles, she admits an alternative view, that the building had never been truly finished; that Sir Frideric's aims were not yet achieved; that the Institute is as any living thing, that is, a dynamic equilibrium, a constantly shifting armed truce between small-scale death and resurgent life. A closer inspection gave the lie to this, however, the scaffold poles are pocked with rust and twined with brambles; the sand piles garlanded with nettles and red-blemished dock, and girt all round with couch grass. The building has died, then, and so have the final attempts at restoration. Just for an instant, Sheepwool sees herself and Fitch, in the understated costume of detectives on duty, walking into a flesh-strewn orifice of a gigantic corpse.

Now Fitch and Sheepwool stand before the great oak doors, each of which bears the kind of stained-glass window seen in Edwardian villas up and down the country, but whose subjects here must be unique: marine life in profuse array, what look like sea-serpents and tentacles curling round one another in a silent yet urgent frenzy. The design reminds Sheepwool of the alarming window-dressing in 'Secrets of the Sea', and finds herself simultaneously fascinated and repelled. Her reverie is short-lived, for the door is opened by a housekeeper, a tiny, bright-eyed woman of indeterminate age whose smallness is only emphasized by the edifice that surrounds her. She neither asks their names nor introduces herself, but beckons wordlessly for them to follow. And so they enter the maw of the great building.

The long skirts of the housekeeper conceal her feet so that she seems to glide rather than walk, and, even so, she moves surprisingly quickly. Fitch follows her with decision, as quickly as high heels and a pencil skirt will allow, her steps clacking on the marble floor of the entrance hall. Sheepwool, however, is distracted by her surroundings, forever drawn aside by details, and soon falls behind. She notices, first, an imposing statue of a man whose handsome face suggests some evil, barely concealed yet proudly worn. She takes this to be the Institute's eponymous founder. To the right, and down some steps, is a thick door marked 'Private', already barred with police-lines tape. The SOCOs were up early. That must be the scene of the crime, if such it is.

She looks up just in time to see Fitch ascend marble stairs to a long, carpeted vestibule hung with large, darkened portraits and chandeliers, dusty in the light of morning filtered through windows from adjacent rooms, and she stirs to follow. But Fitch is too quick for her: as Sheepwool reaches the top of the stair, her colleague has disappeared. The movement of the corner of a tapestry in air reluctantly stirred into motion suggests that Fitch has turned through an open door, second on the right off the wide hallway.

Content in this knowledge, Sheepwool takes time to linger. Her first impression of the hall is of the rampant clutter of natural history. Preferring calm and minimalist order, almost messianically so in her new life, scrupulously shorn as it is of personal complication, this is not a place to which she would gravitate, still less call home. She wonders, though, why she doesn't find such artfully displayed carnage detestable, even creepy, and also why she is not more outraged than she is at the antics of people, evidently unable to leave the works of nature well alone, but driven instead to catch, kill and rip them to pieces, only to put them together again in grinning tableaux that can never be more than cynical simulacra of unvarnished reality. No, rather than outrage, she feels wonder at all this perverse industry, her mind forming a host of questions about science as the expression of some human urge to control, to dominate. But she's not convinced by that line of reasoning either. For a moment, she wonders whether her lack of engagement with such issues is a reaction to what she resolutely refers to only as 'recent events'.

Perhaps, she thinks, her detachment is more than the consequence of such events, but simply goes with her job. She is here, after all, not as a tourist, but in the line of duty. As it always does, this thought gives her more than a little solace. And so resolved, she sets off to follow Fitch.

Once through the imposing square arch through which she's convinced Fitch has passed, Sheepwool finds herself in a great display hall, presumably the main exhibition space of the Institute. Like the vestibule, the walls are crowded with specimens, from the statues and cabinets at floor level to the tapestries and trophies hung so high that reading their labels is impossible from ground level. Much of the intervening parqueted floor is similarly covered, with hardwood-and-glass cabinets displaying various examples of sea life trapped like exhaled exclamations in vials and jars or beneath watch-glasses. The hall faces south and somewhat eastward, such that the winter sun now peers through the tall windows, shafts riding on motes in the great space and glancing, distractingly, off the many panes of glass that separate the visitor from the specimens. Whenever Sheepwool tries to read one of the yellowing labels beneath a specimen, the words always seem half-obscured by reflected sunshine and dancing rainbows of refraction.

Thus squinting, she comes to a cabinet at the very centre of the room, a towering, hexagonal mausoleum divided into six, separate, prism-shaped display cases, each one reaching from knee height to well above, she thinks, the height of a tall man carrying a toddler on his shoulders. Like Nick did, that day when... No, she reins herself in. Not now. Not here. Not anywhere.

The cabinet is central to the Institute in more ways than one, it seems, for it is here (Sheepwool reads through half-closed eyes) that the pride of Sir Frideric's collection is displayed, the many artful taxidermic 'follies and fancies' (Sheepwool smiles at the phrase) for which the Institute is famous. Starting in the welcome shade of the most north-facing pane of the hexagon, she is invited to wonder at a display of 'arctic trout' in fur coats, and other oddities. One of these, the platypus, is a kind of double-bluff, a genuine work of nature discovered when the fashion for taxidermic artistry was at its height, and so naturally assumed, at first, to have been something of the same kind.

Feeling herself edified, Sheepwool works clockwise, to the next case.

This displays, in its upper half, a line of stuffed cats, some with wings, in a grotesque display she cannot immediately understand. Many of the cats are in fact kittens, invariably white, and in costume, some as Victorian Ladies and Gentlemen, booted and bonneted, but others in the clothing of other eras. There is a Roman centurion, and a cat dressed in furs and a club, the cartoon caveman. But other cats, adult ones, all black, and with the chiselled faces of Siamese or Abyssinians, are bat-winged and unclothed, suspended above the line of penitents: yes, penitents, that's what they are, grimacing horribly and waving, what are they? Pitchforks? Tridents? When she sees the direction in which the queueing kittens are headed, downwards, through an open set of shark jaws, she realizes what she is looking at.

It is Hell.

Literally so, for the lower half of the display reveals a cavern, roughly made from plaster and gaily lit with orange fairy-lights, in which the bat-winged cats are subjecting the white kittens to all kinds of torture, everywhere the silent screams preserved for posterity by the skill of the taxidermist; other kittens are being dissected 'alive', in a simulacrum of extremis, by grinning, drooling cats. And there are all manner of other delicacies of feline interaction which Sheepwool can hardly imagine any teacher, or any parent, subjecting a school party. She feels her face, her neck, and the skin beneath her blouse prickle in a cold sweat.

She turns to the next panel. The exhibits in this cabinet, now half-facing the sunlit windows, are initially hard to make out amid the glancing glare. The label, however, is in shadow, and more easily read: from it, Sheepwool learns that in this case, six of Sir Frideric's finest specimens of mermaids might be viewed. Two or three he made himself, the label informs her, whereas others were received from other connoisseurs. Just as she finishes reading the label, stooped down low to make out the finer print, the sun is covered by a scut of cloud, and the reflections of sky in which the case had been wrapped now vanish. The mermaids, she is disappointed to see, are quite small, and almost laughably crude. Although each one is suspended in alcohol in a tall glass jar, it is easy to see that they are no more than the front halves of monkeys, crudely stitched to the back halves of fishes.

On a closer look at one of two of the larger specimens, however, the division between fish and monkey is harder to make out. But these examples, Sheepwool notices, are the more decayed ones: the eye-sockets are untenanted, the faces disfigured, and gluey globs of matter float in the jars alongside the specimens.

Sheepwool finds herself relieved, heartened, even, that the mermaid cabinet is such a comedown after the nightmare of the kitten-hell, and so turns to the next cabinet, the one facing more or less southward, towards the high windows, with more composure. But the sun has emerged from its veil, and strikes the cabinet full on. All she can see in the thick glass is the sun's disk, reflected back at her, hardly ameliorated by her own silhouette. Behind the sun she can just about make out a pair of arms and the bifurcating end of a large, fishy tail. Dazzled by the glare, Sheepwool looks down at the label, mercifully in shadow. The large, coal-black italics, picked out on the wrinkled, sun-baked card, read 'Pickled Lily'. Ah, Sheepwool thinks, this must be the specimen Fitch was on about in the car. Interest heightened, she reads further.

> Many tales surround this famous specimen. The most celebrated is that it was a real mermaid, caught in the South Seas at some time in the eighteenth century by one Obed Marsh, a whaler from the port of Innsmouth in the Commonwealth of Massachusetts. The story is that the specimen, soon named 'Pickled Lily', despite being killed and preserved in white rum, had cursed Marsh's crew, many of whom died during the voyage, and that Marsh was very keen to sell her as soon as he made landfall. She was acquired in Valparaiso by an agent for Sir Frideric and made her way to this Institute.

A likely story, Sheepwool thinks. But being the policewoman she is, though, habit propels her to read further in search of corroboration. At first, she thinks she finds it.

Modern scholarship suggests that this tale is fanciful, and that Pickled Lily is less a genuine mermaid than a very fine example of the taxidermist's art. It is now generally believed that this specimen was created by Sir Frideric himself. If so, the tales that have grown up around Pickled Lily are a tribute to the skill of a master at the peak of his powers.

However, as is so often the case in police work, there are always loose ends that no amount of tying-up can ever seem to resolve.

It is however notable that Sir Frideric's will explicitly forbids the examination of 'Pickled Lily' to establish the truth of the matter.

Sheepwool pauses to consider this. Never mind how skilful Sir Frideric's artistry, nobody, even he, would ever doubt that the specimen before her, still obscured by glare, was a fake. Taxidermy is all a matter of illusion, of bluff, of convincing one, in the same way that a conjuror might, that the canonical Beautiful Assistant really has been sawn in half, even when you know perfectly well that she hasn't. So why then, if it were well known as such, would Sir Frideric seek to prevent the exposure of his skill, even after his own death?

But before she has had time to assimilate this, a cloud once again covers the sun and she can see Pickled Lily for the first time, and when she does, her skin crawls with the miasmic horror of it.

Her hands fly to her face.

"Ma'am?" Fitch's voice echoes from the far end of the gallery, as if from the bottom of a well.

"Ma'am?" Now moving closer, heels tick-tocking on the hard floor , now right beside her. Fitch's pale blue eyes turn to her inquiring, concerned. "Ma'am, I turned round and you weren't there. Ma'am, are you all right? You look as white as a sheet!" Fitch quite pointedly does not look at the specimen, but moves, hand gently on elbow, to chivvy her immobile superior away from it.

"Yes, quite all right, thank you, Fitch. Now, remind me, whom should we see first?" Sheepwool removes her arm from Fitch's light grasp with the waspish, exaggerated care of an old woman who despite her infirmities feels she can manage quite well on her own, thank you very much.

Fitch, stung, looks at her quizzically. "We're going to see the Director of the Institute, Ma'am, who reported the discovery of the body."

"Which was … of whom?" Fitch looks puzzled, as if Sheepwool has lost her mind.

"Just remind me please, Fitch." Sheepwool hopes she doesn't sound as sharp as she thinks she does. She hopes that she can plead in mitigation, as it were, that her mind still feels as if it is surrounded by cotton-wool, and that Fitch seems to be speaking to her from a very great distance.

"That was Dr Evanston Bland, the previous Director."

"But the new Director? His name?"

"Yes, Ma'am, it's a Dr Morrison. Marion Morrison."

Sheepwool pulls herself up sharply: "Is Dr Morrison a woman?"

Fitch falters: "I … er … don't actually know, Ma'am … with a name like that, I kind of assumed that she … he …"

Sheepwool feels slightly cross with Fitch, but realizes in an instant that she should really feel cross with herself for not finding all this out for herself. The gender of Dr Morrison could be important, especially if allegations about the late Dr Bland's sexual predation were related in any way to his death.

"Well, no matter, we'll soon find out."

Fitch smiles weakly, feeling that she has been absolved of some misdemeanour she didn't know she had committed, and the two detectives turn to where the mute housekeeper waits outside a white-painted door at the end of the hall.

The distance is a matter of no more than ten yards, but to Sheepwool it might as well be ten miles, or ten light years. Before her shocked eyes, her mind, as if imprinted by the glare of the sun, is the after-image of Pickled Lily. Her tail: well, that was as fish-like as one would expect. Her torso, though. Her face…

The door is now before them. The detectives halt before it, before the white door, the brass plate inscribed 'Dr Marion Morrison, Director'. The housekeeper knocks on it with a tiny fist.

The torso was white and hairless. Creased and desiccated by time, but plainly not the torso of any monkey or ape. And her face …

"Come in."

The face was surrounded by a halo of grayish hair that looked like it might once have been long and dark, but now waving in the preserving fluid like blind weed. The arms, white, dead white, the white of bleached coral, and reaching out as if imploring, begging. The breasts, gray-white flaps like dead-men's fingers, but which once looked like they might have been full, and soft, and human.

The door opens. The first impression Sheepwool gets is of a rich blue carpet and, abruptly, the too-strong odor of cologne.

The face. There is no avoiding it. It is the face of a mummy, with chapped, rotted lips stretched back over prominent, blackened teeth. The nose sunken between high cheekbones, peaked by death. But the eyes. Deeply, hugely blue in that shrunken face, pleading for absolution, for relief from some terror that Sheepwool, helpless in their gaze, cannot name, still less, grant.

A man - it *is* a man - small but exaggeratedly well-groomed, as if a well-dressed but ordinarily-sized man were shrunken, his tailoring condensed, concentrated, walks towards her, hand protruding from tailored crimson-and-white-striped cuff, extended in greeting.

Sheepwool knows that whatever else this specimen is, might be, the eyes, at least, must be fakes. But why do they seem so alive? Why do they follow her across the hall as she moves, flees, with Fitch, towards their appointment? And why does she get the distinct impression that it is not just the specimen's eyes that turn to follow her, but its whole head, an expression painted on its dead features of anguish, of … disappointment?

"Detective Inspector, Detective Sergeant, please come in, take a seat." A calm voice, beguiling, disconcertingly deep and, well, masculine, for the small frame. A smile that resolves from the rot of centuries to the clean lines offered by modern dentistry. Extreme lines, actually. For as Dr Marion Morrison smiles, Sheepwool feels that his lips, as they draw back to expose his teeth, might as well just keep on pulling backwards, until the edges of his mouth encircle his head so that it falls from his body, as if unzipped. Morrison, perhaps sensing Sheepwool's stare, closes his mouth abruptly. At one glance, Sheepwool knows she has seen that sneer before, on a statue, in the lobby of this awful place.

It has taken a few minutes for her to learn to hate the Lowdley-Purslane Institute.

But Dr Marion Morrison she hates on sight.

5: The Perennial Survivor

"Detective Inspector, Detective Sergeant, please come in, take a seat." And so, obediently they sit.

Morrison returns to his desk, and as he does so, he sees himself, for an instant, as a mouse in the gaze of two cats. He is grateful to be able, finally, to interpose the solid Scandinavian pine (his own touch, that) between the policewomen and himself. But Morrison is no passive rodent, and in those few seconds when the policewomen arrange themselves in their chairs, in which their eyes are not on him, but on their skirts, their bags (Ye Gods! Female impedimenta!) he has a chance to get his story straight. And yet he feels his mind scrabbling for purchase. So maybe he is no more than a hamster on a wheel, vainly trying to escape the cool gaze of these predators. Morrison, he says to himself, get a grip. Be proactive.

Strategize. Morrison's clean, efficient mind rolls out Truth, Version 1.1.

Strengths. Morrison sees himself as the perennial survivor, having been through just one too few close shaves as you'd need to end a career, but coming out on top as a Director of this Institute, and still surfing the wave of opportunity. Whatever doesn't kill you makes you stronger: had Morrison a coat of arms, that would be his motto.

Sure, he is a little nervous right now, he admits, but that's probably natural, and anyone would feel the same were the police to visit one in one's office. The police make you feel guilty if they feel you up on the street for some perfectly innocent reason, don't they? Sure, it's unfortunate that a member of your staff is found dead in the lab at some ungodly hour in what may, or may not, be suspicious circumstances, but Morrison feels, - *knows* - that he had nothing to do with it. Well, 'knows' might be too strong a word, no such word as 'never' in science, nor marketing for that matter, but 95-percent confidence limits would surely bracket certainty. 'Surely'? He hates that word. When anyone in his old team used the word 'surely' in an argument against him he knew his adversary had left solid ground for special pleading. That's when he went for the jugular.

Just like the Detective Inspector is about to do now.

And there's enough uncertainty, just enough, to put him on his guard. Just in case any uneasiness should creep out, and the Detective Inspector should get the wrong impression.

Problems. He has the distinct impression that the autopilot of politesse is at an end and that Sheepwool is asking him a question.

"Dr Morrison, you'll appreciate that we have to ask you some questions. If you don't mind?" The Inspector's eyes are blue-gray and cold. They're rather like Alex Beach's eyes, he thinks. But unlike hers, he can see nothing behind Sheepwool's eyes at all. No warmth. No yearning need. Nothing that might offer him any advantage.

"Yes, Inspector. Of course." He tries his most reassuringly resonant TV-ads-voiceover voice. The one that always astounds people, as its ballsiness seems so surprising given his physical stature. Despite a certain constriction in his throat, he thinks, he hopes, it's working as well as it usually does.

"For example, could you tell us where you were last night?"

"I was at home, asleep, Inspector. I live up the road in Tribenham. Barn conversion. Decent job. Lucky to get it at the price." He immediately senses he might have said too much: gibbering about nothing is always a sign of inner guilt. Sheepwool, across the desk to his right, shifts fractionally forward in her chair, as Fitch, she's the curly-girlie-blonde one across the desk to his left, sits back, allowing her superior to take the lead.

Yes, that's the problem. There are two of them, and only one of him. They'll be able to dissect his story later, between the two of them, bouncing it between them like a volleyball (he is not sure whether the mildly pornographic image created by this simile is pleasant or disturbing). They will have the chance to probe every hole, even if the hole doesn't exist. But on the other side, his own, there'll only be one of him, just talking to himself. No objectivity. He could talk some of this over with Alex, for sure. But not really as equals. Not right now. Not now that he's landed her in it.

"Can anyone vouch for your presence at your home?"

Opportunities. Morrison reminds himself that he's a survivor: that after a spell as a scientist that lurched from disaster to near catastrophe, he rose to the surface in marketing, and more than surface, to dominate. That's how he got here. Director. By his achievements. That, and some insider knowledge of the less well-known features of Truth, Version 1.0. He can do this, he tells himself.

"Well, Inspector … it's, you know… private…"

"Perhaps, Dr Morrison, but we have to rule out everyone, even the Director."

But Morrison simply stonewalls and looks down at his desk. It's a game of chicken, between the Inspector and himself. It's a game which he has never let himself lose. Ever. And this time is no exception. The Inspector sits back. Morrison has got away, this time.

Threats. Threats? No, not really. It suddenly strikes Morrison how tall the Inspector seems, and yet how awkward, even in the well-cut suit she's wearing. That's because she's so thin, he thinks. Not slim, *thin*. There's a difference. She's been through something. Something dreadful. Morrison guesses that she's not quite as tough as she'd like to think she is. In which case there's no need for her to play him like a fish.

Not when he can do the same to her.

"Would you like to know what happened last night, Inspector?" Sheepwool looks up at him as if she's been aroused from sleep.

"Yes, please, Dr Morrison. Do go ahead." Sheepwool's eyes look huge in her too-thin face. Morrison relaxes a little. Fitch gets out her notebook.

"I didn't actually discover poor old Bland's body. That was my colleague, Dr Alex Beach. She was working late in the lab, and she found his body at about, ooh…"

Fitch looks at her notes. "… about 3.30 this morning."

Really, Morrison thinks, this is just too easy.

"Yes, thank you. And the first thing she did, being a loyal member of the Institute, is phone me. Never mind that I'm at home, everyone here knows that I'm on call, twenty-four-seven. Absolutely. So after Dr Beach called me, I called you at… ah…"

This time Fitch simply waits for him to fall into his own trap: his voice topples into a grave of silence "At about… ah … ten to four."

Bad move. Oh, yes. Fitch peers at her notes.

"Our record says it was a little later, Dr Morrison, at four-thirteen."

A pause. The wind picks up again outside.

"Can you account for that discrepancy, Dr Morrison?" prompts Sheepwool. He decides to brazen it out.

"No, Inspector, I can't," he says, injecting a measure of asperity into his voice. "I've been woken up with the news that a senior colleague lies dead in his lab. I'm afraid I didn't keep an exact check on the time. And I have had very little sleep since."

"Of course, Dr Morrison." Sheepwool again. "Please continue".

"Thank you, Inspector." If Morrison is trying to look as though his amour-propre has been offended, the policewomen do not seem to be taking the bait. They remain motionless, looking at him. Once again he has the sensation that Sheepwool and Fitch are two cats, playing with him before striking.

"Dr Beach told me that she had been woken by the storm, decided she wasn't going back to sleep, and so went to do some work instead. Have you ever been a junior postdoctoral fellow, Inspector? You have to put in the hours, and sometimes it's just more efficient to work at night when there's less chance of interruption."

"She lives here, at the Institute?"

"Yes, Inspector. Some of our more junior and visiting staff live … ah … over the shop."

"Dr Beach works in a laboratory a few doors down from Dr Bland's own laboratory?"

"That's right, she …"

"Can you tell us what she works on, Dr Morrison?"

"I … ah … well, I could, but perhaps you'd do better asking Dr Beach that question?" Morrison has a sense that Sheepwool is at least three more steps ahead of the game than he is. He feels a bead of sweat moisten the collar of his shirt just under the nape of his neck, and start to roll slowly, accusingly down his back.

"Yes, Dr Morrison, quite right. But what about Dr Bland?"

"Hmm?"

"Let me put it this way, Dr Morrison." Sheepwool's eyes are no longer expressionless. They appear to have acquired a note of intent, of deliberation, almost of … malice. "Dr Bland doesn't, didn't, live 'over the shop', as you put it. Do you know where he lived, Dr Morrison?"

Morrison suspects that Sheepwool knows the answer to this perfectly well. But he'll have to trot out the answer like a schoolboy pulled up in front of the headmistress, or come up with some pathetic evasion. Game to Inspector Sheepwool.

"I … uh … he lived in the town, Inspector. A nice little bungalow in Halberd Park. I visited him there once or twice."

"Quite so, Dr Morrison. So what, in your opinion, given that you weren't there, might have Dr Bland been doing in the Institute, perhaps two miles from his home, in the early hours of a very stormy night?"

"I regret to say that I have no idea, Inspector."

"Was it usual for Bland to be at work at that time of day? As it was, apparently, for Beach?"

"No Inspector. Bland didn't usually roll up here much before ten or eleven in the morning and had gone by the staff afternoon tea-break at four. But he, well, he was retired, and was probably keen to finish up a few things. Bland was Director-Emeritus, with his own key. He could come and go as he pleased. In any case, Inspector, that's just me, speculating." Morrison feels himself climb back on that horse.

"Yes, of course, Dr Morrison. And I wonder if I could ask you to speculate on another matter?"

"Inspector?" Morrison steels himself against a move four, perhaps even five ahead. Sheepwool shifts again, slightly forward in her chair. He sees her knees press white like knuckles of raw meat against the inside of her stockings.

"Do you happen to know if Dr Bland was worried about anything before he died?"

"Worried, Inspector?" He tries to stifle a slight croakiness in his polished-walnut voice.

"Yes. Worried. Concerned about something? Under stress? Such things do occasionally drive people to climb out of their beds and go to work on stormy nights." Morrison is almost convinced he is imagining it, but Sheepwool seems to get, if possible, even thinner as she asks the question, which, in any case, she seems to be addressing more to herself. Morrison is grateful for Sheepwool's introspection, for he has broken into another sweat which he thinks could probably pass as radioactive, had the detectives had Geiger-counters.

Morrison does not answer the question.

And, amazingly, Sheepwool does not press him. "Well, perhaps, Dr Morrison, it is speculation and thus not fair to ask you such things.

But if I may, Dr Fitch should like to make some arrangements with your receptionist..." Fitch rises as if on cue, nods to Morrison and Sheepwool and leaves. "And, if I might trouble you further, might I show you something, Dr Morrison?" Sheepwool beckons Morrison out of his own office. He can do nothing but follow her lead. As if he is a puppet. He resigns himself to this dance, this charade, wondering what will happen when the music stops.

Without having to be told, Morrison knows that Sheepwool, her eyes boring into the back of his head as they walk, wants him to take her to Bland's laboratory. He cannot understand why she wants him to accompany her.

So, leaving his office unlocked, he leads Sheepwool back through the gallery and into the main hall, down the steps past the statue of Sir Frideric, and to the laboratories. There he waits, like a pupil waiting in the corridor for his teacher, for Sheepwool to catch up, and when she does, she moves some of the police tape aside to let them pass. They have exchanged no words since the abortive interview in his office. Now, at the lab complex itself, he opens his mouth to ask whether they really should be fiddling with the police tape, but receives an icy stare in response to this half-formed question. No more is needed for Morrison to grasp who's boss. Christ, she may look as stringy as a sick turkey, but her mind is like the proverbial steel trap. And yet there's some kind of protocol thing going on here, for once a gap is made in the tape, Sheepwool ushers Morrison through first. Taking a small bunch of keys from his trouser pocket, Morrison selects one with what he hopes doesn't look like too much practiced ease. He is the Director after all, and doesn't come down to the science complex more than he can help.

"Ah, here it is." Trying not to fumble, he unlocks the door and bows Sheepwool through, in mimicry of her earlier gesture. She does not seem to pick up on this, but clacks down the shiny linoleum of the central corridor ahead of him, until she gets to Bland's open door, looks in, and then turns to look at Morrison, still at the proximal end of the corridor. Her eyes are silent, but imperative. Meekly, he follows.

The door is barred by a single line of striped adhesive tape. Sheepwool does not touch this, but instead she and Morrison look over it, like two farmers peering over a neighbour's gate.

So, thinks Morrison, this is what Alex must have seen in the early hours. Beyond a bench he can see, on the floor, two well-shod feet and expensively-trousered legs, only partly covered by a sheet. One of the trouser legs has ridden up to reveal skin as insipidly pale as a frog's belly. Why had Alex made such a fuss? Well, I guess you can't see his face from this angle, he thinks. And to come across a body, unexpectedly, at three-ish in the morning, and in a place as spooky as the Institute: well, no wonder she was upset. He'd have to make it up to her. Eventually. Women whose expectations you have crushed are gratifyingly undemanding.

But now he has a tiger at his side, which seems to be searching all the pores in his face, one at a time, calculating the best moment to pounce. Through the corner of one eye, Morrison can see Sheepwool's every tic, and she seems more interested in him than in the Late Dr Evanston Bland, philanderer, squanderer and pompous pillock of the first order.

Really, the world is better off without tossers like him, always too distracted by a tasty figure or a pretty face to keep his eyes on the prize. If that's death, then it's not as worrying as he thought it might be, and indeed, it is much as he had expected. When Bland had confronted him to have what he called His Argument, he'd been popping pills (he said they were heart pills) like they were Smarties, and he was still as red as a beetroot and clearly agitated. Evidently, the pills couldn't take the pressure. Bland had presumably come to his laboratory at this unlikely hour to think things over and his ticker had finally stopped ticking.

What was the big argument about?

Morrison struggles to remember. Oh yes, amazing! He'd wanted to argue about Alex! Like they were a pair of bulls slugging it out over a heifer. Pathetic. What a sad old fart Bland was. He remembers now, what he'd said, how he'd told Bland to (how did he put it?) Ah yes, 'Futue Te Ipsum'. This had had quite some effect on an old man in who'd enjoyed a classical education. Anyway, that's all he'd said, in response to Bland's futile ravings.

And now Bland was dead. Ah, well, that's life.

And, then again, death.

Morrison suppresses a smirk. A coronary, plain and simple, when it could have been so much worse. So very, very much worse. But for now, he's in the clear. Relaxing, he realizes how tense he's been, and turns to Sheepwool, whose gaze remains on him, unwavering.

"It looks like a case of an old man who had a heart attack, don't you think, Inspector?" Morrison smiles, hoping to soften the chill. He fails.

"Possibly, Dr Morrison. That's for the pathologist and the coroner to establish. What I need to know, however, is why Bland was here rather than at home in bed, a question which, you will remember, we could not address to our satisfaction, along with the related question of whether Dr Bland had been under some kind of stress, which we could not answer in any way whatsoever. If Dr Bland had suffered a heart attack, this becomes all the more pressing". She turns to face him, both eyes, full on. Like blue holes. "And also, if I might add, we need to know who the last person was who saw Dr Bland alive."

Morrison feels the nape of his neck prickle again, as it did when Sheepwool and that other policewoman, the blonde one, were interviewing him in his office.

"That was Alex, Dr Beach, wasn't it?"

"No, Dr Morrison, it was not. Dr Beach discovered Bland when he was already dead." She clips every syllable, as if addressing an especially stupid teenager. But then, her voice softens, and Morrison sees her eyes taking on a misty glaze: "though perhaps he'd not long been dead when she found him. Dr Morrison -" she turns to him again with some urgency. He feels himself draw back reflexively in her gaze. "Dr Beach reported the death to you first. Your report to us was, in effect, at second hand. It's important that you now give a statement to us recalling everything she said, in as much detail as you can. And we'll be interviewing Dr Beach, of course."

"Of course, Inspector."

He's off the hook again. But for how long?

Elaine Fitch can't get away from Dr Morrison's office quickly enough. What a horrible man! He was good-looking though, with clothes like that, and the cool Swedish lines of his office made a refreshing change from the antique clutter of the rest of the Institute. But he made her flesh creep. She shudders involuntarily as she thinks of his ingratiating smile (all those teeth), the constant bead of sweat on his brow, and (ugh!) his clammy handshake. Jason always laughs when she gets home and the first thing she does is scrub her hands, hard, with a nailbrush. But her Jase always had the dry, hard hands of a builder and craftsman. It was one of the first things about him that attracted her, when they'd finally finished all that teenage pratting-about and got it together. That, and the fact that he'd look good in anything, and didn't feel the need to dress up. That's because, she realizes, Jason Fitch is as open and honest as the day is long. He has nothing to hide.

Unlike some people.

Actually, come to think of it, Morrison reminds her of her previous boss, now retired, all testosterone and after-shave, and of how glad she is to have hooked up with Detective Inspector Sheepwool. She'd never worked for a woman before, and wasn't sure she'd feel really comfortable about it, but really it's no trouble at all, and sometimes she feels that she does more of the looking-after than Sheepwool does herself. Of course, Sheepwool was just wished upon her (ours not to reason why!) but Fitch has the feeling that Sheepwool has had a rough time. You know, she thinks, it's just a feeling, such as when sometimes she seems right on the case, really on the money, but then collapses inwardly, as if consulting some deep, internal resource? And then she snaps right out of it, gives a little, almost apologetic smile, and makes two and two make five, which was the right answer all along? Fitch is looking forward to asking Sheepwool what she thinks of Morrison. But that's for later, down at the Station.

Now she's got other fish to fry. As she walks towards the front of the building, looking for the side-office behind the reception desk which she knows houses the general office of the Institute, she consults her notepad for a name.

She finds it: Mrs Janice Squearn, Administrator. She'd just jotted it down before they came, and hadn't given it much thought.

Now the name screams out at her as if framed in blazing neon.

Elaine Fitch stops dead in the gallery, right in front of Pickled Lily (something she'd definitely not intended to happen) and all of a sudden she's Elaine Southfield, aged eight and a half, and giggling because Bobby Honeypott is fooling around on the floor and trying to look up her skirt. From far above comes a voice, stern but kindly. It's Mrs Squearn. Squirmy Squearn. Trying, mostly in vain, to shepherd her unruly flock of Year-Fours past Kitten Hell and in front of the mermaids. That's when Elaine loses it, when the world, the world of Squirmy Squearn and Bobby Honeypott and that nice new boy, Jason, recedes as if visible only through the wrong end of a telescope. For Elaine, all Barbie-girl froth and bouncing curls, has locked eyes with Pickled Lily.

And Pickled Lily says to her: remember.

And Pickled Lily says to her: help me.

Fitch blinks, swallows hard, and all of a sudden she's much taller, in a businesslike suit and all alone, no Bobby or Jason or Mrs Squearn, but still in front of Pickled Lily. Fitch has the disconcerting sense that it was then, back in Year Four, that the seed was sown; that the course was set for her to become a policewoman, because her task in life was to solve the mystery of Pickled Lily. Until then, she'd had no inkling that there was a mystery to solve. How silly! All because of that name, Janice Squearn. She shakes her head to disentangle herself, as it were, from this web of thought that's wound, spider-like, all through her hair while she's been locked in reverie. Surely, she thinks, the Institute's Administrator can't be her old teacher? But then there can only be so many people called Squearn, and not many of those can be called Janice. Yes, the chances are that's what happened to her old teacher.

And so it proves.

"Elaine Southfield! Who'd have thought it?" Janice Squearn, a neat, slender middle-aged woman, looks up from her desk in the cramped cubbyhole of her office, a radiant smile breaking through what looks like a fogbank of fatigue. She gets up, abseils round an overloaded desk and grabs Fitch's hands with both of hers. "I had no idea it would be you, I didn't make the connection … "

For the second time in the space of ten minutes, Fitch is a schoolgirl again. She feels herself flush, and shuffles her feet. Close-up, Squearn is very much older than she'd like to pretend. Careful make-up and precision-engineered hair have ensured that only someone who had known her in a former life can track the emotional scars that time has trampled all over this woman's theater of a face, across which smiles flicker on and off, intermittently, like a fluorescent tube on the point of failure. When it's off, she looks like she's been dead for years. When it comes on again, she is reanimated to a degree that might convince almost anyone.

Anyone except Elaine Fitch, née Southfield.

Fitch does not even have to open her mouth, still less to frame a question. Even as Squearn sweeps aside a pile of dusty papers and beckons Fitch to sit down in a fraying easy-chair opposite her desk, it all comes out, as if Squearn had been waiting years for precisely this audience to turn up.

"Oh, Elaine, you can't tell how pleased I am that it's you. How you've grown! And you still have those lovely curls! It was because of Dr Bland, who died, that I left you all. So suddenly. I'm so terribly, terribly sorry."

Fitch now remembers now: (how could she have forgotten it?) the disorienting abruptness of the departure of a much-loved teacher who had been her idol since she'd been too tiny to — well, for as long as she could possibly remember, anyway. It was halfway through Year Six, just before graduation from Deringland Primary. The pain of loss at the time was indescribable, and of betrayal, too, that Mrs Squearn would leave, mid-term, marring the neat conclusion of all their Junior-school careers before the big leap to High School. Classes disrupted. School plays rescheduled. A succession of supply teachers who could not possibly fill such a gaping wound. But the minds of children are fickle, callous. Very soon other things came along to take Mrs Squearn's place. Halberd Park High, intimidating, huge. New friends. Boys. Exams. Jason.

From a distance of twenty years, she recalls with only a vague sense of unease the announcement from the Headmaster one morning in Spring that Mrs Squearn had gone, and subsequently, what seemed like very careful efforts by the teaching staff never to mention her name again.

But for Mrs Squearn, the memories are still pristine, unworn by repetition, only waiting for the right moment to bloom. However long that might take.

"It all began when I brought you all here, to the Institute, in Year Four. My! I remember it now. You were all gathered in front of Pickled Lily, and I was just about to tell you about Sir Frideric, when I turned round ... and there he was..."

Her eyes glaze, and for a moment she is lost. She brings herself back with a start. "Dr Evanston Bland. The Director of the Institute. He'd heard some noise; must have been Bobby making a row, and all you girls giggling! He'd come out of his office to see what it was ... and, oh well, it was just like in a silly novel, but our eyes met across a crowded room. And that was that." Her face hides itself under deeper clouds of anguish. Regret. Guilt?

"Mrs Squearn?"

"Yes … sorry … and to think, me, married for eighteen years, a teacher for twenty-five, teenage children, never even so much as looked at another man, and Evanston came along and swept me off my feet. He pressed and pressed me to leave my life behind, move here. With him. There was great work to be done. Scientific work. Together. So after more than a year of indecision I did it. I did what he asked. Of course, he played on my vanity." Her voice hardens. The edge is surprising. Fitch doesn't recall Mrs Squearn being this stern, ever.

"I always wanted to become a research scientist, you know? Change the world. But in those days it was very difficult for a mere woman to do such things. Especially one already married and with children. I'm so glad you've succeeded in breaking into this world, this man's world, for that's what it is, Elaine, and don't you forget it. Anyway, I drifted into a kind of part-time half-world of being a research assistant. Hours and hours sexing fruit-flies, that's the lab equivalent of tea-girl, and being patronized by these men who I knew hadn't half the commitment or talent I had. So in the end I became a teacher. I don't regret it, mind, it was never second-best …"

She pauses to take a breath, sighs.

"So, silly me, I gave it all up, threw it all away, to follow science, here, with Evanston."

A longer pause. Fitch is conscious of how heavily the silence drapes this small, windowless office. And of how stifling it is, how it smells of dust and mould; how dim the light; how scruffy the carpet, such fragments of it as can be seen through the crowded furniture, the computer equipment perched in nooks and corners designed for a pre-electronic age, the snags of wiring, the bundles of printouts, the careful inventories of neglect.

For the first time, Fitch notices something odd, that there is not one scrap of anything personal in this room, such as you'd expect in the office of every middle-aged career administrator she'd ever seen. No family photographs. No ornaments. Not even a dead spider-plant.

"It never happened, of course. Evanston kept promising that we'd start a project, but it was always next week, next month. And then I discovered that Evanston's eyes had wandered … and wandered again. But by that time I couldn't go back. I don't think I could have borne the shame, then. I don't think I could, even now. I left town, I had to. Made a new life for myself. I didn't dare leave this job, though, I was stuck! What kind of references would that deceitful man have given me? And the school, before that? The closest I've been to Deringland in all these years is this office. And having to work in the same place as Bobby Honeypott, you know he's here? Well, not everyone turned out as well as you, Elaine, that's for sure. I wish Evanston had done something decent for once and got rid of him, but of course I was hardly in a position to complain." Fitch perks up for a moment at the thought of a new connection in a frustratingly elusive case. "Now poor Evanston is dead, but I still don't think I could show my face in Deringland again."

At this, Janice Squearn collapses like a discarded marionette: Elaine leaves her seat, inches her way past shoals of detritus to Squearn's side of the desk, and puts her arm round the cardiganed shoulders of her old teacher.

"Oh, Mrs Squearn…" She is surprised how bony and delicate she seems, like a tiny bird. "If there's anything I can do …"

Janice Squearn now collects herself, pulls herself up, gently, but firmly, brushing away the younger woman's arm. She now effects a personal transformation as remarkable as that of a caterpillar into a butterfly.

"No, my dear, I'm afraid there isn't. In any case, perhaps it's all for the best. But that's enough about me. I'm sure you didn't come here just to hear the ravings of a foolish old woman. Tea? Coffee?" Squearn turns round to a squirreled niche Fitch hadn't before seen, containing a tiny kettle, a few boxes, and what looks like a small collection of very dirty cups. Fitch politely declines, picking her way once more to the more businesslike side of the desk.

"Well, yes, actually, Mrs Squearn, I'm here as … well, in my professional capacity."

"I understand. And please, call me Janice."

Squearn's attempt at calmness is good, but perhaps a little too forced. Fitch remembers her old teacher as the very picture of grace under pressure, and imagines that she must be feeling a little ashamed, now, of her outburst. Fitch feels she's in two worlds, a little girl and a detective, both at once. To concentrate on the latter she breaks eye contact and fossicks around in her bag for her notebook and a ballpoint.

"You see, Mrs Squearn … Janice … Dr Bland's death was probably just a heart attack, but I, we, need to know what everyone at the Institute was doing… where they were … when …"

"When Dr Bland died. Well, you'll not have any worries on my score." Squearn now seems to have regained her poise, the calm, polished waves of equanimity closing over the wreck of her past as if it had never set sail. But perhaps it's all an act, perhaps, Fitch thinks, her presence in this mean little room has pitched Janice Squearn into the long-lost role of schoolmistress, a role she threw over so impetuously and forever regretted leaving. "Last night I was chairing a meeting of the Sutton-next-the-Sea Evening Women's Institute."

Fitch reflects that Janice Squearn's new life will have had a couple of decades to have become established, and that after her humiliation, for that's what it was, she'll have filled every minute with activity. Just standing still would have been an admission of defeat. Fitch notices, quite suddenly, that the glitter in Squearn's eyes, the defiant set of her jaw, reminds her of DI Sheepwool. It would be a mistake to see Janice Squearn frozen in time as a schoolteacher, preserved like a mermaid. Squearn, like everyone else, like time itself, moves on, in ways that museum specimens don't, which can only look on with a kind of inanimate envy, or spite.

"But Dr Bland probably died much later," Fitch interrupts, "in the early hours. I'm sorry to have to press you, but can you say what you doing … account for your time … until about dawn this morning?"

"I was just coming to that, Elaine. I was in bed. And neither asleep, nor alone. Between around two and five I was enjoying some … ah … relations with my partner."

"Your partner?"

"Yes. After Evanston deserted me, I was desolated for quite a long time. Several years in fact. I ached with longing for my past life, my husband … and my children, none of whom I've seen since … since I left home. But after a while I met Frankie. Eventually, after a long while in which I learned to trust such matters, as sharing one's heart, one's feelings, we moved in together. There have been times in which if it weren't for Frankie I think I might have gone quite mad."

"I'm sorry, Mrs Squearn, Janice, can I have some details for … Frankie? We'll have to corroborate your alibi. He lives at your address…?"

"Yes, of course. I'm sure Frankie won't mind. Francesca Honiton is the secretary of the Sutton Evening Women's Institute."

Fitch is, unusually, lost for words. Janice Squearn's eyes blaze fiercely in the shabby gloom of this office. "I haven't asked about your circumstances, my dear. I see from your ring that you are married. I hope it is all going as well as you always wanted." Fitch thinks warmly of Jason, as she does about once every five minutes, and her three gorgeous children, and, as ever, can't even begin to imagine how anyone could want to change anything about any of them in any way whatsoever.

"A marriage is all about trust," says Squearn. "I betrayed the trust of my own, and Evanston betrayed my trust in his turn. I don't think I could ever trust a man again, nor expect a man to trust me. Indeed, I'm convinced that men and women are different species."

Fitch feels wretchedly small. She opens her mouth to speak, but nothing comes out. She is cast back to her wedding day. A lovely, perfect white wedding, with Jason looking so handsome in his dove-gray tailcoat, her parents so proud, all her colleagues in uniform. And yes, the tiniest, teensiest regret at thinking, just as the photographer took another shot of her and Jason outside the church, whether her old schoolteacher might not have been invited, but crossing her off the list as she'd no idea how the long-lost Mrs Squearn might have been contacted.

6: To What's Submerged

The best view of the Institute, thinks Fitch, sliding the stick into second, and then third, is in the rear-view mirror, driving away. As for its inhabitants: well, her mind is fizzing with possibilities that she's just dying to share with DI Sheepwool. Her boss, however, is actively silent, sunken into her seat, quite still, and apparently staring at nothing.

Fitch changes into fourth, then fifth, and she's away. She decides to sublimate her frustration by concentrating on the driving, something she's superbly good at, and which always gives her solace. At times like this, while she's waiting for something to happen that might get her closer to some kind of resolution, she likes to remember the fun she's always had on the advanced and defensive driving courses the force occasionally offers.

Wonderful!

The expression on Jason's face when she does screaming handbrake turns in the supermarket car park; the admiring approval of Dean, her eldest, and at eleven, passionate about cars; the squeals of mingled terror and delight from Eric and little Bryony.

"Mum! You might get arrested! By the *police*!" Eric had said.

"Mum *is* the police, stupid." Dean had replied, not entirely unreasonably. Fitch basks in the memory. She adores driving, but at work, at any rate, it's a private pleasure. DI Sheepwool either hasn't learned to drive, or has, but chooses not to: and whenever Fitch mentions anything about cars, Sheepwool either ignores her or changes the subject. It's as if the entire subject is taboo. Strange. Oh, well, Sheepwool is not your usual Detective Inspector. Resigned, Fitch turns her attention back to the road ahead.

The wind has dropped now, the last threadbare clouds and swirls of mist have gone, replaced by the kind of unearthly, clear blue sky usually seen only in brochures for ski-ing holidays. This blank blue-ness drops around the car on all sides, as the Institute and then the Deringland Light fall over the rear horizon and once again the two policewomen seem to be amid an apparently endless prairie of grass. Fitch doesn't like this blankness of sky. It's eerie, nightmarish. She longs for a cloud, even a small one, to break it up and give it scale. Her unease is short-lived, however, for she has to use all her driving skills to negotiate the sharp, scarcely-surfaced scree of the final, downward plunge of the track as it meets the main road. She stops, exhales, signals right, and feeds the car on the road towards Der-ingland. A moment later, Sheepwool speaks, but her first word seems completely meaningless.

"Magritte."

"Ma'am?"

"That's what occurred to me, when I saw this lovely blue sky. René Magritte. Surrealist painter. He painted perfectly clear skies, like this one, and then filled them with clouds shaped like everyday objects. Birds. Chairs. And then he gave very strange, teasing titles to the paintings. *Threatening Weather*." Fitch has no idea what, if anything, she should say to this, so she pretends to concentrate on the driving, making a fuss about looking in the rear-view mirror.

"Magritte always puzzled me," continues Sheepwool. "But just now, after our visit, it all seems to make sense. The clouds, the skies, are just portraits of the mind. The clouds you carry around with you, inside your head."

"Ma'am, I…" Art history, still less philosophy, did not figure very highly on the curriculum of Halberd Park High. Psychology, though, she studied that at University in Norwich (her first and only extended stay outside Deringland, if you don't count family holidays and her honeymoon in Thailand). She liked psychology, and got a degree that was good enough for graduate entry to the police, but there were depths and subtleties to it that always seemed just beyond her grasp, and her lecturers' ability to explain. She preferred the crisp certainties of law.

And, oh yes, driving.

"Oh, don't worry about me, Fitch," says Sheepwool, reassuringly, "just thinking aloud."

Fitch now knows her superior sufficiently well that this counts as an invitation to share confidences.

"I checked with Mrs Squearn, the administrator," she says, not taking her eyes off the road, but all the same acutely aware that she rests in the full, lamp-like gaze of her superior. "Most of the scientists and staff were away from the Institute last night, Christmas holidays. Some of them will be back later today - I'll have to go back later to nose around, check alibis and so on, but I reckon it's a heart attack, Ma'am. Open and shut. But, you know, this Bland..."

"Hmm?"

"Well, you know I checked him out? His form? It turns out that he lured Mrs Squearn herself to the Institute. She gave up husband, kids, home, the lot, just for him. But he was all mouth and trousers. Never delivered. He sounds like a right old ..."

"Your point is...?"

"Well, Ma'am, it's like this." She shuffles her feet nervously. Of course, she can always claim she is riding on the clutch. "When I saw Mrs Squearn I nearly had a heart attack myself! She was my old primary school teacher. I loved Mrs Squearn. But she left when I was in Year Six, just disappeared, no warning, and I never knew what happened to her. Nobody knew. And, goodness, she threw it all away, all because of Bland, and never went back. Even after he dumped her." Fitch feels herself reddening with anger at the injustice of it. "All I had to do was turn up at the Institute office and it all came out -- whoosh!"

"It sounds like she has ample motivation for getting back at Bland," says Sheepwool. After a pause, she adds: "all the same, I don't think she did."

Fitch feels unwonted relief course through her arms and legs. She was afraid that Sheepwool would want to interview Janice Squearn herself, forcing Fitch into a cleft stick, between past loyalty and present duty. Now, light-headed, she feels she can play devil's advocate.

"Ma'am? How so? Have you met her ... talked to her?"

"No need. The question is this, if she had the motivation, why didn't she act on it years ago? Why now? Of course, something could have pushed her over the edge, just in the past few days, but what? I think one can have too much opportunity, as well as too little. No, I think your first instincts are correct. Probably a weak heart. But that'll be for Jim Levy and later the coroner to decide."

More silence. The first buildings of Deringland appear: they seem to grow from the verges in disconsolate huddles.

"Ma'am, you remember our last case? Customs and Excise, Bob Honeypott and all that?"

"Yes?"

"Well, I'm sorry it never struck me before, but you know I said Bob Honeypott was in my class at school? Well, Janice Squearn taught him as well as me. So there was somebody who knew what happened to her. She said something, when I talked to her, about having to work alongside him at the Institute. How uncomfortable it was. I wish I'd known she was there, made the connection... she could have been really useful."

"That case is not yet closed. Thank you, I shall mention it to Super-intendent Methwold." Sheepwool smiles. So encouraged, Fitch is sucked upwards into the dewy realms of hypothesis.

"Ma'am, I wonder if, you know, Honeypott and Squearn, maybe there's a history. Could he have had a hold on her, somehow?"

"What? Blackmail? Could be. Money to keep him quiet, perhaps. About his little fiddles and finagles".

"Yes, Ma'am, but do you think he ..."

"Do you think he did away with Bland? Well, anything's possible. But I don't see why. More likely that Honeypott found it convenient to have Bland as a boss, given what seems to have been his casual style of management, allowing Honeypott to do all sorts of things on the quiet. No, I think that if anything, it was the other way round. Honeypott had a hold on Bland. It was in his interests to keep Bland alive. I don't fancy his chances now there's a new broom."

The buildings of Deringland resolve from occasional broken teeth to a sullen, gray density. A few other vehicles join them, a parade constrained to funereal pace by the narrowness of the streets. Fitch is forced to stop behind a bus that blocks the entire High Street to admit a few teenagers and disgorge a small gaggle of pensioners. Just for a moment, she imagines the bus as a kind of time machine, sucking in children and spitting them out as old people, draining them of entire lives in mere seconds. To make it worse, she imagines that all of them, teenagers and senior citizens alike, have the same, fishy heads. Cri-key, this isn't like her at all. Not even after watching *Dr Who*, when she has to keep Bryony company behind the sofa, peeping out over the top so she doesn't miss anything important. Fitch hopes she doesn't have to visit the Institute too often. It does funny things to your mind.

Sheepwool, like the bus, has stopped, but it seems clear that she hasn't finished.

"On which subject…"

"Ma'am?"

"I wonder, what did you make of our friend Dr Morrison?"

Fitch cannot help herself. "I thought he was just horrible! I -- so sorry…"

"No need. I didn't like him much either."

"So, well, slimy!"

"Well, yes. But there's no crime in slime…" And before she can stop herself, Fitch subsides into giggles, right there, in the traffic jam, behind the bus. Sheepwool cannot help but join in. Two detectives behaving like typists on a spree. Decorum is soon reimposed, however, as the bus signals to pull out and the cortège continues through the town, but Fitch feels that an important bond has been forged between herself and her troubled, enigmatic superior officer.

"What I meant, Fitch, was that you have to look past all that. Beneath the surface. To what's submerged."

"What's submerged, but how can you see that?"

"Exactly."

"I'm sorry, Ma'am, I don't …"

"Well, just think about our interview. When I asked him whether Bland was under stress, he didn't answer the question. Didn't try to lie, didn't give some evasion, he flat-out didn't answer. Now, I don't know about you, but I reckon Morrison isn't telling us something. Something important."

"Like, he knows that Bland really was under stress?"

"Yes. But if so, why didn't Morrison just say so?"

"Because … maybe … Morrison had something to do with it? With Bland's death?"

"Well, yes, of course, it's all speculation, but when you went to visit Mrs Squearn I took Morrison to see Bland's body. He didn't look shocked, surprised, nauseated, you know how people look when they see dead bodies."

Fitch felt that this probably wasn't the time to admit that dead bodies were sufficiently rare in Norfolk for her never to have seen one, in the flesh, so to speak.

"No," continued Sheepwool, "if anything, he looked *pleased*. Just for an instant. And he tried to cover it up, I'm sure. But that's how he looked."

"Maybe he was no more pleased than Janice Squearn was, though? After all, Bland seems to have got up everyone's noses. And anyway, Morrison was at home at the time. Just like Mrs Squearn was."

"So he says. All we have, right now, is his word for it. Hers too, as a matter of fact."

Fitch says nothing: she mustn't let her fondness for Squearn and her dislike of Morrison get the better of her.

"In any case," Sheepwool continues, "heart attack or not, we really ought to see this Alex Beach person. She discovered the body after all."

"We only have Morrison's word for that too, Ma'am!"

"Indeed. But I'm puzzled. From everything we know so far, doesn't it seem odd that Alex Beach, who is the only person we definitely *know* to have been at the Institute last night … Morrison wasn't lying about that … just happens to be a few doors down the hall from Dr Bland, just as he expires?"

"… and what was Dr Bland doing at the Institute at that time, anyway?"

"That's also a very good question. I rather think that when you go back this afternoon, I'll ride shotgun. I'd like to meet Alex Beach for myself. Sooner rather than later."

Sheepwool is now sitting up straight, eyes bright. The car inches to the end of the High Street. Fitch turns left at the roundabout opposite the Three Kings. They make their way up the hill to the police station with the resolve, and something of the fear, of the lone gunslinger on his way to meet the noon train. It is January in Deringland, but that calm blue light has something of the Old West about it. The calm of approaching menace.

"Ma'am…. Bland …. Beach …. Do you think…?"

At that moment Fitch brakes hard, reflexively, as a small child runs into the road in front of the car and falls over. It is followed by a squat, brick-faced young woman. Fitch realizes it's the same one who crossed the road in front of Woolworths on their way out that morning. Sheepwool and Fitch watch as the woman yanks the child onto the pavement and smacks it hard round the head, bathing it in a soundless torrent of abuse. The child gives a silent yell of pain.

Danger over, Fitch restarts the engine and looks round at her boss, to see if she'd been hurt by the sudden stop. Sheepwool has turned an ashy white, entirely drained of colour, as if she'd aged twenty years.

She looks the same as she had done when she first saw Pickled Lily, and Fitch had, gently, to steer her away.

"I try not to think, Fitch. Not too much. Not if I can help it."

Deringland Railway Station is a mausoleum to a past which never quite arrived. Spires poking through a January fog like a gaunt arm trying to shake itself free of ghosts, it was built for an earlier, more optimistic age, when the railway was meant to bring tourism to Deringland, and with it the comfort and civilization that was the high-water mark of Victorian England. Hence the façade of enamel, beetle-shiny in buff and blue; the ornate buttresses, the steeply-pitched roof, wedding-cake colonnades, battlements and turrets that would look overdone in Disneyland, all that once bade welcome to the metropolitan seeker after the healthful breezes of north Norfolk.

The boom was short-lived, though, a rosebud consumed by mildew, snuffed out by economic recession in the 1880s. And because of a feeling that whereas visitors were something Deringland badly needed, they were not always what it wanted. What the seeker so often found was a thin veneer of enforced charm and jollity beneath which lay the hollow-faced poverty of a remote region in long-term decline; whose breezes brought icy knives more often than refreshment, these alternating with unpredictable, fog-bound chills that could last for days, even weeks; and whose custom was greeted with embalmed, fish-eyed smiles devoid of warmth.

Tourists left Deringland with the sensation, rarely articulated, that it was always cold. Even on those rare, blessed days of July, when the wind dropped and the fog cleared, and when the Sun stood high in the South, baking the backs of those who, on the West Promenade, would sit on the plentiful municipal benches and gaze to seaward, a passage into shadow, perhaps behind a building or in the lee of one of the crab-boats pulled up on the beach, or when the Sun would disappear behind a scrap of cloud, would create a chill which always seemed more profound than merited by the moment: a chill that would run, like mercury, deep into the bones, affecting one far longer than one could imagine for such a transitory phenomenon. Nobody said it at the time (indeed, nobody would say it now), but Deringland played host to an active kind of cold, a cold that deterred all but those hardy few accustomed to the region's natural state, seals, and bitterns, flat salt marshes bounded by vertiginously wide beaches of shingle uninterrupted by any overtly human construction. Certainly not one as profligately, as pathetically, ornamented as Deringland Railway Station. Few tourists visited Deringland more than once.

Therefore, and as if in acknowledgement of its fundamental uselessness, Deringland Station now welcomes far fewer trains than its structure would suggest, its large but deserted ticket hall; its small news kiosk, which never seems to be open; its waiting room, until recently the haunt of indigent youth and drug addicts and now boarded up. Indeed, over the Christmas holidays it has welcomed no trains at all. The first train of the New Year arrives just after sunset in the afternoon following Bland's very private, Deringland death, and carries a handful of passengers. The clear, unearthly blue of the day has faded to a woollen gray, and now black, as clouds once more congeal upon the town.

The few passengers alight and disappear, faceless, coalescing with the night. All except one, a small, fussy middle-aged woman struggling with a roll-along suitcase almost as large as she is. On the Station's cobbled forecourt she waits for a cab, reckoning that even here, one will arrive to meet the train and tout for custom, as reliably as vultures gathering over a recent kill. But the post-Christmas torpor, like the fog, always takes longer to lift than one thinks, so it takes ten or fifteen minutes or so for the rust-pocked Peugeot estate that is currently Deringland Cabs' only vehicle to arrive. The driver seems cheerful enough; in response to which the prospective passenger chokes back the several acid comments she'd been brewing as a way to stave off the damp, the cold, and the boredom of waiting. Moreover, and not a little disconcertingly, the driver knows the passenger's destination without even having to ask.

"The Institute? Sure. Can't have you walking all that way on a night like this, with all that lot to lug around!" The driver, a big, round man, balding, with sandy hair and a moustache that makes him look like the Carpenter's Walrus, nods at the enormous bag. He gets out of the car and heaves it into the back with practiced ease, then opens the passenger door for his fare. The woman smiles weakly, as if smiling is a habit in which she does not usually care to indulge, and lacks the practice to do it with any confidence.

The car grumbles out of the forecourt and onto the road, taking a left, down the hill and into town. At length it passes the police station on the right, thereafter taking precisely the same course as that followed by Fitch and Sheepwool. The late-afternoon vista could hardly be more different. Mist and blackness obscure almost everything from view. Today is half-day closing, so all the shops are blank and shuttered. The street lamps of Deringland are widely spaced, and many do not work at all, turning the short journey into a voyage in space between scattered stars, each surrounded by a foggy penumbra like a halo of comets seen from an immense distance. It is barely four p.m., but it feels like midnight.

None of this penetrates the exhausted, shrouded mind of Dr Maureen Boynton, a Visiting Fellow at the Lowdley-Purslane Institute, currently on sabbatical from the University of Leeds, and who has just returned from a conference in the United States. It had been an awful trip. Just awful.

Dr Boynton has been a regular attendee at the annual meetings of the American Association for Algal Ecology for almost twenty years. The AAAE is a touchstone, a marker for her year, and, being a spinster with no immediate family (at least, none she's prepared to tolerate), the thought of the AAAE keeps her going through the dismal hole that is Christmas. Come the second or third of January she jets away for a week of collegial pleasantries, interesting lectures, a week during which she can review ongoing collaborations and forge new ones, what her younger colleagues, over-fond of pushing the present participle into uses for which it was not intended, would, no doubt, call 'networking'.

The American academic schedule means that the best time to hold a conference is in the first week of the New Year. The academic semester has yet to begin, and algal ecologists are less likely to be doing fieldwork than would be the case in the summer or fall. Perhaps a greater consideration, Boynton thinks, is that hotel block bookings immediately after Christmas are cheap. Algal ecology, after all, does not rank among the most conspicuously well-funded of disciplines. Indeed, Boynton reflects that she tends to go to AAAE as part of her annual holiday, funding it from her salary, grants for attending such conferences being hard to come by.

Winter conferences are all very well if they are in places that are pleasant, or at least pleasantly *warm*, with opportunities for field trips.

But this year? They say that travelling hopefully is better than to ar-rive, but to have the culmination of a trip much anticipated - much cherished even - take place in a motel on a freeway on the outskirts of Pittsburgh?

Oh dear. Best put such things down to experience.

The cab chugs through Deringland and out the other side, climbing the eastward hill, streetlamps fading altogether into what seems like intergalactic darkness.

But perhaps every cloud has a silver lining. For she's returned with a nugget of information. Disturbing information. Something she really ought to tell Lars Johansson as soon as possible. Whether she should tell Alex Beach, too ... well, that's something she'd have to think about. Lars would know what to do.

She'd escaped for a quiet lunch at a Chinese restaurant in Pitts-burgh with a colleague, Professor Britta Sonnenschein of the Univer-sity of Oregon, with whom she's currently preparing a paper. Al-though Boynton is spending a year at the LPI, living in a room barely better than the one at the conference motel, she tells herself that she's at the Institute for the reference collection of kelp hauled from the North Atlantic by the *Spaniel* expedition, and nothing more. As for the Institute itself, she loathes it and can't wait to go home to her neat flat in Harrogate. However, she cannot quite understand why she seems so reluctant to tell Sonnenschein where she's currently located, as if she's ashamed of it.

But the truth will out, and the effect of casually slipping in the words 'Lowdley', 'Purring' and 'Institute' into the conversation, while they're waiting for the Dim Sum trolley to arrive, is disconcerting.

Now, Boynton would be the first to admit that she and Sonnen-schein make an unlikely pair. Whereas she is slight and neatly dressed, Sonnenschein is blousy and, frankly, obese; whereas she has nondescript hair on the verge of graying, and somewhat sallow skin, Sonnenschein has wild masses of hair the colour of mango chutney and a complexion that supermodels would die for; whereas she dis-appears easily into a crowd without raising a ripple, Sonnenschein dominates a room and, in the words of her devoted astrophysicist husband, is a 'walking focus of entropy increase'. If asked to summa-rise Sonnenschein in an epigram, Boynton would say she's a pre-Raphaelite model gone to seed -- gloriously. But despite their differ-ences, they have been collaborators for more than a decade, and Boynton counts Sonnenschein as one of her few, close friends, almost a confidante.

This is why her reaction to news of the LPI is so peculiar. Sonnenschein, who is a diabetic and has been rifling through her disordered purse in search of insulin, stops as if caught in a flashlight, looks up, and says "Morrison!" with as much drama as if she'd said "Nevermore!"

"Morrison? He's the Director …"

"For *sure* he is, Maureen! *And* the rest!"

"The rest? Of what?" Boynton is puzzled. The question hangs in the air for frustrating seconds as the Dim Sum trolley draws alongside their table. The waitress receding, Sonnenschein plays Earth Mother and dishes up for both of them.

"You should watch that one, Maureen. That's all I can say." Sonnenschein's arrestingly emerald-green eyes sparkle with conspiratorial mischief.

Boynton laughs, a shrill and nervous sound that is rarely heard, perhaps mercifully so, as it sounds like a small skylark being sucked, very politely, into a jet engine. Sonnenschein looks around the restaurant stagily as if to check they're not being overheard, bundles of coppery hair loosening with each turn of her head. Now she leans over the table as if to offer a confidence, revealing a mountainous, flawlessly white cleavage beneath her loose, Indian-print dress. Boynton thinks that the entire restaurant, which has the size and character of an aircraft hangar, would have no trouble overhearing, had it wanted to.

"You remember I told you about that conference I went to in Atlanta? Drug discovery and natural products? 'Secrets of the Sea', it was called. Not really my scene, but, hey ho, a girl has to make a living…"

Boynton nods her assent.

"Yeah, well, it was just *full* of suits. More like Wall Street than any conference *I've* ever been to." Boynton imagines how Sonnenschein couldn't help but have stood out in such company, like a pole-dancer at a funeral. She suppresses a smirk. "But there was this one guy, little guy, couldn't help noticing, because he only came up to my chest. Got fed up of him staring, frankly. Anyway, he was the most suited-up of the lot. Quite the dandy, he thought himself. Don't want to be talking out of turn, Maureen, but *that* was Morrison. And when I heard his full name, well…"

"His full name is Marion Morrison. Why…"

"Don't you get it? What kind of a guy has a name like *that*?"

"What's wrong with it?" Boynton confesses herself nonplussed.

"Oh, nothing's actually *wrong* with it. It's just that nobody is born with a name like that. Not these days." Sonnenschein looks at Boynton's confused expression and laughs. Reaching over the table, she pats Boynton's hand.

"Oh Maureen!" Sonnenschein puts on a voice of affectionate exasperation. "'Marion Morrison' was the real name of a Hollywood actor. *Stagecoach? True Grit?* With me now?"

"So what? If …"

"Sure, that could be his real name, but I bet it isn't. I'm only saying this because you're only there a few months and it's clear you don't much like it…

"Me? I …"

"Hey, Maureen, this is *me* you're talking to! *Sure* you don't. But this Morrison is a front. A phoney. And you know what? He was acting the real big shot at this meeting, giving it the full John-Wayne swagger, chatting people up, taking them out to dinner, cocktails, throwing parties. Like he had money to burn. I kept asking myself, whose money was it?" Maureen had to admit that it sounded strange. Staff at small, provincial research institutes, even private ones, rarely had an entertainment budget that would stretch further than a bottle of warm chardonnay and a few cheesy dips.

"At first I didn't think much of it. After all, he wasn't the only one. Some of these big-pharma types might as well be hedge-fund managers for the money they throw around. But then I was at the bar one night, waiting for Harvey, I think: we were going to discuss that East Pacific Rise idea I told you about…" Boynton nods in recognition of a mutual colleague and another possible collaborative project.

"And there was Morrison, staring at some young girl's tits, which he couldn't help doing, as she was a lot taller than he was, and telling her like some wise-guy that as her doctorate was so good, she should come and work at his place on … what was it now? Ah yes, 'carnostomids'. So there am I putting two and two together, and recalled the *Voyage of the Spaniel* from some history-of-science course I taught years and years ago. So, naturally, I eavesdropped.

"He said he had plenty of money from some set-up called Ma-gusPharm and he could easily take her on for a postdoc, if she wanted. Well, that name, MagusPharm, kept coming up at this meeting, you know? It's some new pharma company that's made it big, though nobody really knows how or why, and has scared the shit out of the established players. And yet that's the company that seems to be raining money on this Marion Morrison character. But that's not what struck me most."

There was a pause, as if Sonnenschein were trying to recreate the scene clearly in her own mind before passing it on. "Now, Morrison always seemed to be schmoozing with some young girl or another, but I got the impression that they all thought he was some clown, never took him seriously. Not this one, though. She seemed to be easy meat. Sure, she was no waif, tall, Cindy-Crawford-curvaceous, you know? But she just gazed and gazed at him with these big blue eyes like she'd been hypnotized. *Don't do it sister*, I yelled on all telepathic channels, you know? Turned my world-famous fempathy up to the max, but then Harvey arrived and I never saw her again."

The sound of the cab's tires scrunching on gravel jolts Boynton back to the present. She pays off the taxi driver; the cab, graying in the deepening shadow, scrunches off down the track. After the fug of the cab, which smelled vaguely of old tobacco and wet dogs, the sea breeze is quickening. The Institute, illuminated by the slow pulse of the Deringland light, looms massively before her in the darkness. The sea, invisible from here, makes its presence felt in the low but wide-screen noise of surf, and a smell which Boynton finds irresistible, casting her back, if she lets it, to happy memories of a lost childhood, long ago. Useless to speculate, she thinks, setting her head high and dragging the roll-bag over the gravel towards the front door.

Perhaps it is the effort of having to haul the luggage that prevents her from looking around, from noticing that a police car stands on the drive closest to the doors. Two women are emerging from the car. One is tall, willowy, with a rather abstracted look, as if her mind spends most of its time on some remote plane. The other is shorter, a smiling face framed with blonde curls. It is this woman who intercepts her.

"Hello there ... before you go in... I'm Detective Sergeant Fitch, Norfolk Police. I have some bad news, I'm afraid."

7: Speaking Ill of the Dead

Sheepwool wonders which kind of interview is better: the one in which the interviewee says too much, or the one in which she says nothing at all. In Alex Beach's lab, a mote of relative neatness in this efflorescently horrible place, she realizes that this is a false dichotomy. No, the most problematic interviews are those in which the answers are ambiguous. Or, worse still, in which the interviewee seems entirely, readily cooperative with the answers she gives to straight questions, but her eyes, her whole body, seem locked in a tetanic scream of contradiction.

Dr Alexandra Beach seems to belong in this latter category. Sheepwool, who finds it hard to order the parallel thoughts that rattle round inside her brain into a coherent line of argument, wishes (not for the first time) that Fitch were here to do the talking. Any questions she asks seem to falter, half-done, into nothingness, and if there is one thing Sheepwool dislikes, it is incomplete sentences. But Beach is just there, impassive. Whether Beach is standing, or leaning, or sitting, all Sheepwool sees is a tall, voluptuous young woman who, in another age, and except for her eyes, blue-gray rather than brown, would have made a good model for Renoir. She has the same pale, clean limbs, the same curves, and, most pertinently, the same vacant expression.

Yes, it's her expression.

That's it, thinks Sheepwool. That's what's so, well … so disturbing. Perhaps some sympathy would be in order here. Here is a woman who lives in what passes these days for a haunted castle, who has gone down to the dungeons at some godless hour and stumbled over a body.

Vacant.

It's a coping strategy, she knows. She looked like that once, not so very long ago. If Sheepwool softens her hitherto somewhat business-like and yet abortive line of questioning, she might begin to get re-sults.

"Dr Beach, I know it's hard. Really, I do. You've had a terrible, ter-rible shock. And, as far as I know, no support. Would you like me, or DS Fitch perhaps, to arrange for some counseling? Someone you could talk to?"

Breakthrough.

Beach sits down on a squashy sofa in one corner of the lab -- the sofa, with its coffee table cantilevered with journals, reprints and gen-eral paperwork, that would serve as a communal relaxation area for the lab's three residents, were there to be three, and not just Beach, alone. No, not so much sits, but slumps, her empty eyes now popu-lated with a fleeting wetness.

"Thank you, Inspector. That would be nice. And would you mind, please, if you called me 'Alex'? I've only just got my PhD, you know." A pause. A shy laugh. The hum of machinery in the background. "Sometimes I think I haven't really earned it. Or that it's so new they still might come along and take it away. Oh, this *place* ..." Beach's voice is the calm, assured contralto of a newsreader, but it is, Sheep-wool suspects, merely a rainbow-skin of oil on troubled depths.

"This ... place? The Institute, you mean?"

"Yes, Inspector, that's exactly what I mean. When I simply *hated* it --the specimens, the crowding, the damp, the feeling that you couldn't move anywhere without knocking something over -- well, that was easy. But now, now that I've been here a few months, it's more diffi-cult."

"How so?"

"It's hard to put into words, and I've never really tried, but I guess it's like this. I am beginning to fall in love with it. You know, like those hostages, who fall in love with terrorists, or whatever?"

"Stockholm syndrome."

"Yes, Inspector, that's it. And now ... now you're here ... do you know that you're the only person I've had a real conversation with for weeks?" Beach is all smiles now, and talks, and talks, like a rescued castaway, and Sheepwool begins to think that perhaps the most diffi-cult interviewees are in fact the most voluble. Beach talks of science, and of her fascination with the improbable variety and abundance of marine creatures, and of how little we know about them. And without even waiting to be prompted, Beach answers the question that she had asked Morrison.

"My job! Well, I'm just trying to learn about things called carnostomids, they're a kind of marine worm. This place has the best collection of carnostomids in the world. Perhaps the only one. Problem is, nobody really knows anything at all about them, so I am starting from scratch. At first I thought it was frightening, but now, well, I'm getting over it. Yes, it's still frightening, but everything I find out about these things, every little thing, might be completely new. I've just had this idea, you know, that carnostomids aren't adult animals, but larvae …"

"Larvae?"

"Yes, immature creatures. Babies. Things that might grow up into something else."

"Do you have any idea what?" Sheepwool is now as far from any plausible line of questioning as Timbuktu. But to have Beach talking, even if too much, might be better than her not talking at all. Sheepwool admits that her classification of interviewee difficulty might require yet further revision. And as Beach talks, Sheepwool can cast a surreptitious eye over the journals and papers before them, on the coffee table. Her eyes take in some letters. A letterhead. She has seen that letterhead before. At first, she cannot place it.

"No! That's just it. The larvae of marine animals can grow up into just about anything. That's the problem, Inspector, and, really, the thrill of it all. You know, Inspector, when I got my doctorate, I thought I'd be working on some problem that had already been mostly sketched out. I'd be working in industry, you know, refining things, filling in gaps, making drugs whose properties were already pretty well known, work slightly better. I never expected, not in a million years, to be actually discovering things. Totally new things. Sometimes it fills me with amazement, on the days when it doesn't, frankly, terrify me." Beach deflates again, her torrent stopped, her expression blank once again. It is as if a light has gone out.

"Alex?"

"That larvae thing. It came to me, that idea, moments before, before I …"

"Before you discovered Dr Bland?"

A long pause. Alex had mostly been talking into space, releasing a flood of words as if Sheepwool were only the catalyst, not an interlocutor. But now Alex turns her head, looks directly at Sheepwool, and, with an almost imperceptible movement, nods.

"Of course I don't mind, Detective Sergeant, come right in."

The exceptionally tall, elderly man with the swirl of white hair (Fitch can't help but think of an ice-cream cone) stoops, offers a winning smile and ushers her into his office. This is almost, but not quite, as small and cramped as Janice Squearn's glory-hole. It does, at least, have a window, overlooking the sea. And that's all it overlooks: there is no land, no foreshore to give it scale. Now after dark, the view is of utter blackness, or, rather, it is a view more audible than visible, for the surf can be heard to scour the cliffs directly beneath them. For an instant Fitch imagines she's lost her moorings and is in fact on a ship far out at sea. Or it could simply be a tremor in the building. She holds on to the back of a chair, as if to steady herself. She must have let something slip, for the man proffers a solicitous arm and guides her to a simple, pine chair.

"Yes, Detective Sergeant, it can be somewhat disconcerting, can it not? Believe me, it is even more so in daylight!" His accent is foreign but unplaceable (Fitch knows from her dossier that he is originally from Sweden), but his English is as clipped as a box hedge. "One feels that it is a little, one might say, romantic? Up here, with nothing but my own thoughts and the great sea out of the window, I am on a voyage of discovery! Might I offer you some tea?" Fitch nods, palely, remembering at the last minute to murmur a thank-you. She decides to let Dr Lars Johansson make his own way into this interview.

"I am, however, directly above the kitchen. Sometimes the smell of chips on a Friday afternoon destroys my cheerful maritime fantasy, but one cannot have everything. And, believe me, I have quite a lot! I am blessed with, as you might say, independent means, so I can do what I like. Come and go as I please."

"Were you…?"

"I am pleased to say not! No, I was not here when the unfortunate Dr Bland met his untimely end. No, I have been spending Christmas with my parents in Umeå, that's in Sweden, you know, and arrived back only this morning." Fitch ticks the mental box marked 'alibi' -- this one should be easy to verify -- and suppresses amazement that Dr Johansson, who looks to be at least sixty, has both his parents. But then, Swedes, don't they live practically for ever? Not like her Dad, hacked to death by cigarettes before his fifty-third birthday. And her Mum, who is barely fifty-five but looks seventy, poor love.

"What do you do here, Dr Johansson?" Fitch asks as a way of making conversation, and immediately regrets it. For this is Dr Johansson's cue to expound on his favourite subject, the marvellous diversity of creatures that live their entire lives inside barnacles, a subject for which he clearly has an obsessive love.

"Darwin -- you are familiar with Darwin, yes?" Fitch nods gamely. She remembers vaguely having heard of Darwin in biology lessons in school, when she wasn't too busy making sheep's eyes at Jason and giggling whenever the teacher mentioned sex. "Ah! Darwin, like me, loved barnacles. His work on barnacles still stands as the definitive treatise. But about the societies, kingdoms -- empires! -- *inside* the barnacles, the man had no knowledge! Imagine, had he been privy to such information, he could have based his *Origin of Species* entirely on examples drawn from within the valves of his beloved barnacles.

"It is the barnacles and their little friends that keep me here. The Institute has possibly the best collections of the parasites and commensals of barnacles anywhere in the world. I would not be here otherwise. In this place." His voice darkens for an instant, as if a small black speck has temporarily occulted the Sun. Daylight is soon restored: "But enough of that! The kettle. See? It boils. We must have tea. Milk and sugar, yes?"

Fitch nods assent and, her equilibrium restored, decides to venture a toe into the conversation. "Pardon me for asking Dr Johansson, if it's not too rude, but did you say 'independent means'?"

"Not at all, Detective Sergeant. Not at all! You will know of course how this Institute is funded? None of the scientists who work in places like this receive any money from the Institute. It is, in fact, the other way round. They bring money from other sources, government grants, for instance, or universities, or philanthropic organizations, or even corporations, and buy time and space here, so they can use the Institute's unmatched collections. This money pays all the support staff at the Institute, and keeps the building from falling down, inasmuch as it can … as *anything* can." He laughs, Fitch thinks it polite to join in. They are, by now, both familiar with the precarious state of the Institute, perched on the very cliff-edge of an eroding coastline.

Johansson continues: "You did not, of course, imagine that it got much from visitors!

"This is what we in science call 'soft' money. But some money is softer than others, and I have the softest, or should that be the hardest? It is perhaps hard to say. For I am blessed with what is, I believe, called inherited wealth. My grandfather was a chemist who with my great-uncle founded Johansson and Johansson, which eventually came to be a very large and very profitable drugs company. It is still a private company, not quoted, and as a family member I am ashamed to say that I live off its profits. Although, I have to say, that these aren't as great as they once were, and the company is currently being pursued by the jackals of the marketplace. One particular jackal, in fact." Worry streaks his countenance. "Did you hear of a company called MagusPharm?"

Fitch confesses that she hasn't.

"Few people have, outside the pharmaceuticals industry itself. It appears to have come straight out of nowhere. Nobody seems to have any idea how it rose to prominence, or on which product." There is a pause. Fitch has a hard time reading Johansson's face, but for an instant she could have sworn that she saw in it a flash of agony.

"But still, no matter, I have plenty of funds to indulge my modest cirripedophilia."

Fitch has no idea what he is talking about. She sips her tea, and, putting it down on a corner of Johansson's desk, decides to steer the conversation back to the shores of relevance.

"Dr Johansson, what were your impressions of Dr Bland?"

"Bland? Not much. One does not like to speak ill of the dead, but I confess I thought him foolish. He did little work of any scientific merit, and that long ago, and he tended to let the administration of the building slip. You know, Detective Sergeant, much as one appreciates this building as a picturesque folly, it is a death trap, and the Institute should really have moved to somewhere more secure years ago. I am amazed that the authorities haven't forcibly closed it down. One reason I spend so much time here, rather than, oh, I don't know, playing golf, is that I wish to research the Institute's collections, and believe me, Detective Sergeant, these collections are priceless ... before they fall into the sea.

"Bland should have been moving the Institute to a place more secure. He was not a bad man, far from it, he was always pleasant enough, but he was too easily distracted."

"Distracted? By what?"

"By... well, there is no sense in being coy ... by women. It was, if I might say so, his great failing." Fitch has been here before, Bland's form is well known to her. But on a sudden she thinks of her conversation with Sheepwool, their brainstorm in the car before she almost ran over that toddler. Of how it was that Bland happened to be in his lab at an unaccustomed hour, and just up the hall from Beach.

"Do you think, Dr Johansson, that this ... er ... distraction ... had anything to do with his death?"

"I could not possibly answer that, Detective Sergeant. After all, I was not here!"

"But would it interest you know that when he died in his laboratory in the early hours of the morning, Dr Alex Beach was working just along the hall?"

A small fracture appears in the scientist's polished poise.

"Yes, Detective Sergeant. I regret to say, on reflection, that it should. Dr Beach is a pleasant young woman. And, now I come to think of it, Dr Bland did spend an inordinate amount of time pursuing her. I can understand why he might, but at his age, as at mine, one should exercise some decorum, should one not?"

Fitch senses that this rhetorical flourish marks the end of the interview, at least for now. She thanks Dr Johansson and rises to go. Just as she is about to gather her coat and bag, there is a soft knock at the door.

"Ah! Please excuse me, Detective Sergeant." Johansson rises and shambles for the door. "Nothing for ages, and then it is like Victoria Station in here!" The door opens to reveal the neat, middle-aged woman with the rather sour expression Fitch and Sheepwool had met alighting from a cab.

"Ah, Maureen! Please come in. This is Detective Sergeant Fitch. About this terrible news. Have you met?"

The woman mumbles something inaudible.

"We have met, but not actually introduced," says Fitch.

"Allow me. Detective Sergeant Fitch, this is Dr Maureen Boynton, who is, like me, a visiting fellow of this Institute. Do you ... have you ...?"

Fitch, moving to the door, looks at the expression on Boynton's face. The sourness is sharpened with what looks like urgency. And conspiracy. Whatever it's about, Fitch thinks, she'll have to find out later. Boynton enters as if Fitch had been nothing more than a stuffed animal in a glass case.

"That's fine, Dr Johansson. I really must be going now. Thank you for your …"

The door closes behind her.

" … time."

Really. Some people are so rude! And Johansson seemed such a nice person, very polite. Like something out of an old movie. No, it was that sourpuss, Maureen Boynton. She looked like she had to say something soon or she'd burst.

Fitch has hardly gone five yards along the narrow, shadowy corridor when she realizes that she's left her purse in Johansson's office.

"Who else is on our list?"

Fitch pauses as she slips up into third and looks keenly around into the encroaching night that the yellow-white beam of the lighthouse seems powerless to penetrate, as if her own eyes can do any better. Her face looks ghastly, pallid in the beam, cut up into shards of darkness by the fractured illumination, her hair pale and stringy like the dead-men's-fingers that is all that passes for seaweed on this part of the coast. Sheepwool is cast back to the shock of Pickled Lily, hair floating and awry in that horribly amniotic medium. Abruptly, Sheepwool turns away, looking through the windscreen at the blankness ahead, picked out by the car's too-weak headlights.

"Just two, Ma'am. I checked in with Janice Squearn while you were with Dr Beach. There's an American, a Professor Garrison Williams, and a Dr Heather Franks. Apparently, from what Janice told me, Williams got back from America last night, so we need to check his alibi. He sounds like a live one…"

"Hmm?" Sheepwool hears Fitch's voice as if through static, or from a long way off.

"Well, Janice says he, that's Williams, was due back yesterday, but didn't actually show up. This means, she says, that Professor Williams probably went straight from Heathrow to the Dazed Haddock. And Ma'am, get this, that's where he lives."

"What? At the Dazed Haddock?" Sheepwool sits up, incredulous: Fitch's voice swims back into focus. Perhaps Williams is one of those canonical Americans who'd look at a tumbledown ruin or, in this case, some seedy dive, and see only olde-worlde charm.

"I know. Unbelievable. A place like that. He's a bit of a shark apparently. Of the pool-playing variety." Fitch sounds disapproving.

"Is that a crime, Fitch?"

"No, Ma'am, it's … well, Janice said he's well in with Bob Honeypott, and you know what she thinks of him. And, well, you know what *I* think of him, and what Gerry Rammell, and, well, just about everyone else! Anyway, I thought we could go there now."

"Good idea, Fitch. I think we deserve a drink." Sheepwool turns to Fitch to read her expression, but Fitch's face is now out of range of the Light. Only the set of her jaw is visible, reflected from the pale strip of the track.

"And what of Franks?"

"Ah. Well, Ma'am, she might be harder to pin down. Janice says that the last time she saw her it was December the twenty-first. Franks seemed in a great rush to leave the Institute. Janice says she wanted to get some idea of her plans, you know, when she was going to return in the New Year, just to write down in case anybody wondered, but Franks seemed distressed or worried about something, so …"

"So we have no idea of where Franks went, or when she might be back?"

"No, Ma'am, I mean, yes, I'm afraid so. There's certainly been no sign of her."

Sheepwool sits back, drawing a shroud around herself with her own thoughts, letting Fitch pilot the car, a tiny mote in this vast and active darkness. Like all city dwellers, she finds the intensity of the rural night threatening. She is a creature of light. Unlike Fitch, who seems born and bred to this murk, as sharp a driver at night as by day. Even if she herself still drove … even if, by day, she…

No, Percy. Keep your mind on the present.

So, what do we have? Still-life with corpse, by Peter Brueghel the Elder, at the very least, although she'd settle for Matthias Grunewald. The grisly extravagance of the Isenheim altarpiece would have suited the Institute nicely. But the corpse itself? Could be heart failure. In fact, could be anything. No obvious foul play.

So why are we interested? Because Bland was acting out of character. Why was he in the Institute at night? Nobody knows. Though she thinks Morrison knows something and isn't saying.

And was it coincidence that Alex Beach was just yards away from Bland in his lasts moments, in that worm-casting of a cellar, surrounded by the purr of machinery (which would have driven Sheepwool round the bend) and the too-still air? She feels sure that the ever-reliable Fitch will be able to find rock-solid alibis for everyone, even this Williams person and the elusive Dr Franks. Of all of them, only Beach was there at the time.

That is, in fact, the only thing we know for certain.

And then, there's Morrison. He has an alibi, too. Only … well, Sheepwool trusts him no further than she can spit.

Percy, she says to herself: it's just a feeling. No more than that. There's no crime in slime, she'd reminded Fitch (she warms to the memory). But this feeling nags her because it's something she can't place. She rummages in the heaving handbag of her mind, the outside world quite forgotten. Ah, that's it. This goes way back, before she ever heard of Deringland, or the Institute, or Morrison.

It started on that school run, pieced together later, vicariously experienced. A car, zooming from right to left, carrying … what was it carrying? Machinery in Sheepwool's head, buried beyond awareness, grinds into life. It seems like only a moment later when the rasp of a handbrake pulls her back into wakefulness.

"How is it you live here, Dr Williams, here at the Haddock?" Fitch's voice is high, strained, but makes it clear that the Dazed Haddock is a place she'd rarely want to visit, much less call home.

"Oh, Detective Sergeant, may I call you Elaine? Please just call me Garry." Williams flashes a big, cheesy all-American smile at Fitch and eases his frame into a more comfortable leaning position on the bar. He is standing, bottle of German lager in hand, while Sheepwool and Fitch perch on stools.

Sheepwool feels uncomfortable, exposed, here at the bar. She'd have preferred a table in some quiet corner. But quiet corners at the Haddock have an intensity of purpose which their occupants are often reluctant to share, swathed half in shadow, whispering furtively between themselves in nameless transactions, and glancing towards the bar with obvious resentment. Sheepwool feels as if she has a sign saying POLICE written in flashing neon on her head. Only the prevailing gloom, softened by cigarette smoke, offers any kind of a shield. That, and the appalling noise, the ping and clang of the fruit machines; what sounds like a particularly lively pool tournament in the adjoining bar; and the juke box, provide a curtain against what would otherwise be an aggressive silence.

Sheepwool takes what solace she can in the jukebox. Hardly classical, but then again, nothing very much later than the mid-seventies, either. The sound of the juke is muffled, sodden, a result either of the acoustics of the pub, with their general conspiracy against easy conversation, or because the treble speakers have been shot as a result of three decades of playing 'Smoke on the Water'.

It's now playing 'Hotel California'. The song's atmosphere of enigma and loss strikes Sheepwool as apposite. It takes her back, and back, and back. She shakes herself once again into the present, but remains, for all that, detached, watching the drama of the world evolve, unseen, as if from an upstairs window.

Fitch, back half turned to her, is talking energetically to Williams, struggling to be heard against the ambient surge. Williams does not seem to find the atmosphere uncomfortable in the least. In contrast, he seems quite at home. He is lean and grizzled, in jeans and faded black leather jacket, face very pale and somewhat scarred beneath a full head of silver-gray hair. His eyes, beneath white brows, are pale blue and a little watery, but sparkle with a dangerous intelligence. Something about his face: he doesn't look burned, exactly, but perhaps a lifetime spent in labs turns one's complexion to driftwood. That, and smoking. Williams has a pack of Marlboros at his elbow and is never without a lit cigarette.

"Hey, well, you know, it's a place. And cheap. Sure, I could've afforded to rent or even buy somewhere, but when I first got off the train and pitched up here, a few years back, I came here for a drink, and … well …. I never left. They do food here, and beer, and I like pool, y'know? And the surfing, here at Deringland. It's just fine."

"But the cold? And the fog?"

"It gets real foggy at Half Moon Bay, too. And inland, the woods, with those big, big trees and the moss just hanging down." He laughs. "After that, the Institute is nothing to be frightened of. That mermaid though, Pickled Lily. She's scary! Scares the living crap out of me. Wooooh!" He hams it up as a pantomime ghost. "Do you ladies want another drink?"

Fitch declines, regretfully. She drives a police car, she explains. Sheepwool nods a polite refusal, thinking that being a disembodied mind, watching the scene from far, far away, is sufficient excuse. From this distance she can see now, quite clearly, that at least some of Williams' demeanor is an act of bravura. People confront their grief in different ways.

"I am sorry that you lost your wife," she says. "And might I change my mind, Dr Williams? I'd very much like a white-wine spritzer."

The change in Williams' face is remarkable. His cheeks sink, his skin turns a weird, pale green. He stands straighter, but looks much older and exhales from every pore the memory of the stink of death. Fitch turns to Sheepwool, looking shocked, mouth open as if to say something that doesn't quite emerge.

"My ... wife?"

"Yes. I'm sorry. Terrible, terrible shock, losing her like that. Just when you first returned to England."

Williams crumples. His eyes flicker towards the bar. The barman seems not to notice, but to Sheepwool's eyes, this nonchalance is entirely theatrical. "Let's find ourselves a corner, okay?" Williams says.

8: Easy Access to Liquor

The corner in which Sheepwool, Fitch and Williams now find themselves is dark and smells faintly of something unpleasant that a bottle of bleach hasn't quite managed to dispel. They are in an alcove, almost completely enclosed by high and grimy stained-glass partitions, at a square table of worn planks, sticky to the touch with the detritus left by too many under-age Saturday-nighters. Fitch and Sheepwool sit on one side, Williams on the other. Sheepwool has a window on the world here, she can see the bar, but feels enclosed, secure. She wonders if she was a cat in a former life. Illumination comes from a sconce high on the wall, throwing faces into shadow but hands into the spotlight, infusing all and any gestures with a significance they perhaps do not deserve. In this half light, Williams unpeels his life before them, the ageing surf-dude image now put aside, his hands like puppets in a child's toy theater.

"I'm fifth-generation Californian, never left the State until I was twenty-one and came to England on my first post-doc. Thomas Hunt Morgan was my idol, ever heard of Morgan? No?" The policewomen shake their heads. "Invented genetics. But his first love was marine biology. Worked his summers at Moss Landing, California, worked on how little animals like hydroids can grow themselves whole new bodies from just a piece."

"Like worms, when you cut them?" says Fitch, helpfully. Sheepwool wishes she had Fitch's ability to plunge in, without shame, with all the seeming naïveté of a small child, or by playing the dumb blonde. That's an act, too, of course.

"Yeah, kind of. Well, when Morgan retired from genetics he went back to studying regeneration full-time. I'm following his footsteps. Here, now." Williams' words scrabble for the present, but his eyes tell a different story, of a career that scaled the heights, of amazing advances in genetics at CalTech and at Berkeley, with enormous teams of scientists unlocking the deepest secrets of heredity: teams orchestrated and conducted by his own vision. Of a career that might have secured a Nobel, were it not for a black dog at his heel. Sheepwool had read the dossier Fitch had compiled -- of course she had -- but only she had read between the lines. It had not occurred to Fitch, Deringland born and raised, how incongruous it was for a man like Williams to close an illustrious career in a crumbling research institute at the ends of the earth. But Sheepwool, like Williams, is a fugitive, an exile. She knows what that feels like. She and Williams, she thinks, seem, by instinct, to have reached an understanding.

"It's more than footsteps, isn't it, Professor?" Williams recoils slightly, as if in fear.

"Footsteps? Well, yeah, I suppose. You see, my wife, Beverley, came from these parts. I met her in Cambridge, when I was a postdoc. She came back to California with me. She was with me the whole time."

"Beverley?" In this one word Sheepwool conveys a lifetime of meaning. Of the lists of young female research students, research assistants and colleagues commemorated on the notches of the Williams laboratory couch while Dr Beverley Williams was away, and yet faithful; and of the glittering prizes which, late in life, eluded Williams and his circle.

"Yeah. Beverley. Bev. I promised her when we married that we'd eventually come back to England. Well, we did. But not long after we came back she … she …"

Sheepwool resists the temptation to complete his sentence, but instead starts another. "So, Dr Williams, if I might clarify: when you came to England you didn't live above the pub immediately, as you said. That came later. After your wife died."

Williams hangs his head. "Yeah. Oh hell. I'm sorry. It's just, you know, when something like that happens, you just try to paper over the cracks, reinvent yourself. Backtrack to that fork in the path. The road not taken." Fitch looks up now, mouth pursed, eyes moist. Sheepwool can see the name of Janice Squearn in her eyes. Sheepwool feels a tug of sympathy towards this tortured man. She suppresses it now. She is, after all, on duty.

"But it was horrible, horrible. We hadn't been back here for more than a few months when Bev wakes up in the night, we were renting a house along the coast, real pretty, and tells me that she's pregnant."

This is a revelation that even Sheepwool doesn't expect. The clink of the bar, the clank of the one-armed bandit, the woolly throb of the juke box, all fade into the sweat-stained wallpaper.

" 'Pregnant?' I say. 'Bev, baby, that's not possible', I say. Look here, ladies, if I can be frank: we had a good sex life. Something about the atmosphere here made it better. More urgent. Like, fateful, as if something was gonna come along and take it all away. But, damn it, I'm quite a lot older 'n Bev, and she always kept herself in good shape, but she was pushing fifty, post-menopause. But no, she says, she's done the tests and everything. I'll never forget her, that night. She broke out into a sweat and looked at me with those big brown eyes. Eyes you could just fall into. Sometimes I wake up in the night and see Bev's eyes. That's why I like to live above a pub. Good access to liquor when you need it." Sheepwool has a jarring flashback to Methwold. Eyes as bottomless wells of pain.

"So, that night, when she told me, I came over to her and held her, and held her again, until she stopped crying and fell asleep. We never exchanged another word. She threw herself off the cliffs next day. After a few days, and the police investigation, the hounding, I moved in here. It was Bob's suggestion. He fixed it up for me."

"Bob? Bob Honeypott?" This from Fitch.

"Yeah. He was real nice to me. Genuine, you know? Not like some."

"Some?" Sheepwool again.

"Yeah, okay, on the level, that klutz Bland." Williams sits up straight, his shaggy brows joining into a frown. "Some friend *he* was. He just ignored me. Shunned me like I had some disease. When you told me he'd died, I don't deny it, I was pleased. I'd've been first in line to throw him off the cliffs too, after what I'd been through."

"*Did* you, though, Dr Williams? You were in Deringland at the time. Didn't you arrive yesterday afternoon? We'd need to eliminate you from our enquiries."

"Oh, shit. I haven't yet checked in at the Institute. Poor Janice! When I got back I was up all night drinking with Bob. After closing time we went to his flat. It's above that funky shop, 'Secrets of the Sea'?" Fitch looks at Sheepwool as if to interject, but Sheepwool halts her with an incremental gesture as if to say that yes, this is another link, but in a different chain. "But Inspector, do you suspect that

Bland was … murdered?"

"At present we have an open mind. At least until the autopsy. And there will need to be an inquest."

"I see. Anyway, Bland had it coming to him. After Bev died I saw it all. There was some kind of triangle going on. Bland was pursuing a young postdoc at the Institute, one Alex Beach. Arrived last fall. Sweet girl, very dedicated. Bit ditzy, though -- I get the impression she doesn't know which way is up most of the time. But she kept re-buffing him. I had -- still have -- the impression she's spoken for, though I don't know if that was a front to put Bland off. She was real cut up about it though. Came to me for advice. She does some work for me, you know, a bit of tech stuff. I'm like the father-figure. You know, I reckoned she needs it."

"Yes, Dr Williams. But don't triangles have three corners?"

"Huh? Oh, yeah. Bland got his come-uppance all right. He was be-ing chased by Heather. Oh, Heather!" For the first time, Williams laughs. It's a big, fruity sound that would, in any other part of the world, make the sun come out in an instant.

"Heather?"

"Heather Franks. Another postdoc. Have you met her yet?"

"She's next on our list," says Fitch.

"Well, ladies, there you have a treat in store. A very determined… uh … person, is Heather. She was chasing Bland. But Bland was chas-ing Alex. Quite the carousel. Or, as you Brits might say, a lobster qua-drille."

"The story so far," declares Sheepwool, pouring coffee from the brown-choked jug at the corner of their brown-choked office.

Neither Fitch nor Sheepwool have much stomach for police can-teen coffee. Even when they'd had a canteen. Sheepwool prefers a cup and saucer, but gives Fitch hers in a stained mug bearing a bold pink-and-yellow decal advertising that the drinker is the 'World's Most Marvelous Mum'.

At the close of day, Fitch's mind is indeed maternally occupied. She'd texted Jason to ask if he could collect the kids and dig some-thing out of the freezer for their tea. Only now, a moment belatedly, does she look up at Sheepwool, now craning over her, literally her superior, and forces a guilty smile. She knows what she must look like. Pasty, lined, as crumpled as her suit. It's been a long day.

"Ma'am?"

Sheepwool takes her cup and saucer, pure white, and perches on the edge of her desk. Fitch has noticed that Sheepwool is ill-at-ease in a chair, fidgety, as if sitting is a painful activity that compels one to get up and move around. Ah, she thinks, we Mums know that sensation, and it is purely physical. If only she'd toned up more after Bryony had been born. It occurs to her, then, that she has absolutely no idea if Sheepwool has ever had children. Sheepwool's desk, unlike hers, shows no sign of personal adornment. No family photos. Holiday snaps. Just like Janice, then ... But now does not seem the right time to inquire about such things. Not when Sheepwool seems to have been seized with a demonic energy. A second wind. Like a foxhound on the trail.

"Thoughts, Fitch? It's been a busy day. But you know what they say about first impressions."

Fitch takes a little time to think it over. Sheepwool sips her coffee and grimaces at its bitterness. "It just keeps going round and round in my head, Ma'am, 'Bland and Beach', 'Bland and Beach', like they're a holiday company. Like they're joined at the hip. I mean, Ma'am, why was Bland in the lab at three in the morning? Why is *anyone* in the lab at three in the morning? Me, I'm always at home in bed!" Cuddled up against Jason's broad chest, she adds, silently. She wishes she was there now.

"Following the passions of science?" Sheepwool suggests. "That's certainly why Beach was there."

"Okay, granted, but people keep telling us, don't they? Janice and that Dr Johansson told me, and Williams told the both of us, that Bland wasn't all that interested in science. He was more interested in Beach, so ..." Fitch adds it up. Sheepwool does not intrude on her calculations.

"Could it be, Ma'am, that Bland and Beach arranged to meet then, for some ... oh, I don't know ... rendezvous ... and either Bland had a heart attack, which seems most likely, or Beach ... killed him?"

Sheepwool smiles. "It's the best we have yet, Fitch. Assuming it was a murder, which we don't know. But I think it was a genuine co-incidence. Yes, Bland was chasing Beach, and Beach didn't want to be chased, but something our lonesome cowboy said in the pub sticks in my mind. Now, I think Williams is a lousy liar..."

"Yes! All that stuff about moving straight to the pub when you knew his wife had died. How did you… ?"

"… but he seems to be an excellent judge of character. You haven't talked to Beach, and I have, and she is, how did he put it, 'ditzy'? Her mind seems everywhere at once. Lost to the realms of science. Bruises easily on contact with reality."

"But maybe, Ma'am, she was in shock? Or could she have been putting on an act?"

Bless you, Fitch, Sheepwool thinks to herself. Don't we always put on an act? Every minute of every day? As she often has cause to re-mind herself, giggly dumb blondes don't get to be detective sergeants.

"Hmm. Yes, Fitch. That's a point." Fitch, encouraged, retrieves an-other scrap from her day.

"And, Ma'am, oh yes, before I forget. There's Morrison, isn't there?"

"Morrison," says Sheepwool. Her smile fades. "What about him?"

"Yes, well, silly me, when I left Johansson's office, I bumped into that Maureen Boynton woman. You know, the one who turned up in a cab, just when we did?"

"Yes, thank you, Fitch: we'll have to interview her, too."

"Well, Ma'am. She just barged past me into Johansson's office and slammed the door in my face. She was really keen to tell Johansson something, just bursting with it. I was about to leave them to it, come and find you, when I realized I'd left my bag in the office. Notes, purse, the lot." Her face pinks with the memory. "So I go back to the office but something makes me pause at the door. I didn't knock, but I listened closely. Johansson and Boynton were having a conversation. Quite loud it was, and, do you know, it was all about Morrison?"

"Say on, Fitch."

"Boynton was telling Johansson that she'd come back from some conference, where someone had told her that Morrison was being paid a retainer from a drugs company called MagusPharm. Far more than he would be getting as a Director of a small private museum. This stuck in my mind, because Johansson had told me that his drugs company, a private firm called Johansson and Johansson -- he's part of the founding family and very rich, or so he told me -- was being threatened with take-over by that same company. So, anyway, that's when I knocked, went and grabbed my purse, and ran for it."

Sheepwool has turned parchment white. She stands, like a tableau, coffee cup halfway to her mouth. Small dots of pink appear at her cheeks, and then she unfolds, like a blooming flower, and, slowly, a smile dawns on her face, as if illuminated from a window high in the nave of a Church.

Fitch drops her at the door of her apartment block, waves her goodnight, and zooms off into the thickening fog. Just time to read Bryony and Eric their bedtime story, Fitch says, something about Harry Potter and the Temple of Doom, or the Geranium of Fear, or something.

Nick would have done the same thing, if … when…

Right there, in the tall lobby, in the darkness by the mailboxes, she is immobilized, caught in a vice of dry, wracking, sobs. It always gets her like this, at the end of the day. She is grateful to Fitch for taking her home, as she does most days, but the combination of the drive and Fitch's family chatter is sometimes too hard to bear.

But the thought of walking home through the foggy darkness is worse. Perhaps, when the days get longer, she'll walk herself home, if there is any season in Deringland other than winter.

Avoiding the dubious invitation of the elevator, she clatters up the stairs to the comfort of her flat. Oh, to shuck off these shoes!

Later still, in bed, in Winceyette pyjamas and bifocals, she puts down her book, turns off the light, and stares at the ceiling. She hears the swish of the surf, much gentler now after last night's rages, and when her eyes have accommodated, sees the cheerless dim swell of yellow street lamps through the foggy murk, and the swags of the curtains drawn part-way across the window.

It all clicks into place now. She closes her eyes. That's what she'd seen in Beach's lab, a short letter confirming that funds had been approved for the postdoctoral fellowship of Doctor Alexandra Susan Beach, administered through the Trustees of the Lowdley-Purslane Institute. And the letterhead?

MagusPharm SA of Zurich, with offices and facilities in Cambridge, England; Mountain View, CA; Trenton, NJ; and Guangzhou, PRC.

It's not Beach and Bland, Fitch's holiday company (Sheepwool smiles inwardly, she can practically hear the TV adverts). No, it's Beach and Morrison, but doing what? Not holidays, certainly. But now, Percy, get this: Morrison was certainly cagey about what Beach worked on, but he must have known. Must have. Especially as Ma-gusPharm was under-writing it.

And what was Beach working on? Sheepwool wracks her mind hard to pick out the eseentials from Beach's stream of enthusiastic sci-ence-speak. Ah yes. 'Carnostomids'. Worms so obscure that even most zoologists had never heard of them.

Sheepwool wonders why a drug company should be interested in such things.

Later still, it could have been many years, but was in reality no more than a few seconds, Sheepwool's mind slips a little further to-wards the lip of sleep. MagusPharm. Where had she heard that name before? Eat me. Drink Me.

Lobster Quadrille.

TubeWave.

She jolts, startled on the cusp of oblivion.

The many impressions of the day cascade through her head, cas-cade and fade, sentences breaking up like rotten snow, into words, fragments. Here's a word, though: 'womanizer'. Used as applied to Bland, and also Williams. Odd, though, isn't it? We use it as a noun, describing a man who pursues women for sexual conquest. But not far below it is a transitive verb: 'womanize', as in 'weaponize': not in the sense of the pursuit of women, but of their creation, by transfor-mation from other things.

Women from men.

It's odd how two names she's seen today that belie their owner's gender. Alex. Marion. To be fair, she calls herself Percy, but at least she knows who she is. Doesn't she?

But it goes further.

Women from fish.

The horrible, yearning face of Pickled Lily swims into view. She tries to put it out of her mind as she tumbles into sleep.

Off With Her Head!

She could never work out why anyone would like Hieronymous Bosch. But perhaps there is one corner of the world where his visions will ever be a reality.

You are on the beach again, but it is night, deserted, and there is no light at all save from the stars and the gas platforms that ring the ho-rizon like a necklace. The surf pounds and retreats, pounds and retreats, and you hope that this will soothe your mind, wear away the corners of your secret. You have told no-one that you were there that night, watching from your high window at the Institute. Nobody knew you'd never left, but you wanted to be alone, to grieve for your lost love, an orgy of self-flagellation, sitting there in silence and darkness, spending Christmas in your room, starving, thirsty, punishing yourself. But for what? And now he's dead, dead! How dare he escape like that! But you are so stricken you want to die yourself, to walk into those welcoming waves and never come back. The urge is strong within you, but something inside stays you. It is your grief. It has yet to run its full course. And there's something else, too. That from your high window that night, you saw someone leave the Institute in the early hours, creeping away, across the forecourt into the dark lane beyond. At first you couldn't see who it was, until the beam from the lighthouse caught him.

It was Morrison.

Part Two

1: Like Bindweed in the Garden

"Most unfortunate, Mr Willoughby, that she had to die like that. Most unfortunate."

The speaker is a big, ruddy man like a butcher, with a mass of gingerish curls and extravagant side-whiskers. His sleeves are rolled up, his arms are big and beefy, and he spreads them wide in a massive gesture of the acceptance of life's realities. In one hand he waves a large knife. It is dark with blood. His butcher's apron, also, is more red than white, and words of Shakespeare come to Willoughby's mind about seas incarnadine, about blood that would not cease its spread until it had covered the Earth. Fresh blood covers the bench between the two men completely, and runs in great washes down the sides. Blood, in fact, is this scene's prevailing colour. Counterpointed, it must be said, by the whiteness of the corpse on the bloody bench, the corpse of a woman, bare to the waist. Willoughby, whose curiosity has always overcome squeamishness (perilously so, he now thinks), moves forwards to take a closer look, his boots now treading red prints from the splashes of blood on the floor.

Two, perfect arms lie to either side in a gesture of peace, or submission. Two, perfect breasts, nipples palest pink knots, lie symmetrical to each other, resting softly over the upper arms; the breasts are spread far more widely than is natural. It is only then that Willoughby can accommodate the most egregious fact of the corpse, that the ribs have been exposed and forced apart like clam shells, exposing the chest cavity. One cannot see the heart and lungs, though, as the cavity is now nothing more than a crucible for a flat sea of blood.

The woman's face is covered.

"Sir Frideric, you have not tried…"

"Yes, Mr Willoughby, I had to. Her symptoms demanded more than simple physic. Sadly, I was unable to save her."

Willoughby backs away from the blood and looks again at the corpse, as if it were one of Sir Frideric's masterful taxidermic specimens. The skin is flawless. No sallowness that might indicate underlying malaise; no sign of pox; in fact, no blemishes whatsoever. He cannot imagine why such a person would need such strong medicine as surgery. But Sir Frideric's reputation as the best surgeon in London has not been achieved by lack of boldness. He has long told Willoughby, the latest and keenest of his gentleman pupils, that the key to curing people is to understand the underlying causes of their ailments, not merely to assuage their symptoms with the potions of countrywomen. "Weed it out, Mr Willoughby, weed it out!" he had often bellowed. "Like bindweed in your gardens! Pulling off the flowers will not do while the plant still spreads underground, unseen." To expose the unseen, said Sir Frideric, will occasionally mean surgery. And if the patient did not always recover, well… that was the risk one took.

Except that Sir Frideric has been taking greater risks of late. Risks that even his closest disciples, such as young Ralph Willoughby, are beginning to question, at least among themselves. But the husbands and fathers of some of Sir Frideric's invariably wealthy, young and female patients have been less reticent. Matters are now coming to a head.

Sir Frideric drapes a sheet over the corpse as if it were no more than a sculpture of the same marble whiteness as its skin. The fabric sags into the open chest cavity and immediately takes up blood. Sir Frideric shrugs and looks up at his young acolyte, who has the high-coloured air of urgency.

"Well, Mr Willoughby, I trust this is more than a social call?"

"Yes, Sir Frideric, I'm afraid it is. It is, again, I regret to say, a matter of most pressing urgency, and …"

"If that's the case, then, spit it out, man, spit it out!"

Willoughby shuffles his feet. His hands knot together. Sir Frideric is as intimidating as he is undoubtedly brilliant. Willoughby draws breath. In Sir Frideric's rooms he is accustomed to breathing through his mouth. The odors that assail his nose are still very often too unpleasant to bear.

"Sir Frideric, you will remember the … um … exhibition you presented at your most recent open-house?" A ridiculous question, thinks Willoughby—Sir Frideric's latest cabinet of the follies and fancies of nature, unveiled at the same Kensington mansion in whose cellar they now stand, had been the talk of the season. Sir Frideric, however, glows with the memory that Willoughby has disinterred. It had been a high point. Especially the mermaids: they were always a great success.

"Well, Sir Frideric, you will remember that a Mr Castle was there, whose daughter you had been treating, and who, sad to say ..."

"Ah, the fair Marina," interrupted Sir Frideric. Willoughby did not dare counter him before his master's disquisition had come to a close. "She had quite plainly the earliest signs of consumption, you see, like our fair body laid here before us. Signs too faint to be seen by the inexperienced, but which nevertheless betoken rot to the lungs. Rot that simply must be removed by section, simply *must*: before the malady progresses further, because, by then, death is inevitable."

"Yes, Sir Frideric, and I am sure that Mr Castle accepted this, but ..."

"But what, man? But what?" Sir Frideric's icily blue eyes show more than a flicker of impatience. He turns away and starts to gather his bloodied instruments, placing them in a metal bucket. Willoughby now feels as though he is a stand-in curate at the pulpit, preaching to a bored and disappointed congregation who had expected their regular and more charismatic minister. But having started, he can hardly stop now.

"Sir Frideric, it's like this. Mr Castle was at your exhibition and saw your latest creations. He was struck by the similarity of ... um ... parts of one of your sports, with ... with ... oh, hang it all, it must be said: with parts of his late daughter. He is now putting it about that you did not return her entire body for Christian burial as you had said, but instead, you ... you..."

Sir Frideric now looks up, his face darkened and serious. Willoughby, suffering from exertion brought on, no doubt, by this outburst before his master, as well as from more continual exposure to this house of death, feels light-headed, as if he were disembodied, floating, having shed an accumulated load which had started as a mere grain or two and had become insupportable.

"Oh my dear Willoughby," says Sir Frideric. "We pioneers on the frontiers of knowledge can hardly expect complete understanding from the common herd. Look at Galileo; look at Socrates! Now go upstairs and ring for some refreshment, there's a good man. I think you need it." Willoughby nods minutely and then turns to flee as if he had been stung.

For the first time since she discovered Bland's body, Alex Beach has returned to some measure of contentment. Sensing that she needed a gentle reintroduction to laboratory life after her shock, Garry Williams has taken her under his wing, offering her a space in his lab, next door to hers ('a home from home', he'd called it) where she could work alongside another warm body, and, if she wanted to, to do a little work for him—as she sometimes had before. Nothing very exciting, running a few gels, mainly, but it would be company of a sort.

Garry thinks he's hot on the trail of proteins expressed in hydroid polyps as they regenerate after injury. He thinks he's on to something big. You know, Elixir of Eternal Youth stuff. Alex thinks he's on a hiding to nothing, and tells him so.

"These proteins could be the consequences of regeneration—their by-products—and not what kicks the cells into division, differentiation."

"Proximate or ultimate causes? Truth or consequences?"

"Yes, Garry. Or just some correlation. Nothing to do with regeneration at all. You know, I read ..."

"About the storks, Alex?"

"Storks?" Alex is nonplussed.

She had been about to mention an immense, multi-authored microarray study showing that cells when they are dividing express just about every protein in the genome. As if the control of cell division is precisely what the genome is for. Division, and differentiation: development. The genome is that agency that guides a single cell so formless that it could be from any creature imaginable, into an adulthood unique to each species. It is not one single, selfish gene that is the guide to fate, but all of them, working together in seamless concert. Unweaving that concerto is still, even now, a task for very large research teams, funded by very large grants.

Which is why, here, in a laboratory of one, Garry really hasn't a hope.

Alex suspects that Garry hasn't quite got used to the implications of retirement, or exile, in that he no longer has that vast budget and teams of postdocs to do his bidding. Perhaps that's what drew them

together: both refugees from the machined elegance of science, un-
used to their new but more primitive circumstances. And it was just
like Garry to bowl a curve-ball. Storks?

"Yeah. Canonical example of spurious correlation. That the birth
rate of Germany goes up and down with the breeding success of the
European stork. You never heard of that one?"

Alex laughs, and says no, she hasn't.

"Well, the correlation has unbelievably high statistical significance.
And a funny thing—nobody has ever done the obvious test on the
availability of gooseberry bushes. I mean, do they even *eat* gooseber-
ries in Germany?"

This time they both laugh. It is a tonic for her. That, and a return to
lab-tech stuff, the kind of work she'd been used to, is like a holiday, a
comfort after the frightening unknowns of carnostomids. But, she
knows, she must return to these, sooner or later. Preferably sooner.
Halfway across the lab to get some reagent or other, she pauses in
mid-stride.

"Hey, Alex, you OK?"

She has just had one of those insights that makes the routine of scientific lab work worthwhile.

"Genome..."

"Huh? Hey, Alex, you look white as a ghost. Come on, let's sit
down." Garry lopes off his perch on the other side of the bench from
Alex and guides her to his own relaxation corner—somewhat like
Alex's own, next door.

"What's up?"

"I could run some simple gels, of course. Just like I'm doing here.
You know, I don't know if anyone has ever done that. With ... them."

"Sorry, you lost me."

Alex turns her head and looks straight into Garry's eyes for the
first time.

Garry thinks he's never seen anything so arrestingly beautiful, nor
so highly charged. No—not with sex, not quite: but with something
he'd say was higher. Beatific. Her eyes are huge and blue, streaked
with gray, the pupils shrunk to points, luminous in a bone-white face.
Her lips part in a kind of yearning.

"Garry, you couldn't help me, could you? Please?"

"I'll do what I can. But as I say, you lost me."

Alex shakes her head as if twisting herself through some kind of foreign dimension and returning to reality. She laughs, her pupils dilate, and to Garry, just for a minute, it looks like this face could light up the Universe.

"Oh, Garry, I'm sorry. I was thinking of carnostomids. You know, those things from the *Spaniel* Expedition I'm working on. I don't think I've seen any genomic work on them at all. No comparisons, no ESTs, no *Hox* genes or anything. I had been thinking of getting into that, ages ago, when I first started, but I got, you know … delayed. And now I am not really sure what kind of creature they are. Just before … before … well, I had this idea that they were larvae, and what with the kind of work we're doing here with your hydroids, maybe, I thought … if you didn't mind…"

"Larvae, huh? Cool. Sure, Alex. I'll help you. Set you up. Show you what to do."

He thinks he could sink into those eyes, to follow their fleeting changes of expression, from anxiety, to unbridled joy, and back to thoughtfulness, all helter-skelter in a matter of shavings of seconds. It is strange he'd never seen Alex so close-up before, but this evanescence of expression reminds him of the beating hearts of small birds, a romantic cliché which he imagines would make any man want to put his arm around her and protect her. No wonder Bland made such a fool of himself over her.

But there is, well, something that goes with the package. Their faces are close enough now that he can feel her breath on his face as they talk, and in the set of her eyes, her cheekbones, the angle of her face, he sees a haunted look.

Driven, anxious, as if she is forever looking over her shoulder, ever on alert for some nameless pursuer.

This anxiety has corrupted her otherwise perfect face, as if her image has been stamped with every age and condition of humanity, from girlhood to extreme old age. A kind of Turin shroud, as if something mysterious is trying to peek through; as if Alex's face is a Western storefront onto our own, cartoon inexistence, a window on an older, harsher and more concrete reality that is altogether grimmer and grittier than our own, sanitized version.

For an instant he sees in her eyes the face of death, growling at him. He feels as if he's been slapped, but before he can recoil, Alex grabs his hands in hers. Garry knows better than to respond too willingly to what is, after all, once he catches his breath and rights himself, a simple gesture of thanks.

A knock at the door is a jolt that makes them both sit up straight.

Alex turns and sees Morrison in the doorway, and lets Garry's hands go as if they were hot plates fresh from the oven. Garry, caught out by Alex, is now wrong-footed by Morrison, who always looks ridiculously tiny when framed in a doorway. But Garry knows that his constant surprise at this — Morrison's seeming smallness -- is conditioned by his prior knowledge of the man himself. Morrison is as large as life. Larger.

"Morrison."

"Garry ... Alex." Morrison smiles like a tiger shark. "Sorry to break up the ... er ... conference." The smile narrows, as do his eyes. "Alex? Might I have a word?" And Alex rises from the sofa and walks out of the lab without a backward glance. Garry sits there, gutted, and wondering.

They are next door, in Alex's own lab. Morrison has ushered her in, locking the door behind them with a snick, and now spreads himself well back on the sofa; arms, Jermyn-sleeved and Asprey-cuffed, flung across the seat backs, suit jacket wide to reveal red striped silk tie and a shirt front as white as a penguin's. Without so much as a word, or even a movement, he makes it clear that Alex should sit down next to him. She perches, primly, as knotted as he is expansive, as tense as he seems relaxed.

Alex muses abstractedly that she never really knows what Morrison is thinking. The corollary of this is that she cannot know what he might say or do next. She had once thought this unnerving. In fact, she still does. But a rebellious part of her — or is it the enslaved part? She's not sure — finds it obscurely thrilling. She now finds that the rebellious part of her is taking more of a hold, and has done so ever since Bland's death, an event which seemed to damage the more cautious part of her beyond repair, so that it now ceases to care. As if Bland's death were somehow both her own fault and also a harbinger of worse things, and that in the face of a remorselessly oncoming doom she should just release herself from any kind of prior bondage while there is a world still to inhabit.

On a sudden she has the impression she is being spoken to. At first it seems from far away, but it is, in fact, closer: it is Morrison's voice, speaking to her, against the background hum of the laboratory. But she can't quite shake her head back to reality, as she had in Garry's lab, whenever that was. No, her head feels like it's encased in a warm blanket. Warm, soft, inviting, like the tartan rug her father always kept in the car for long trips when she was a child. She wants to sleep. She has wanted to sleep for ages but all effort is thwarted by dreams, of Bland's bulging, fish-dead eyes, Bland's blood. The contrast with Bland's big, groping hands like kelp, his old-man's breath, when he at least acted like he was alive. She has not seen or talked to Morrison since Bland's death, and, surprising though it may seem to the more cautious but rapidly crumbling part of herself, she knows that only Morrison can put it right, say the right things, grant her absolution. Of course, she always knew.

"Alex! Alex? Are you all right? There is no need to worry. I'm so sorry I haven't had a chance to catch up with you, since ... well, you know. I really am. I should have made more of an effort."

And with that she knows that Morrison has broken the spell: or has replaced it with a new one. But who cares? She sags, as if all the springs holding her taut have been released at once, and collapses next to him, so that his right arm can rest on her shoulder. She folds herself in towards him and starts to cry.

"Morrison, I..."

"Hush now, Alex. Really. It's not your fault. You've had a terrible shock. You have been all alone when I should have been with you, to help." With his free left hand he strokes her hair. She sits up a little, shakes his left hand free, pulls the tears back in to her eyes and looks at him.

"It's just, you know, not what I was expecting. What it would really be like, once it happened."

"No, nor I."

"Dr Bland ... that he should be in the lab when I was. Why? He's been chasing me for ages. I couldn't get free of him. I hoped he'd just go away, leave me alone, but that he'd find me in the lab... at night ... and be dead! I feel so awful. So guilty."

"Guilty? But why?"

"Guilty that I'd wished it, and that it happened."

"Well, don't. And don't worry about him being in the lab, Alex. How could he possibly have known you'd have been there?" He pauses: his voice takes on a more businesslike note, but still full of the warmth of reassurance. He allows her to come closer into his embrace. Her right hand meets his chest, just inside the left lapel of his jacket.

"I do have a reason for coming down here, Alex. It's to reassure you that Dr Bland's death can't be seen as a casualty of your work, of mine, or of ours." Briefly, Alex looks up into his eyes and sees an expression of distant worry. She has not seen that expression before.

"Ours?"

"Yes. Your work on carnostomids, and my ... well... efforts to secure the future of this Institute, through MagusPharm. Your work on carnostomids is vital to that future, Alex, you can't afford to be distracted. I should say that MagusPharm is impressed with your progress. Very impressed. And so am I."

"Yes, Morrison... but sometimes I feel, you know, like it's always back to square one. Like I am having to learn everything from the beginning. But, well..."

"Hmm?" His smile. Like a father. Like a confessor. Like a lover. She basks in it.

"I've got to admit it but ... well, I *am* starting to enjoy myself. The discoveries... the possibilities ... the ... well, everything, really." Her smile opens in submission, to mirror his.

"I know, Alex. I can see it. I always said, didn't I? That you were the right person for this job. Someone who could see the problem with new eyes. And don't worry any more about Bland—that's an order!" They both laugh. "I know it sounds horrible, but now he's out of your way, out of your hair..." He strokes her hair again, now. "You can make much greater progress, more easily. And if you need anything, I'm here to help."

Her smile crumples, but there is a command in his body for it to revive, for her to straighten up, for her to approach him yet more closely still. She watches herself as his face moves in with the inevitability of a docking spaceship and they kiss.

The cautious part of her wants to scream that this is all wrong; that this is disgusting; that the tongue squirming around inside her mouth is a slime-hag that will burrow down into her guts and gnaw her alive from within; that the hands weaving around and over her breasts and thighs and hips, awakening her skin and senses, are morays about to strangle her, drag her down, rip her to shreds, body and soul.

But the cautious part of her is now in long retreat and is now visible only as a thin line in the far distance, like low tide on a muddy foreshore. Now the rebellious part of her is in the ascendant, and it is this part that propels her to try to loosen his tie and his shirt, an effort that soon peters out before Morrison's more expeditious removal of her own clothes, so that she is now unclad and on the sofa beneath him, his teeth and lips in and around her throat like a burning neck-lace; the leatherette of the sofa pulling and sucking and stinging at her exposed shoulders and backside; his jacket rubbing her hardened nipples raw; the expensive wool of his trousers scraping the insides of her thighs as he moves inside her like a branding iron.

2: Two Kinds of Dark

Ah, how evocative smells are. Evocative, yes, but sometimes very hard to place. This one, though, is not quite Proust and his madeleines. What smell is this? Is it … urine? Deserted, ill-lit concrete alleyways flash before her mind. Slumped rubbish; resentful, deceitful faces. No, not urine. Sweeter, smoother. Smugness and triumph: not quite sweat, either, because this smell … ah, this smell … contains none of that sweated anxiety of thwarted escape.

Dreams tumble in on one another.

Sheepwool now sees the teeth of sharks, jaws opening to reveal the enormous blue eyes of a frightened girl. Sitting with Nick in some scratchy-seated cinema in Camden before … well, *before*. Watching some Japanese anime. She sees a car forever moving from right to left, from right to left, and she comes to it at last.

TubeWave. The new designer drug distilled from the sea.

She remembers how she laughed when she first heard the name of the company that made it;

She remembers how her team was looking into suspicions that the company did not seem as worried as it should have been that its new drug had hit the street; that it was undergoing, for want of a better phrase, real-world testing;

She remembers, now, how she couldn't help humming the company's name all that day at the Station, to a defiant tune: ain't gonna work at MagusPharm no more.

Only now she's not laughing. No, not laughing, but … waking.

She wishes her brain could switch off when she's not actively on duty. Too much time alone means too much time to brood. She looks across at her bedside clock, which quietly tells her that it's five minutes past midnight, and envies Elaine Fitch, whose mind is blessedly compartmentalized; who turns for home at the end of the day without a backward glance: to children, and fish fingers and turkey dinosaurs and potato waffles and peas. And a husband. Someone she can talk at, instead of the echoing insides of her own skull.

Her mouth feels as gritty and sour as the bottom of a birdcage. Creaking, she rises and totters to the kitchen, swirls water into the kettle and rattles around in her box of herbal teas. Something with ginger in it, to scour away this fetid corpse taste.

But ah, that smell. She remembers it now, from when she and Nick had not long met. Long, lazy nights and early mornings in his college rooms; taut, winding-shrouded sheets and the befuddling stink of it, and the slick euphoric moisture that went with it. Oh, Nick... how I miss you. And now it makes sense, of course. It is the smell of sex.

That was what she'd smelled in Alex Beach's lab.

Sheepwool had decided to call on Alex Beach at the Institute. Not wanting to trouble Fitch, she had decided to walk there, and had put on jeans, sweater, mackintosh and sensible low-heeled pumps for the purpose. It seemed to take her hours, battling the breeze with every step, a breeze which for all its rawness did not manage to dispel quite all the shreds of night that clung obstinately to the alleys and doorways of Deringland.

As she struggled, she wondered whether there were not in fact two kinds of darkness. One, by far the most common, is a simple absence of light, found in places where light simply does not penetrate. Then there is the second kind of darkness, much less common but more robust, and which is actively inimical to illumination. The first has driven the second almost to extinction, for whereas the first only needs the absence of light to propagate, the second requires additional nourishment. And yet it lurks, nonetheless, in isolated places such as wind-scoured moors where humanity fights and yet clings limpet-like to the brutality of existence; in old buildings whose labyrinthine human history feeds into their decrepitude, and seaside towns largely cut off from the tide of human intercourse, and where the humans that exist there prey largely upon one another. In other words, where such darkness is afforded additional adhesion by the memory of human misery.

The kettle steams and clicks.

The worst part of the journey was the last, across that seemingly endless grassland, at that place where the track disappears behind a knoll, and the Deringland Light and the Institute have yet to be lifted into view. A place of endless and disorienting sky where, at one point, Sheepwool half expected some vast and leprous moonrise in the blear daylight sky, a moon with the accusing, half-rotten face of Pickled Lily. She could hardly credit the relief she felt when she saw the Light and, behind it, the Institute: home, she is convinced, to several very fine and ancient examples of that second species of darkness. But she resolved then and there, that as soon as she arrived she'd ask Mrs Squearn to arrange a taxi home.

She pecks around in a cupboard for a clean mug. Not finding one, she washes up the few things stacked on the draining board.

Alex Beach had looked somewhat out of sorts when she'd arrived at the laboratory, angry with herself, like it was mid-morning and she'd only just started arranging her notes, her slides. Her clothes were crumpled and askew, her hair spiked and disarranged, and the scientist herself broadcast an edginess counter to the pale smoothness of her face. Glancing only in furtive jags at Sheepwool, Beach smoothed down her sweatshirt with the nervous obsession of a startled rabbit and had said that if she'd wanted Dr Morrison, he'd just left. The words were weighted with all the cowed sulkiness of a bored teenager.

Now Sheepwool can connect with that smell, and her recollection of that interview can be seen through its roseate light. Only now, hours after, is she conscious of the flush to Beach's face, and the nipples standing out through her sweatshirt as she'd tried to straighten it. Ah, but was that a genuine recollection, only now honestly recalled; or an elaboration, created by the filter of memory through her own further mental processes, colored as they are, now, with her own associations, her own liquid desires? How fickle memory is: how ill it serves. How memory changes with exposure to any and every subsequent thought; how it is winnowed on the bed of past experience; and yet how it fools one into an impression of archival permanence. How are its animal origins and drives antithetical to the reason and logic with which we fancy we form our daily lives, our interactions with others? And yet it is memory, an object whose color is not known; whose size and weight are unguessed; whose location is a matter of conjecture; and whose very existence as a discrete object is a subject of debate, which must suffice as the principal tool of any investigator. For what is forensics, what is corroboration, but to provide concrete authentication, a placeholder in reality, for this most evanescent of things?

"Actually, Alex, I wanted to see you, not Dr Morrison."

Beach had looked up, then, brightening slightly, as if her mental journey had climbed up at last from a dank and thicketed ravine to a clear, windswept upland. Sheepwool had wanted to take her ease here, especially after her long walk. But the only convenient place was the sofa in Beach's laboratory, and this, somehow (she now knows why), did not lend itself to sober recollection. She could think of no-where else to conduct an interview. Perhaps inspired by the unaccus-tomed practicality of her own clothes (she is not sure) but it popped into her head to suggest that she and Beach went for a walk outside, perhaps down to the shore below the Institute. Beach readily agreed to this, picking up a bulky anorak without further prompting.

Sheepwool finds a lemon-and-ginger teabag and flops it into the mug.

Was Beach's enthusiasm conditioned by the thought of welcome fresh air: or relief that she was not being arrested, or cautioned, or be-ing brought to the Station for the canonical Helping-Police-With-Their-Inquiries? This question nags at her as the seconds and minutes of night wear away, vapour rising from the slowly swirling herbal infusion as she stands at the kitchen counter, staring into a space that only she knows or can inhabit. Slowly swirling: the self-similarity of stirred tea and distant pinwheel galaxies. And of memories, imper-fectly recalled.

The phone rings, as surprising and unwelcome as a cuckoo to a meadow pipit.

Beach strode before her, as keen as a dog let off the leash. Sheep-wool, whose lean frame tried its best to keep up with a woman per-haps half her age, reflected that this savage, childlike eagerness did not suit Alex, as if her body were too large for it, and that she should affect a mood more circumspect, reticent, even (she kicks herself in-wardly for having thought this) more womanly, becoming. Perhaps, though, Alex Beach is primarily a creature of mind, and does not think too much about how the image of her body is projected onto the canvas of reality.

Leaving the Institute, Beach found a path, to the right and seaward side of the car park, that led through a brake of gorse, down wood-framed earthen stairs, and into a deep, wooded cleft in the cliff. Trees clung to the steep slopes, tense roots standing proud of the ground as if physically braced against imminent collapse. Their branches were hung heavily with creepers, and ivy and brambles scarfed over the leaf-moulded ground from which snowdrops were starting to emerge. This was a world closed in: out of the wind, the air stood still, damp and unusually warm, laden with the scent of mould, of fungi burrowing beneath bark with beetles in their wake. As she walked, Sheepwool felt that this wood was a realm of secrets that would remain undiscovered, as one could hardly stop to admire the view, even were there one to descry, for it was impossible to negotiate the twists and turns of the perilous descent without ceaseless vigilance. You had to watch where you put your feet: the treads of each step were of uneven height; some had rotted away, whereas others stood proud from eroded earth like teeth whose gums had receded. In places the stairs gave out completely, especially round switchback corners defined by trees, the treads replaced by laddered roots. But even so, Sheepwool's eyes, looking up to anchor her eyes on Alex, well ahead of her, got fleeting images of brown, shadowed depths, populated, she was sure, by that second kind of darkness, foundering sullenly in abandoned rabbit holes and the puddled hollows of rotten stumps.

At no time during this descent could she see the sea: and even the sound of it, stridently audible from the Institute itself, was muffled, muted by the same vegetation that shielded it from view. Until, quite suddenly, the path ended, blocked by a gravel berm on which Alex Beach stood, beckoning. Sheepwool swished and dragged her way upwards through the gravel to meet her at the top of the ridge, and there was the sea before her all in thunderous array, thirty yards down the beach and from one horizon to another, surf crashing and gravel clattering and foam flying: the sea, with all its light; and rich, weedy tang; and endless, endless, deafening roar.

"It's quite a view," Alex yells.

The phone rings, as surprising and unwelcome as a cuckoo to a meadow pipit.

Sheepwool, still standing at the counter, removes the tea bag from the cup and raises it to her lips for an exploratory sip. She remembers how Alex beckoned her along the shore to the westward, where, beneath the cliff itself, a reddened buttress of eroded earth clad in sea buckthorn afforded a relatively quiet hollow, no more than a foxhole, in which they could talk.

"Sometimes I hike down here to have a think," Alex had said. Sheepwool decided then, for the moment, to postpone any discussion of what promised to be an exhausting ascent, were they to have re-traced their steps. "I don't know why, but it's something about the sea. It's magnetic. You know, Inspector, when I wake at night and hear it, when there's a storm, it is somehow a comfort." Beach's ex-pression flashed from eagerness to happiness to remote thoughtful-ness, as if there was something she wanted to say, but couldn't quite put it into words.

It was then that Sheepwool decided that the time was right to jump right in and tell Alex how Morrison had been, when Sheepwool had shown him Bland's body. Yes, as if he were pleased. And, the mem-ory having brewed and matured in Sheepwool's mind, as if such a circumstance were not entirely unexpected. This was the point, Sheepwool recalls, taking another sip, to which the entire exercise had been building: she wanted to see Beach's face on hearing this news: Beach's face, a faithful mirror of every thought and feeling that passed through what, to Sheepwool, seemed a troubled mind.

The phone rings, as surprising and unwelcome as a cuckoo to a meadow pipit.

And the expression that met her was of an anguish that Sheepwool would have had difficulty putting into words. There was conflict; there was the realization of betrayal, and the dawning knowledge that a lifeline still existed, standing before her.

"Inspector … you've guessed … you know…"

"What do I know?"

"That Morrison … I … he…"

This is where Sheepwool had come to a fork in the conceptual road, and her reassessment of that conversation is weighed, and turned over, in the light of competing hypotheses, none substantiated. Beach soon recovered her composure, changed the subject and sug-gested (to Sheepwool's relief) that they both walk towards the town along the seashore.

Beach's split-second reaction, when she dropped her guard for one hot second, seemed to have let something slip -- but what? That Beach and Morrison are lovers is something that Sheepwool had guessed, in which case Beach could have been reacting to a secret that her lover had kept from her. If Sheepwool is correct about Morrison's character, then this would be no surprise. On the other hand, there could be some deeper force at work, and what she had witnessed was the very edge of a confession, a journey right to its rim, that Beach and Morrison were complicit in something more. More, even, than both being employed by MagusPharm.

Something more, which could explain why Bland was in the laboratory that night, and why his visit had been repaid with death.

But there Sheepwool dared not go at present: not until there had been an inquest. Although foul play had not been ruled out, neither had it been ruled in.

It's at times like this that she wishes she could bounce such ideas off Fitch. But Fitch, if she were sensible (which she is) will have long since read an episode of *Harry Potter and the Temple of Doom* or whatever to her children and curled up on her own sofa or in bed with the solid and dependable Jason.

The thought goes through her like a skewer.

Provisionally, though, and as a working hypothesis, she selects the simplest: that Beach and Morrison are complicit only to the extent that lovers are, and if they both happen to be funded by MagusPharm, then it should be no surprise, either, that people working in the same line of business should forge more intimate relationships. That being said, there is an uncomfortable residuum: for Sheepwool is sure that Morrison is up to something, and the question of why Bland was so uncharacteristically in the Institute at night remains unresolved.

The phone rings, as surprising and unwelcome as a cuckoo to a meadow pipit.

Standing at the kitchen counter, mug in hand, Sheepwool notices that the phone is ringing. Her mind's butler, ravelling rapid recall, suggests that the phone has rung no more than four times. The answering machine will interrupt after six. It takes no more than half a second for Sheepwool to pick up the kitchen extension.

It is Fitch.

"Ma'am? So sorry to disturb you so late."

"Not at all, Fitch. Mulling things over. What's up?"

"We've had a tip-off. The Station just phoned me, not five minutes ago. I …we … that's Jason and me … were just getting the kids' school bags ready for tomorrow when they called. That's Angie on the front desk. That's who called."

A pause. A distant, muffled rattle like some nameless insectoid infestation faded into what could have been low, daemonic muttering, punctuated by the eerie whistle of a distant ghost train. The Deringland telephone exchange, Sheepwool had read in the *Mercury*, was one of the last in the country to hold out against the digital revolution.

"Yes? Fitch? Are you still there?"

"Yes, Ma'am, sorry. Well, Angie said that somebody phoned in, not a quarter of an hour since, to say that they, that's this somebody, had seen another somebody -- somebody *else*, that is -- leave the Institute in the early hours of the morning when Alex Beach discovered Dr Bland's body."

"Somebody?"

"That's just it, Ma'am. Angie said it was a woman, that's all, who wouldn't give her name or details or anything. She wanted it to be anonymous, seems like."

"Pity. Did they say any more about the person this anonymous source had seen?"

"Yes, Ma'am, Angie was most definite about that. The caller said it several times—it was Dr Morrison."

Sheepwool pauses to digest this news, mug halfway between mouth and counter. "And when, precisely, did the caller say she'd seen Morrison?"

"Well, Ma'am, the caller was quite definite about that, too. It was around three a.m. That's when …"

"That's when Dr Morrison told us he was at home in bed. And when did Dr Beach call him?"

"I don't have my notes here, Ma'am—they're all at the Station …"

"I understand."

" … But it can't have been later than three-thirty."

Phantoms and sprites: analog to digital. "Fitch, I have an idea."

"Ma'am?"

"We know that Morrison raised the alarm when Bland died, because Alex Beach called him. I bet Alex called him on his mobile, assuming he'd be at home …"

" … because, well, where else would he be?"

"But the thing with mobiles is you can be anywhere."

"Well, Ma'am, the landlines in Deringland are a disgrace, so everyone has one. A mobile, I mean. Both my boys have them. Jason, well, he has two, and even Bryony says she wants one. Quite a few of her classmates …"

"So, Fitch, Beach just assumed Morrison was at home, when he could have been at the Institute, or anywhere else for that matter."

"Do you think we should arrest Dr Morrison, then, Ma'am?"

"Whatever for?" Sheepwool's reply is decided and definite. "Yes, he appears to have lied to us about his alibi. Yes, this might be critical. But we do not yet know if Bland died from anything more than a heart attack." Sheepwool pauses. She remembers Morrison's expression when he saw Bland's body for the first time, and Beach's agonized rictus when she told her of that same incident.

"Ma'am?"

"Yes, Fitch. Sorry. You're right. We should keep tabs on Morrison, but let's bide our time. When you get in tomorrow, see what you can dig up about his past."

"I could interview Johansson again, and catch up with Boynton. And I still have to track down this Heather Franks person."

"But there's one more thing. Now it seems we have an eyewitness report that Morrison was at the Institute when he said he was at home. Now, it's anonymous, and it could simply be malicious gossip, you know how things are."

"Ma'am?"

"Well, if it's true, it means that there was at least one more person in or around the Institute that we don't know about."

Fitch, artlessly as ever, throws out another idea: "Ma'am, do you think it might have been Dr Beach? You know, she finds the body, calls Morrison assuming he's at home, then looks out of the window and sees him, and ..."

"Hmm. Hadn't thought of that." Sheepwool, thus intrigued, now thinks, and having thought, her conclusion is clear. "No, Fitch, it can't have been. She was down in the lab at the time the caller says Morrison was seen, which was before Alex called him. Have you been in the labs at the Institute, Fitch?"

"No, Ma'am... I've just been in some of the upper rooms."

"Well, you see, the labs have no windows. If Beach were there the whole time, and there's no reason to say she wasn't, then she couldn't have seen anything. But you're right. We have to keep an open mind."

"So, Ma'am, that could be two people whose alibis might not be solid."

"Two people. At least."

"Ma'am, you know what I think? I think we have to find Heather

Franks. If it's not Beach, then it has to be her. But whoever it is—whoever it was - had to have known Morrison well enough to have recognized him."

Sheepwool is convinced that Fitch is completely unaware of her own acuity. Long may it last, she thinks—long may it last, for such gifts sometimes wither in the harsh light of self-knowledge. For, irrespective of the mystery caller's identity, she—it is a she—had to have been able to know Morrison sufficiently well to have identified him, from a distance, from the back, in the dark, and during a storm.

"Yes, Fitch. I agree. We must track her down."

"And, Ma'am … before I forget … my mind's like a sieve! … before we can interview anybody, Jim Levy's calling in tomorrow. The autopsy. Bland. Will you be at the Station, Ma'am?"

Sheepwool is amazed at herself that she had forgotten this. She curses herself inwardly for being so wrapped up in hypotheses and counterfactuals to neglect the plain fact that there might be no case to answer, by Morrison, Beach, Franks or anyone else.

Smiling ruefully to herself, she assures the thrice-blessed Fitch that she'll see her in the morning, wishes her good-night, and hangs up.

Her mug now as empty as her soul, Sheepwool watches helplessly as the darkness of night closes in. She walks to the sitting-room window to adjust the curtain. Looking out, there is already a hint of fog.

3: The Madman in the Fog

In general, Deringland has two kinds of weather. Either there is a wind blowing that rips into anything that isn't nailed down, scouring anything that is. Or there is The Fog (Deringlanders always use the definite article and audible capitals), rolling in from the North Sea, smothering all in a thick blanket of cold. The small, luminous speck of it that Sheepwool had seen the previous night, something so small that she thought at first that it was no more than a smudge on the half-moon spectacles she likes to wear indoors, has, by this morning, grown into a rampant contagion that swamps the streets.

Sheepwool's walk to the Station has been a disorienting journey through freezing cloud, starting with the total white-out that greeted her at the front door of Bordfield Court, as if, like Dorothy's shack, the entire building had been plucked by some freak weather and was in the process of being transported to a magical and sinister kingdom. She herself has made the connection at once and spends most of the journey looking down at her fur-lined boots (having left her heels in the closet) because these are all she can see, as if they might transform themselves at any moment into red slippers, and a click of the heels will be all she needs to send her safely home.

Although she sees nothing, she hears the gruff grumble of cars just inches away, chuffing carefully through the near-zero visibility and betrayed only by clouds of deeper condensation and smears of red and white light that pass her, slowly, like geriatric comets.

All in all, she is pleased with herself that she made the journey without mishap, relying on little more than proprioceptive dead-reckoning and the few hints offered by buildings and street furniture when a gable end, or a window-frame, or a pillar box, emerge very briefly from the dead-eyed murk. Each one not much in itself, and possibly confusing to a complete novice, but Sheepwool is now just sufficiently well-acquainted with the landmarks of her new home, however unconsciously noted, to have been able to place each in its context. And so, as she greets the warm ground-floor office she shares with Fitch, she congratulates herself, and puts on some coffee in celebration. The machine is soon gurgling away.

There are, however, two things that worry her, clinging to her clothes like spent dreams. The first is the shudder at the recall of having met just one other person on her commute: a shaggy, mad-eyed man who had loomed out at her like a sudden standing stone, just outside the Three Kings. He had grimaced and yelled something incomprehensible that was sucked forcibly into the fog before he, too, followed his crazed imprecation into the white oblivion.

The second is that there is no sign of Fitch. This is unusual, for Sheepwool has become used to her Detective Sergeant always arriving well before she does. Sheepwool is, in truth, rather ashamed at herself about this, given that Fitch has a family and a school run to organize and a drive across town whereas she only has a short walk, irrespective of its occasionally alarming signs and portents. Sheepwool has always prided herself on her ability to work on her own, to work things out in her own mind. But now, she finds, she's grown so used to having Fitch around that she has become dependent on her. Without her, here, now, Sheepwool becomes irritated and paces the room, arms crossed, wondering what to do.

And then, Fitch arrives, harassed, anorak dripping, blonde curls flattened and greyed with drops of water. Sheepwool looks up and, just for an instant, wishes to reprimand her for being late, but this small and (she admits) thoroughly ungrateful impulse is soon overwhelmed by one of gratitude. Fitch has arrived—normal life may once more resume. In Fitch's wake is a stocky man in a hooded parka. He throws it back, shedding water, revealing a mass of wild hair and bloodshot eyes. Sheepwool is amazed: it is the man who, roaring like a polypheme, briefly ambushed her outside the Three Kings.

"Sorry to be late, Ma'am, it's this weather!" One sudden shock after another—Sheepwool realizes that Fitch must have driven here. "And on the way I met Dr Levy. Have you met him?"

Sheepwool confesses she hasn't (resolving not to mention the raw and fogbound ambush) and introduces herself.

"Nice to meet you, Inspector. I got the train in, from Norwich. Glad I did. But when I got out at the train station I got lost immediately. If it hadn't been for DS Fitch, who heard my bellowing, I'd still be out there wandering about like a ghost ship."

Fitch smiles. She hangs her coat on the bentwood hanger where Sheepwool's mac is already resident, takes Levy's parka, and heads, instinctively, for the coffee jug. Sheepwool had, at least, had the presence of mind to have put it on. She could manage that much, at least.

The office being too small to accommodate all three of them at once in any comfort, they relocate to an interview room that is larger but more sparse. Not one for interrogating suspects — more for consoling the anxious parents of miscreant offspring or the relatives of people whose lives had been suddenly ripped away, leaving their dependents as washed up as driftwood. Not that this place makes many concessions to homely comfort: it looks like an annexe to the waiting room in any hospital emergency ward. The seats are metal, rectilinear. The walls, painted an institutional blue, are decorated with improving notices about the dangers of drugs, alcohol and driving too fast.

"Well, I'm puzzled," Levy begins, crouching before the low coffee-table on which their mugs are placed. The pose forces him to lean forwards, conspiratorially. Sheepwool notices the incongruity of his appearance. Although he is wearing a suit as neat as anything that Dr Morrison might affect, the impression of style contrasts rudely with the rest of him: long, dirty gray waves of hair wash over a greasy collar and around a hedge-bearded face. His cheeks and nose are rough, ruddy and lined with the thin tracks of burst vessels. His teeth are testaments to many long years of indulgence in pleasures of the kind which the puritanical writers of this room's wall posters might regard as deeply dangerous, if not actually sinful.

But beneath this near-paleolithic neglect lie eyes that are arresting in their sea-green intelligence, and an animation in his body that threatens to burst the buttons on the neat jacket, as if suits do not feature greatly in this man's mental wardrobe. Summing up, Sheepwool pictures Levy most succinctly as a spaniel with clothes on.

Thinking of this, she has a brief but nasty recollection of Kitten Hell and wondered what Sir Frideric and his friends did with dogs. The horror must have been broadcast on her face, for the next thing she sees is Fitch's concerned face, close to hers, asking her if she is all right. Just like that day with Pickled Lily. And just like that day when … different female officer, room very much like this …

"Ma'am?"

"Inspector?"

"No, sorry." She takes a breath, straightens up. "I'm all ears. Please continue, Dr Levy."

Levy had come as quickly as he could from the autopsy — Bland's autopsy — which had happened yesterday in Norwich. He wanted to fill them in before they received anything official, and to explain any delay in the forthcoming inquest.

"To be honest, I thought it was a coronary, at first," he says. "Elderly man, unsocial hours, stress, you know." Levy waits for assent, as if the policewomen really did know. But for Sheepwool, this is news of a sort, corroboration that Bland was indeed out of place, out of time, for reasons yet to be discovered. But Sheepwool feels her eyes widen, that she nods fractionally to acknowledge Levy, urging him to continue. Inwardly, she feels herself boil and hunger for any concrete facts that the pathologist might wish to impart; any secrets at all that he might share; any bones on which she and Fitch can hang their incomplete rags of supposition and conjecture. Not for the first time, Sheepwool feels a strong kinship with Alex Beach, scientist, in the rawness of her realization that the puddle of knowledge is insignificant compared with the ocean of ignorance, and in the frustration that to gain further knowledge, the ocean must be examined drop by drop, stewed, distilled, rather than swallowed in great gulps in the vanity that one might ever begin to assuage that impatient and never-ending thirst.

"Well, a coronary was what I first thought. But then I examined his skin, and it looked odd, kind of blistered, and then, I thought, there was more to it. 'Aye aye', I thought to myself — looks like some kind of allergic reaction. Whether that had anything to do with the coronary ..."

"Allergic reaction? To what?" asks Sheepwool, leaning forward. In the corner of her eye she sees Fitch leaning back, getting a notepad from her bag.

"Can't say, as yet. Could be anything. Unlikely to have been a bee, or pollen, at this time of year. His medical records say nothing about the usual things - peanuts, penicillin, latex. At this stage it could be anything." His voice becomes darker, more stern, as if a steely mind is shedding its usual coat of affability. "Anything, especially in that ... that place."

"The Institute?"

"The world is full of allergens, Inspector. I've seen people who've died, or nearly so, because of a brush with quite normal things like coins or wallpaper paste or particular brands of deodorant. Now, think of the Institute: it's Allergy City in there. That place must be absolutely chocka with allergens. Lousy with them. Not just the dust and dirt of it," Levy wrinkles his nose in distaste, which Sheepwool thinks mildly ironic, given Levy's appearance, "but the specimens themselves.

"I guess you've been there, Inspector. Piles and piles of old tat from around the world, lots of it biological and nobody really knows where it's from." The shade of Pickled Lily hangs briefly over all of them. "But that's no crime. Not in itself. What I don't like, speaking professionally, as it were, is that it's so poorly looked after. Yes, Inspector, I've seen the rotting seals on some of those jars, the cracks in the cases, oozing goodness-knows-what. Who knows what's been leaking out over the years?" Sheepwool notices that Levy's cheeks redden and his eyes sparkle with a barely suppressed and pitiless fury, like the reflection of halogen headlamps in chips of gravel. "Really, I'm amazed that Environmental Health hasn't closed the place years ago. So, goodness knows what Bland was allergic to."

Fitch scribbles a note.

"He was allergic to something, though?" prompts Sheepwool. "Something that might have been related to the coronary?"

"Well, yes, Inspector... yes, and no. Sure, Bland's nasal membranes and windpipe were inflamed, as you'd expect if he was allergic to something—the tests are probably being done in the lab even as we speak—but there is more to it than that. I hope you're both sitting comfortably." He himself sits back, his expression unfathomable.

"Dr Levy?"

"Well, yes, first it's a coronary. Then it's an allergy. And then what? Both might be right, or, at least, contributory... to the death, that is. But when I opened him up, it was like nothing I'd seen before. You know, don't you, that when you do an autopsy, you take all the bits out of a body, weigh them and have a general poke around. So when I thought 'coronary' and 'allergy' you'd think I'd want to see the heart, the lungs, the major blood vessels; open up the stomach and intestines to see if he'd eaten anything that disagreed with him; not forgetting a good butcher's at the liver and kidneys, in case he had been poisoned or if there were any long-term problems, diabetes and so on?" Levy sounds as if he had been doing nothing more unpleasant than servicing a car.

Fitch is absolutely still: Sheepwool, glancing around, notices that her colleague's face has faded from its normal rose to a pinched, chalky white. Sheepwool begins to turn towards her but a movement of Fitch's hand, too tiny for anyone else to notice, signals reassurance, and that for all its promised grisliness, her desire to hear Levy's testimony without interruption. Fitch is as keen to pursue this chase as she is, no matter what the cost.

"Well, I was prepared for all that. All in a working day, you might say. But when I cut him open, this is what I saw—nothing. The windpipe got more and more inflamed as it went down, so did the oesophagus, but not far below the collar bone it all faded out into a homogenous crimson goo. No internal organs. It's like Bland swallowed a blender, tuned it on and left it running."

"But what …?"

"What caused it, Inspector? No idea. Not an earthly. Of course I bottled up some samples and sent them to the lab. They're working on those right now, too. But heaven knows if they'll find a cause. I have never seen anything like it. Actually, thinking about it, that's not true. I did see something similar, once." He leans closer. Their three heads form a triangle over the table, coffee quite forgotten.

"Not long after I graduated, I picked up some work in West Africa. First the Niger delta, then the Gambia. No names, no pack drill, but there are some tropical diseases that do things like this. Liquefy the internal organs. Hemorrhagic fevers. Very rare. Very, *very* deadly. It's only the fact that Bland hadn't been abroad for many years that has prevented the whole Institute being put off limits by … well, not to put too fine a point on it, higher authorities than mine. That, and the fact that the same higher authorities seem as pig-ignorant of the dangers of things leaking out of old and creaky museums to think that what might have pulverized Bland's insides could have been in the Institute for years. Decades, even."

"But, Dr Levy, if Dr Bland's insides were … well, all messed up," Fitch frowns as she asks what seems a disarmingly naïve question, but which, as always, exposes uncomfortable lacunae in our understanding. Sheepwool smiles inwardly as Fitch continues. "If his heart and lungs and such were all scrambled, Bland couldn't have been … well … walking around like that. Could he? He wouldn't have been able to breathe. Yet he seems to have got into the Institute, you know, all on his own, and …"

Levy sits up. "Yes, Detective Sergeant. The time course. You're right. Whatever killed Bland must have done so rather suddenly. But I don't think he could have breathed something in, then and there, or got poisoned, and suffered such an instant … well, instant liquefaction. I think he'd been infected some time before and whatever was doing it had slowly built up until it had reached a crisis point, a threshold. Then he would have just keeled over.

"But now I'm speculating. That's all I have to say, except this: whatever killed Bland, the coroner will say that he died of natural causes. And I'd have to agree with him. Doesn't matter if those natural causes remain to be identified, but at present -- and of course I'd have to defer to your knowledge here of the people involved -- I can see no case for foul play here. Unless he was poisoned by somebody with the kind of amazing occult knowledge and truly evil mind that you don't see outside … well, did I mention higher authorities?"

"Dr Levy, you used the word 'infected'," says Sheepwool.

"Did I, Inspector? Slip of the tongue. Thinking of my African days. I saw some things out there, Inspector. Things that would make your hair stand on end. Things …"

"But if you meant what you said, could we have some new disease? Surely, caution …"

"Should we close the Institute? The word from the higher-ups is that we shouldn't act too hastily. Balance of probabilities, you see. The Institute has been open for decades, people walking in and out, and although Bland could have caught something off a pickled mermaid or something, nobody has ever seen anything like this before, so it's just as likely that he caught it elsewhere—if 'caught' is the right word."

"And what's your view, Dr Levy?"

"Me? I think the Institute should be closed down right now and placed under what our American colleagues call Level-Four containment. Totally sealed off. Martian suits. Disinfection. And not just because it's a crumbling death trap. Just between us, and strictly off the record, you'll remember BSE, and Foot-and-Mouth, when the cat got out of the bag, if you ask me, as a result of too much higher-level farting around and not enough action."

"But what about Bird Flu?" asks Fitch. "Every time they talk about it on the news, it's headlines for weeks."

"My point exactly. All it takes is for a swan to sneeze and even Posh and Becks get blown off the front page." Fitch smiles, but Sheepwool looks puzzled. Clearly, she and Dr Levy had very little reading matter in common. "But has anyone said anything at all about Dr Bland's death? Hmm?"

Silence. Publicity was the last thing that had occurred to either policewoman. Usually, when there was a dead body, there had been a press conference. The Super would have coached them in what to say, and what to leave out. But this was Methwold, not the Met, and there hadn't been even half an inch in the *Mercury*. Sheepwool is left alone in her own head, more puzzled now than at any other time since the investigation began.

To the outside world, the death of Dr Evanston Bland, as mysterious as it was in many ways, would have to be put down to a freak of nature. So the inquest would say, and the funeral that would follow. Sheepwool is convinced that the case will soon close, at least as a police matter, and that she will be moved to other duties.

She is unhappy though, at the loose ends. Morrison's lies; the role of MagusPharm; what drove Bland to the lab at such an unaccustomed hour; the identity of the mystery informant; Alex Beach's possible complicity; the bizarre results of the autopsy. And most of all — mainly because it had never occurred to her before — why there had been no public announcement of the death. The reasoning part of her brain, the part that likes things cut-and-dried, tells her that she will have to accept things as they are, because no case can ever be as neatly resolved as you'll find in a detective story, isolated and separated from other cases as separate gift-wrapped parcels under the Christmas tree. One event leads to another until they form a massively interconnected ramifying network of happenstance. In the real world, there is no such thing as coincidence, and there is only one crime.

The meeting with Levy now over, Sheepwool is gripped by a compulsion, strangely strong, to return to the Institute (despite Levy's warnings) as a tourist. As she works her way through a morning of routine, the thought coalesces that a closer look at Pickled Lily, now she knows what to expect, might help her sort things out in her own head. So, leaving Fitch to catch up with some paperwork, she calls for a taxi. She could have asked for a police car and driver, but does not wish to attract undue attention.

And so it is, in mid-afternoon, the battered Peugeot Estate that is the sole vehicle of Deringland Cabs inches through the thinning but still considerable fog and deposits Sheepwool in front of the Institute. That so little of the hideous building can be seen through the blind murk is a blessing, and Sheepwool climbs the steps with unaccustomed lightness of heart. Perhaps it is her instinct, as a professional, that despite her misgivings, this case will soon be closed, taken from her, her responsiblity no longer. Or, perhaps, that the fog is shielding her from some watchful malice.

She trips past the statue of Sir Frideric with the impudent glee of a schoolgirl and heads towards the main public gallery. But the spring in her step fades and finally crumples as she reaches the great hexagonal case and inches round to the southern side. Pickled Lily limns into view like the dark side of the Moon.

The fog has bathed the gallery in an even, pearly light. There are no shadows within which objects might hide and generate spurious menace. Likewise, there is no glare to obscure details in blinding shafts of sudden light. Sheepwool notices that the polished parquet floor immediately in front of Pickled Lily's case is bare (the word 'tank' had fleetingly occurred to her, as the mermaid is, after all, suspended in fluid) and that a large, padded bench stands facing it, about six feet away. A bench for the ease of Pickled Lily's audience, perhaps: or for those who might view her as an oracle, her case a kind of shrine. A comfort in times of trouble, a source of inspiration and advice.

Our Lady of Deringland.

Sheepwool's mouth hardens and twists. Even though she has accommodated the shock, knows what to expect, the sight of Pickled Lily is still disquieting. In her presence the padded bench seems a necessary relief, rather than an optional comfort. Sheepwool now sits on it, squarely in front of Pickled Lily, and feels the last vestiges of cheerfulness ebb through her toes and into the floor. In her grim tableau, her arms outstretched, pleading, her chapped lips stretched, her teeth bared, Pickled Lily reaches out to Sheepwool as if trying to communicate some hidden agony, some secret but devastating message that will bring down this place, even from beyond the walls of night. A message of hideous abuse, of appalling injustice, of dreadful crimes committed long ago and never punished.

Sheepwool gazes at the specimen, and past her, into space. The ambiguities of the Bland case swirl around her head like buttered tigers chasing one another's tails. There is only one crime, she reflects, for in a sense, all crimes are identical: someone is done a disservice, and there must be recompense, but that recompense leads to further crimes, further injustice, and these multiply exponentially with each loose end that is not cauterized.

But all loose ends, like all crimes, are the same.

Such are her thoughts as she leans forward and studies Pickled Lily's label, and reads once again of the exploits of Obed Marsh, the curse on his crew and the selling of Pickled Lily to Sir Frideric's agent. But that's all rubbish, Sheepwool says to herself—the label admits as much. The salient point is this: Pickled Lily is thought to have been Sir Frideric's greatest achievement as a taxidermist. Only 'thought to have been', for as the label implies, Sir Frideric hardly bragged about it, as he had with all his other, inferior sports, and his secrecy extended to a ban on any further study, even after his own death. Sir Frideric Lowdley-Purslane clearly had something to hide. Something horrible: and he had got away with it. And as crime begets crime, cause begets consequence, she strongly suspects that Morrison has secrets too. Whether he has committed a crime in the past, or his misdemeanour remains as yet lost in the future, Sheepwool is sure that he, like Sir Frideric, has secrets that he would rather remain so to the grave, and beyond it.

No, more than sure. She is absolutely certain.

4: An Exile of Secrets

The mind of Lady Felicity Lowdley-Purslane was now wholly given over to internal conflict, the opposing sides in such balance that she was effectively frozen immobile.

On the one hand, she had been forced to leave her comfortable home in Kensington, her friends, all but a few of her servants, society in general. Forced out—by scandal, could she only admit it to herself—and banished here, to the ends of the earth.

For any woman of her station this should have been a one-sided argument without compromise. Deringland was a squalid village populated by what seemed to be savages, remote in a dark region, as far from the tides of fashion and gaiety and social intercourse as the meanest hovel. To have exchanged Kensington for Deringland was more than exile—it was punishment.

And this house, Ketchingham Lodge—this rambling, draughty, mis-shapen building, such a contrast with the elegance of her old home -- was not even in the centre of that tiny village, its paltry services to command; but on its periphery, and even then, was not a proper house, for all that it dwarfed her former home in size. It was in fact a kind of gatehouse, a decayed Restoration folly, the last and southernmost outpost of what (she had been informed by Ralph Willoughby) had been a medieval estate, long ago, whose manse had long since crumbled into the still-encroaching surf. The present cliffs now ran sheer across the grounds like a gash, not fifty yards from the back windows. It was said (again, Mr Willoughby had much delight in imparting this information, though his eyes were directed more towards Rebecca than to her) that when the weather was especially severe, one might hear still the peals from Ketchingham church bells, faintly, from beneath the pounding waves.

But Lady Felicity was not as outraged by her present fortunes as one might have at first supposed. Pallid, somewhat reserved, with somewhat protruding eyes and wide, flaccid lips, she was—if she were honest with herself—as glad to have left London as she would have been to have remained there, with its noise, haste and bustle, its crowds and stink. She had never liked it so much as to call it home in her heart: nonetheless she had been fearful to leave it, for it was all she had known, at least since she had met Frideric in girlhood and later married him.

She had furthermore taken ill the dark rumors about her husband, the whispers of people who had thought her back turned; whispers that had depopulated her London house of visitors so that it became as effectively deserted as any seaside retreat in winter. The public tale was that it had been Lady Felicity's delicate health and need for the restorative airs of the sea that had directed this migration, and not any of the affairs of Sir Frideric, and such should be made plain to anyone.

Many in their shrinking circle had politely assented to this fiction. But it was the rumors—about Sir Frideric -- that had finally driven them out.

Rumors to which she quite deliberately had paid no attention whatsoever.

But now she'd left, she was glad. All fictions should to some measure be earthed in fact, and it was true that in Deringland she had found clear air, and cool; a revival of her spirits, and a relief from the cruelties that the well-meaning words of friends might afford. Such slights as she had lately suffered had been supplanted by the noise of the sea, from which she derived such delight as might be scarcely credible in one who had never seen any more of the sea than the tamed and neutered waves at Brighton. She would sit in her morning-room in the clear north light, listening to the many voices of the sea. And it was on more than one occasion that they found her—Frideric, or Mr Willoughby, or even Rebecca—sitting near the very edge of the cliffs as if she were a kittiwake, deaf to all entreaties to return.

These, then, were the two balanced sides of her demeanour. The one, which enjoyed with a quiet appreciation the sophistication of London; the other, hating it, all of it -- that gained comfort from this wild shore.

If there was one thing that tipped her heart in Deringland's favour it was the lighter manner of her husband, who seemed in Deringland to have shed a great weight. To be sure, to her he always presented a cheerful face, whether here or there, but she was his wife, and their move to Ketchingham Lodge had been accompanied by a slight lessening of those intimate habits to which he had become prone to an excessive degree in their final months in London. She consoled herself that all husbands were, she believed, wont to vent their frustrations in such a manner, and covered the scars and wounds as best she could.

Indeed, Sir Frideric had found in this lonely house the space and lack of interruption he required for his researches; to display and extend his cabinets of curiosity, and to practice his formidable taxidermic arts.

Had she paused to consider any of these things even for a moment, and the connexions between them, Lady Felicity might have realized that her knowledge of her husband's activities was variable, both in degree and in kind.

His cabinets, of course, were open for all to see, and Lady Felicity found, to her pleasure, that she was a hostess once more, at least to those few persons of refinement who lived in that part of Norfolk, or those others sufficiently idle or curious, who came to marvel at Sir Frideric's collections. Often had she heard him boast in company, especially after dinner when the Halberds or the Bordfields were there and Rebecca was invariably required to sing at the pianoforte (accompanied by the redoubtable and attentive Mr Willoughby, their sole remaining London connection, who had served as Frideric's agent and confidant) that Frideric's aim was nothing less than to create a repository of knowledge of all things marine.

"The greater part of the Earth's surface lies under the wave," he would say, throwing his great arms wide, face shining and ruddy with snipe, venison and claret. "Not over it, Under it! And of its secrets we know vanishingly little. Let us expose the secrets of the sea to the light of knowledge! Let us expose them!" And he would raise another glass of claret and the company would all cheer, she herself not the least.

Of his taxidermic arts she knew only of what finished products might adorn these selfsame collections. He had been much engaged with cats of late, and had asked her to communicate to the servants and thence to the village at large that here would be a home for unwanted kittens, and sorry specimens would be delivered in sacks to the kitchen door, anonymously and under cover of night. She wondered whether any arrived alive, and drew back from the manner of their dispatch, had they arrived alive and were then rendered otherwise.

Of course she knew little or nothing of how Frideric practiced his arts, or even precisely where, for there were parts of the house to which she was, if not quite forbidden from entering, then at least strongly discouraged from going. She fancied that it was her own reticence -- her own fear of what she might find -- that was a greater bar to her curiosity than anything that Frideric might actually do or say.

Though, she recalled, one evening when he had found her strayed into a narrow corridor that she had not realized existed — a corridor dominated by an enormous, fanged and black-furred creature, and from whose walls hung tapestries illustrating people and animals engaged in activities which she could not at first discern, because she had thought such things unimaginable — following which Frideric had led her away with gentleness, repaying her later with more than his usual degree of amatory extravagance and force. (The act of sitting down had presented various problems for several days following). She had not been tempted to venture into that corridor again, or near it, though she at times fancied she heard peculiar sounds emanating from what were presumably Frideric's private rooms at the far end.

Sometimes, even, screams.

Such rooms were, she presumed, the location for Frideric's researches, but of these she necessarily knew nothing whatsoever. She knew better than to ask Mr Willoughby about them, and on the one occasion when she had mentioned the matter to Rebecca, her daughter had responded as if she'd been stung by a hornet, and changed the subject.

There were clues — signs — but a natural caution drew her away from thinking too much about them such that she might read into them a coherent picture. As the Lady of the house she could not help but notice the relatively rapid arrivals and departures of servants, especially the younger girls. And as a local notable, albeit one reclusive in spirit, she had been witness to much discussion in recent weeks of disturbances in the graveyard at St Christopher and those in adjacent parishes, which had increased the commissioning of lockable, lead-lined coffins. The 'Sack-'Em-Up' men, among the many scourges of

London, or so she had heard, seemed to have followed them to north Norfolk, presumably in search of fresher prey, and easier.

She was likewise aware of the frequent deliveries by cart of large packages for the sole and expressed attention of her husband whose contents he would never discuss (and concerning which she was prudent enough never to inquire).

She was, in the main, shielded from furtive and largely nocturnal meetings between her husband (like as not accompanied by Mr Willoughby) and various visitors who for some reason did not make themselves known at the front door, but insisted on less well-publicized entrance and swift egress through the kitchen. She was aware, however, that transactions of a similar nature happened with fair regularity on the beach, given her habit of strolling along the shore at night, under the stars, but all she ever heard were voices, rather than any words exchanged.

No—all these things she let pass. But if her own mind was in a state of careful balance, perhaps swayed towards contentment by the evident satisfaction and pleasure that the move to Norfolk had given her husband, then there might be one thing that would direct the compass of her mood back towards a guarded equilibrium. That was the state of her daughter.

Rebecca, tall, shapely and lively, with a clear complexion, wide gray eyes and dark hair (much like herself in her youth, she reflected with pleasure), had been as happy in London as one might expect for any handsome, well-connected girl of seventeen, and equally as sullen as any such girl might become were she forced into exile many miles from her home and acquaintances. Lady Felicity felt that Rebecca's mood would alter to the good, given time. But Rebecca had remained unhappy, and her unhappiness had deepened. She spurned company, and often failed to appear at the dining table. Her voice had declined with her spirits so that she sang now rarely, if at all. Frideric, when the subject was raised, would make light of it. Mr Willoughby, who had expressed some affection for Rebecca -- and indeed doted on her slightly more than was strictly proper, she thought, for all that this might compensate for the dearth of girls of Rebecca's age and position in the immediate locality that might serve her well as friends—took Rebecca's seeming malaise more seriously, but seemed impotent to turn it around.

Lady Felicity soon found such avenues as existed for the exploration of her daughter's state swiftly exhausted, and was left only with hope and prayer. She did notice one thing, however, and that was Rebecca's mood at any time when her father might appear. Whereas once, as a young girl, she had joked and played with Sir Frideric as boisterously as any boy, eyes sparkling in her pale face, her father's entrance into any concourse at which she was already present now rendered her unusually silent and mulish. At first Lady Felicity had dismissed this as a symptom of any girl her age—she had seen such things often enough in London, and perforce such moods were also Rebecca's answer to having been uprooted.

But as the months passed, and a chill and windy winter gave way to a wan spring and the promise of outdoor activity, Rebecca's spirits still failed to improve. Whereas Lady Felicity deliberately forbore to examine her husband's activities too closely, she lavished much greater attention on her daughter. Because of this she noticed a closer connection between Rebecca's moods and the presence of her father, such that were Sir Frideric to approach Rebecca directly, she would recoil, as if stricken. This was a circumstance for which she could offer herself no explanation, and at the same time she was reluctant to discuss it with anyone else.

"So, now we have the long-expected result of this much-delayed inquest, there's nothing more to say, is there?"

Methwold tents his fingers and shifts in his chair as if about to say something else, but the question, rich in sarcasm, is almost rhetorical, and requires nothing more than the conventional response.

"No, Sir." Sheepwool, not wishing her irritation to show— irritation that would stray, were she to let it, to the border of fury -- resists the urge to shuffle around in the chair opposite. But this morning she senses some small risk that she might lose that battle. Stalling it, she gets up and leaves, without a word, not looking back, thinking that as the atmosphere in Methwold's office gets thicker with every step she takes, she'll have to move fast if she is to escape at all.

Case closed.

In the corridor, back to the cooling wall outside Methwold's door, she grits her teeth in frustration. The corridor is dingy and dark—the fluorescent bulbs in an overhead cluster of lights have gone out, all except one, which flickers like the wing of an injured pigeon. Loose ends, she keeps telling herself. There are—and will always be—loose ends. As if that were satisfactory in this case, for Morrison had out-foxed her by loudly tying one of them while conspiring to bury an-other: hidden, it seems, from everyone. Except her.

Three days earlier, Sheepwool and Fitch had cornered Boynton in her laboratory. Cornered — there was no other word for it: the woman had the prickly hauteur of a duchess and clearly regarded the pres-ence of officers of the law in her sanctum sanctorum as akin to having to tolerate the servants tracking dog shit on the floor. Boynton man-aged to bring herself to talk to Sheepwool, just: she all but ignored Fitch. Nevertheless, they managed, between them, to drag out a tale of Morrison being funded by MagusPharm (which they already knew); tittle-tattle about MagusPharm's attempted hostile takeover of Dr Johansson's family firm (which Fitch had already had, first hand); and some snide, second-hand academic gossip about Morrison's first meeting with Alex Beach (which amounted to very little).

It was then that Sheepwool and Fitch had confronted Morrison, as brazenly as they dared, given that the cause of Bland's death was still yet to be established — but murder was looking less and less likely.

It was this, on reflection, that fuelled Morrison's cocksure attitude, that whatever he was hiding (and Sheepwool remains convinced, even now, that he did indeed have things to hide), such things could be hidden by diverting attention away from them. So when Sheep-wool had asked him about his funding by MagusPharm, he had not denied it. In fact, he had admitted it fully, and at length, and also told them, without prompting, that Alex Beach was funded by Ma-gusPharm, too — thanks, in part, to his arrangements — and that he and Dr Beach were currently engaged in what he called a 'relationship', "not that the fact that I'm fucking Alex Beach is really any business of yours, Inspector, is it?" Sheepwool clenches her fists at the memory. She feels her long nails excavate small holes in her palms. Stigmata. No wonder Methwold looked like he wanted to crucify her. The final bulb gives one last, pathetic flash and dies above her head.

But that wasn't all.

Morrison, again, without prompting, had then launched into a long and passionate exegesis on why major funding from Ma-gusPharm was necessary. "The collections at this Institute are irre-placeable, Inspector. Priceless. But the Institute is falling down. Liter-ally. The Trustees' surveyor has just sent me this report" — Morrison brings out a massive sheaf of papers which he lets fall on his solid pine desk with a dramatic thump—"which says, not to put too fine a point on it, Inspector, that the whole place is likely to go arse-over-tit within two years, maybe sooner. Over the cliff. The county's Environmental Health people, who goaded the Trustees -- lazy sods, every one -- to commission this report in the first place, have been on to me and—quotes—'recommended' that this place is closed down and evacuated as soon as possible. And I have to say, I agree. What's more, they'd said as much to Bland, years ago, but he was more interested in porking the staff than doing the job he was paid for. At least I'm trying to do the second as well as succeeding in the first, which is more than Bland ever managed—on both counts. So if you want my opinion, Inspector, I think it's a good job that Bland is out of the way. About fucking time, if you ask me. And you can quote me, all right?"

Sheepwool had glanced at Fitch, who had turned white and sat in her chair, immobile. Morrison seemed to be aping the words of his own scientists—the scientists who, according to Fitch's investigations, seemed to have had one up on Morrison. But now Morrison was showing why he got to be the Director, and they didn't. By playing a hand of calculated recklessness. By sheer bloody politics.

"But MagusPharm wants those collections to survive," Morrison continues, his voice, quiet and authoritative, shot with a measure of righteous indignation. "Just like the Trustees only pretend they do. MagusPharm wants to use them. To fulfil, if I may say so, the wishes of Our Fucking Founder."

Sheepwool wonders about the degree to which Morrison's high colour, his tone of determined annoyance, his well-placed injections of profanity, were synthetic. She confesses that she still has no idea whatsoever: the man has her outmanoeuvred.

"So you see, Inspector, much as I'd like to help you investigate the death of my completely useless tosser of a predecessor, I'm actually working twentyfour-seven to find somewhere—anywhere—that I can move a huge collection, much of it irreplaceable, all of it delicate, a high proportion of it preserved in highly inflammable and toxic liquids, much of which would, these days, constitute a biohazard—in the next few months. I've found places that want to take bits of it, but the shit-for-brains Trustees insist that it must be kept together, like some debutante's legs, and nobody has room for the whole lot, so nobody wants any of it. Not the County Museums Service, not the Natural History Museum, not even the American Museum of Natural History — but if I did that, you can imagine the unholy fucking furore there'd be about Britain's heritage being shipped abroad and such bollocks.

"And there's no time to build a new Museum, even if we had the money and the planners singing from the same hymn sheet, and didn't have years to waste on planning inquiries — which there would have to be, Inspector, because nobody is going to want *our* spirit store at the bottom of *their* garden. MagusPharm — who is paying for all this — is spitting fire. But at least they are still paying. Without them we'd be bankrupt. Totally fucked. And the collections would have to go off piecemeal no matter how loudly the Trustees squealed. And the fucking tragedy is that if the late unlamented Bland hadn't thought with his cock the whole time, there might even have been a way out of this mess. At the very least, the Institute wouldn't be quite so far up shit creek as it now finds itself."

Sheepwool had opened her mouth to interject, to divert Morrison on to the question of his movements on the night Bland had died. But, once again, Morrison got there first, steaming ahead, always one move in front.

"You want to know who last saw Bland alive? It was probably me, Inspector. Bland found me that night — yes, that very night — to have some stupid teenage confrontation about Alex, saying that he'd seen her first and I was stepping on his turf or some such tripe — yes, Inspector, that's what he said, 'stepping on my turf'. As if Alex Beach is only good for one thing, and that's for lying on. As if there weren't other more important things to worry about. I told him not to be so ridiculous, to get a grip — and fuck off. Which he did. So now you know. The stupid prick probably went down to his lab to lick his wounds, and keeled over. You're asking me if I'm sorry? Well, in public I have to parade the usual platitudes. But in private — which this is, Inspector — I couldn't give a flying fuck. Now, if you'll excuse me…?"

As Sheepwool and Fitch rose to leave, Sheepwool tried one last, desperately Parthian shot, asking Morrison where he and Bland had had their argument. "I was at home, Inspector. As I've told you before. The moron came and pounded on my door. What's that got to do with anything? Now, I really do have calls to make. Pull this place back from the fucking brink. Literally." Morrison picked up a phone as if to emphasize the point and Sheepwool and Fitch, without quite knowing how, found themselves in the public gallery, outside his closed door.

Outside doors. In corridors. Alone, humiliated, gutted. At least, Sheepwool now reflects, she hadn't dug herself in further by blurting out the eyewitness report that Morrison was at the Institute at the time, not at home. Especially when they still hadn't tracked down the witness, or even knew who she was. Sheepwool, cowed, hobbles along the corridor to the office she shares with Fitch. She collapses, winded, into her chair, and kicks off her shoes. The tension in the soles of her feet begins to ease.

God, these heels.

Fitch isn't there. Something about a school concert. Bryony playing the violin. And it wasn't as if they'd had much else on at the Station at the moment, was it?

As soon as the policewomen leave, Morrison puts down the handset (the phone call being a ruse, though he'll have to make one for real, soon enough) and sits down. He takes a deep breath, relaxes, and as he does so he feels sweat pour from him: sweat suppressed throughout the fight-or-flight confrontation with the policewomen. The small of his back is sodden; his armpits slick; and if he doesn't do something, the inside of his suit will soon stink like a rat's arse.

Luckily, the solution is at hand.

Wiping his brow, he rises, turns, and clicks open a door behind his desk — a door disguised as a wooden panel. It opens on a dressing room with a small, modern shower cubicle and a surprisingly deep closet. The dressing room is furnished with a chaise-longue spacious enough for one. But, on occasion, just squeezable for two.

This small but convenient space had once been a store-room but Bland had had it converted for the Director's private use, and whatever he now thinks of Bland and his private life, this had been one of his better ideas. When he'd first discovered it he'd found a stash of quaintly old-fashioned soft porn and several packets of condoms, unopened, possessed more in hope than expectation.

Morrison strips and showers, feeling the anxiety peel off him, with the sweat. He imagines Alex -- in the shower, her fabulous curves glistening in the wet, her gorgeous, snowy-white tits, her ... how had Bland put it? 'Turf'? Normally he'd feel himself hardening massively at such thoughts. But, unlike Bland, Morrison is proud of how he can direct his energies, arrange his priorities. So he suppresses an urge to pay Alex another visit in her lab (that girl is just too easy!) because, for now, there is other work to be done. Not that he can't use sex as a goad, but no -- he looks down at his small and shrivelled tackle, whose wretched state confirms to him that the problems he is now facing are as arse-clenchingly pressing as he'd told the policewomen.

Yes, he thinks he's put on a good front with the police, turning his Aggrieved-Suspect Act all the way up to eleven, perhaps enough to throw them off. Inspector Sheepshit might be shrewd, but he thinks she's on to a loser, for two reasons.

One, because—from what he's heard—the inquest will probably say that Bland died of natural causes, and that will be that. In the clear. Free. And La Dipshit certainly didn't seem quite so on-the-ball (on *his* balls, anyway) as she'd been last time.

And, two: the fact that the problems he'd told them about were largely true, which only made his performance all the more convincing: the Institute really was on its last legs, and his job was to find a new home for it all.

Well, not entirely, perfectly, squeaky-clean, honest-to-God true.

Morrison turns off the jets, towels down, splashes on a liberal measure of cologne and selects a new shirt, tie and suit from the closet. He'll get the housekeeper to take the rest to the dry-cleaners later. But on top of that he finds a crisp, pressed lab coat. One with the MagusPharm logo embossed on the top pocket.

The MagusPharm people, he consoles himself, really don't give a shit about the whole collection remaining together. All they want are results, especially from carnostomids. And if, after that, the collection falls into the sea, so much the better—nobody else will be able to get in on the act. If Alex, true to the talent in her which he's recognized and on which his reputation at MagusPharm increasingly depends, can isolate active compounds from carnostomids and find ways to recreate them synthetically, MagusPharm's investment will have paid off. Especially if they are anything like TubeWave. Oh yes, Big bucks. Big time.

Big time. If there is time at all. Which is why he now thinks he's been caught between the proverbial rock and hard place. Alex, he now knows, is undercapitalized, and he won't be able to screw results out of her as quickly as MagusPharm would have liked, or as their remaining time at the Institute will allow—no matter how talented she is. He's thought about and around this problem many, many times, but can only ever reach one conclusion.

Sure, he could outsource some of the work—but to whom? And when? Finding more people of Alex's calibre takes time, which he doesn't have.

Yes, and he could move Alex to another lab, better equipped, somewhere else - but not with the carnostomid collections, and not without enormous security risks, especially if she'd be working in a University lab where secrecy is less important than in the commercial sphere.

Of course, he could pack her off to one of MagusPharm's own facilities, in Basel, Seattle or Shanghai, visiting her now and then for a luxury weekend fuckfest at MagusPharm's expense ... but seriously, the logistics don't bear thinking about, and the Trustees would never release the material she needs if they thought it was going to be exploited commercially.

So, Alex is better off here, well away from prying eyes and any sticky fingers but his own, and where she and Morrison can continue squirreling out the secrets of the sea from under the Trustee's pig-like noses.

Now then, if that's the case, he could always bus more staff in here to help Alex—but this would be hard to do without arousing suspicion. And even if he could find anyone suitable in a hurry, where would they go? There is room for two more in Alex's lab, and Bland's lab is obviously free, but he doesn't want to move too fast without arousing suspicions, especially while the Trustees have the nod on all appointments, even if they are on someone else's money. And the Trustees, he's learned, have two speeds—dead slow, and stop. Except that they have three, for if they smell anything they think is fishy they go into full reverse. Even if—*especially* if, it seems—the Institute they govern is quite literally on the brink of collapse.

All other options exhausted, Morrison always comes to the same conclusion. If you want a job done, you have to do it yourself. Only this time, he swears, he won't get caught. He steps into the closet, parts the massed ranks of Armani, gently lifts aside a curtain at the back, and steps into another world.

When he first found it, he swore that there really was a God.

Not long after he had first joined the Institute and was exploring the Director's secret closet, he was trying to find a jacket or tie or something, tripped, and fell very hard against the closet's back wall. But rather than bouncing off hard stone, his shoulder made a large crater in what was not, as expected, masonry, but a thin screed of wooden laths and horsehair plaster. When he'd recovered from the shock it didn't take him long to make a hole in the back of the closet big enough to walk through without too much trouble. No need to call that berk Honeypott—an evening's work with a torch and a few simple tools was sufficient.

He remembered that night as if he were Howard Carter and this was the Valley of the Kings. The hole he'd made gave on to a sheet or hanging of some kind, ancient and heavy with dust. Pushing himself through what must been a slit deliberately scored in the heavy material, he found himself in a corridor, utterly dark, but dry, with no hint of the sweetness that betokens damp and decay. Turning the torch back on the tapestry between whose leaves he'd emerged, he saw a depiction of a frenzied bacchanale, with—well, not something you'd want to show school parties. Turning again, he almost collided with a vast mass of blackness. Stepping back, alarmed, he realized he'd almost collided with some massive stuffed, furry … thing. Kind of like a bear. Except bears don't have hands like that. And beyond the bear, there was a door. Ajar, hanging amid what looked like a shallow sea of dust.

He walks through that corridor now, conscious of an unmeasured height teetering into darkness, a galleried landing halfway up on the right hand side, hemmed in with dark, uneven bookcases. This thought is, for the moment, fleeting, for it is the door at the end that welcomes him now. The door into his very own chamber of secrets.

When he had first found it, his first thought was that it was a medieval torture chamber. Or maybe an abattoir. Dimly lit from two grimy skylights far above, the room was dominated by two monumental wooden benches, punctuated with various metal and leather stanchions or fastenings. The wood was pitted and made darker by swathes of some ancient stain. This same stain marked the filthy flags on the floor. Dark wood cabinets were arranged around the walls, filled with ancient glassware—all broken—and all kinds of iron and brass instruments whose purposes he could not fathom. There were, however, several large buckets full of knives, probes, pokers, forceps and other tools, all of which were stuck together, and to the bases of their containers, by some unnameable, blackish mass. At one end there was what looked like a forge, with a hearth, anvil, and enough chains for a Gothic sadomasochism convention.

It took a few secret visits for him to work out that this laboratory — if that's what it was — must have been Sir Frideric's private den. So private, that he — or someone coming after — had blocked it off. Morrison was sure that nobody had broken into it for more than a hundred and fifty years. When Bland had had his closet fitted, the workmen had obviously not bumped into the thin false wall that divided the old store from the corridor with the black beast and the tapestry. Its very presence went unmarked, undetected.

Until now.

It took just one phone call to MagusPharm to set the ball rolling. No strangers to setting up laboratories in odd places with the utmost discretion, the company had transformed the old room into a compact laboratory in which Morrison could shadow Alex's work, but fast-tracking it into more immediately fruitful directions. He was worried that Alex was becoming waylaid by the joys of zoology, mesmerized by the diversity of it all — when what he and MagusPharm needed was results that could be turned into drugs, as quickly as possible, without worrying too much about their precise zoological provenance.

Not too many weeks before Bland's death, he was beginning to get somewhere. His first, rough extracts from carnostomids, filtered from a jar from the *Spaniel* Expedition he'd lifted from the spirit store, appeared to exert strange effects on human tissue. Squirt some on a smear of blood and the erythrocytes shrivelled as you watched. Or, at least, it worked with his own blood cells, which was all he could get. He found the same things with squamous epithelium (cheek swab, again his own) and semen (ditto: Bland's porn collection did have some use, after all.)

But when he did the same thing with Alex's cells, something very strange happened. Or, rather, didn't happen. Morrison didn't like to recall too vividly how he'd obtained such a sample without Alex's consent — that was the sort of thing that had pitched him into the shit before — but the results were clear. Carnostomid extract nixed his cells, but not Alex's. Purified extracts did the same thing, only more so. A purer carnostomid extract made Alex's cells positively glow, while reducing his to membranous rags. The effect of carnostomids on unprotected human cells wouldn't be hard to imagine — provided they were male. Provided, of course, you could generalize from a sample of two, divided into two groups of one each. Phooey.

But that's as far as he'd been able to get. When Bland died, Morrison's first worry was that through some unforeseen contamination he'd upped his male sample to two, and had confirmed his hypothesis, all at once. When Sheepshit had shown him the body, just one sight of Bland's eyes, his skin, had provided all the backup he'd needed. Bland had died from natural causes, all right—he'd been infected with carnostomids. Morrison was sure of it.

The gut-churning worry was that, somehow—he had no idea how—he, Morrison, might have been the unwitting agent. He kept telling himself how nobody at the Institute knew of this lab, and how he hardly ever saw Bland. But Bland could hardly resist keeping his hands off Alex—could Morrison have transmitted the carnostomids to Bland through her? And how long did it take for carnostomids to kill a whole person? Could he have infected Bland on the night they'd had that argument, hours -- minutes -- before his death? Surely not: although Morrison had rushed out of the lab so he could meet Bland in his office, Morrison was as scrupulous about lab hygiene as anyone. More so, in fact. And he and Bland hadn't touched, hadn't even shaken hands—

Only now does Morrison think back on something that Bland had said in that final showdown. "Morrison, I know what you're up to," he'd said. And Morrison thought he'd been talking about Alex. Truth dawns, with a sickening, blinding light.

5: The Dead Below

Fitch has heard all sorts of gruesome stories about the Old Graveyard at Deringland. She'd always thought they were just silly tales the boys at school (boys such as Bob Honeypott) had used to scare the girls (and themselves), but reading up on local history — as she has done, to get some perspective on the Bland case — she realizes that they might contain some measure of truth.

The Old Graveyard (she'd read) was situated on the cliffs behind the Church, and had been the town's burying ground since time immemorial. Remorseless coastal erosion had rotted the cliffs for decades, depositing the occasional grisly morsel in the rock pools beneath. The final knell was struck during a gale in March, 1845, when an entire chunk of cliff collapsed, obliterating the graveyard right up to the lych-gate and raining corpses on to the beach.

It's certainly true (she had been amazed to find, and making a note to keep this particular cutting away from Eric and Bryony, though Dean lapped it up with relish) that human remains are occasionally washed up on the East Beach, even today. ("Cool!" Dean had said, taking the library-loan photocopy to his room). Such remains are usually so worn and weathered that they cannot usually be recognized as such (thank goodness!) but sometimes there are perfect teeth in crumbled, barnacle-crusted jaws, and even skulls, crabs living in their eye-sockets (Dean read this part aloud to Bryony, who'd only said "yuck!" and wrinkled her nose.)

Only last year, apparently, a small child had emerged from the summer surf, triumphant, with a bucket of shrimp in one hand and most of a human leg in the other. This had been written up in the *Mercury* at the time, but Fitch had missed it — perhaps because the editor had buried the story on page 26, between adverts for the Koh-I-

Noor Tandoori (Fully Licensed) on one side and the Restful Paws Luxury Cat Hotel (Ditto) on the other.

In the 1880s -- many years after the Old Graveyard had slumped into the sea and into local fancy -- the town elders, all of whom had had railway shares and were thus keen to attract tourism, had decided to build the pier, more or less on the same spot. There had always been a wonder—a question mark, you might say—about the outbreak of a still-unidentified disease among the workmen building the pier. Some authorities suggested that it had been cholera; others, anthrax; but nobody had been able to find out with sufficient certainty to satisfy all.

And then, of course, there'd always been the stories about the Gaiety Theater at the end of the pier being haunted, but then she'd always thought that the Theater had used this as a gimmick: nobody would ever really believe that stuff, would they? Fitch now remembers being told such nonsense by Bob Honeypott, which itself tarnished any truth these myths might have contained. She recalls vividly when Bob had told her: she'd been fifteen or sixteen, and he'd been trying to feel her up behind the science block, when Jason had come round the corner on his bike. She saw only a knight on a white charger, and then, well... Bob never groped her again, so she'd heard no more about skulls and stuff.

But now, to her horror and fascination, she discovers that Bob really had known a thing or two, and perhaps more than that, for there was the fact (fact!) that the very last person to have been buried in the Old Graveyard before it fell had been none other than Sir Frideric Lowdley-Purslane: syphilitic, half-mad but by then definitely dead, interred the very day before the storm. His body had been carried away before ... before, well, it had been decently rotted, and was never seen again. And she's doubly amazed (given the things that Bob had tried to scare her with) that she'd never heard the local lore that the burial of Sir Frideric had somehow triggered the storm, as a way of cleansing Deringland of some pernicious evil.

After the catastrophe the town elders and the diocesan authorities had had to find a new burial ground. They chose a field on the bald north slope of Federal Hill, just south of the town, a cautious mile from the encroaching sea. She's standing in the New Graveyard, now—of course!—next to Sheepwool, and scientists from the Institute, and scattered oddments of friends and relations, and they're all buttoned up against the cold wind, like the huddle of penguins she remembers seeing in one of the documentaries Jason and the kids like to watch on the Discovery Channel. The view's fantastic, but the continuo of wind has shorn the half-hearted shelter belt of pines and yews into contorted, demoniac shapes. Even on relatively calm days, like today, a wind whips and veers round the stones, blowing scraps of paper and old crisp packets to decorate the drifts of leaves, leftovers from last autumn, lying in sodden heaps against the walls of the brick-and-flint chapel of rest -- itself long abandoned, stained glass broken, windows boarded up against night intruders, the boarding itself peeling and flaked.

The coffin bearing the last remains of Dr Evanston Bland is lowered gently into the earth. Fitch, however, pays this event relatively little attention, being more concerned with her own internal equilibrium, jarred—as it has been—by the sudden shock of being forced to see familiar things in unfamiliar ways. When you've lived all your life in one place, as she has, you tend to take it for granted, to think well of it—to take pride in it. That other people might think of your home town as something out of one of Jason's Stephen King novels simply does not occur to you. But then, she reflects, pulling the lapels of her coat up to shield her reddening cheeks from the biting cold, if you're born and raised in a place, you just don't see things in the same way that a stranger might.

A stranger like Sheepwool.

Until they'd sat together in the nave of the Church, she had not quite grasped the sundering chasms that separate their lives, their experiences. Fitch had always seen the Church in a rosy light, full of happy memories of childhood carol concerts and, most of all, her own wedding day. Now, all of a sudden, she looks at the Church through Sheepwool's eyes—it is dim, cavernous, threatening, and much too large for the town it serves. The funeral service has attracted perhaps thirty congregants, but the totality is swallowed by this immensity of space, as if the Church can accommodate a very much larger number than this and still feel empty. Funny—she thought her wedding had been full, and cosy.

The warm bodies, each now occupying a small island of humanity in the long and pitiless pews, and each giving off its own misty exhalation into the frigid gloom, is not a person overlain with an album of memories, cross-referenced with those elicited by most of the other people present, but a bare cipher, constrained and individual, a well of unanswered questions, of possibilities. For example, she herself had not met Boynton and Johansson until recently. Looking at them now, in the Church, she'd think they were an old married couple, heads canted together in whispered conspiracy that pays no polite regard to the address of the minister, nor to Morrison's eulogy of hastily arranged blank platitudes from the pulpit. And who knows — perhaps they are? Married, that is? Even though she's a policewoman and has greater licence to inquire into the details of peoples' lives than most, she is unceasingly amazed by the fact that one simply never knows what goes on behind closed doors.

And there's Janice Squearn who, sharply relieved of the burden of warm association, looks shrunken and, quite plainly, very ill, for all that her eyes spark with marble-hard defiance. She sits next to the silent, long-skirted housekeeper who'd admitted she and Sheepwool to the LPI on their first visit (Fitch realizes with a shock that the housekeeper had never been questioned — even her name was a blank). Next to them in his own pool of loneliness is Garrison Williams, his solitary state piqued, she now thinks, by the frequency with which he steals glances at Alex Beach, who is in the front row, but nowhere near Morrison. Neither Beach nor Morrison (when he is seated) look anywhere but straight ahead, each in a private steeple of their own thoughts. Morrison, she thinks, just looks bored — Beach's face is unreadable. Or so she assumes: from this angle Fitch can mostly see just the back of her head.

And there's Bob Honeypott and his formidable Ma. And other people from the town she recognizes, and several she doesn't. There's a woman, tall and heavily built — rather mannish, she thinks — sitting near the back. Fitch suspects that this woman has tried to slip in unnoticed, but if so, the effort was futile. There is something about this person that sparks off hard jags of insecurity, uncertainty, even fear. Fitch notices that this woman has not made the journey to the graveyard itself, but left the Church just before the end of the service, in a state of some distress — red-eyed and brimming. In her haste she'd almost tripped over Fitch's bag (left carelessly in the aisle — one of her bad habits, as Jason likes to remind her) and a few quiet words of mutual apology had been exchanged. Fitch wonders who she could have been.

Such thoughts were summarily ejected following the arrival, almost at the end of the service, of Jim Levy, who'd perched, out of breath, on the end of the pew next to Sheepwool. Fitch had given them both a lift up to the graveyard. Sheepwool had ridden in the front, Levy in the back, leaning forward to talk to both of them through the gap between the front seats. Levy had told them the news that very little of Bland's body actually made it to the coffin. None at all, actually—Bland's remains had finally (finally!) been considered a health risk and had been incinerated. No, the family hadn't been told—it was something of a state secret—and he'd be obliged were Sheepwool and Fitch to keep it to themselves, too. Fitch says nothing but fixes her eyes on the winding road out of town. Inside, though, she's appalled. She's heard those stories about hospitals making free with the bodies of dead patients without consent, and hates to be a part of such a conspiracy. She cannot see Sheepwool's expression, but senses that she, too, is less than pleased. Levy must have responded to this body language, for his spoken response is almost apologetic.

"I know, I know," he says. "It's dreadful. But the Higher Authorities—no names, no pack-drill -- ruled that even in a case of death by natural causes, which this is—no doubt about it—some precautions should be taken. In this case, anyway, when no-one has any idea what these natural causes might have been."

"But why not simply advise the family to cremate the body, based on the autopsy findings?" asks Sheepwool.

"For one thing, Bland's will specified burial. But it's as we discussed earlier." says Levy. Fitch thinks his answer is a little waspish. "This is an isolated case. We have no idea if what killed Bland is an infectious disease, but inasmuch as we can extrapolate from a sample of one, it doesn't look like it. And the last thing the Higher Authorities want to do is spark off some panic when it's not warranted. And I agree with them—on that, at least. So all we can do is watch and wait, and hope that this really is what it looks like—a one-off."

"Watch and wait," says Sheepwool, but this time Fitch is convinced that her superior is talking only to herself.

Then it hits her: that woman who'd left the Church. It was something she'd said. An excuse, about having to make an urgent phone call. A phone call. A call made, by an anxious, unknown woman. Thoughts writhe inside her head with the rapid-fire urgency of live snakes on a griddle. This was the woman who'd phoned in with the tip-off that ruptured Morrison's alibi. This was Heather Franks.

"There's something I think you should read," he says. She looks at him then, enormous eyes glistening in the jagged shadows, as if pulled from a dark dream into happier but still uncertain wakefulness.

Garry Williams has, at last, got Alex Beach on her own. And here they are, together, in the secluded carrel at the Dazed Haddock where he'd tried and failed to grandstand before those two policewomen. He'd suggested a drink after the funeral — anything but having to attend the small family gathering at Bland's bungalow — and Alex had readily agreed. Her smile of assent had wrung his heart out like an old rag. He is convinced that he's never seen anyone or anything more beautiful. It's the fact of her distraction, her evident preoccupation with things seemingly beyond his powers to apprehend, that he finds so alluring. Had she simply shed all these things and paid full attention to him — well, it would be sexy, but not quite so achingly lovely. For he knows that Alex can never be his, and never should be. Therefore, he reasons, what grabs him cannot be the thrill of the chase, because that implies that the hunt might yet be won: but some older, more courtly instinct, that she is actually, as well as theoretically, beyond his reach, and he is her champion. That here is a young girl surrounded by encroaching horror, hurtling headlong (had she known it) into doom, a girl whom such things should never have the chance to sully, and he has the means to protect her. Because he, perhaps better than anyone at the Institute, knows the danger she is in. Well, almost anyone.

And that's exactly the problem.

"Mmm?" She turns, as if half in sleep. Her lips part slightly. He is aware of the pale freckles on her white cheekbones, the way the flesh of her lips lazily unzips as she parts them, her white teeth beneath. His tight-sprung heart winds up another notch.

"Yeah. Did you read Houghton? *The Voyage of the Spaniel*?"

"Banneman Houghton? No. At least, not yet. I've had a request to borrow it from the Institute Library but their copy always seems to be out. It's hard to get otherwise — and as I assumed it's just background, and I've got other things to read in the meantime…"

"I've a copy of my own, if you want." He'd wanted to add 'upstairs, here, at my room above the pub, come and look at it', but caught himself in time—it would sound far too much the cheesy pickup line. As it is, the line is left hanging in space. But just before Alex can retreat, once again, behind those immensely filmic fish-blue and silver-gray eyes, Garry catches her on the hooks of his words. He hears himself say them and hopes they don't sound too desperate. At the same time, he does not want to give too much away. For her sake, as well as his.

"Knowledge is power, Alex. Right now, you need both."

"I...? Why...?"

"You know—sure you do -- that all those things you're looking at—those carnostomids—all come from the *Spaniel* Expedition? Well, it sure was an interesting expedition. Just thought you should get into it, that's all. Give you some idea of the ... uh ... whys and where-fores." He is conscious of sounding enigmatic. He doesn't want to tease. It could be an ingrained academic habit of coaxing students to find things out for themselves, rather than dishing it all up on a plate, and where would be the fun in that? But it's clear that Alex's mind is too often far from the matter in hand, and that she'll need a little push. Otherwise she'll just be led, unseeing, uncomprehending, to the slaughter. And he's also conscious of not spilling any beans, or even of not wanting to be even seen to be thinking of doing so.

He knows who has *The Voyage of the Spaniel* out on permanent loan. Oh, yes. He is sure it's the same person who, he suspects, is—somehow, God only knows how—stealing a march on Alex's work. And if his hunches are right (and Garry Williams didn't get to his near-Nobelian eminence without trusting his hunches), it's the same person whose disciplinary proceedings he'd once reviewed under the strictest terms of anonymity. Proceedings that enumerated in neces-sarily guarded language (the circumlocution making the facts all the more chilling) the trail of lost or missing regulatory instruments which, when reconstructed and followed, had exposed this person as one of the surprisingly few scientists who abuse the trust without which the scientific enterprise cannot function.

It had started as a case of data massage. Something which most scientists, if they are honest, find themselves doing (albeit almost un-consciously) if their concentration strays for just a moment. But things had evolved, exposing further and deeper and more hideous strata of infraction. Shadowy funding from bodies fronting for other bodies, still unidentified; unauthorized experiments, after hours. On humans. Without consent: unsurprisingly, given the results.

Death.

And things much worse than death. Some of those pictures — those events he's seen, first-hand -- still haunt the marches of Garrison Williams' soul.

Somehow — God only knows how — the person had managed to bargain his way out of legal action. Perhaps because he was a relatively small fish in a larger pond, and had fingered others yet more shadowy and powerful. But nobody would — should - ever let this person near a laboratory bench again. He'd left science, gone into marketing, and then management. But lab work can be addictive. He knows that for himself, all too well. And he thinks that Marion Morrison has found a new fix. If so, Alex is in terrible, terrible danger.

But how can he tell her? Even were he not to break confidences and a variety of more specific injunctions framed in brutal legalese, she would hardly fall for a direct approach, given that she and Morrison are an item, or seem to be, and that his attentions towards her might so easily be … misconstrued. All Williams can do is keep watch, and drop the most tangential of hints. He only wishes he hadn't fallen for her so badly himself. After three wives (two divorced and, with Bev, one death) he really should learn not to be such a walking heart. Love, he's found to his immense cost, only makes things more complicated.

Related concerns are, perhaps, in the mind of Detective Inspector Sheepwool when Methwold calls by her office in the late afternoon of the day following the funeral. A day of closure, he hopes — for the reports he's been hearing from Levy (oh, that man should see a barber: and clean his teeth) have disturbed him; raised old ghosts he'd hope he'd never have to confront again. Only just now he's caught himself looking at that silver-framed picture of Allie, and suddenly realizes that he's been doing that a lot lately.

Giving up the fight, he decides to leave for the day, coat over his arm, and heads for the forecourt. An early night would do him good, anyway. Just him, a quiet meal, listening to the big-band jazz programme on Radio Norfolk. Ah! Allie used to love that programme.

Before … well, before.

Before shutting his office door he looks outside and notices that a wintry rain has started to fall and he wonders if Sheepwool should like a lift home (he knows Fitch usually does this, but she'd had to rush off and immerse herself in domesticity). Methwold been amazed at Sheepwool's persistence, actually: walking to work, the ferocity of the weather a more than adequate trade-off against the shortness of the distance travelled. He lives in North Canterton, a few miles west along the coast, so driving really is his only option (unless he fancies waiting hours for the reliable yet highly infrequent Coast Ranger bus service).

He knocks on her door and enters, and it's as if he's strayed into a tableau. Fitch has gone, of course, taking her animated clucking with her (sharing an office with Elaine must be like living in a chicken coop, he thinks to himself, not without affection). Sheepwool is there, though, shoes off, stockinged feet on long legs crossed, taut, atop the desk. She is sitting back in her reclining chair, face turned from him, looking out of the window as if hypnotized by the renewed rain: he can see, in the window, the reflection of her round, blue eyes, like twin planets, unblinking. Her left hand is on the arm of the chair; her right, nearest him, has fallen over the side, grasping steel-framed spectacles by her fingertips only. The slight downward motion of the spectacles is the only movement in the room and, with the practiced grace of a weekend crown-bowls player, Methwold stoops downwards in a smooth arc and retrieves them, just as Sheepwool's grip fails.

She starts, turns, sees him, and — afraid of falling — grips his hand. Her hand is warm within his, but firm, dry, authoritative: he does not let go so long as she needs his hand to right herself, to wake from her reverie. Then suddenly, and as primly as she'd just come in for her first interview, she pulls her legs off the desk, straightens up, smooths down her blouse and jacket, and starts flustering apologies.

"Never mind that, Sheepwool."

"Sir?"

"You were miles away! Just wondered if you'd like a lift home, that's all."

"Sir, if it's no trouble…" He thinks that the little-girl-lost act, so vulnerable, might appeal to some. But it occurs to him that it doesn't suit her hard-edged frame, optimized more for the rigors of decision. Sheepwool wants to see closure, too.

"None at all. I'm going that way anyway. Drop you off outside your door."

As he drives, he can see Sheepwool in the corner of his eye and (to his relief) she has regained composure. His instincts are proven right when she says, without prompting:

"Morrison. There's something about Morrison. Her, and Alex Beach."

"It's closed, Sheepwool, *closed*. You know that. *I* know that. But yes, I think you're right. He's up to something. But Dr Beach is a grown-up. She can look after herself. And you know as well as I do that there are always loose ends."

Loose ends.

"Yes, Sir. I know." The rueful sigh, as of a foxhound denied the chase.

A silence. But in this silence Methwold is absolutely sure that they both share the same unspoken conviction. That there is something in the air, a heavy, congealed essence, that speaks to both these experienced police officers of careering, unstoppable fate. In this certainty he is gripped by the terror of one used to exerting control, who feels that something just at the edge of vision is slipping away from his sweated grasp, and he can do nothing about it.

Nothing!

He knows that Sheepwool feels precisely the same terror. He can feel it. Methwold says nothing of this, partly through the simple economy of not repeating something they both know very well, but also for fear of saying too much, revealing things still too raw and private. Of those last weeks and months after Allie said that she was pregnant—and at her age!—and very quickly spiralled into a mental state he'd describe only as mad, until he'd had to restrain her from rushing out towards the sea. But finally, in all conscience, he could no longer, and she had gone. Tousled early morning bedclothes; a mug of tea, half-drunk; not even a note. In truth, the Allie he'd loved had vanished with the arrival of that thin blue line.

Still, even now, washing up and listening to the radio, he looks out towards those cliffs.

6: The Voyage of the Spaniel

'After the expedition had passed the latitude of the Chiloes, during which time some extensive and profitable trawls of deep-sea sediments were essayed and many interesting specimens of fauna catalogued and bottled,' Alex reads:

> several members of the crew fell to a sudden, severe and indeed fatal illness such that by the time the *Spaniel* had reached the latitude of Valparaiso, the Captain was obliged to seek harbour for the purposes of rest and recuperation and — perforce — recruitment. The first case was American Gothic Midshipman Lawrence, who had been my most recent assistant. He performed his duties without demur but was on a sudden seized with a violent agitation and collapsed in a dead faint, not to be revived. Anyone else who fell to this fever also died, such that the crew came almost to the edge of mutiny.

Alex shifts around in bed. The sheet has become tangled, thrown into tight coils and ripped from the bed through her constant febrile movement and increasingly futile attempts to achieve rest and comfort against its hot and gritty surface. Her pillow, now rank with sweat, is knotted and lumpy.

She feels terrible.

Nights are haunted by rain-spattered dreams; the days, drear and wan, her tiny, dirty room littered with crumpled tissues, books, notes, scattered clothes, remains of meals half-eaten, coffee cups; hating herself for not even trying to tidy it up, but utterly spent of any energy except that required to fuel a generalised, low-level self-loathing. She cannot remember how long she's been like this. Any tiny movement she makes seems to demand the accumulated energy of centuries.

Some of the men, being very superstitious and hardly Christian, bayed for a scapegoat, a sacrifice. Look at your baby, Alex! When a mulatto called Hawkins was suspected of witchcraft and put overboard, the Captain felt constrained to have several men flogged. Well done! Well done! It's a... It's a .... Morrison, he's dead. But the causes of this sudden ailment were never found. After departure from Valparaiso with new rations and crew, cases ceased, and the ship and its company went forth in a fresh wind full of new resolve: but far from easing men's minds, this new hope caused not a few to whisper that the despatch of the unfortunate Mr Hawkins had been justified. It's all your fault, Alex!

She is desperate to lie down flat and forget herself in cool sleep, but whenever she tries, viscid mucus snarls into her sinuses and her head throbs. And so she sits up, and sits up, and sits up again, still desperate for sleep. The turbid sweat springs into her armpits and runs slick down between her breasts and over her abdomen and between her legs; down the channel of her spine, pooling beneath her upper thighs so she feels she's floating in a fetid pool of her own effluvia. By keeping her ringing head as still as possible she tries as well as she might to follow the lines of tiny (very, tiny; very, very tiny) print in Garry's copy of *The Voyage of the Spaniel* (subtitled *A Philosophical Memoir of a Voyage of Discovery to the Americas and the South Seas with Remarks on Topography, Natural History, Navigation &c.*, by Banneman Houghton, F.R.S., published John Murray & Co., first and only edition 1837, this copy octavo, slight wear on boards, inscribed 'To Mr Chas. Darwin' on flyleaf) as the words writhe across the fragile, brown-spotted pages, sometimes so close she can see every pore in the paper, sometimes so distant she thinks she is reading them through air of unnatural clarity across a vast plain—but finding in them no more meaning than were they ancient runes.

After a brief call at American Gothic, the Captain set a course westward, across the Pacific. This gave me the opportunity to roll it out, run it up the flagpole, set new targets, resolved to order some of the Chiloes specimens and attempt some preliminary notes.

Alex has no idea where she might have got this hideous infection.

It is like the flu—except that she cannot recall having been breathed on by anyone with a cough, or who later went on to develop one, and she hasn't been beyond the Institute's gates for a fortnight—not since—well, not since Bland's funeral. Perhaps it's this place: something in the rank, unmoving air, full of silent, invisible spores; the blank glass eyes that seem to stare from behind dusty panes wherever you look; eyes that follow you round the room, cursing as you pass; or, worse, preserving in a silent smugness a knowledge of your own fate with which everyone seems to be familiar except she, herself.

She slides; the lines of the book cant upwards and out of reach. The Spaniel swishes and washes in the cold Chiloe currents as Banneman Houghton, F. R. S., plunges both hands into an oak barrel whose contents she can't quite see, and pulls them back as bones bleached bare. Alex sinks, and slides; and sinks; and as she does so the sun comes up, and ascends into the vault, and falls as a drop of deep red ink into the blind fog; and the moon rises and careens across the sky pursued by mildewed clouds, and the sun once more rises and falls, pursued again by the moon.

At the third dawn (or it might be the fifth, or the ninth, or—who knows?) Alex wakes—but refreshed, renewed, like a phoenix reborn, as if her past is a memory of something she cannot quite grasp. Her head feels that peculiar lightness conferred by an absence of pain; her body is smoothly and uniformly calm, passive, receptive, but encased within a seamless shell of encrusted sweat. She is unbelievably hungry. She looks around the room. It is filthy. But it will have to wait.

Later, her room once more as tidy as it'll ever be, she takes *The Voyage of the Spaniel* down to the common room. It is night, and the great cold space is deserted. She stretches herself on a worn chesterfield, its button-pocked back a foxhole against the constant draught from the tall windows; she looks up at the damp-streaked cornicing and the eggshell cracks as they trace their way across the ceiling far above. Chandeliers, glass corroded as if with some mineral smallpox, hang down on immense chains, and, as she looks up, she has that curious sense of inversion, as if she were floating at the sea's surface, looking downwards to the shadowed sea floor, forests of kelp straining up to meet her. As she floats, she thinks of what she's read, piecing the feverish fragments together of the many deaths that befell the crew of HMS *Spaniel* as they rode the Antarctic swell up the west coast of South America. They had just trawled something from the depths—specimens whose identities were not clear. Or, not so far, at any rate—Alex hasn't read the extensive appendices of the book that catalogue the findings made at each stage of the voyage.

What strikes her about all the deaths described is their suddenness. That, the abrupt outpouring of blood from the eyes and mouth, and a description which Alex cannot shake free from her mind, of the victims

> ...being possessed of a round-eyed blood-circled stare, were their last thoughts on this world either of some great revelation, or of a witness to horrors too great for any one human mind to encompass, and, in so trying, expiring.

Later still, the wind blasting against the thin panes of the common-room windows, she admonishes herself for not realizing precisely why this description seems so real, so vivid. It is because she has seen it herself, that look of dawning horror on the face of a corpse, that only *in articulo mortis* can the truth of our pasteboard lives be laid bare. When there is no going back. Bland had looked like that. His face. When she had found him.

The sediment at the base of her mind stirs with vermiform thoughts, sparked into as yet sluggish life. The deaths aboard the *Spaniel* seemed so much like Bland's death. But she'd never seen a dead body before .... before ... well, how's she to know that all dead bodies don't look like that? Maybe that's why people close the eyes of corpses. Put coins on them. So the eyes don't spring open into that unnerving, thousand-yard stare. But here, in the night, in the gloomy penumbrae of the chandeliers, she feels quite strongly that she is just casting around for excuses—and that there really are genuine factors in common between Bland's death and the ones reported aboard the *Spaniel*.

Two things. Two reasons, chasing round her brain like dogs chasing each other's tails.

The first is that Garry has been so insistent in pressing this book on her. And why is that? To make her realize the second thing, that the Institute where they both work is where all the *Spaniel*'s collections are housed. The unspoken subtext is that we are the same as Houghton's crew, exposed to the same risks.

All the same, she thinks, if Bland had suffered the same complaint as the *Spaniel*'s crewmen, why had his death occurred just now? The *Spaniel* collection has been here for a century and a half — and she has no knowledge of any greater frequency of death here at the Institute than that observed in the population generally. But this complacent musing is immediately overwhelmed by a surge of doubt: she has no information that might bear on this fact. None whatsoever. And discovering it might be extremely difficult — the population of the LPI is largely transient, its constituent, coffeespoonerish lives allotted in the neatly parcelled parsimony of research visits and grant applications. Pinning the deaths of former LPI staff and visitors onto a sojourn at the Institute itself would probably be quite impossible.

She gathers these thoughts somewhat distractedly, a beachcomber raking stray weed with a branch of bone-white driftwood, reflecting that the impossibility of making any such connection probably explains why Garry is being so evasive about it. In some ways that's just like Garry. Despite the surf's-up posing he's a scientist through and through: he is fastidiously cautious about anything that really matters, about ascribing causes to effects.

Consider: whenever Garry has mentioned the *Spaniel*, it's been a far from casual affair. It's as if he's worked to choose his moment in otherwise routine exchanges, framing each word with uncharacteristic intensity, to be sure she wouldn't miss it. Garry has been trying to tell her something — trying so hard that the effort has been as painful as shouting at her from a great distance through a headwind. It's vital that she knows, that she understands — but for some reason he cannot simply come out with it.

Alex shakes her head, which on a sudden feels full of bees. She adjusts her position, propping herself up against the arm of the chesterfield, and decides that at times like this, one must try to put aside all speculation until more data are acquired. She flips forward a few hundred pages, to the Appendices.

It takes her a while to make any sense of these at all. They are printed in type hardly big enough to be readable without a hand lens, and that ornamented with numerous even smaller indices and superscripts. She wonders whether these spidery ornaments might not be further qualified with superscripts too small to see without her microscope. The cumulative effect of these crabbed tabulations is frustrating and eventually exasperating: the constant necessity to swish pages this way and that to trace an argument through a skein of notes and references.

She gives up.

This calls for desk work: she abandons the common-room, but leaves the chandeliers on in her retreat, illuminating the corridor beyond so she can begin the tortuous but now familiar ascent to her own quarters. And as she climbs, she thinks, so that by the time she arrives in her own room she has forgotten precisely how she came to be there. She settles a half-full kettle on the hob, scurries around for a match, lights it. The gas ring spurts into an orange simulacrum of eager life. This is comforting, as if she has managed at the end of a long day in the wilds to light, with a few sticks, a camp fire to stand as a private beacon against the elements beyond the black panes of the arched dormer window beyond.

Standing, hands in pockets, she reflects that the Appendices to *The Voyage of the Spaniel* (in a pool of light on a desk now partially cleared of detritus) are not meant to be read in the same way as the adventure story that comprises the first half of the book. No, the key is that they are more like lab notebooks, undigested, written not so much in transparent language designed to be read and understood by anyone—like a novel—but girt round with conventions peculiar to these notes only, unique symbols and meanings. It is as if each lab notebook records a new language in the process of formation, starting with the most primitive runic scratches and progressing by uneasy stages to that most refined nuance of passive voice and subjunctive mood suitable (with some small erosion of the facts allowed by the necessary loss in translation) for publication.

This should be no surprise, really, for if science records any kind of advance into realms previously obscure, the leading edge of that science, in its reptilian, fractal detail—that is, in terms of the figures and notes and signs in a lab notebook—will in its nature document that obscurity, and—if it is honest—find new ways to translate that obscurity into meaning that can be understood. But it is in the very nature of unknown things to stretch familiar concepts, and to demand new ones, new ways of thinking—and new symbols in which such concepts might be expressed succinctly.

Therefore it takes Alex, in her pool of light perched four stories above the sea, some little while to cross-reference the dates, designations of packages, sample numbers and so, on to discover that most of the specimens trawled from the deep sea immediately before the fatal outbreak on the *Spaniel* had been

> ...microscopical in nature (see barrels SCT.LXXIV-LXXXIX and vials and microscopical preparations derived therefrom (*ibid* and p479; table 102[a]); concentrated by sieving through a fine grade of Egyptian muslin; stained as described elsewhere[k] (see p505 and table 12c for general microscopical techniques). Many small vermiform creatures of previously unknown form unequally bifid or segmented the larger part consisting of a body or *sacculus* of simple undifferentiated cellular matter attached to a smaller and more dense particle of more intricate arrangement in which the presence of paired bowed that is *arcuate* arrangements of *denticles* is characteristic (see Plate XXXVIII[j-q]).

Alex rifles through the book for Plate XXXVIII, which she has not noticed before, buried as it is among a cramped tangle of engravings at the back of the book. The pages here are sometimes ragged at the edges and of uneven thickness, the stiffened paper of each engraving interleaved with a blank sheet that clings to its as if reluctant to allow it seen; so that it is hard to turn the pages, to open the book fully without risk of breaking the spine -- and so individual plates are easily missed on casual inspection. When she finds the plate she sits back in her seat as if slapped. Looking at her, straight out of the page, grinning with hideous knowingness, are the same carnostomids she's spent several weeks drawing.

The kettle whistles.

She has seen enough, and replaces the book in the plastic wrapper and buff envelope as Garry has instructed, switches off the reading lamp, and makes her tea. Carefully, slowly — so as not to re-awaken any lingering germs of contagion — she undresses and purses herself gently into bed. She is glad she'd finally found the energy to change the sheets, giving them to the sepulchrally silent Miss Honiton to wash (how strange — she had been her only visitor during her fever, and was a great solace, for all that she never once spoke.) Miss Honiton had brought new sheets, as starched and white as old linen napery, within which she now enfolds herself as tight as an oyster.

She closes her eyes, and carnostomids dance before her like fairy lights. Carnostomids, then, are the connection. Carnostomids killed all those sailors, that midshipman and all the rest. And carnostomids had killed Bland. Was that what Garry was trying to say? If so, why didn't he just say so, drop it into their daily conversation?

No, there was more to it than that. The only carnostomids she'd looked at were preserved, primped, mounted on slides in a way as contrived as any taxidermy specimen. Like Pickled Lily. And, like Pickled Lily in her tank, they were covered in glass cover-slips edged with thick layers of Canada balsam and gutta-percha. All the slides she'd seen had been pristine, uncracked. The sailors on the *Spaniel* must have drunk them raw and alive, in unfiltered water, perhaps if some of the filtered seawater had got into the drinking supply, or (now here's a thought!) if specimens preserved in rum were filched and refiltered for drinking.

Specimens preserved in rum. The spirit store. At the end of the laboratory corridor. Had Bland been siphoning off the spirits? Surely not—the very thought was ridiculous. Though, come to think of it, she'd heard something somewhere about that very thing, but couldn't place it. Her brows furrow: she rubs her closed eyes, and the carnostomids dance in phosphene specks before her, like carnival dragons. Oh yes, she remembers now—it was Mrs Squearn ('Just Call Me Janice') arguing with that creepy janitor, Bob, or whatever his name is. The one who seems to get on remarkably well with Garry (she suppresses an upwelling spike of—what's that? Jealousy?) The same Bob who only ever looks at her at chest height before shuffling off, leering like an old Carry-On movie. The thought of Bob sets her mind racing in an unexpected and unpleasant direction, rich with images of eroticism and fear, and rising up behind all of these, like a thunderhead behind a parade of dancing Bob-goblins, is the face of Morrison.

The blood in her face congeals with fright: her hands break out in pins and needles. She sits up with a start and clicks on her bedside light. The sheet falls away from her like a plasterwork mould. Look at your baby, Alex, look at it. She is a scientist, damn it (she hates it that she now has to continually remind herself of this, something she'd hitherto taken for granted). She must consider all the options. No matter how improbable. No matter how ... unwelcome. She must not flinch. And so, at last, cold with terror, she looks down at her baby. There in her lap, lying in a pool of stale seawater, is Pickled Lily, not frozen in time and space, but animated, thin arms clothed in sagging, white flesh clawing at her own arms, her shoulders; long finger-bones raking her neck; the thin face with sunken nose and bared teeth—

teeth gnashing up and down, up and down, like carnostomid teeth, searching blindly for something (the icy glass eyes, being sightless, are there simply for decoration). It is just for an instant, though, before the mermaid churning glutinously in her lap is washed out by a kind of monochrome static and is replaced, for an eternal quarter-second, by the head of Marion Morrison, jaws clamped on to her right nipple and sucking, sucking, sucking, but the head has been severed, and the more it sucks, the more blood spurts from the sectioned arteries in his neck, spattering her face and shoulders and the bedclothes and the room beyond. This vision, too, disappears, and she looks down at the amazing whiteness of the sheets in her lap untainted by any vision or contagion, and surveys her own off-white belly, her breasts, her arms, as carefully as any leper doing her daily round. Only her nipples betray her, rucked and rose-red. She looks down at them, lifting her breasts and examining them, as if they belonged to someone else.

Later still, and finding she cannot sleep, Alex rises and dresses. The first signs of dawn are revealed as a lighter blueness against the black, a dimness which nonetheless causes the awful fingers of fading disease to vanish like dew. Rationality rises with the sun. Alex is a scientist (oh yes she is!) and must consider all possibilities, no matter how odd they seem at first. That's it -- Garry is trying to tell her something about Morrison. About what he thinks he's doing. Trying to tell her in as devious a way as possible, to spare her feelings — which is sweet of him — and not look like he's coming on to her.

Which is sweet, too, kind of.

But there's a time and a place, and now it's she, Morrison and carnostomids, a kind of eternal triangle, twined in a way she cannot yet fathom. She picks a few memories from the past few weeks like a hen pecking choice grains from the threshing floor — of Morrison's increasingly insistent questions about her progress, but not — strangely - as if he were in some kind of a hurry, but simply — how had Garry put it? Ah yes, 'sizing her up'.

And that's just it. 'Sizing her up'. Like broodstock. She stands facing the dormer, looking over the brightening sea, and feels her eyes glaze with a film of moisture. 'Sizing her up' has been about right, she thinks, now biting her lip. How could she have been so blind as not to have noticed, when Garry so obviously has? It has been Garry's hunches, the instincts of a scientist of far greater wisdom than she, which, she knows, are far better judged than the results of her own experiments, her own controls. For only now with the shock of the dawn does she realize that each sign of progress on her part is marked by some sexual favor from Morrison in proportion to the perceived degree of advance. If 'favor' is indeed the right word, for Morrison's attentions are as brutally efficient as they are controlled, such that after each encounter she feels as spent, as used up, as – broken – as so much litter discarded at the roadside.

She remembers their first encounter, in Atlanta, when he'd had her up against the wall of the shower-cubicle in her hotel room, when despite his small stature he'd raised her off her feet with each thrust, but vanished as soon as he'd climaxed, leaving her hot and cold and dizzy and bruised on the cubicle floor nursing bloody bite marks in her shoulder.

Every encounter since – and that's the word, 'encounter', that she finds her mind using, with all the self-delusional euphemism of the possessed -- has been much the same, so that she is no longer able to distinguish one from another, even the different degrees of pain left by each kind of humiliation her mind minutely records and, dispassionately, details.

Except, perhaps, that time quite recently, when she'd told him of her discovery – now, it seems, only a re-discovery – of some new detail of the bow-like tooth rows of carnostomids. She'd rushed – rushed! – to his office to tell him, as eagerly as a child in search of praise. He'd smiled that big smile and said he had something to show her too, which was the now too-familiar cubicle behind his office, and before she could do anything else, he'd made her strip and kneel on the floor, gripping her hair, the back of her head, with his hands, with his teeth, and again, and again, and more … and … well, all she can now really recall was being left like a newborn calf on the floor in its own slick, marbled residue, and, when she'd recovered somewhat, aware of kneeling up in the blood and God knows what else and looking down at her own body, and feeling that she would not be able to stand the shame of it were anyone else to discover this mess and clean it up other than she herself, who was, after all, responsible; and most of all the humiliation she felt within herself that, despite the pain, despite everything, she enjoyed it.

The sun rises – were she able to lean over the chipped sink, the dripping tap, and lean to the right, she'd see it as an orange bubble cresting the flat horizon. And as it rises, she feels herself as a worm, turning, turning as yet slowly within the heavy oil of her self-loathing. She dares not now reveal to Morrison what she now knows from her fervid nocturnal investigations into the writing of the late Banneman Houghton, F. R. S. There is a reason she's been unable to get hold of the Institute's copy: Morrison is way ahead of her, it seems. As the first rays of the new rising sun hit her eyes, forcing her to step back into the shadows like the lowly invertebrate she feels she has become and surely deserves to be, she wonders whether Morrison has anything in particular to do with Bland's death, certainly caused by ingesting carnostomids. The scientist rising with the sun reminds her of the principle of parsimony, that you should only act on what reason tells you is the simplest course, and that course does not directly implicate Morrison.

No, with the knowledge she has now, it is more likely to implicate *her*. But what angers her, more than anything, is not that Morrison uses her so ill, physically — because she is convinced that this is entirely her own doing -- but that he has deceived her, as a scientist; failed to recognize her as a collegial participant in the whole carnostomid project. The worm inside her turns, and having turned, tells her that she must reclaim an intellectual stake of her own.

7: Saving The Mermaid

It was a warm night of summer when I chanced on Rebecca walking on the beach below the house. She was dressed all in deep purple as was her wont, as indeed was her habit to walk along the foreshore at evening, looking westwards towards the sunset.

Many times had she marvelled volubly in my presence at the reflection of the golden light on the rock pools, the effect the waning light had on enriching the blues of the wave, picking out the whiteness of the foam. On one occasion when I had caught up with her, I remarked that she had the instincts of an artist. After that she had for some reason spurned all my attempts at conversation, which puzzled me — such is usually read as a compliment.

On this occasion, however, I felt that nothing was to be lost by further hesitation. Giving chase, I wondered which of my many verbal darts I should first unloose, but she forestalled me. Turning, she looked at me with a most alarming hardness, hands clenched into two fists at her side. Then I felt like the poor Actaeon who had spied the Huntress, chiding myself — happily, before I voiced the remark — that Diana had at that point been unclothed, which had been the essence of the story, and unsuited quite to the present encounter.

"Do not talk to me of Art, Mr Willoughby," came her stern imprecation, loud against the water. I saw that she stood on the very edge of the surf, the hem of her gown soaked and taken up like weed by the waves' flowing margin.

"I shall not if that is your wish, Miss Lowdley-Purslane — but I should advise you to step out of the waves!"

At that she looked down, and far from an expression of concern, her face told of an emotion I shall not here try to describe, and she moved from out the waves with languid unconcern, to take my arm. "Walk with me?"

And so we walked towards the west. We talked not, but as we walked I was conscious of the grip of her arm on my left elbow (I had taken the seaward side), the rhythm of her breathing. She seemed preoccupied, as if not so much at a loss for something to say, but, in contrast, in possession of so many topics for discussion yet unequal to the task of choosing between any one and any other. All at once she stopped, drew apart and looked at me, her eyes like brilliants, causing me to flush from my neck to the roots of my hair.

"Rebecca …"

"Do you believe in mermaids, Mr Willoughby?" There were hot tears in her eyes, making them sparkle in the sunset.

"Do I … what?" I was now aware that had I not watched my temper with the greatest circumspection I might indeed suffer the fate of that unfortunate huntsman. For although I knew of the predilections of Rebecca's father, Sir Frideric, to favor the unusual, I was not entirely sure the degree to which his likes and dislikes were communicated to the rest of his family.

"You heard me, Mr Willoughby. Mermaids. For that, I believe, is what you and my father hold in highest regard as Art. Not the play of sunshine on water, Mr Willoughby, but the rough severance of natural life and its conjoining in … in …"

"Rebecca?" I held my hand out towards hers. She did not take it at once, but, after looking at it for a moment like it might have been some snake set to strike her, she placed her arm once again in mine and we continued our walk. I gave no explanation in answer to her outburst. She had known for years—must have known—that Sir Frideric was acclaimed as an artist of the flesh. But something had of late stirred her into some hitherto unbroached emotion. A few paces on, she sighed.

"I am sorry, Mr Willoughby—it's just … well, it is Mother. My father and I had thought that the sea air would revive her spirits, and so it did when we moved here. But lately, well, you have seen, surely."

I nodded. Lady Felicity had lately grown morose and silent, spending her days and increasingly her nights staring wordlessly at the waves from an upstairs window. But I did no more than nod, for, as I have noted, I was in possession of some of Sir Frideric's methods of working and procuring artistic materials, which I did not feel sure I could discuss with Rebecca. Though I fancied that Lady Felicity had divined what some of these methods might have been, which could account for her present state. Methods which had required, of late, many deliveries in the early hours of the morning, with coin given in exchange for silence.

And there were other things I felt I could hardly discuss with Rebecca with any propriety, such as the frequency of the screams of a woman in the fastnesses of night—screams which to my ears seemed too much like Rebecca herself, *in extremis*. The radiance of her eyes had within it a taint of madness, enough to confirm suspicions to which no one at the house had yet dared give voice.

Yes, these two things together gave me much pause before speaking. It was, I reasoned, more than my life was worth—here, in this remote region—to reveal too much of the sacrifices Sir Frideric had made for his art. The young Actaeon, on stumbling on divine secrets, had paid with his life: Diana's hounds had torn him limb from limb.

Alex had not intended this—subsequently, she felt it perhaps a consequence of her own shrinking and changing state. That she would often find herself on a bench in front of Pickled Lily and not be able to remember how she got there.

It would seem as though she'd wake with a jolt, and, disoriented, be conscious of a smoothly but rapidly fading dream in which she'd received information from the mermaid, not just the self-pitying self-advertisement she'd expected (how had she expected this? On what basis?) but deep and detailed knowledge. What Alex could only describe as instructions. Protocols. A part of her, small as yet but shrill, told her that she must leave this place. The Institute. Morrison. None of this was doing her any good at all. But Alex, like most people, sets the consequences of a shot in the dark against the pursuit of one's present course which, while wretched, is, at least, known.

But more than that—she was fascinated by what Lily had had to say, and how she—Alex -- had come to learn it. That same small and shrill part (which now sounded increasingly like her mother) warned her of voices in the head, that such a reaction only proved the case for putting as many miles as she could between her and the Institute, as soon as possible. In any case, there was a rational explanation. Alex wasn't hearing voices, because everything that Lily said was right there, on the label, in plain sight. Alex must have read the label a hundred times, but only now does it seem to make sense. Lily is telling her about Obed Marsh, a whaler of Massachusetts, and of a terrible, terrible crime. A crime she must now solve. She can no longer save Pickled Lily, she reasons—but she can do her best to save herself, and the course she must choose is not flight, but confrontation.

The Institute Library would satisfy any curator of the more austere species of nightmare. A small door just off the main hall at the opposite end of the building from the main entrance—a door one might easily miss—gives on to what must have been a substantial space, with a ceiling as high as that of the common room and with wide windows which, in times past, revealed dramatic cliff-top scenery to the eastward. This space has always been a library, but the press of books, periodicals and papers accumulated over a century and more have led to an unplanned metastasis of shelves which over many decades have divided and subdivided the room both horizontally and vertically into a labyrinth of narrow, ill-lit corridors, chambers, staircases and carrels such that the original lines of the room might no longer be made out. When Alex first ventured inside, she imagined that the boundaries of the space circumscribed by the library might be far more extensive than that of the room in which it had been created, and had been initially fearful of going too far in.

At first, this was in case she became lost. This concern subsided after her first few visits there, after she had established landmarks as she'd done with the rest of the building, though there were sometimes moments of panic when she looked up and could not recognize her surroundings. More recently she had become afraid that she might turn some corner and come across Morrison, and have to endure another encounter. Lately, however, she surprises herself that she has, without really trying, managed to sublimate that fear into an image of discovering Morrison in some dusty, yellowed corner, engaged in some procedure—or rite—the details of which she cannot not quite make out, but when he turns to look at her, his dead-eyed face is stained with blood running from his jaws. The image is horrible, but the Morrison it contains is neither triumphant nor controlling, but an abject thing, a husk of humanity. Alex has never been one for analyzing such things too deeply, and she does not do so now. But she does wonder at the change in herself, and derives solace from it. As a result, she now sees the Library as her haven, her friend, a place more welcoming than anywhere else in the Institute with the exception of her own laboratory. No, more, even than that, for in the lab she is too

much on show, where others can find you too easily; the mazy interstices of Library are in that sense more private, a tangible extension of
her own thoughts, a place in which one neither easily be discovered,
nor violated. Over the past few months, she has came to know every
tiny passageway, every lintel under which she has had to stoop, every
incomplete run of every obscure leather-bound journal crammed into
its dark-wood shelves.

And so it is that on a shelf in an upper-floor corridor so narrow
that one can only shuffle along it crabwise, she finds what she consid-
ers to be more than a book, but a key to her salvation. Generations of
even fairly diligent scourers of the library might have missed it, for
although it is catalogued, it had at some point been re-shelved
wrongly and had been listed as 'lost' some time in the 1960s. Alex
counts herself blessed that she has found it, by chance, wedged between two much larger volumes of some near-forgotten marine biology periodical. Alex pulls the little thing from the shelf, along with a
small puff of dust and mould, and, in a shaft of sunlight narrowed by
the grime of a skylight just three feet above her head, opens the thick,
blackened boards to a pocket-sized book whose bindings have decayed so much that even the act of her opening it shatters the spine
into a choking explosion of dust, so that in the end she holds no more
than a thick sheaf of roughly cut paper kept together solely by the
pressure of her hands. With great care she takes it to a small table at
the end of the row, equipped with a creaking office chair and an old
anglepoise. There she sits, and reads, and when she looks up, she
finds that hers is the only pool of light in the labyrinth, for deep night
has fallen. But now, she knows secrets which she is sure Morrison has
never known—or if he has, he has dismissed as ridiculous impossi-
bilities. But she knows differently now, and no amount of darkness
can change that.

It takes Alex a little while to become accustomed to the rough and
uneven type of An Account of the Voyages, Adventures and Opinions
of Captain Obed Marsh, Innsmouth Whaler, With Divers Observa-
tions and Remarks of the Secrets of the Sea, As Reported to Mr Urth,
Gentleman, of Arkham, Mass. But the pages are small, the print is
large and crude, and she finishes the entire book at one sitting. As the
title suggests, it is less a book than a kind of diary or annal, taken
down secondhand by this Mr Urth from a source who seems to have
made up in robust vigor what he evidently lacked in literary style.

The text is rambling but racy, the events reported intermittent and selected more on the basis of lurid content than any testable veracity or unbiased observation of nature. Life onboard is a series of floggings, keel-haulings, disease, starvation and mutilation, all of it directed with gusto by Captain Marsh; life ashore is an uninterrupted bacchanale of drinking, battle with variously exotic and brutal indigenes, whoring and more drinking in which Captain Marsh plays the leading role, whether as drunkard or fighter or lover, and all described with a degree of attention to explicit detail which (Alex thinks) might even have shocked a Regency cartoonist. The promised Secrets of the Sea are little more than a medieval freak-parade of witch-whales, orcs, rocs, sea-serpents, kraken, mermaids, cyclopes, basilisks, maelstroms, anthropophagi and sirens, some of which are rip-offs from mythology, obvious even to one as relatively unlearned in such things as is Dr Alex Beach. Clearly, sex, violence and the great unknown were as potent as ingredients of cheap literature at the dawn of the nineteenth century as they are now, or at any other time. And, as everyone has known since stories were first invented, the old ones are the best.

Central to the account, though—and presented in far greater detail -- is the graphic description of the capture of one mermaid in particular, described as a 'she-witch', with 'weedy hair', who ambushed sailors attempting to land their small skiff on an unnamed Pacific Island, killing one of them by drowning—after which the boatmen gave chase, finally ensnaring the mermaid after a breakneck pursuit lasting several exciting pages. When finally netted,

> The she-demon was hauled aboard, a-thrashing with her fishy tail as powerful as a tunny, a-squirming and a-biting with her sharp teeth, but the Men shewed her ther boots and ther oars and ther boat hooks, and she a-took to a-mewling like a puss-cat and became obedient to their whims on a sudden, smiling with her sharp teeth and parting her long weedy hair. The Men who had long been at sea pawed and prodded at her comely shape and she did not protest but seem'd to encourage it by bringing the Men to her close in turn, one after another, and this merriment was continued once the mermaid was taken on board ship.

There followed a passage in which violence, licence and general fantasy are combined in a thoroughly phantasmagorical stew. The mermaid, it seems, was kept in a large water-filled barrel on deck, and the Men were invited to 'seek certain pleasures' from her at prescribed times, tasks which she evidently discharged to the general satisfaction, the details of which are set out with such pornographic frankness that Alex feels herself sweat and squirm while reading them, and is grateful that there is nobody around who might peer over her shoulder. During this extended exegesis of seven (or possibly eight) adventures in which the sexual appetite of mermaids in general, and this mermaid in particular, is more than fully explored, Alex learns that the star of this particular live barrel show is called 'Lily' or just 'Lil'. No reason for the appellation is given.

A few pages on, however, and the horror, ever lurking as background to this bestial revelry, comes to the fore: there is an account, as ever luridly detailed, of a sailor enjoying the company of Lily in her barrel, but this time things seem to have gone too far. Screams are heard, and crewmen rushing on deck find the sailor yelling for his life amid a boiling morass of what looks like blood, trying to avoid being pulled under. His struggles are unsuccessful, and when his fellows haul his corpse from the barrel they find that

> his breeches were gone and with them his manhood, there remaining a hole whence gush'd forth a torrent of blood like the water from the barren rock struck with Aaron's rod.

With of without the consent of Captain Marsh, the revenge of the crew is terrible. A mob surges on deck armed with boat hooks, ropes, chains and anything else handy, thronging around the red-filled barrel, thrashing at the water, probing it and prodding it, until, eventually - inevitably - the mermaid is dragged to the surface by the hair. Her screams of anger and dread are horrifying to hear—many sailors retreat, dropping their weapons and covering their ears. But a doughty few avoid the nails, the pointed teeth, and—standing over the slithering, muscular form on the deck, restrain her, pinning her, cruciform, to the planks. Captain Marsh is called for and he dispenses summary justice with a sharp blow of a boathook to the creature's head. And so she ends.

Had the book been true to form, this event would have been

swiftly submerged by a flood of further adventure, as if the entire mermaid episode had never been. Instead, Alex finds the text taking a more pensive tone, detached even, as if the writer is trying to hold the events at arm's length even while he is telling them.

The remainder of the story is swiftly told. Captain Marsh orders Lily to be immersed in a barrel of rum, so that she might be preserved and sold or traded in Valparaiso with

> a gentleman there who acted as an agent for an English Lord much famed for his interest in the secrets of the sea which few others vouchsafe to themselves even had they known them.

The voyage continues, but the previous mood of riot and rumpus is replaced by one of static, reflective lassitude. The only other events are these—a worry about the diminution in rum supplies, now that most of the rations have been used to store the mermaid; and an epidemic of deaths among the sailors, whose bodies are found, eyes wide and blood-rimmed with the same infinite stare with which Alex is now only too familiar. Marsh's voice now forces its way through the measured tones of Urth as the text reaches the last page.

> We earnestly hoped that there would be men still aboard in sufficient numbers and in a condition still hale to steer the boat into Valparaiso: men who had avoided falling to the Curse of the Mermaid.

And with that, the text reaches its abrupt close. Alex knows better than to expect any measured account (or any account at all) of the epidemiology of this 'curse'. But she has become used to reading between the lines. The sailors, otherwise deprived of rum, had been drinking from the same barrel in which the mermaid had been stored. If science has any victories, if it has any spur, it is the satisfaction of connections forged, even ahead of the evidence, between previously disparate areas of enquiry. Alex, alone in a pool of yellow light in the library attic, feels that addictive thrill now, the same which, as a teenager, first turned her into a scientist. There is a link between carnostomids and mermaids; between Obed Marsh and Banneman Houghton.

That connection is Pickled Lily, the specimen left in a tableau of writhen agony three floors below. With growing shock — and supreme fascination - Alex now knows what carnostomids grow up to become.

8: A Metaphor for Death

On returning to her eyrie, the Voyages of Obed Marsh concealed in her bag like the smug prize of a jackdaw, Alex finds a text on her mobile. It is an invitation to dinner. 'My Treat', it says. A small part of her fancies that it might have been from Garry Williams, and this embryonic wish could, she imagines, be a part of her long road back to the surface: but it is not. It is from Morrison, and she obeys, with a mixture of resignation and the hope, perhaps beyond hope, that there will be a change in the weather, something more to this assignation than brutal expediency. But she is armed now with new knowledge of which Morrison is surely unaware—and were he made so, he'd dismiss it as idle rubbish.

Mermaids? Honestly!

But Garry is right—knowledge is power, and it coats her in what she imagines is a sheen of impenetrable diamond, proof against whatever Morrison might throw at her.

Put on Posh Frock. Meet Lobby 7.

At first she is blindsided, but soon loses herself in an unaccustomed fluster of grooming. She is forced to admit that this very act is therapeutic in itself. However, the only frock she has that is remotely posh is the strappy red one she had worn for her doctorate graduation. Audacious, she had thought at the time, even though it had been concealed by an academic robe. She had worn it, then, as a kind of rebellion, or as a way of pleasing herself and no-one else. The wearing of it brought with it, as if it were an accessory, a memory of being a teenager in Marks and Spencer in Marble Arch, watching agog as a parade of Arab women in full burkas solemnly passed by, each pushing a supermarket trolley piled high with the sheerest lingerie. She felt akin to those women then—more so, now, concealing a significant new discovery in her mental underclothes alongside her own true self, beneath the pretence of her corporeal shell.

And so she arrives, beneath the Founder's statue, as promptly as they both knew they would.

She finds herself disarmed of her pre-emptive steel even before it is deployed, for when she peers through the glass of the Institute's main doors, there is Morrison on the gravel forecourt, suited and floodlit in the sleety weather, holding open the door of his red sports convertible, the tails of his tan raincoat flapping in the northerly squall.

"Ma'am - your carriage awaits!" he declares, yelling against the wind, but managing, all the same, a self-deprecating flourish that is quite out of character—but Alex is so charmed, so relieved, that she decides to ignore this, for the moment.

Morrison drives, with assurance and great speed through the wet, to a discreet but extremely expensive restaurant in Tombland, on a small cobbled square opposite the gates to Norwich Cathedral. He leaves the car on the kerb, tosses the key to a valet (she is amazed at this) and shepherds her into the restaurant, all in one, commanding swoop. She is quite bowled over, and it is not until they are some way into their first glass of wine, that she can begin to attempt the policy of confrontation she'd resolved to pursue. She feels, even as she starts, her resolution crumbling at the edges.

"I've managed to do some reading. Background."

"Hmmm?" Morrison fusses with the menu. He does not meet her eyes, but Alex is not sure whether this owes more to his perusal of the very long list of francophone fare or to something deeper, more strategic.

"Yes, I..." her voice quavers. "I've read up on Houghton. The *Spaniel*. The first records of carnostomids. The ... deaths. They remind, me, you know..."

He looks at her then with a blue stare so penetrating that she stops in mid-sentence, all possibility of further speech taken away. But then he smiles. That big, welcoming smile that forgives everything.

"Oh, Alex. Alex! I told you not to worry when you stumbled across Bland's body, your poor, sweet thing..." Another part of Alex wants to curl up, then, at this small crumb of affection, for him to tuck her up in bed and read her a bedtime story. "But yes, I have something to share with you -- I really ought to have done so earlier, as part of our respective contracts — and I apologise. I really do." She feels herself swell with relief (and pride, and vanity) as another part of her fissile and treacherous soul is now thrust into command: a colleague, yes, but first among equals.

"You may have noticed that I've been hogging the Library copy. I'm sorry you've had to dig out another." Alex notices that he does not ask the source of her information. "But yes, I've known about carnostomids for, well, a little while…"

"But why…?"

"Because MagusPharm asked me to. First, to track your work, as a kind of check — not that you aren't doing great stuff — but if you'd known what I was up to, that would have spoiled some of the controls, wouldn't it? Especially as I'm … we're …" A third part of Alex wants to pull the little lost boy to her breast and hug him.

"Because we're … an item?"

"Well, yes, Alex. That's just it. That part *wasn't* in our MagusPharm contracts." They both laugh. "Though it's — I hope you agree — a very nice extra." Her emotions on hearing this are both so violent and so conflicting that she feels that to say anything risks disgorging a treatise. So she remains silent, and hopes that her smile is not too sickly.

"But better to be hung for a sheep as a lamb," he continues. "As Director I've … er … loaned some of our carnostomid material to our masters at MagusPharm. So they could do some tests — exploratory, mind — on human cell lines. Just to see what they'd find. And, well -"

But Morrison is interrupted by the waiter, who arrives to take their order, and amid much flourishing and gesticulating about the chef's specials in what Alex is certain is a very fake French accent, Alex and Morrison make their choices (with much solicitation on Morrison's part), and the waiter retreats. Alex is now desperate to hear the end of Morrison's account. So desperate, she recalls later, that she'd believe anything. Just to be vouchsafed this information is to receive the food of the Gods.

"What did they find, Morrison?" She is conscious, now, of the blood retreating to the core of her body: her skin is cold. Morrison stares back, with a different face — a flash of the old reptilian. His pupils shrink to points like black lasers. Alex wonders if she has stepped too far — across the line that says one should never, ever question Morrison about anything, not if you know what's good for you, and she has the sudden sensation of being quite naked before him and inwardly recoils.

"Well, I'd have told you about it eventually, but you know, what with one thing and another …" He leaves the words hanging as he refills her glass. Alex remains mute and still. "But, yes, rough extracts of carnostomids did have the most remarkable effects. Something like a super-antigen. But, you know…" He shifts in his seat. Alex dares to venture another question.

"Anything specific?"

"Well, no. I … they … they haven't managed to get anything pure, not enough to home in on specific agents — well, that's all they've told *me* — so we don't know much about mechanism. And they haven't scaled things up to an *in-vivo* level yet. Mice. Rats. You know the drill."

The waiter, as if on cue, arrives with their order.

"But I can guess, and, well, Bland and all that. I think you're right, Alex." She has the curious sense of having dropped into a conversation several steps ahead of where she thought it was. "Bland was killed, I think, from exposure to carnostomids." Alex's mind races ahead to possibilities. Connections. The *Spaniel* Collection. Pickled Lily. Had Morrison had the same intuition she'd had? Had he already disrobed her of her new and precious secret, before she'd known it herself? She feels herself blanch, and once again the sensation of cold panic freezes her limbs. She feels she wouldn't be able to move even were the tablecloth to ignite.

"But how…?"

"Alex? *Alex*! Don't look like that. But yes, I confess, it worries me too. How could Bland have been infected with carnostomids, unless he'd been drinking the preserving fluid? Who'd do that? It's crazy. And Bland may have been many things, but I'd never have marked him down as that kind of a drinker. No-one is that desperate. Not even Bland. Not when you can get a drop as decent as this Sancerre, anyway." Morrison laughs as he tops up their glasses once more, but Alex detects a remnant coldness behind his eyes. Not of remorseless control, but of fear, of a world beginning to slip from his grasp. Without knowing or caring why, she reaches her left hand across the table and rests it on his wrist. He looks up, then, his pupils once more enlarged, vulnerable.

"There's something else, Alex. The night Bland died. That same night. Well, he and I had an argument. I might well have been the last person to have seen him alive. The police kept on about it, but, well, I had to be evasive." He puts down his fork and rests a hand on hers. His fingers find the warmth in the pulse-point of her wrist where the radial artery almost breaks the surface, and strokes her skin with an almost imperceptible movement that makes her catch her breath.

"Morrison? Why? What about?" She remembers her own meetings with Inspector Sheepwool, and guesses that even as skilled an operator as Morrison (she is under no illusions on that score) would have had to have chosen his words with care.

"Believe it or not, Alex, it was all about *you*." Morrison tries to laugh, but it is forced, and brittle: "he came on like the alpha male, ranting on about how you were his, or something. I said that Alex— you—were your own woman, and didn't belong to anyone. But he wouldn't have it. He said a lot of other things, too, shooting off in all directions, saying things about me, how I wasn't fit to be Director, not with my scientific record, blah blah blah, not that he'd stirred himself to very much on that front. All bollocks. So I told him to … er … get lost. And, well, he did. Pity he had to do so just then." It is here that Alex sees a glimpse of things darker, secrets of whose existence she's not been aware, but Morrison now seems to be talking more to him-self than her—so she does not feel entitled to question him further.

Nor does she dare.

But he looks up then, pinning her to her seat once more with that icy stare, a shocking contrast with the warmth of his hand round her wrist.

"Good job the coroner came up with that natural-causes verdict. Because if he hadn't, the Police would make two and two equal five and conclude Bland was done away with as part of some scientific cover-up. You know what people think of us scientists, Alex, don't you? Especially those of us who've bought into the pharma dollar. Well, what with our work on carnostomids, I'd really be in deep doo-doo. And so, Alex, would you. What a mess.

"But we have to keep working on them, you and I. Carnostomids. Given what I … we … MagusPharm knows of their potential immu-nological effects, we could be onto something big. But you've read the small print. Tell no-one what you come across." His gaze is relentless, stripping away layers of her mind, in search of anything she might be concealing. She feels her lips part as she struggles for breath. "No-one except me, of course." He smiles again, the same big old smile, and she asks herself, as he pays the bill with his MagusPharm platinum card, why she always falls for it.

She lies now, half on her back, half on her side, half awake, in his bed, cradling him to her. He is asleep, faintly snoring, his face cushioned between her breasts.

The relief she'd felt—that he'd confessed he'd felt too, of a problem shared and thus halved, but mostly that he'd at last confided in her, bringing her into the fold. That whatever they were in, they were in it together, as a pair, as a gang, as a couple. So that when he'd whisked her back to his house, they'd made love as partners, and not as she'd become wearily accustomed, as if he were some kind of mechanic, and she the soulless machine. And yet, even though she'd known she'd had too much to drink, her mind was alert—braced—for his violence. That his lovemaking was, uncharacteristically, anything but violent caught her unawares and, she reflects, made her participation all the more willing, more forgiving, as if compensating for having been so uncharitable to have thought Morrison anything but gentle and considerate.

She remembers little of it, now, except in isolated, pinkly-fogged flashbacks.

Of his big sofa in the huge, upstairs living room, the walls still brick-and-flint rough. And after that, of his big bed downstairs.

Of his hands again, his electric fingers, rucking up the rebellious red dress and parting the scratchy fabric of her knickers, his palm curved around her warm, wet sex, his fingers sliding inside her, her whispers of pleasure, willing him on.

Of his tongue, around and inside her, as his hands—his hands, again—kneading her breasts through the same rebel dress and raising her nipples, and her whispers of pleasure, willing him on.

Of his body as he rose above and on top and inside her, and her own self as she pulled up her bare legs and crossed them over his back, his shoulders, so she could feel him within, as deeply and as hugely as possible.

Of his movement, as measured and as relentless as the sea, in crimson waves of surf that seemed to last forever, bringing them both to tidal climaxes.

Of him now, close to her, unmanned, vulnerable, like a baby in her arms, the half-light of dawn through the French windows. Look at your baby Alex. Look at it. And not like Morrison at all. She drifts once more into seamless sleep.

Rebecca is in her room once again, a room that overlooks the long-shadowed lawn and the clifftops, waiting for the familiar knock, and dreading it. Every evening she prays that it is anyone else—Mr Willoughby, her own maidservant, her mother, even—any one but her father's valet with his message, a message that bears the same wearisome words, a summons to Sir Frideric's private rooms, a place she now equates with hell itself.

She can hardly bear to think about the transactions that occur within those walls, and when she screams, as she does, inevitably, her soul unable to contain her suffering, she now—after long habit—hears these utterances with detachment, as if they were the screams of someone else, some other tortured creature. Yet this offers scant solace, as it is after all the point of view of a witness complicit in the dreadful actions therein committed: a witness sworn to silence, however unwillingly held.

It is a summons she dare not disobey. She knows, from experience, what would happen to her, should she refuse it.

It is fully light, the silver of an overcast dawn washed with recent rain, when Alex wakes. She is cold, and turns over into a dead space. Morrison has left, silently. Disoriented, she sits up and wonders. But Morrison is a creature like any other animal, true only to himself. This is something she knows she should simply get used to. But did last night count for nothing? She rises and finds a bathrobe, the bathroom, the stairs and the kitchen, the air chill around the glow of a cooling kettle on the gleaming steel of the range. It occurs to her then how flawless the kitchen is—indeed, how spare and brand-new everything is in Morrison's house. As if it had been delivered yesterday. Not a proper home: a show-home, devoid of personality, revealing no more of its occupant than it might an alien. She has been here before—of course!—but she has never been left alone here, and only now, in this gray morning, does she notice the absence of books on the teak shelves; the absence of CDs or DVDs around the big plasma screen; the absence of any photographs that might indicate some connection, however exiguous, with human beings. Family. Friends. Colleagues. The absence of any conventional clutter whatsoever. The surfaces are spotless: even the bins are empty—it could be a set-up for a particularly well-heeled sting operation.

Or a metaphor for death.

She feels the walls close in and draws the robe around her as reflexive protection. Drawn to the kettle as a stone-age hunter—or a moth—might be entranced by a fire, as the only sign of homeliness in a pitiless Universe, she notices a mug already set up with coffee (instant) and milk, and a folded sheet of paper. It is Institute paper, bearing the single line:

Duty calls. Make yourself at home. Love M.

The amatory declaration foxes her. At first she reads it only as some impenetrable glyph; then as an imperative, a command. Finally it dawns on her that it's the only time either of them has said anything of the sort, but rather than being warmed by it, she remains confused. Nobody could make themselves at home here. Nobody except Morrison. She boils the kettle, fills the pre-arranged mug and takes it to the sofa. The same sofa on which, the night before, they had started to make love. But even that bears no stigma of the previous night's excursions. No creases, no residual heat, no musky smell. It's as if she's woken up in a different house.

The realization hits her so hard that she almost up-ends the entire mug on the pristine berber-twill carpet. That she has walked into a trap. She is not a colleague, not a lover, not even a friend, but a specimen trapped in a designer cage, and she expects at any moment huge faces to peer in through the windows, leering.

Yesterday her most earnest wish was that Morrison would confide in her. Today, she wishes that he had said nothing, for now he has confessed—the parallel work on carnostomids, the experiments on human tissue, his suspicions about Bland's death and what that might imply for them both: and now, apparently, his love—she has become nothing, no-one, expendable. His tenderness of the night before was therefore as cruel in its deception as his previous violence had been to her physical frame.

For now she is soiled, tainted, compromised - bought. For whatever else might happen, Morrison knows perfectly well that she, Alex, can never say anything to Sheepwool for fear of saying too much.

Had she been any other person than the human nullity she knows herself to be, she would have raged, then: spilled her coffee on the carpets, ripped the stuffing from the cushions, beaten chips out of the granite worktops, smashed in the TV, anything to impose some personality on this mockery of a home. But she doesn't, and Morrison knows she never would.

But before Alex can give herself up for lost, a small bubble of hope rises to the surface of her mind. She still knows something. Something that no-one else knows. She clings to it as a shipwrecked sailor might to a broken spar.

In the same dawn light, five miles to the north, Detective Inspector Sheepwool stands at a different counter-top, nursing a different cup of coffee. The mind, she reflects, is a wonderful thing. Her beloved surrealists had known it—that life is no more than the plane on which we blithely skate, unaware of the surging forces beneath, the subterranean connections between one life and another, connections which are so easily made, provided that one detaches one's mind sufficiently from the banal prejudices which so often obscure them. Sleep, she finds, is the medium in which such links are forged. Sleep, the gift beyond price which, just a few months before, had been stolen from her, and only lately regained. This is why Sheepwool, more than anyone, appreciates its value.

Connections.

Something that American scientist said—Wilson? Willans? Williams, that was it—about his wife. Middle-aged and pregnant, and a victim of the sea.

And something earlier, much earlier, something that Fitch had said in the car, about Sir Frideric. His wife.

And closer to home. Much closer. Something that Methwold said, or, rather, the shape of something he has never said, but defined in negative by his every action. His glances at the woman in the photograph. Middle-aged. A suicide.

Connections. In the deepest, bluest holes of her mind, she fancies she can see, just on the edge of vision, a yet deeper blue. A flick of a tail, and it's gone.

Part Three

1: Whisper of the Surf

Deringland, as has been noted, suffers from formidable weather, with one exception—it rarely snows. Even in the deepest vaults of winter, black-freighted clouds roll from the sea to offload their cargo at least ten miles inland, leaving most Norfolk residents with prospects of crisp whiteness under morning sunshine, while Deringlanders scurry about their business beneath a close pall of gloom.

But there comes a time when the proprietorial cloud lifts, even here, and it is in her office one day in the last week of April when Sheepwool looks up to be assailed by a light from her window so white, so blinding, that she cannot help but cover her eyes in fearful apprehension—only to realize that what she sees is the first sunshine of Spring, whose radiance she has long forgotten. She lowers her hand from her eyes and smiles, basking in the warmth, staring straight at the beams until her eyes water. She fails to notice the door to her right open and snick shut, and it is only when Fitch bends low over her desk, obscuring the sunlight, that she looks up and takes notice.

"Ma'am? Are you…?"

"Mmm? Yes, Fitch, thank-you—I'm fine. You?"

"Yes, thank-you, Ma'am. Do you mind if I….?" Fitch waves vaguely at an armchair. Sheepwool wonders at Fitch's stiff formality. To be sure, after the Bland case closed, Methwold had put Fitch on other duties that have taken her away from the Station most days. Another advanced-driving course. Study leave, too—Methwold knows a bright spark when he sees one and, on Sheepwool's recommendation, has encouraged the younger woman to aspire to the heights of Detective-Inspectorhood. Sheepwool and Fitch, therefore, have moved apart, and the companionable ease they were just starting to enjoy during the Bland case has stiffened somewhat, from lack of use.

Sheepwool, for her part, has been managing a portfolio of somewhat lesser duties. But there are loose ends—loose ends which she acknowledges must often stay that way, for all that their frayed edges catch on the inside of her soul.

A flash of blue.

She wishes she had a legitimate excuse to visit Alex Beach again.

Fitch takes a seat and perches uneasily on it, knees pressed together as tightly as her lips are pursed. Sheepwool looks up with added interest. She feels—has felt—that she has not come to know Fitch as well as she'd have liked to have done, and now her junior is swimming off to newer, broader waters.

"Fitch?"

"Yes! Well! I must say, Ma'am, that these new courses … these exams … they're quite a challenge, aren't they? Not that I can't cope with them—of course not! Sometimes I think I'll never get my head round them, but then—whoosh!—there I am, on the school run. Of course you do, you *must* do—and it suddenly hits me, and I just *know* what to do, I can *see* a way through, I …"

Sheepwool's amused stare brings Fitch to a sudden halt. "I'm glad you've taken to it so well, Fitch. Really, I am. I think you'd make a first-rate DI." Fitch smiles, and relaxes, all in one gawkish movement. Sheepwool is inwardly alarmed—do such young girls make DI these days? Hang on—when she herself went for promotion she was only— what? Hardly any older than Fitch is now. Maybe a little younger. And Fitch isn't really as young as she seems: it's her freely animated nature that makes her seem the green girl, not any lack of talent or experience. But she'll have to pull herself back, now and then, if she's to succeed. Now is not the time to say such things, though, and it occurs to her, belatedly, that Fitch has come to see her for a reason. She sits back in her chair and cocks an eyebrow in Fitch's direction. Detective Sergeant (for now) Elaine Fitch takes the hint.

"Yes—Ma'am—sorry to go on. But I came across something that might interest you, kind of 'off the record', really." Sheepwool perks up. "You know, Ma'am, we never got to interview a few potential witnesses in the Bland case, before it was wound up? Well, one of them was Heather Franks, you know?"

Sheepwool nods. She has the sensation, as jarring as it is brief, of a trapdoor opening beneath her feet.

"Well, there I was, pushing the trolley round the supermarket, and

I bump into her. Literally, just like that."

"Franks?"

"Yes. We were stuck in the dairy aisle. Bryony was whining about yoghurt, as usual. Eric was running around—he can be a holy terror!—and then—bang!—we run straight into this tall, dark woman who's just stood there, in a daydream, right in front of the specialty cheeses. She turns, you know, and there's the usual I'm-sorry-no-I'm-sorry-no-think-nothing-of-it routine, when her face just—just—well, just *changed*, as if she recognized me.

"Then I recognized *her*, of course—aren't you Heather Franks, from the Institute, I asked? She went all a-fluster and tried to change the subject, so she never told me, but I'm convinced it was her. Tall woman. Big feet. I remember from the funeral, when she tripped over my bag in the aisle of the Church. Poor woman—seems we're *always* bumping into each other. But then she said the weirdest thing." Fitch pauses, brows tense in recollection, making sure she recalls precisely the right words.

"She said 'I'm sorry, do I know you? I have a call to make. A Christmas call. From a window. No, from the sea. That'll show him.' And then she looked at me as if she'd said something she shouldn't've. She went as red as a beetroot and ran for it. I wanted to call after her—she just abandoned her trolley, food in it and everything—but what she said was, well, so strange…"

Sheepwool sits back. A broad ray of sunshine spotlights a beam of dancing motes. " '*I have a call to make. A Christmas call. From a window. No, from the sea. That'll show him'*", she echoes, but more to herself than to Fitch. As she does so, she sees herself, briefly, as small as a speck of dust herself, smaller, riding on one of those dancing rays. But she brings herself back with disorienting force and looks directly at Fitch.

"Fitch …"

"Ma'am? I thought—well—it must have been Franks. The mystery woman who countered Morrison's alibi. All about making calls, and from a window—that's where she saw Morrison, from her window at the Institute. Just after Christmas—well, still in the holidays, at any rate, and …"

"But wasn't Franks away for the holidays?"

"Yes, well, that's what we *thought*. But all we know was that Janice Squearn saw her rush out on the twenty-first of December, and nobody saw her until the funeral. So who's to say she wasn't here—in town—all the time? We know *someone* saw Morrison leave the Institute at the time he said he was at home. It could've been Franks. After all, what was *her* alibi?"

Sheepwool smiles. Fitch will, indeed, make a very fine DI. But she has a question of her own. She has been nursing it for two months now, unable to articulate it in any way without seeming ridiculous. But the longer the words remain unframed, the more ornate the question seems to become, until she despairs of being able to ask it at all, ever. Perhaps—now that the case is closed—she can take Fitch into her confidence. "What about the 'from the sea' part, though?" she asks.

"Yes, Ma'am, I have to say, that puzzled me."

"You know, Fitch, I've been turning things over in my head. All about the sea."

"The sea?"

It is then that Sheepwool realizes how much one takes for granted. People who live by the sea—live by it, and die by it, and have it shape their entire lives—spend most of the time barely conscious that it is there at all.

She'd read somewhere that the first thing that humans did as soon as they'd evolved, in the parched hinterlands of Africa, was head for the beach, where they learned how to harvest the bounties of the sea. That's where they'd discovered art, and the beginnings of culture, and had taken the first steps on the long road to humanity. Even today, millions pay homage to their ancestors by re-enacting that ancestral journey: for all that they are laden with buckets and spades and deck-chairs, they are every bit as sincere in their pilgrimage as those who advance on their knees to the shrine of Santiago de Compostela. (There's a painting by Dalí that sums it all up, beautifully, she thinks - Christ, St John, and wide, deserted beaches...) But Fitch is one of those seasiders who have never lived far from the whisper of the surf. It is, perhaps, because she—Sheepwool—is an incomer, an inlander, that she is aware of the pervasive power of the sea. The power to pull people under, with inexorable, irresistible force. The power to leave others behind, keening forever on the strandline, like gulls.

"Yes, Fitch, the sea. Do you get time off for good behaviour these days?"

Fitch looks confused, but then she smiles and scans her watch.

"Yes, of course, I ..."

"Well, so do I. Far too much time, in fact. So how about the Three Kings at lunchtime? I rather fancy a spritzer. My treat."

As evening falls, Alex Beach is in the lab. Morrison has pulled some strings and her room is now much fuller than it had been just two months earlier: instead of two empty spaces, each with the potential to house a colleague, the lab now seems crammed to bursting.

Almost a third is occupied by new equipment, humming quietly, and the remaining space is more than filled by a technician called Valentina, small and dark, who is there to operate it. Which she does, with cold expedition, despite the occasional curse levelled at it in what Beach supposes is some eastern European language. Beach has never heard Valentina say much more in recognizable English than conventional phrase-book salutations, and her brooding countenance does not invite further intimacy. At first, Beach thinks that she would find the presence of another person in her laboratory intimidating— especially one with whom one can have no conversation. But she soon finds that Valentina understands instructions well enough, whether spoken or written, so Alex (to her shame) finds herself regarding Valentina as another piece of equipment, a computer, perhaps—an entity with whom one can have that kind of relationship made uneasy by mutual incomprehension, and limited by the constraints of the operating system.

Despite this (or, perhaps, because of it) Alex tends to keep different hours from Valentina, and has now become very largely nocturnal. She knows that Valentina lives somewhere in the Institute, in a room perhaps rather like her own, but she does not know where this might be and has made no effort to find out. Annoyed and perhaps slightly afraid of the technician, and finding herself (yet more shame!) jealous of breaking a solitude with which she has achieved some hard-fought accommodation, Alex now works from around eleven in the evening to around mid-morning the next day, after which she either shuffles up to her room or, as often as not, reclaims her long-unused bike and pedals the few miles inland to Morrison's barn conversion. She likes the exercise, she tells herself, puffing through the brooding prairie between the Institute and the main road.

Nothing she might do to change things can ever make any dent on the robotic sterility of Morrison's house, and she feels it would be unwise to try. But the hours she now keeps, and the toll taken, make its anonymity more welcoming than her cold and cluttered attic room, in the same way that travelling salesmen often prefer the bland calm of commercial hotels to their inevitable return to family life, when they are first greeted by the barely disguised reproach of spouses forced to manage a house alone, the mulish children, the endless chores left undone by way of retaliation. And even when she and Morrison happen to coincide long enough to have sex, this, too, seems drained of any color: she has almost begun to regret the absence of the sudden violence which characterized their earlier encounters, and they now pursue the act almost without thought, still engaged in conversation, as if they were making tea or loading the dishwasher.

One evening, when Morrison had returned before she had left for the Institute, they had gone to bed, and afterwards, when Morrison was doing up his fly, his back to her, she had asked for the equipment she needed to get to work on carnostomid DNA, and his response was businesslike and immediate—sure, he had said, just write me a shopping list and I'll have MagusPharm get it for you.

As simple as that.

And then he'd put on his jacket and left the bedroom, leaving absolutely no sign of his presence but for a faint smell of cologne.

The equipment had been installed barely ten days later, and Valentina along with it. And here Alex is now, in the lab, sitting on the sofa at dead of night, reading the childlike scrawl of a person whose first alphabet was probably Cyrillic, spreading printouts before her, on the coffee table, and—first and last—reading an unsigned note in a different, slyly masculine hand.

Carnostomid DNA is like nothing she has ever seen, and at the same time it looks awfully familiar. At first she didn't know what to make of it, until she dared take Garry Williams into her confidence. Williams, who has had a lifetime of genomic research and can read sequences like a virtuoso pianist can read Rachmaninov at sight. It is Garry's note she's now reading, and she is grateful that he has not signed it. Nonetheless, she'll shred it as soon as she can.

Just in case it gets into the wrong hands.

'Alex', the note reads,

> I've checked and double checked this and it's the darnedest thing. You <u>must</u> repeat this, two or three times, in case of contamination. It's vital that you get the work replicated someplace

else to make sure. If I can do some runs for you on the sly, I shall, just ask. Or we can ship some to Berkeley, no questions asked. So I ran the BLAST searches and what you've got here is <u>human</u> DNA. Nothing else - no bacteria, no fungi, no nothing — not even any sequence that pops up as unknown. It's weird. But it's been shuffled up real strange, like all the exons have been taken out, introns excised, and the whole lot tied up with inverted repeats and put back in the wrong order like someone packing a bag in a hurry. Kind of like VDJ recombination, but then, not like that either. Let's talk over a drink. After this I think I need it.

The reading is clear, Alex thinks. She and Valentina have sequenced their own DNA by accident, haven't done enough to check for the constant bugbear of contamination, and Garry is chiding her for it as gently as he can. But it's a blow. But rather than do any more work, she leaves the lab and pilots a course up to her own room, now rarely visited. She blows dust off a mug and puts water on for some tea. This will have to be black—the milk in the fridge, neglected, is clotted with white, foul-smelling sediment and she's had to sluice it away. While she'd about it, she finds herself tidying the small space and cleaning it to a sparkle it hasn't seen in months.

It is only when she is sitting at her desk once again, with her tea, a smell of bleach in her nostrils, that she realizes that this is only a kind of displacement activity. Carnostomids with a smorgasbord of human DNA? With weary resignation she realizes that she's back to square one. She sighs, and closes her eyes. Look at your baby, Alex. It's all your fault.

And then, two rows of tiny, grinning teeth, in human shape. With enamel. No, she was right the first time. Yes, she'll do all the work Garry has suggested, but no, she was right. And perhaps it is the smell of the bleach, or the rancid residue of the milk, or the excitement she feels, or a combination of all these things, but she feels her gorge rise and has to turn to the sink to throw up.

A minute later, pale and wobbly, she sits at the table again to sip her tea, hands round the warm mug as if it were a talisman. She hears the percussive bark of rain, re-started, on the window. And there's a larger noise, more insistent, which takes some time to penetrate her fogged consciousness. It is a knock at the door. It is Valentina, eyes wide, vulnerable, haunted -- an expression so unlike the habitually self-assured scowl, that Alex first takes it as belonging to a different person entirely.

"Please, Doctor Beach, you come," she says. At Alex's evident confusion, the tiny, dark woman becomes agitated. She seems to jump up and down on the spot, like an imp on a hotplate.

"Please, you come—you come *now!*" repeats Valentina, pulling Alex by both hands and dragging her from the room by main force. "I saw her fall!" she cries, turning, not waiting for any further questions. Alex has no option but to follow.

The corridors, the book-lined intestinal stairs, the main hallway in the half-light of failing chandeliers, all pass by in a blur as Alex chases her technician through the interstices of the building. And suddenly they are out, in the rain, the salt breeze an assault of refreshment after the building's chronic claustrophobia. But Valentina does not pause for even half a second to appreciate this, and rushes out into the downpour. Without stopping, or even slacking, Valentina heads to the staircase through the woods and down to the shore beneath the cliffs on which the Institute stands. The treacherous switchbacks of the steep, winding path are dangerous enough in daylight: but in this rainy dark the treads have become slippery, and Alex—no stranger to this twisting path -- loses her footing several times during the descent, and saves herself from falling by grabbing hold of the occasional handrails—all of which are drunkenly loose through rot and rust, but still just about holding—and fortuitously placed vines and branches.

Alex and Valentina are now on the beach, lit only by the glow from the Institute far above and the gas platforms on the distant horizon. At last, Valentina stops, and looks down at what Alex at first thinks is a pile of weed or dead-man's fingers. The clotted clouds are picked out in charcoal shades as the rain eases, and the moon and stars emerge from the murk. But Alex, the pursuit over, is soaked through, covered in mud, her clothes stuck to her body in filthy, sodden planes, angry at being taken on what seems to have been a wild goose-chase by a madwoman. Panting for breath, Alex stands forward, hands on her knees, pulling in oxygen. But Valentina, as wet and dirty as she is, simply stands over her prize and bawls at Alex over the howling surf. "Doctor Beach! You come! You come *now!*"

And so she does, staggering the last dozen yards of scrunching shingle.

At their feet, crumpled, broken, in a pool of what in the shadows Alex takes to be dark blood, is a body, limbs thrown and broken, eyes open in red-rimmed pools.

It is the body of Heather Franks.

2: Unearthing the Bottomless

Sheepwool's caseload unravels until it fades out altogether. More liaison with Gerry Rammell from Customs and Excise concerning the adulteration of spirits at the Dazed Haddock had once again come to nothing. So she decides to take a couple of days' leave, just tidying up, reading, and thinking.

She treats herself to an exhibition of Max Ernst paintings at Norwich Castle Museum, finding them satisfyingly unsettling—but the more she looks at the ghoulishly animated picnic feasts, the elephants made of giant vacuum cleaners, the mice and small girls in mazes of what look like melted candle wax, the more her mind turns inward on itself, catching the frayed ends in the Bland case.

Which is why, the evening before she is due to return to work, the arrival of Methwold at her front door seems less unexpected than the working out of a premonition. He offers flowers, but even from behind the ramparts of his glasses, he finds it hard to meet her gaze, as if he were an errant husband seeking absolution for some infraction too minor to be worth consideration. She stifles a smile, invites him in, and looks for a vase.

On the threshold, he says "I owe you an apology".

"Whatever for?" She is busy in the kitchen, heedless that he seems to stand in the hall, lost in space, as if seeking further permission to enter. She returns to the hall, and they stand there, as motionless as sculptures, looking at each other, each daring the other to make the first move.

"Sorry to disturb you on your holiday."

"That's quite all right, Sir."

"Off duty, Sheepwool. Off duty. You can call me 'Ivan'."

"Then … Ivan … you have to call me 'Percy'. And please, do, come in, sit down," -- she indicates her living room with its spare but stylish

211

sofa and armchairs—"and I'll make tea."

"Thank you … Percy. That would be lovely." But instead of taking his lonely course towards the living room, he follows her into her kitchen and sits at the table. Ever the policeman, she thinks: never as comfortable as in an interview room, in an upright chair, at a plain table, solid protection against criminals, suspects, and the Great Unknown.

As the kettle boils, he tells her of the Institute's latest victim.

"I didn't apologise for disturbing you, Percy, not really—though I did, I mean…" He makes as if to start again. "You see, the thing is, I'd like you to handle this latest case. Probably nothing to do with Bland, you know, but two deaths at the same Institute in just four months, well…

"And then, you see, Elaine Fitch came to see me this afternoon. Don't know how she finds the time, with her exams, and her family, and her caseload…" (Sheepwool knows that Fitch has been investigating a midnight knifing outside a kebab shop in Thetford, forging a new self-confidence from the blood and the violence) "… but she's been adding two and two, and, well, maybe some of those loose ends we let hang. You know, last time. Bland."

Methwold looks so unsettled—had she known better she'd finger him as guilty, though of what, she cannot imagine—that she restrains herself from loosing the torrent of questions that she has been forced to keep to herself.

About how they failed to pin down Morrison's alibi, a failure which could, if examined critically, have led to this, a second death. And about the late Dr Franks' strange encounters with Fitch, in which the plainly (it now seems) troubled academic practically admitted that she was the informant who had blown Morrison's cover. Most of all, of their failure to trace Franks at a crucial time, leaving questions open that cannot, now, be satisfactorily resolved. Could Franks have murdered Bland? Or at least contributed to his death in some way? And if not, given the circumstances, what, precisely, *had* killed Bland? 'Natural Causes' is no more a solution than any other universe of possibilities—Sheepwool has learned that much from the extravagant profusion of nature displayed at the Institute. Franks had had the opportunity and possibly even a motive, and successfully sent the police up what might have been a false trail. And now she is gone. Even suicide is doubtful, for, as (Methwold explains) Franks left no obvious note. And if not suicide, then...?

Dead men tell no tales. And dead women are just as silent.

But Sheepwool says none of these things out loud. Instead, she sits down at the table opposite Methwold, reflecting for a fleeting moment that the strange blue thoughts she's been having, as if glanced from the corner of her mind, are too unformed to share with Methwold, even if one can extend a confidence to a junior colleague — and friend — in the pub at lunchtime. Or try to, at any rate. She had done her best to explain her vague unease to Fitch, but the blueness in her mind did not translate very easily into words, and, feeling foolish, she had let Fitch steer the subject of their infrequent conversations to more routine matters.

"Fitch ... Elaine ... came straight out with it," says Methwold. "That Morrison and Beach are up to something, together. Beach was the first, or almost the first, to have found the bodies both times, and the fact that Morrison lied about the first time raises more suspicions now..." Methwold pauses, hands waving weakly in the air, as if he were a sea anemone confronted with a Platonic ideal.

"Even if there wasn't enough to go on last time?" Sheepwool does her best to keep a hardness from her voice. Much to her surprise she succeeds, for Methwold smiles, unexpectedly. It occurs to Sheepwool that she has rarely seen Methwold display any kind of emotion that might fall outside the compass of professional self-assuredness. This stirs a mixture of emotions in her, in response — of fascination, and also of terror, as if discovering flaws in something taken for granted as utterly reliable.

"Quite. Yes, perhaps, but there's more. Fitch. She's been digging around a little, even after the Bland case closed. Digging after Morrison." Sheepwool smiles, partly to encourage Methwold, but also in satisfaction. Good for Fitch. No detective ever succeeded without, sometimes, a strategic disregard for standing orders.

"Fitch told me that the fact that she's been ... well, otherwise occupied, has delayed things, but the more she unearths, the more she finds it a bottomless pit. I should never have doubted you, Percy, there's something shady about Morrison. He was dismissed from an academic post a few years back for something nasty, unethical... though the closer Fitch says she gets to it, the harder it is to pin down."

"So, he *is* up to something."

"Possibly. Or, at least, he *was*. But what it has to do with Bland's death—or Franks'—is not at all clear. Not at all. That's what you and Fitch should find out. Starting tomorrow morning."

"And my other caseload? And Elaine's…?"

"…Will be taken care of."

This time they both smile, a coincidence that strikes them both at once, and from which they both recoil.

Methwold's departure a few minutes later leaves Sheepwool at once deflated and, curiously, content. She puts this down to the sensation of being put back in harness, self-esteem restored after weeks of idleness.

Nothing like the thought of a job in hand to raise one's spirits.

As she clears up the tea things, she remembers that what irked Fitch the most about the closing stages of the Bland case was their seeming inability to learn anything much about Franks. Now was the time to make amends for that omission, if it were not too late. Something that Methwold had said, just before he left, rolls round her mind. About Bland's previous, and something else Fitch had recalled, from talking to Janice Squearn, perhaps. That Bland had been pestering every woman at the Institute: all except Franks, and that was because *she* had been pestering *him*.

Finally she arranges Methwold's flowers. Chrysanthemums, a dull, dusty pink. The colour of municipal funerals.

Deringland must be taking mysterious deaths in its stride, for hardly have Sheepwool and Fitch put down their coats and bags and fired up the coffee percolator the next morning than they get a call. Fitch takes it: Sheepwool, looking across the room, notices a new poise in her junior colleague.

"Ma'am? That was Jim Levy. He says that if we're not 'too busy'"—she smiles as she says this, but the smile signs experience rather than levity—"then we should meet him in a couple of hours. 'Something to our advantage', he said."

"Very good, Fitch. Where? The Haddock?" Sheepwool remembers the discomfort of meeting Levy in the cramped and inhospitable Station, and earnestly desires somewhere else for their conference.

"No: somewhere else. Have you ever been to the Barking Lobster?"

The Barking Lobster is tucked away in a tiny mews in the centre of Deringland. Although a matter of yards from the seafront, its seclusion borders on the secretive. The pub does not open on the street, but is found at the blind end of a maze of dirty, bin-strewn back alleys which one is always surprised to learn are public thoroughfares. Girt all round by fisherman's cottages — some derelict, a few restored by incomers to a state of embalmed kitsch they never enjoyed in real life, so to speak — the tiny door to the public bar gives on to a cobbled lane so narrow that it is impossible to get the measure of the building from the outside, by virtue of one's inability to step far enough away from it to look at all of it at once. For the Barking Lobster is, as it happens, fairly extensive, burrowing from its deceptively simple ground-floor bar to occupy several rooms upstairs and in adjoining cottages. The resulting warren of half-shadowed nooks and snugs would be attractive to a predictable clientèle, Sheepwool thinks, wondering why, as a police officer, she has never heard of it before.

She stoops to pass through the street door, unmarked save for the unconventionally adulterated licensing sign on the eye-level lintel:

> Gerard Franklin de Nerval, licenced to sell intoxicating liquors for consumption on or off the premises or wherever you bloody well like.

The interior is as black as the inside of a poacher's pocket, and even after a minute or so, Sheepwool can discern very little amid the gloom. She hears Jim Levy's voice as if it is jarringly, intimately close, for all that she cannot see him:

"Ah! Here you are! An odd choice, I know, but the beer is better than the Haddock".

Sheepwool is not really conscious how, but in a moment they are seated in a small upstairs room, big enough only for three worn armchairs, a small dark-wood table; peeling, scabrous paint the colour of bile, and a print of marine life which cannot be clearly seen in the weak light offered by a small, low-silled window looking over a courtyard full of barrels and refuse. From the little she can see of the picture — just a small corner, really — Sheepwool is grateful for not being able to see any more, Max Ernst notwithstanding. Three pints of bitter ("no half measures here, Inspector, and whatever you do, don't ask for a spritzer!" Levy had cautioned) are on the table to greet them.

Sheepwool cannot remember having seen a barman, nor indeed of Levy having placed an order. Such are the perks of being a regular, she imagines. But the beer is every bit as good as Levy promises.

Levy sits closest to the window: later, Sheepwool wonders if she had imagined it, but at the time she was convinced that the pathologist stole a glance through its grimy panes before speaking. Just to be sure. He turned to the two women, conspiratorially: "To business." The subsequent pause falls between them like a shroud. Fitch is first to catch its falling corner.

"Doctor Levy ...?"

Sheepwool sits back and says nothing, content to let her Detective Sergeant take the lead. Slightly irritated with herself, her mind is full of a kind of non-specific yearning, punctuated by the image of dusty pink chrysanthemums, multiplied and rotating as if in a child's kaleidoscope.

"Well, it's like this. The SOCOs got to the beach beneath the cliffs as soon as they could—much later and the tide would have swept everything away. They had to bring the body to the morgue in Norwich. So, naturally, they called me." Levy pauses to draw on his pint. Sheepwool weighs the balance between theatricality and thirst, and chooses the former. Levy wipes his mouth with the worn cuff of his tweed jacket.

"When I say 'fell', that's exactly what I mean. The injuries— compound fractures of both legs, mainly—are consistent with a fall from a great height. Franks lived in a room on the fourth floor of the Institute, which has a sea view, you might say. It could hardly be closer—that's where the building stands directly on top of the cliffs. Leans over them, really—if you knew that beach you'd say there was an overhang. You can even see parts of the foundations poking through. Really, they should close the place down—certainly, that stretch of beach should be off limits—the Institute is only a storm away from toppling. But then, that's just my opinion."

Not just yours, Sheepwool thinks to herself, remembering Morrison's own candid analysis of his dilemma as Director.

"But I digress. Franks' window was hanging open, and from there she'd have a clear drop to the beach of eighty, maybe ninety meters."

Fitch leans forward to echo the pathologist's pose. "But did she jump? Or was she pushed?"

"Was it *suicide*, Detective Sergeant? That's really your business. But

I think I can say that she *didn't* die from a fall. Neither was she pushed. But were *I* pushed, I'd say she was *driven* to jump. She could even have been dead before she hit the ground."

Another pause for effect. The sun peeps between the clouds and sends a timid shaft through the window, illuminating Levy, and nothing else except for a faint blonde halo around Fitch's crown. Sheepwool smiles to herself — this man has missed his métier. There must be an Am-Dram group, somewhere in Norfolk, desperately short of a pantomime villain. Sheepwool is content to rest in the shadows.

"When I got to the morgue, I had a kind of sneak preview. A biopsy."

"Were you...?"

"Allowed? Probably not, strictly. But — now, you didn't hear it from me — well, you know, Higher Authorities. After the Bland case. Basically, we have to get on with it. Not to beat around the bush, but Franks' insides are a mess. Just like Bland's were. Some kind of massive reaction resulting in the total liquefaction of the body cavity. I reckon Franks felt it coming and pitched herself through the window to... er ... ease her passing."

The sun goes in again and the room is plunged into dusk, as if the light were suddenly sucked out of it. This time both Sheepwool and Fitch sample their beers. Fitch looks up immediately, with a sour face: Sheepwool finds she rather likes the taste. It has an astringency she finds appealing. "Yes, Doctor Levy," she says, "you're right. This beer *is* good. What's it called?"

"We're lucky. It's a guest beer they get in just now and again. It's called 'Merry Mermaid'. Watch it — it's stronger than you think! And before you ask, Detective Sergeant, yes, I think that the two deaths are linked. The pathologies, the symptoms. Too much to be a coincidence. I'd say the same in court. Here's to 'Merry Mermaid'. Cheers." Levy raises his glass.

"And that's why I was able to get in so quickly. One baffling death is just that — a one-off. But two? Well, I've taken some samples to send to the various laboratories, but frankly, they've still to get over being foxed by Bland."

"I suppose the Coroner ..." Fitch starts, uncertainly, her resolve wavering.

"'Natural causes'. You're dead right, Detective Sergeant. But we know that there's a great world of nature out there, most of it unknown, some extremely dangerous, and a lot of it crammed into the Institute. Just imagine if it all fell into the sea—it hardly bears thinking about."

"So if it's not murder…"

"Most unlikely, Detective Sergeant. But it's no fluke either. There's something in that Institute that's got loose and poisoning the people who work there. We'll probably never know what it is. By the time we've sampled and tested everything that place contains, we'd be buried up to *here* in corpses." He waves his hands above his head, to indicate total immersion. "Well, you already know *my* opinion on the Institute. It's got to be shut down. Now. Not that anyone would ever do so, on this evidence—it's just too strange."

Not for the first time, Sheepwool feels that the coast of Norfolk really does stand at the very lip of the abyss.

"Anyway, drink up. I've got to get back to Norwich. I wish you well in this case, I really do. If you need me, you know where to find me." Levy drains his glass in a final, luxurious draught, and gets up to leave. Sheepwool and Fitch, their beers half drunk, start to follow, but Levy waves them down. "No, don't get up. Enjoy the Merry Mermaid. While you can. She really can't be hurried!"

Framed by the doorway, he turns abruptly. "Oh yes—silly me!—I almost forgot. When I took a biopsy, I took a cheek swab, for routine identification purposes. DNA database—you know the score. Didn't take me long to run up a karyotype. And, well, the plot thickens."

Sheepwool reckons Levy is good for at least three curtain calls. The pathologist turns and resumes his seat—another ray of sunshine joins him, this time illuminating the rags of foam as they slither slowly down the inside of his empty glass.

"Did you know that Heather Franks is a genetic male?"

Fitch sits up, the fleeting passage of shock across her face replaced with hard realization, eyes bright, jaw set in the triumph of certainty.

"I *knew* it. You only had to look at her feet. *His* feet, I mean." She giggles. Sheepwool laughs, too, and so does Levy. He decides to stay for another pint. And so they remain, while the sun circles, dancing on the edge of the unknown.

3: The Scarlet in Her Mind

This time Sheepwool and Fitch take no chances. They interview everyone they can think of, as soon as possible ... and get nowhere. Fitch digs once more into the Morrisonian hinterland, and is often on the phone until well past her usual clocking-off time. Every time she delves into the inquiry that saw Morrison dismissed from his earlier scientific post, she hits a dead end. She desperately wants to interview those whose evidence damned him—but their identities are buried behind a wall of anonymity which not even the Police can shift.

As for Franks, everyone has a cast-iron alibi, even Morrison, who was at a MagusPharm-sponsored seminar at the University of East Anglia when Franks fell. Alex, ever a prime suspect, convinces Sheepwool and Fitch that the first she saw of Franks' body was when Valentina had shown it to her, on the beach, just after midnight. Valentina herself provides corroboration.

Heather Franks' room—just down the hall from Alex's garret—has been combed, to no avail. No suicide note. Not even (as they had half-expected) deranged letters to Bland, unsent. And definitely nothing to implicate Franks in Bland's death.

All that they are able to discover is that the person who had achieved a first degree under the name of Harold Franks had, by the time of gaining a doctorate, changed his gender completely and convincingly. All (as Fitch loves to recall) except for his feet.

The inquest is even swifter than that for Bland, but comes to the same conclusion.

The case is once more wound up, and this hits Sheepwool with some force the very next day, when she arrives at the Station, full of energy and expectation of a full day's work, and—just in the act of hanging up her coat on the back of the door—realizes that she has,

219

once more, nothing to do. It catches her, freezing her in a kind of self-made tableau. That restless unease, that depression, that …void.

No, Percy, she says to herself—you cannot go there, you cannot even look at it. You must find something else to do instead.

At that moment she decides that the long-postponed chat with Alex Beach should be postponed no longer, but as she turns to reach for her coat, she sees it, out of the corner of an eye.

A flash of blue.

She turns to look at it directly, but it has gone.

"You're lucky to have caught me, Inspector", says Alex Beach, hardly turning from the bench as Sheepwool enters, face focussed fully on her task.

To Sheepwool, Alex seems to be depositing tiny but precisely measured quantities of a clear liquid into a honeycomb stack of very tiny plastic vials, using what looks like an oversized syringe. She could, for all the world, be an ichneumon injecting her own eggs into the pupae of some larger and less fortunate insect. Only now does Sheepwool notice that the lab seems much busier, fuller, than it had been the last time she called. Benches crammed with shining equipment are surmounted by racks to which all kinds of tubes are pinioned, with shelves above bustling with white plastic jars with big green lids. It looks like a color negative of a hotel kitchen.

Task completed, Alex turns, and Sheepwool notices the change in her. No more the slightly distracted ingénue—now the fully fledged scientist, big blue-gray eyes shining with new confidence in the cream-white face.

First Fitch, now Alex Beach.

These young women are growing up. Taking over. Soon be time for the slippers-and-pipe routine, Sheepwool reflects. But what would she do *then*, to keep the demons at bay?

"I was just clocking off", Alex says, and in response to Sheepwool's raised eyebrow: "I usually do the night shift. Fancy some fresh air?"

Rather than take the long switchback through the woods and down to the beach (Alex confesses that since the Franks business, she's rather gone off it) the women leave the Institute, cross the car park and take a level path directly to the rim of the cliffs. There, in the lee of a large bank of gorse bushes, is a wooden municipal bench. This has been fastened securely to a monumental slab of concrete, and decorated with a brass plate reading 'To the Memory of Ralph Willoughby'. No dates are given. As they sit down, Alex says that she always wonders who Ralph Willoughby might have been, that his heirs should dedicate a bench to him in this lonely place (for all that the view over the sea ahead, and the town to their left—the west - is spectacular).

Now that they are here, now that Sheepwool has Alex all to herself, she wonders where to start. It had been hard enough trying to explain her intuitions to Fitch. That the death of Bland was not a murder—how could it have been, given the symptoms?—but must have had some direct connection with the sea. Something unknown, but equally, something with which the Institute was familiar. Indeed, something for which the Institute was well-known, and in which its founder took pride.

Something which rose to the surface of her mind, something last heard bathed in Gerry Rammell's honey-voiced chatter. He was so convinced that the liquor at the Dazed Haddock had been spiked, he said, that he was sure he couldn't account for where it all came from. For all he knew, he said, he'd not be surprised if someone had been skimming the preserving fluid from Pickled Lily!

She had tried to explain it all to Fitch, several times, but the words seemed to clog up in her throat: she seemed half ashamed of it, as if she were admitting some secret vice, pleading, trying to seek the approval of one's subordinate. Fitch was plainly discomfited by this unaccustomed note of—what was it? supplication?—in Sheepwool's voice. That flash of blue kept on teasing, laughing at her.

Sometimes, Sheepwool thinks, you go through life completely blind to some feature of environmental furniture so common that your senses tune it out, until the moment when the subject comes up, and, sensitized, you see it everywhere—billboards, newspapers, T-shirts, the shapes of clouds. You hear snatches of conversation—on the radio, in the street, at work - in which the very subject just happens to be mentioned.

The other night, for instance, she found herself at home and sufficiently bored to have switched on her television set. When the picture swam into view, she realized it was a commercial for a car, in which the shining vehicle was plunging in and out of waves accompanied by mermaids. She'd switched off before the commercial had finished.

The very next day, in town, she had passed a shop displaying sea-side wares for those tourists robust enough to brave Deringland's late-spring weather. Buckets and spades, blue or red, with images of mermaids picked out in cheap gold paint. And then there was Jim Levy's favourite drop — Merry Mermaid. It was all too much.

But then there was Franks.

At this point Sheepwool looks up, tunes herself back into the world, sees the rim of the cliffs just a few feet ahead of her, startles, and then realizes that Alex Beach has taken the problem away, for she is already far ahead in what seems like a ceaseless monologue, of ti-tres and aliquots, of plates and gels, things called 'gilsons' and 'micro-arrays', and other technical impedimenta of science.

"…isn't that strange, Inspector?" she concludes.

"Strange? I'm sorry, Alex … what is?" Alex turns round and smiles in a way that Sheepwool can only interpret as indulgence. She notices that Alex's face glows even more warmly out here, in the open air. Perhaps it is only the freshening wind, but Alex's cheeks seem fuller, pinker, than they had before.

"What you've said. That Heather Franks was really a genetic male."

"Yes, Alex. It is. Strange. But what …?"

"Don't you see, Inspector? It all fits, now."

"It does?"

"Yes …. Well, it's only my wild theory, anyway. That all the deaths — everything that's happened — happened to genetic males, and…"

"*All* the deaths? I was aware of just two, Alex. First, Bland, and now Franks. Are you telling me that there have been more? More - that we've missed?"

Alex first looks confused, then slightly — what was it? Affronted? — and then sighs. That indulgent smile again — Sheepwool is beginning to think she's back in nursery school, with a fresh young teacher not as yet disabused of that lets-all-be-bunnies voice reserved for the most diffident toddlers. But Sheepwool soon has cause to forgive Alex, for what she then reveals is interesting.

Very interesting indeed.

About the *Spaniel*, the ship during whose research voyage Alex's specimens — carnostomids — had been collected, and in which several sailors died from a mysterious contagion whose symptoms looked very like those described by Jim Levy.

And even more interesting (if even more difficult to corroborate), the wild tale of Obed Marsh and the mermaid, after whose killing — murder - the sailors seemed to start dying in much the same way.

Mermaids and cars. Mermaids on seaside buckets. Merry mermaids. Merry, murderous mermaids.

Sheepwool tries to keep it all in focus.

"Don't you see, Inspector? All the people who died were men. This is a kind of illness that affects men only. Sure, all the sailors were men, but there are accounts of women, too — especially in the Obed Marsh story — but there is no mention of their ever getting any disease. Not even the ... um ... prostitutes in the various ports, and..."

"Mermaids," says Sheepwool, interrupting.

"The ... what?" Alex replies, and the sickly smile is instantly replaced by a species of hardness, eyes glinting. Sheepwool senses that she has hit the spot, as wild and as unlikely as it seems. Alex flusters, then, and backtracks.

"Of course, it's only a silly idea. This link between the Spaniel, and Obed Marsh's story — completely over-the-top — and the deaths of Dr Bland and Dr Franks..."

"Did you know her? Heather Franks?"

"No — not very well. She seemed very wound-up. She was clearly in love with Dr Bland. Perhaps her death could have been suicide, if it hadn't been for..."

"But it wasn't suicide, was it, Alex? She was poisoned — infected — with these things, these ... carnostomids. How do you think that might have happened?"

"Well, I suppose she must have drunk some. But I can't imagine how she could have got hold of them, except from the preserved specimens in the *Spaniel* collection that Morrison and I have been working on. But, you know, in the Obed Marsh account, they talk of the mermaid being preserved in rum, and the sailors, maybe, drinking from her barrel, and ... Oh my goodness, Inspector." Alex flushes. Her eyes widen.

"You know, Inspector, what Obed Marsh called the mermaid? She had a name, you know, it was ... the same as the label ... Surely, it can't be?"

"Morrison?"

Alex looks puzzled, aghast. "Morrison? No, the mermaid was called ..."

"No, Alex, you mentioned that you had been working on the specimens—the carnostomids—with Dr Morrison. Really, I had no idea. I wonder if you'd like to tell me all about it? Perhaps we can walk into town together. To the Police Station. Or I could ask Detective Sergeant Fitch to bring the car round."

Alex directs a brazen stare at Sheepwool. At first, Sheepwool reads it as a look of frankly incomprehending incredulity. But Sheepwool has given up trying to read the many faces of this young woman in whom, she feels, external expressions have become ever more divorced from internal motivation.

Miss Rebecca Lowdley-Purslane has done her best to cover her tracks. Taking as little as possible, and leaving her room at the dead of night during a New Moon, she swirls a travelling cloak around her, gathers up a bag of only those belongings from which she cannot bear to be parted, and picks her way along the cliff-top track which leads, by slow degrees, down to Deringland. There is almost no light, and she can hardly even see her own feet as she makes her careful way along the path. But she knows this path well, and steers herself by sound, for the sea is up, and the crash of the surf on her right seems at first to come from almost directly beneath her feet—and as the path weaves westward, it descends slowly to sea level until she is on the beach beneath the cliffs that lie below Deringland church and its skirted burial ground.

The building now looms beside her, to the left, a patch of deeper shade against the night. Beside the church is the steep, cobbled gangway for the crowded fishing boats. Their shadowed shapes are large and threatening, and the smell that emanates from them—of rotting fish, and the sweat and toil and death of men - is all the more intense in the absence of light. Past the boats and landward, the gangway leads upwards through the small, sleeping town, to an Inn—the Dazy Haddock, she believes it's called, where, at daybreak, she will be able to board a mail-coach to Norwich. After that, she has a vague plan to seek refuge among her mother's relatives in London—she has an address in Bedford-Square—where she will tell all. Of her humiliation. Of her ... shame.

If she can bear even to speak of it.

She settles down in a nook behind some barrels just outside the door of the inn. The cubbyhole is damp, and smells of rot and stale beer, but it will be daylight soon enough: she spends some time reflecting that a person such as herself would never have entertained the thought of crouching in such squalor, in such circumstances, but recent events have accustomed her to such degradation. She is appalled that she might have become hardened to it.

The revelation sends a chill through her body, cold and stiff as it is, but it is followed by a more concrete sensation. Of hard hands, and lifting arms, and a rough rag placed across her face. The rag smells of tobacco and brandy and something sweet she doesn't recognize, and she knows no more, until a sharp blow across her face brings the world into view once again.

Sickeningly so, for as she wakes and looks round, her face, indeed her whole head, is pounding with an agonizing throb, her throat shrieking with the pain of razors, she finds that there is, after all, no escape. She is chained to the wall, spread-eagled, as she so often is, in her father's private rooms.

She looks down. She discerns that her body is slick with blood. She has the impression that she is bleeding from her nose, her throat, and possibly her eyes or her scalp, for she blinks often, and it is through a reddish haze. She cannot wipe away the blood, for her hands are manacled, splayed above her, as are her legs below. She does not need to inquire further whether she is clothed, because she knows, from long experience, that she is not: and that the shape moving — pacing — before her, is her father, and behind him are mounds of the remains of animals, birds, fishes, and people, either whole or disarticulated or in various stages of unnatural reunion.

One corpse, in particular, draws her imperfect gaze, partly because it is set directly in front of her, propped up, as if deliberately placed there for her inspection. It is of a large fish, or, at least, it has the tail of a fish, attached to the torso of a small, wizened woman — or, she assumes as much — with sunken eye sockets, lank hair, skin blackened with decay, and the grinning, sharp-toothed gape of death. Her father halts before her, blotting out the apparition.

"Needs some improvement, what? 'Pickled Lily' she was called! But that rogue Marsh sold me a pup. A real mermaid, indeed! How could I have been so foolish? Not worth the sovereigns I paid that dotard Casares to collect. Hardly worth even throwing away."

Rebecca whimpers as if in answer, but she finds her tongue doesn't work properly, as if it is too small, just a stub of its full extent. Her mouth, too, is full of blood, as if several of her teeth had been knocked out. Instead of saying anything remotely coherent, she lets slip a slaver of bloody drool.

"Nothing to say, eh, Rebecca? That is just as well, for we cannot have you telling people of our little soirées down here, can we? Our little gatherings? And what would we do, Rebecca, my friends and I, without your satisfying entertainment? What would we *do*? Wonderful satisfying, it is, *wonderful* satisfying! In fact, my guests remark that you always give such *perfect* satisfaction. But you cannot tell it, Rebecca—upon my word, you cannot! Which is why I have had to perform a little surgery. On your tongue."

He waves a hank of crimson flesh before her, fresh blood running over his fingers, and then flings it into the general melée of crimsoned refuse behind him.

Rebecca feels faint, as if the room is beginning to slide about. Or perhaps it is she herself. She is not sure.

"And you did not feel it? Good! I have now perfected a technique for rendering a subject insensible during the most egregious of procedures. A chemical technique. And you, my dear, have been the first human subject. I offer my congratulations!" Sir Frideric comes closer, leers, touches a fat finger to a bloodshot, bulging nose. He whispers in her face—the stench of brandy is overpowering.

"Cuts down the *screaming*, don't you know! And that's something my guests just can't abide. Upon my word, they cannot! So while I had you to myself, as it were, I extracted as much as I could of your larynx, too. A very delicate operation, if I say so myself. Didn't want to occlude your windpipe. I wanted you still to be able to breathe, what! After all, my dear, you have to be *alive*, even for just a *little* longer. While we say our goodbyes."

Rebecca closes her eyes. She knows what is going to happen next, and, indeed, subsequent events follow the weary path with miserable familiarity. The rip of her father's breeches. The lurch of her father's body against her own, the sound of his porcine grunts, the stench of his breath -- a testament to many well-fortified meals—until the scarlet in her mind fades slowly to black, and all other sensation gone, she hears him, as if from a great distance: "you were always such a good little girl, Rebecca—such a *good* little girl."

Her last sensation on Earth is the sound of her father breaking down in great, wrack-lunged sobs, as he screams her name—"Rebecca!"

4: Stranded On The Shore

Garrison Williams puts another coin in the juke and selects 'Hotel California'. Something is not right, tonight. Something has disturbed the routine he has so carefully cultivated. A routine which he feels he needs, since Bev died, to keep pointing full ahead, in case he turns and sees that tiny but malevolent shadow, that silhouette, ever on the far horizon, in case it is far closer than he's feared, and it will consume him.

Well, actually, two things.

The first is that he hasn't seen Alex lately. Not that she works in his lab much any more, not now The Dwarf has tricked it out like a proper laboratory. Or more like a lab in an RKO picture. Heck, she even has an Igor to fetch the bodies. But it's sad—he misses her company more than he thought he would. Or, more to the point, more than he feels he can afford. The many facets of Alex Beach taunt him, parading across his mind's eye, across the unsupped bottle of German lager and the untouched packet of Reds on the bar.

The strange way she has of bringing up a topic kind of halfway through, as if you'd missed the beginning, but hadn't really, and he has to ask her to backtrack, and they always end up laughing. And her laugh, and the way her pale cheeks curve and fill and dimple when she laughs, and the way she cocks her head to one side after laughing, and the way she gets up off a lab stool, jeans hanging low; bending over; the way her hips sway as she crosses a room, the way … oh, hell, he thinks, he could go on and on like this, and probably will.

Or would, but for the other thing. And that's more urgent.

For there is a craving deeper, older, and even more ritualized than his private fantasies about Alex Beach.

Garrison Williams is Waiting for the Man.

God, he's tried to kick it, like he kicked acid in the sixties, and horse in the eighties. But this is a habit too hard to break. So now, he gives in. He knows that he only need the flimsiest excuse to advance as justification. His is the fact that Bev has gone. Bev, who used to check him over, police him, confront him with suspicious little packets of white dust (or brown dust, or black dust, whatever)—and forgive him.

Bev, who used to keep him on the level.

Bev, who would find him, in whatever goddamned awful state, at whatever hour, clean him up, bail him out, and cradle his head to her breast like the baby he knows he is, and tell him everything was gonna be OK. Bev, whom he brings to mind every time Alex Beach laughs. How he misses her now. She was the safety net that no longer exists, just when he needs it most. Just when he's fallen in love with the big one.

Surfer's Delight. Splash. Smash. The 'T' You Can Really Taste.

TubeWave.

Oh yes, Garrison Williams is Waiting for the Man, all right. What concerns him—he'd go far as to say that he is now worried -- is that the Man in question is late. And this is the one appointment that the Man, unreliable in so many other ways, never misses. Not ever.

Except today.

The name of this man? Every town has one like him—part-time barman, part-time janitor, full-time backdoor-man, rogue, fence, pimp, smuggler, money-launderer, unacknowledged father of indeterminately many rat-faced urchins, burglar, beggar-man, thief—and pusher. Oh yes, you can find one in every town, if you look under enough rocks. This one is called Bob Honeypott.

Garrison breaks the seal on the Reds, tips one out, and lights up. His right hand shakes, holding the lighter. He tries to ignore the tremor.

"Sir?"

"Sheepwool. No, please, come in. Sit down. What's on your mind? Gerry Rammell again?"

"No, Sir, it's—well, I apologise for raising the issue again, but ..."

"The deaths at the Institute. I think that case is closed. Has to be."

"Of course, Sir. But one or two other things have since come to light. Irrespective of the status of the case—and I agree with you completely, Sir—I felt you should be kept informed."

You, of all people.

The dark-framed spectacles look up at her then, the eyes within imploring her to say more, but at the same time helpless before the wave, dreading it.

"Go on."

"Sir, as you know, I have had a long, on-the-record interview with Alex Beach."

"Thank you, Sheepwool. I have seen the transcript."

"Good, Sir, I am glad. From that interview you will see that Beach and Morrison have been working closely on these agents—these ... er ... 'carnostomids'—which we now think are strongly implicated in the deaths of both Bland and Franks."

"I see..."

"In my opinion, Sir, we should seek an interview with Dr Morrison. A formal interview. For the record. As corroboration, if nothing else."

"On what pretext, Sheepwool, would we do that? We can't just barge in and ... well, like you did with Alex Beach. A bit close to the wind, that..."

"Sir, there is the matter of Morrison's alibi—or non-alibi—concerning Bland's death. And the fact—or, at least, strong supposition—that it was Heather Franks who blew his cover ..."

"And that she was the next to go. From the same supposedly 'natural' causes."

"Yes, Sir. These natural causes being related to the ... er ... specimens that both Beach and Morrison were working on. To which they alone had regular access."

A pause.

"Sheepwool, have you actually charged Dr Beach with anything? Conspiracy? Accessory? Jaywalking? Anything at all?"

"No, Sir." Sheepwool is alerted to the unwonted note of sarcasm in the voice of her superior. She will lose this battle, she knows. But she may yet win the war. If she can put it so baldly.

"Well, then, in this case I think you should just let this one go, too."

Throw it back into the sea, where it belongs. Where some things are best left. Those loose ends again. For the sake of one's own sanity.

Silence. She hopes that it cannot be read as impudence.

"There's another way to read this, Sheepwool. May I? You could put it this way: Morrison's research is entirely legal, but it's proprietary."

Secrets. Secrets of the sea.

"So, he's funded by this company—MagusPharm, is it?—And, as far as we can see, he's brought in Alex Beach on the same ticket, to work on the same things—no, please, Sheepwool, let me go on with this for a minute -- goodness knows what mileage there might be in specimens from the Institute, but there you go, that's their business, surely?

"And we know, or at least can guess, from what the redoubtable Fitch has discovered—she's doing rather well, by the way, sewed up that Thetford Kebab-Shop Knifing nicely—that Morrison has had a shady past. Shouldn't be allowed near a lab again, after something nasty crept out from his particular woodshed, and so forth. Did Dr Beach say anything about that?"

"Well, Sir, yes and no. When she first raised the subject, she said quite clearly that she and Morrison were both working on these specimens. But on the record, she backtracked, and said that he had sent material to another MagusPharm laboratory, as far as she knew, and at first without her knowledge. As a blind test, she explained, independent corroboration for her own work."

That wasn't to say that Morrison wasn't working on them himself, but if he were, there was not, as far as she could make out, any evidence of his physical presence at the bench, so to speak. Perhaps he was simply nothing more than he seemed—an overseer, handling the funds, the admin. But she kicks herself, now, that she let that particular loose end hang free. As Methwold does so now, continuing:

"So here he is, at the LPI, and bodies start to fall. And he lies about his whereabouts…"

"Precisely my point, Sir…"

"Well, my guess would be that he's embarrassed to tell all, in case he might be falsely implicated. So what if he lied about his background to the Institute before they appointed him? We all have skeletons in our pasts. *All* of us. Some we'd rather not have dragged out at every opportunity." Sheepwool wonders if she is imagining it, but she has the distinct impression that Methwold's eyes have become rounder, darker. Deeper.

"All that does is make him a liar, not a murderer. No wonder he went into marketing. Best place for him. He can lie for a living."

"Yes, Sir."

"So, as I say…"

And Sheepwool sees it once again, in Methwold's eyes. She's sure of it — that in his evasion, in his denial, Methwold is trying to tell her something. Finally, she sees the whole thing in full, the grand panorama.

The car, screeching in from the right.

The loyal wife of decades whose head is turned finally, fatally, seawards.

She looks at him more closely, solicitously, and he responds, with a faint smile.

"… Yes, Sir. Perhaps some fish should be thrown back into the sea. Where they belong, Sir."

"Thank you, Percy. I knew you'd understand."

The door closes behind her and she backs into it, panting, submerged in a tide of emotion which at first she struggles to rationalize, until, finally, she finds the appropriate category for this sensation, and it is this — *relief*. Methwold has it all worked out. Some things must be thrown back into the sea. *Must* be.

Else you'd go mad.

Thrown into the great, encircling, forgiving sea, that raging yet silent keeper of all the secrets of the world. Sometimes the sea has a habit of disgorging its secrets, and sometimes these recycled memories are distended, distorted, fragmentary. But that is the sea's way of reminding those of us, stranded on the shore like gulls, keening, that although we must find some accommodation with those who are lost, we should not forget these memories entirely, discard them, turn away.

As every mariner knows, you turn your back on the sea at your peril.

But for now, Persephone Sheepwool has the distinct sensation of shackles having been unloosed, of lightness unaccustomed, of floating. She returns to her own office with a spring in her step.

Janice Squearn catches herself in the act of tidying up for the day. She has been doing a lot of this lately — watching herself, that is, like she is her own subject in a time-and-motion study.

Perhaps it is because she is close to retirement, and feels less and less attached to the Institute, this place that she both loves and loathes. Perhaps it is because Bland is dead, and this is simply her way of reacting to it. Detachment, she's read in a magazine, can be a symptom of shock.

A reaction, perhaps, to bereavement.

Or perhaps—now, this *is* a new thought—she is in fact standing still, but the Institute is finally on the move, slipping away.

She gathers her bag to leave. She wonders how many days she will do this before it is the very last time.

She usually meets Frankie in the car park and Frankie drives home. But this time she starts, because Frankie is right there, standing outside her office. Frankie looks disturbed, troubled, her hands clenched together.

"Frankie...?"

Janice has become adept at reading Frankie's expressions. This is just as well, because Francesca Honiton, the Institute's housekeeper, is mute, the result of a cancer in her youth that had robbed her of her tongue, and later, in some weird metastasis, of much of her larynx. She seems to have recovered completely, though she has to be very careful how she eats. Frankie is as fastidious as a crab: she has told Janice that she would do anything—*anything*—not to have to be fed through a tube again. She has nightmares about Hickman lines, she says -- about choking to death, as if she'd been hooked like a fish. Janice knows and cherishes every one of the ridges and scars that run down Frankie's throat. They are like the battle-plans of a desperate war fought now long ago, but not yet forgotten, and which nevertheless remain intensely private. No wonder Frankie prefers these otherwise affected, high-throated Victorian gowns.

Now Frankie unclenches her hands, pinking knuckles whitened by tension, and beckons Janice to follow her. Janice is infected by her excitement.

Frankie sails before her, rushed, animated, through the darkened public gallery and into Dr Bland's office. As she corrects herself— really, it's Dr Morrison's office now, isn't it?—she wonders how Frankie can just barge in, unannounced. But Dr Morrison must have gone home.

But Frankie is, after all, the housekeeper, and has licence to go anywhere in the Institute she wants, whenever she likes. And it's not as if she is likely to go telling tales. Not really. Janice wonders why it is only now, after all these years, it had dawned on her just how many secrets must lie hoarded in Frankie's mind. For Frankie has been at the Institute longer than she has, and must have seen ... well, all kinds of things.

Frankie moves behind the big, blond-wood desk and moves her small, lithe fingers over a wall panel, and, suddenly, the panel clicks aside, and she beckons Janice through into a kind of bathroom.

Why?

There's more, says Frankie's anxious face, her hands, sharply gesticulating; the tense heave of her hunched shoulders.

She says: follow.

Janice follows — implausibly, through the back of a closet (tailored suits in ranks, towels, a smell of cologne); a dark corridor hung with a tapestry which, after a first glance, Janice thinks she'd rather not look at again; past what looks like a stuffed bear (though bears don't have paws — *hands* — like that, do they?); and into a bright space, a laboratory, arrayed with benches and shelves and machinery, humming.

Janice had no idea that Dr Morrison has a private laboratory.

Neither, it seems, had Frankie. And Frankie is the one who knows — who *should* know — everything. Frankie stands before the banks of polished chrome, the orderly lines of pipettes, of plates, of equipment, and her expression is a study in anxious incredulity. Without having to say anything, without having to be told, Janice Squearn knows that her next telephone call must be to her favourite former pupil, the bright-eyed girl she had so rudely abandoned, once, long ago.

And then they both look up. All thoughts of contacting Elaine Fitch are driven out by a crash of glass, a thump, a strangled, echoing yell, back towards the public gallery. The brooding darkness of the Museum is broken. She and Frankie turn as one, and retrace their steps.

Through the lab, the corridor, the closet, the bathroom, the office, Janice's mind replays — she amazes herself — a nursery rhyme. About the King's Horses and the King's Men, and how Humpty Dumpty might not, now, be put together again. It is the Institute, then, that is slipping away, not her.

It occurs to Janice, then, that she has made a grave mistake about how she has viewed her own life, the guilty, downtrodden refugee. But no, her life has not been a constant tale of flight from one squalid event to another, she sees it now. She has instead been the centre, and the world really has revolved around her. For the first time in her life she feels … she cannot find a word for it, until she thinks of a word that Frankie is fond of. That's it — she feels 'empowered'.

Sheepwool is on the scene as cloudy night closes in about the Institute. Fitch arrives late, a scramble of bag and raincoat, breathless from a long but (Sheepwool assumes) speedy drive from Thetford. Her heels click urgently across the parquet towards the floodlit centre of the public gallery, a mess of broken glass and splintered wood and a lake of sharp-smelling fluid, darkening the floor's herringboned, hardwood staves.

"Ma'am, sorry I'm late, it was … oh heavens, just look at it — at that — it's…"

At the centre of the lake is a body, eyes round and red-rimmed, mouth open, exuding a single, thin, viscous line of pinkish spittle. The SOCOs cluster busily round, and in the pool of light, the general effect is like nothing so much as a painting by Joseph Wright of Derby. See — the moon now peeps in through a seaward window, completing the illusion. Sheepwool smiles, but whether at this nice artistic touch, or Fitch's characteristic fluster, she is not sure.

"Fitch."

Sheepwool turns to look at the body. A man, grizzled, leer still on his face, belying the thousand-yard shock in his eyes; hands and face cut around with glass; clad in a brown warehouseman's coat soaked in the same fluid that drenches the floor; legs and arms and clothing now tangled amid the splinters of an ancient step-ladder which had broken under him as he struggled with what looks like the remains of a demijohn, the kind used for home brewing (according to one of the SOCOs); tottered, fell, and …

"Oh my!" exclaims Fitch, "It's Bob — Bob Honeypott!" Her hands rush to her face. "And, oh no, it can't be…"

No longer able to speak, she points, finger shaking, entangled with the remains of the janitor, in a final embrace, curled, distorted after more than a century in fluid suspension, is Pickled Lily.

Fitch now turns white, and totters. Perhaps it is nothing more than the headlong rush to the Museum from the other side of the county. Or perhaps it's nothing more than overwork. Whatever it is, Sheepwool reflexively reaches out to catch her colleague as she begins to fall. The weight is too great for one arm to bear, so Sheepwool wraps both arms around Fitch, who is trembling all over, the sparrow at bay.

"Fitch," she whispers, so only her colleague can hear, "let's leave the SOCOs to it. I think I need a drink."

"You and me both," replies Fitch, quavering, but regaining her composure almost as swiftly as losing it, disentangling herself from her superior's cradling hold, straightening herself up, dusting herself down. "The car's outside. And mine's a pint."

"Even on duty?" Sheepwool smiles again, indulgently.

"*Especially* on duty," Fitch retorts, turning away, heading purposefully for the darkened exit. Sheepwool can still hear a tremulous catch the younger woman's voice. It is very slight, for Fitch is plainly restraining her emotions by main force. Fitch is, after all, and increasingly, a professional.

But it is there.

Gosh! I've been busy. Fitch takes a long draw on her lager. *Busy.* Here, there, and everywhere. Thank God for Jason, bless him. She looks up, then, at Sheepwool, across the table.

"Well, Ma'am, now we know what Bob Honeypott has been up to. Siphoning off the preserving fluid … I *ask* you."

"Caught in the act."

"Just like Bob, though, isn't it? He'll never be able to make a statement now, will he? Always one step ahead of the game. Of all of us."

Neither woman laughs.

"Desperate times, Fitch. Rammell thinks that Bob knew we were on to him at last, so he couldn't be caught filching fresh supplies like he used to, so …"

"He had to have it … *used.* That's *disgusting.*"

"Yes."

"But what a way to … it was *horrible.*" Fitch takes another swig. She notices that Sheepwool's spritzer remains as yet unsampled. "Ma'am—do you think…?"

"Like Bland and Franks? Oh yes, definitely."

Fitch looks long and quizzically into the gray-blue eyes of her superior officer. Sheepwool seems more self-assured, somehow, more confident, more—well, peaceful, is how she'd put it. Like she'd found something. Or lost something, but found she no longer cared.

The Dazed Haddock's juke box, giving up on the Eagles, now grinds glutinously into another number, the slew of noise resolving into the nasal whine of John Lennon singing 'Imagine'. About how we'd feel if we rid ourselves of all possessions, of all cares. *Free.* That's how we'd feel. That's how Sheepwool looks. But she still hasn't touched her drink.

Sheepwool straightens up, as if about to give an announcement at a school prizegiving, and wondering what, precisely, she should say. The impression of calm contentment is removed as smartly as a conjuror's handkerchief, revealing that the brace of white doves he'd displayed with such extravagance but a moment before had, in fact, disappeared into thin air. "Fitch, I have an idea I'd like to try out on you."

Fitch is all attention. She has the impression that her superior has been trying to share some secret with her for weeks, but has never quite managed to explain it: as if it were outrageous, or silly, and she'd be afraid of embarrassing herself if she hadn't said it all exactly right. Fitch has not pressed the point, for she has seen it so often in herself. She knows what to say, but when it comes to it, she can never find the right words. And Sheepwool's discomfiture always reminded her of Jason's faltering attempts to ask her out, to propose to her … my goodness, she thinks, she hopes Sheepwool hasn't taken her silly grin of recollection as patronizing. So she composes herself, now, as Sheepwool continues, once again, on this uncertain voyage into hypothesis.

"We can agree, I think, that Bob Honeypott died, substantially, of the same thing that disposed of Dr Bland and Dr Franks, can we?"

"The same 'natural causes'? Well, I expect we'll need Jim — Dr Levy — to rule on that, and the coroner, but … well, sure, Bob seemed to have the same symptoms."

"Fine. Well, while you've been away, I've had a couple of long chats with Alex Beach." Sheepwool shifts nervously in her seat. "I've been meaning to tell you this — share some ideas — but the opportunity never seemed to arise, and, well…"

"Go on. Please." Fitch is now straight and serious, as if demanding — yearning for — an answer. So Sheepwool tells Fitch of Alex Beach's theory that both Bland and Franks were killed after ingesting specimens of these tiny sea creatures called carnostomids, and her other theory — more a conjecture, really, that in the wild, carnostomids grow up to become ...

"Mermaids? Ma'am — you can't be serious, can you? Surely..."

"Yes, Fitch. I think I am."

"But ..."

"Yes, Fitch — and please don't let this go any further, just now. I thought it was just a flight of fancy until now. Perhaps it still is. But, you know, there wasn't just Bob lying on the floor just now, was there? There was..."

"Pickled Lily." Fitch looks shocked. Electrified.

"Yes, Fitch, Pickled Lily. Ever since I first saw her, I've been intrigued by the label. You know, on the display case. It says that despite a lot of overblown mariner's tales about Pickled Lily's provenance as a mermaid, it — she - is probably the finest example of the taxidermic art of Sir Frideric Lowdley-Purslane."

"And...?"

"Well, if that's true, why did Sir Frideric never brag about it? Like he bragged about everything else?"

"And, if so — *especially* so — why did he forbid any examination of Pickled Lily to make sure, *even after his death*?"

Sheepwool sits back. She picks up her wine glass and takes her first sip. "Anyway, whatever Pickled Lily is, or was, it all fits", she says, putting the glass down once more. "Bob caught carnostomids from the preserving fluid. And that's that. And whatever else I might think, it exonerates Morrison. He's above suspicion." Somehow, thinks Fitch, Sheepwool's expression suggests that she does not really believe this, but has, in some way, compartmentalized it.

For she knows, as well as Sheepwool, that Morrison has done some terrible things in the past. It was she, after all — Fitch — who'd done the legwork, dragging out those old reports on Morrison's previous. That he should never be let loose in a scientific laboratory again. Not ever.

Problem was, all the evidence against him was given under the terms of anonymity. The perpetual penumbra of peer review. Result — Morrison gets away scot-free. Again.

The two women are lost, briefly, confined to their own thoughts. At this point they are joined by another: the sound of a manly exhalation tells them that Dr Garrison Williams has joined them at their table.

"Mind if I joined you, ladies? Freshen up your drinks?"

Sheepwool looks up, as if jolted from reverie.

"Dr Williams, no—please do", says Fitch. "Mine's a Grolsch, and the Inspector…?" Sheepwool puts her hand up as if to say that she can nurse this warming spritzer a little while longer. Williams is back at the table in less than two minutes, bottles in hand.

"I heard you talking about Bob…. Is he…?"

Fitch explains the situation. About how Bob fell from a ladder at the Institute and died. She spares him the details of the precise location. And what he was doing at the time. But Williams' face is a study in shock—he turns a dreadful, ghastly white.

"Dr Williams?" Fitch puts a calming hand on his arm.

"Goddamn. That's awful. He was a good friend to me. A good friend. When many others weren't. His poor mother …"

Sheepwool remembers the formidable figure at Bland's funeral. The detectives offer conventional condolences. But after taking a long swig of his beer, Williams appears to pull himself together, and, drawing closer to the women, offers what at first seems a very strange confession.

"Ladies—officers—I hope you don't mind, but there's been something I've been meaning to tell you. Something I should have said before, really, after Bland … died … but now Heather, and now poor Bob, well…"

"Please go on, Dr Williams." This from Sheepwool. Fitch is aware that Sheepwool's complete, patient stillness contrasts with what she thinks is a slight tremor in Dr Williams. When she touched his arm, she felt it jolt and shake.

"Sure. Yes. Right. It's all about Morrison. That's Dr Morrison, at the Institute, you know? How a panel of anonymous scientists recommended that he never be allowed to work in a lab again."

Fitch is astonished. "Dr Williams—how—you—how did you know?"

"Easy, Sergeant. I was one of those anonymous scientists."

5: Just On The Edge Of Sight

"We'll need an autopsy, Dr Morrison."

"On Honeypott? That's hardly up to *me*, Inspector, is it?" Morrison looks up at her, from behind the barricade of his desk. Funny, he thought La Dipshit had gone, perhaps as spectrally as she'd appeared, but no, there she still is, hanging over him like a dyspeptic vulture. He sits back, meets her gaze. He had not invited her to sit, imagining that this would earn him strategic points, but now wonders if this has been an error on his part—for she sees in the Inspector's eyes none of the slightly barmy distraction he'd gotten used to.

False sense of security, old boy. This time her eyes are pitiless points, like she knows precisely where to strike, and how hard.

Really, Morrison thinks to himself, he should watch his step. Engage brain before opening mouth. But, much against his better judgment, he feels himself—too often these days—seized with the desperation of someone who knows that they are reaching the end of the road. Alex may be pleasantly dickable (though he preferred it, somehow, when she had been oiled with the smell of fear -- terrific turn-on, that). But he's beginning to think that sex is *all* she is good for: she is getting absolutely nowhere with the carnostomids, not even with that expensive equipment and that technician he's hired for her. No, she just keeps gibbering on about DNA, like genomics ever solved anything, rather than cutting to the chase and using that hardware to isolate the immunogenic activity that he'd found, all on his own.

Stupid, stupid girl. Well, he admits to himself, ruefully, what did he expect from some bit of fluff he picked up in a hotel bar, hmm? Really, old man, you have to stop thinking with your tackle.

But he is forced to admit that *he's* got nowhere, either. At least he might get *somewhere*, more than Alex has, with some *help*, but he could hardly hire a technician for his *own* lab, now, could he? People would, after all, notice. But Alex has all the stuff, so he should at least give that dozy tart a thorough talking-to. Get her to sharpen up her act. If there's any time still left. She's been funny, though, lately, come to think of it. Keeps going off the boil, rushing off to give it the whole pavement-pizza performance.

Speaking to God on the Great White Telephone.

So the sex is going down the tubes, along with the research. Oh, well, screw *her*. Or not, as the case may be. There are other fish in the sea. Yes, what he needs is more people. More time. More resources. He has none of these things. He is cornered. So — what the hell? Might as well rush headlong for the old rat-meets-sinking-ship nexus with as much style as he can muster.

Go for it.

"Mr Honeypott's autopsy is all arranged, Dr Morrison," Sheepwool says. What? The scarecrow is still here? "I strongly suspect that he will be shown to have died from the same — whatever it was — that killed Dr Bland, and Dr Franks."

" 'The same *whatever-it-was*', Inspector? And what do you think that *whatever-it-was* might have been, hmm?" He shoots, he scores. His mimicry — perhaps stronger than he really means it - has the Inspector back on her heels.

"I think you know that better than I do, Dr Morrison."

Oh fuck. Fuck-fuck-fuck-fuckity-fuck.

Who *has* been talking? Has he — perhaps — been indiscreet where he shouldn't? "In any case, you misunderstand me. I request — no, I *require* — an autopsy on Pickled Lily."

Morrison tries to smile, to brush it off. Something has gone tits up, somewhere. He hurls his mind through all its internal cubbyholes, looks under every rock. Not that he gives a damn for Pickled Lily. Probably best to let La Sheepdip have the corpse, if she wants it. But he should at least attempt one last hurrah. He is, after all, even if in name only, The Director. The Grand Fromage. The Big Kahuna. As *if*.

"Well, I'm so *sorry*, Inspector, but that's *entirely* out of the question. Conditions of our Blessed Founder's will. Holy Writ. The Trustees would forbid it. Absolutely. And as much as I think they're a bunch of tossers, Inspector, I'd be right beside them on this one. Shoulder to shoulder. No, Inspector. No. Can. Do."

"Look, Dr Morrison, three people have died at your Institute. On *your* watch…"

"And a fat lot of progress your lot has made with any of them, Inspector. 'Natural Causes'? That stands for 'No Fucking Idea', in my book…"

"… in which case, Dr Morrison, I think you should probably give us a little more help. With our inquiries. Don't you?"

"Do I? *Do* I? Look, Inspector, if *you* want to write to the Trustees directly, be my guest. Go right ahead. But you won't get permission to slice up Pickled Lily before Hell freezes over. No way."

A transformation comes over the vertically over-extended form of La Sheepshit. She seems even taller, somehow, like her head is brushing the ceiling—and darker, like a thunderhead. She really is *very* impressive.

"Fine, Dr Morrison. If that's the way you want it. But when I ask the Trustees, which I'll do *ever* so nicely, I might mention a few other things. Such as your misplaced … er … location on the night of Bland's death…"

"Like I fucking care. I have bigger fish to fry, Inspector. *Much* bigger …" He throws up his hands, exposing two lengths of Jieves and Hawkes and a gold Rolex. That'll show *her*!

" … and the fact that you misled the Trustees about your appointment here. About those various holes in your *curriculum vitae*. Those …"

"Holes, Inspector? *Holes*? What holes are those? As if it's any of your business. But no, I forgot, how silly of me. You're a Police Officer." He spits out the capitals. "I should really be on my best behaviour. *Holes*, indeed."

"I take it, then, Dr Morrison, that we have your permission—and, indeed, your full and willing cooperation? Aren't you, as a *former scientist*, Dr Morrison, at all *curious* about why the Founder made that provision? Hmm? I assure you we'll treat her with all the respect she deserves."

Morrison really should be more on his guard, but Christ, Sheepshit gets very sexy when she's angry, as if all her saggy bits tighten and perk up. Maybe he should ditch Alex and shag her, instead. Morrison, old chap, this time you have really, *really* lost it. Time for a diplomatic retreat, he thinks—to buy some time later on. This isn't the first sinking ship he's been on, he reassures himself. And he's a more experienced rat than most.

Exit strategy.

Morrison emerges from behind his desk, picks up a raincoat and thrusts himself past Sheepwool, heading for the door. "Do what you like, Inspector. Do what you fucking well like."

He leaves rather more quickly than he'd have wished. Not quite the grace-under-pressure he'd hoped for. But he wouldn't want the Detective Inspector to have clocked his stonking great hard-on, now, would he? That would *never* do.

Jim Levy looks up, caged within his pool of light. "It's like nothing I've ever seen before, Inspector," he says through his green theater mask.

Sheepwool, with Fitch, in the shadows, looking on: suited and booted, as they all are.

"And believe me, Inspector, I've seen a *lot* of things."

Alex is beyond Levy, at the tail end of Pickled Lily. Alex ought to be excited about this, Sheepwool thinks, but instead she looks puffy, subdued. The customary chatter has been replaced by brooding silence. And there is something else, too. The few glances she essays at Sheepwool, eyes above the mask, are full of what looks like resentment. Or is it fear?

Levy turns to Alex. Sheepwool can't hear what Levy says, but Alex nods, then Levy turns to the policewomen. "Look," he says, "I've done all I can here. I think I can let Dr Beach have a few samples to … er … take home with her."

"A party bag?" says Fitch. Sheepwool wonders at the edge in her subordinate's voice. None of the usual giggling. But Fitch is looking at Alex with merciless hardness.

"Er … if you like, Detective Sergeant," says Levy. "Probably against the rules. But I won't say anything if you won't. Alex has all the equipment we'd need to tie things up, right there, at the Institute. And the expertise, too. We'd get further, quicker, that way, than if we had to …"

"That's perfectly fine, Dr Levy," Sheepwool says.

"Right then. I'll just sew her up — Pickled Lily, that is. Dr Beach and I can clear up, get changed, and then we can do some hard talking." Levy suggests a pub in the centre of Norwich.

It is a nameless city-centre pub, just off Colegate. Run-down and almost deserted, its clientele having been sucked out by newer, flashier establishments round about. A lone fruit machine is what passes for entertainment, its red lights winking uncaringly into the void.

"At least it's quiet," says Levy, "And the beer's good."

Merry Mermaid. She might have guessed.

The four of them are clustered round a table at the far end, screened off from the rest of the bar. Levy leans forward, conspiratorially.

"It's all very odd. She looks human down as far as the waist. Allowing for ... er ... decay, I'd say she was a woman. A young woman, too, probably no more than sixteen or seventeen — eighteen at most. The teeth are all there, all erupted, but relatively unworn, as it were. None of the usual signs of age. And below the waist, well..." He shrugs.

Alex, who has not said a word all evening, moves as if to speak, then appears to change her mind. She waves Levy to continue.

"Well, as I was saying, below the waist, well, that's another story. The skin of the torso seems to intergrade with the scales on the tail really well. It's beautiful. If it's a fake, it's a bloody good one. Whoever did that was a real expert. But *anno domini*, I'm afraid, has bollixed things up, too.

"And inside — well, that's another story, too. Usually, with a taxidermic specimen, you'd expect all the viscera - the innards, if you like - to have been removed. Not so with Our Lil. Whoever did this did something of a knife-and-fork job. There are bits and pieces of tissue all over the shop. Intercostal muscles still between the ribs, and so forth. Just about everything in the arms, shoulders and face. Apart from the eyes, of course. They *are* fakes.

Sheepwool suppresses a shudder.

"All the tissue's tanned and hardened with age - but, you know, this could explain why Pickled Lily was mounted in preservative - rather than dry, like a stuffed hunting trophy. So she wouldn't... er ... *go off*."

Goodness, thinks Sheepwool. I hadn't thought of that.

"And that explains another thing, too." Levy pauses to sup his pint, as theatrically as ever.

"Which is?" asks Sheepwool, playing up to Levy's mood.

"Well, much of the insides, especially in the tail end, have been replaced with a light framework of wood and wirework, as you'd expect. But the bones are there..."

"Bones?" This from Fitch.

"Yes. Not usual in stuffed specimens. Usually the bones are taken out and mounted separately. Not so Pickled Lily. The top half has all the usual bones—human ones—I think I mentioned the ribs. But the vertebrae—all suspended on a wire that replaces the spinal canal - kind of grade into the tail and fade out. There's no sign of a pelvis or lower limbs."

"Almost like a whale," says Alex, largely to herself.

"The vertebrae look human, too—not at all like those of a fish—right down to the radials at the end of the tail itself. The fin. I'd like to say that there's a join at waist level, but if so, it's hard to see. Like I said, impressive."

"I'm puzzled, Dr Levy," says Sheepwool, her inquiry leading, gentle.

"Aren't we all, Inspector? Aren't we all!"

"Yes. For me, it all comes back to the museum label, not the specimen itself. From the *outside*, you say that Pickled Lily was created by a real expert…"

"Just so. A professional job. Whoever did this knew precisely what they were doing."

"But from the *inside*, it looks like it was done rather badly. Inexpertly."

"That's it, Inspector. As if two people did it—a pro and a novice. An apprentice, maybe. Or if it were done by just one person, an expert, but in a hurry."

"So, as you said, Dr Levy, it's a puzzle. But I still come back to the label. If this were a taxidermic fake—like the other ones we knew Sir Frideric created—why did he contrive to hide it, to the extent that he forbade anyone from looking at it? From doing what we—well, what we did just now?"

"Perhaps, Inspector, he was afraid someone would see the botched inside job. Professional pride, and so on."

Sheepwool is silent for a spell. "But some of the insides *do* seem very well done. The bones, and so on."

"That's true, Inspector…"

"But, on the other hand, if it were a real mermaid…" This from Fitch.

"Why would he hide that, either?" asks Levy. " 'Secrets of the Sea', and all that? The mission of the Institute?"

"Quite," says Sheepwool, "you'd think he'd want to advertise that.

It would be a major discovery."

Fitch falls silent.

Alex stirs, once again, abortively.

"So we're back to square one," says Sheepwool. "If it's a real mermaid, the discovery of Sir Frideric's career - or anyone's career - why did he hide it? But if it were a fake, it looks very convincing from the outside — as you say, Dr Levy, an expert job — so why would he hide that, too? Prevent anyone from taking a closer look?" Her question is left hanging in the air, unanswered. Levy breaks the spell, jarringly.

"Well, I'm as puzzled as everyone else, but whoever heard of real mermaids? Now, if *I* were Sir Frideric, and I'd discovered a real mermaid, I'd have told everyone all about it. So if Pickled Lily isn't an expert fake, the next round is on me."

"It is anyway," says Sheepwool.

"Oh — is it? Same again, I take it?" Sheepwool and Fitch nod. Alex remains a tableau, inert, disconnected. Levy gets up and shambles towards the bar. Not with any reluctance, however, because behind the bar stands the only redeeming feature of this hostelry — apart from the beer itself — a plump, blonde Australian with relentlessly bubbly Antipodean cheer and an enticingly low-cut top. Her flirtatious banter with Levy fades into the background as Alex, then, starts to speak. It is at first no more than a murmur.

"Alex — are you all right — you seem, well ... not quite yourself."

"Me? No, Inspector, thank you, I'm fine. Just fine. It's just..." she places a hand over her belly, and turns to Fitch.

"Something that never occurred to me until we were there, at the hospital, looking at Pickled Lily. The Sea Bathers."

"Sea Bathers?" says Fitch.

"Yes. Funny thing. It's kind of a custom, you know. In Deringland."

Fitch lights up. "Oh yes, so it is ..."

"That every year, on the twenty-first of December, people go for a swim. They're called the Solstice Sea Bathers. Off the beach, you know, below the pier", says Alex. Fitch cannot help but contribute: "That's right: the newspapers cover it, lots of people come. Kind of a funfair, really. Prizes for the Bather who stays in the sea the longest, goes out the farthest, you know."

Alex grins, then, and starts to laugh. It is a strange sound, deeper and more halting than expected: "Hot buttered rum for the swimmers!"

"Alex—why now?" asks Sheepwool, "What is the …?"

Alex turns to face Sheepwool directly. Her eyes are huge, yearning. "Because Evanston Bland and Heather Franks were both in the sea that day. They were both Solstice Sea Bathers. They were there, standing in the sea—I think they were having an argument—but then they both got swept off their feet by a huge wave that came out of nowhere. But it's all consistent, you know. With the *Spaniel* accounts of why the sailors died. The incubation period. A few days to a few weeks. No more."

Fitch chimes in: "are you saying that Bland and Franks were infected by … what are these things? Carnostomids? From the sea?"

"Yes, I think I am. From the sea. At least, they could have been. It doesn't explain Bob Honeypott of course. He wasn't there. He got them from Pickled Lily. I'm almost sure of it."

"Alex," says Sheepwool, as gently but as firmly as she can manage, "how do you know this?"

"Because I was there, Inspector. I was in the sea, too. It was very warm, you know. Warmer than you'd think. And you know what? All the swimmers were men, except me. And Heather Franks of course—but—oh yes! Well, all except me, then." Alex's eyes are filled with an alien kind of blue. Sheepwool has seen that blueness before—in her dreams. And in wakefulness, just on the edge of sight. Only now, Sheepwool sees it clearly, for the first time.

And what she sees makes her sit up with a start.

Sheepwool has often thought that a love of surrealist art, while not absolutely necessary for the training of any detective, is, at least, helpful. It's all to do with the unnerving effect created by the placing together of unlikely objects, or the appearance of objects where you least expect them. Cups and saucers made from fur. Telephones with lobsters for handsets. Clouds in the shape of tubas. Or chairs.

Or, come to think of it, female torsos.

Threatening weather.

Combinations which on the face of it spell paradox, but when thought about, signal uses we had not, at first, considered, or even thought possible—or imaginable. Pickled Lily is just that. A paradox.

Or a juxtaposition.

If she is ambiguous, both a real mermaid and a fake, and yet nei-ther one, or perhaps both at once, then that could be because that is *precisely* what she is. A chimaera of truth and illusion.

On a sudden, she knows why the Institute is the way it is. No mat-ter how full Sir Frideric stuffed it with his specimens; no matter how assiduously he and his successors added to its already overwrought frame; something nasty, something truly hideous, has managed to leak out through its pores.

So, she thinks, *that's* why Sir Frideric forbade further investigation of his prize specimen. It is Pickled Lily herself, both the victim — and the creation — of Sir Frideric Lowdley-Purslane's most terrible crime. A crime which, she thinks, she has now solved.

Jim Levy, exuding bonhomie, returns with a tray of drinks. Reflex-ively, with the unthinking, meandering artlessness of the tentacles oaf a sea anemone, Alex Beach caresses her abdomen.

It is close to midnight, and Sir Frideric Lowdley-Purslane is about to start work. He feels that this will be his greatest triumph — but one which, regretfully, must remain forever hidden.

Upon my word, he thinks, trimming wicks and lighting a few small lamps around the bench at the very center of the room, casting the rest of the great space into coaly shadow, it took no great art to distract Felicity, not that she was not already distracted already — the Lady is more than three parts demented! - and to convince her that their daughter had in fact drowned on one of her mad moonlit wan-derings — her body lost, irrecoverably.

It had then been a trivial affair to have her body (which Sir Frideric had, in reality, thrown into the sea, although with great care) collected by those two singularly ill-favored natives of Deringland, crab-fishers both but hardly more than common footpads, who, despite their regular employ, had been very well paid to keep a secret of their complicity — *very* well paid. But Sir Frideric knows other ways of keeping men quiet, now, and he has impressed this on his hired hands. Oh, yes, the Honeypott brothers had little in the way of wit, but just enough to know when to hold their tongues, lest Sir Frideric hold them on their behalf.

He could easily have disposed of Rebecca's body. Quite easily! Or pushed it into the sea, all by himself, alive or dead, genuinely to have seen the last of it. Or contrived some fatal conjunction which would

have encompassed both Rebecca and that love-lorn fool Willoughby:
to be sure, that man, once so full of promise, is fast becoming a liability — a liability!

But the opportunity was just too fine to pass up.

All that new, young, white, incorrupt flesh.

Almost incorrupt, at any rate, but he could see about such defects
as he himself had lately introduced. Of course he could! And yet, and
yet: by all that's Holy, he knew he should never have gone down this
perilous path. But Sir Frideric loves a challenge, and sees himself as
secure from all risk. And there is that siren call, temptation. Ah, temptation! He can resist anything — *anything* — but that. He laughs, rolls up
his sleeves, collects his butcher's apron from a hook, his saws and
cleavers and needles and so forth from a bucket next to his bench, and
sets to work.

And, moreover, he adds to himself, by way of justification, he has
to make *something* of that specimen sent by Casares. A real mermaid,
indeed! The tail looks well enough, but the torso is all in disarray. He
doubts whether even an artist of the flesh as skilled as he undoubtedly is (Sir Frideric, despite his many faults, is a fair judge of his own
accomplishment) could make anything of *that*. And even if he did,
who would then believe him? A *real* mermaid? One that has required
quite so much restoration?

So, it is the tail, only, which is worth saving. All that it needs is the
torso, the head, the arms, to make it into a mermaid that would be a
fitting testament to his genius — even if only for his own, private contemplation.

Fortunately he has a choice of several cadavers, but, in truth, there
can only be one. Only this -- this young girl, whose flawless skin and
soft curves that only a Greek sculptor might have rendered, and even
then only in the rarest marble, the face of such perfect serenity, will
provide material of sufficient worth to participate in this, his most
signal endeavour.

He makes short work of cleaving the body in half through the
lower abdomen, making sure to collect in a broad, stone basin as
much of the viscera as he can. Ah, he wonders, as he always does, at
the fascination of it! Is it, perhaps, the shining pinkness of it; the almost feminine, folded intricacy of the internal organs, intimately
joined and yet separated by the delicacy of their mesenteries? Or,
perhaps, the slight, quiet sounds they make as they tumble forth, the

gentle suck and slap and slide, as waves on a far shore? He feels himself stirring—but alas! There is insufficient time, tonight, to indulge oneself such glamour, such gorgeous contemplation. At any rate, from this spill of guts—by Jove, the dogs will have some rare offal in the morning!

Ah, the morning. He knows he will have to complete the task by then, for Willoughby is due to assist in some other, more mundane tasks. And Willoughby, above all, must not be a party to this exercise.

Now he penetrates the chest from below, through the diaphragm— so as not to disturb the ribcage—and pulls out the heart and lights. These, too, he slops into the basin. He flenses out the thoracic cavity as well as he can in the sooty lamplight, but he will not have the time he'd usually devote this necessary task. No, Sir, he does not. So he does as well as he is able: for there are the bones to see to, which he must leave in, for want of a suitable armature—he has no time to prepare anything but the most rudimentary framework. By good fortune, he has a few, ready prepared for the mounting of large fishes and creatures of that sort.

And the sewing, and the careful arts required to join fish to flesh. These will require the greatest devotion of all, the most refined delicacy. Upon my word, he declares, the most refined of all!

6: A Pale Simulacrum

Alex is still at her bench as the sun rises, had she but known it. With every passing day she is in the underground lab yet longer after the dawn, as the Sun slowly swings round to the southward. For summer has come at last to Deringland, with a force and ferocity to compensate for the long months of winter. The Sun is a pitiless white hole in the sky, sucking all moisture from the land, shrivelling once-wet grass to splintery husks, annealing all relief into sintered planes. Even the sea is cowed.

But now, after almost four weeks of eighteen-hour days without a break, she can now contemplate her results.

A rack of slides, neatly labelled, testament to her increasing skill, a match for anything that the surgeons and naturalists aboard the *Spaniel* could have mustered; a row of vials, each containing some refined and subdivided portion of the exquisite corpse that is Pickled Lily; sheaf after sheaf of micrographs, radiographs, gels, expression profiles; a well-ordered stack of printouts. And, atop these, an account of it all, her results.

They are startling.

She sits there, amid the stacks of unread journals and unopened mail on the saggy sofa, as yet ignorant of the furnace blast of the outside world, and wondering how — when — she should deliver these results to Morrison, as she knows she must. She is afraid that he will not like them.

This, in part, is why she has gone out of her way to avoid him, returning once again, full-time, to her eyrie when sleep can no longer be dodged; carefully by-passing his office, and ignoring the ringing in her ears of Janice Squearn at reception as she rushes past, not meeting the older woman's concerned gaze; trying to shut out the increasingly shrill calls that yes, she knows Dr Beach is busy, but Dr Morrison should like to see her, please. Alex neglects her mobile; does not answer texts; has not accessed her email for nearly a month. She knows Garry is concerned, but he, too, has been spurned. And always at the back of her mind is a reminder, given as a sidelong hint from Sheepwool—that she should stay out of Morrison's way, if she can. If she has any worries on that score, she should just call.

But that recollection leads to plain guilt, at her betrayal. At her complicity, which has made her into a pallid simulacrum of her former self.

There is yet a third reason for avoiding Morrison—but she is not ready to admit that even to herself—not yet.

These reasons, combined, have eaten away at her. She is sallow, dead-eyed, but with a belly increasingly distended, like an African child in the early stages of malnutrition. It takes an effort of will for her to tear herself away from the all-consuming work, to eat, even to drink. Every part of her aches. Her feet are swollen from hours standing at the bench; her back aches; her guts ache like there are bears crawling up inside her. At least she's stopped being sick.

But now she must pause, take stock.

Pickled Lily, she's learned, is a game of two halves.

The samples from the insides of the tail, from the bones, the scraps of tissue the taxidermist had not removed—but particularly from the preserving fluid in which the mermaid had been suspended—offer a window on the life-history of carnostomids as riotous and grotesque as anything Bosch might have imagined.

Wherever she looks, the samples are absolutely crawling with carnostomids, of all sizes, shapes, states of preservation and stages of development, so much so that she can now create a reliable ontogenetic series, from what seem to be fertilized eggs, exploding into a parade of grinning tooth germs, leading to ranks upon ranks of heads and teeth and tiny eyes and jaws, and then—wonder!—a parade of 'intermediate-stage' carnostomids (for so she terms them, retrospectively) degenerating into formless sacs—from which emerge yet more carnostomids, far tinier than those of the previous generation, and the round continues again, and again, so that a single carnostomid, through cycles of polyembryonic fission, can give rise to almost ten thousand cloned progeny, each only a few microns in length. But each one with set of thirty-two, perfect, enamel-coated teeth. They all dance before her eyes now, her puffy, gritted-sore eyes, even in this waking hour, mocking.

And what then? Behold! She has found another form, found largely within Pickled Lily's tissues but almost never in the super-natant. She had ignored it when it rolled into view on a slide: only when it cropped up in numbers, in tissue samples, did it occur to her to investigate it closely. A shared signature of plasma-membrane pro-teins — but nothing else — betrayed any kinship with carnostomids. Tentatively, she infers that carnostomids found within the mermaid's body, *but not outside* (Alex remembers the exact moment when she made that connection, at her dormer window, the rising Sun outside raking the mirrored sea as if with boiling scoria) can metamorphose into this new form — but how? And into what?

Description, data — the basics of biology. It is a tiny, creeping, al-most formless blob, like an amoeba. Except, that is, for the presence within it of a pair of sacs, each bulging with tiny, tadpole-shaped cells, lying either side of a massive, syringe-like organ, protruding for many times the body's diameter. She fretted over these structures for nine humid, stultifying nights - sectioning, staining, imaging at all angles and at many degrees of magnification, and getting deeper into longer spells of worry and doubt - until, at some metaphoric cock-crow, the clouds parted: she caught one, frozen in time and tissue, in the act of squirting the mass of cached tadpole-cells through the sy-ringe.

This creature is not another larval stage, but an *adult* — transformed by its exposure to mermaid tissue, reduced from its carnostomid form to nothing more than a pair of testes and a penis: a sexually mature male, optimized for its primary purpose, ejaculation. She remembers that moment now, how it filled her with a mixture in equal parts of dramatic wonder and consuming nausea; how she staggered from the microscope to the sink, slick with sweat, wracking her guts out until nothing more came but thin strings of gray-green sputum. How like *men*, she thought, bitterly: *plus ça change*.

Internal fertilization. But of the females subject to the attentions of these dwarfed males, she could find no sign.

After that discovery, and assailed with waves of paralytic exhaus-tion, she threaded her own uncaring carcass up through the build-ing's duodenal windings and slumped, fully dressed, onto her bed, whereupon she was overwhelmed by that same dream, that same old dream, which she had been having with increasing frequency.

Her own knees, flexed like a gun-sight for the arched window beyond, white sashes sharp, *American Gothic*, the farmer, the pitchfork, the wife with her teeth (her teeth! Always her bloody *teeth*!) as Alex strains and *strains* to get this — this *thing* - out of her womb. But the farmer's wife parts her skirts to reveal an enormous, purple-veined phallus that squirts all over her, her face, soaking the sheets - with blood. The farmer's wife, with his (her?) member now deflated, reaches down as the farmer looks benignly on and smiles. The farmer's wife comes back up, now, with a squalling infant clothed in a towel. The farmer has gone, but the farmer's wife says, insists:

"Look at your baby, Alex! " She doesn't talk: she *screams*. "*Look* at it, Alex. It's all your fault!"

Only, this time, Alex looks.

And now, she knows: as she has known, for a long time, perhaps for her whole life. The missing females? She has been looking at one, scraping its insides, boring into its bones. She feels she knows it as well as the hag-ridden ghost she catches herself staring at, in the mirror on her wardrobe.

Internal fertilization.

Alex, slumped on the sofa, contemplating her arrayed results as the merciless Sun climbs outside, now remembers waking from that dream; how she put it aside; how she faced down the disorienting, incipient migraine, the metallic taste in her ever-dry mouth; how she forced her protesting form along the corridor of shadows, down the labyrinthine stairs, back to work.

She had turned, then, she recalls, to the torso of the mermaid, but the results are disappointing and few. Carnostomids of any stage are rare, and the male — *things* — are absent. And there is another puzzle. She's checked and rechecked herself, and with Valentina. She hardly dares broach it with Garry. But the DNA from Pickled Lily's torso — when corrected for the usual fungal contaminants — has none of the bizarre rearrangements she's become accustomed to seeing in carnostomids.

No, it's all there, in good order. Human. 99.99 per cent.

That was three days ago, since when she has been awake for all but two hours, writing it all up — or, at least, as much as she can. For Morrison. For all her apprehension, for all her fear, she knows she cannot avoid Morrison much longer.

Internal fertilization.

The sofa sags beneath her, and after sitting still for this length of time, her aching knees have locked. A spasm of cramp wrings out the calf muscle in the right leg: she staggers to her feet, tottering, a pile of papers sliding to the floor. She hops around, loosening the knots in her muscles, and when this is achieved she acknowledges that she is dying to pee. There is a small bathroom just across the hall, and in she bolts, the pain in her right calf leaving no more than a stain of its passing. Seat up, knickers down, the luxury of release, the raw, clean burn of the urine as it passes. It occurs to her only later that she can no longer see down over her protruding belly.

Internal fertilization.

Relieved, she washes, and leaves.

Wham.

The blur outside the door is Morrison. She has had no time to register the pain across her face.

Wham.

There it is again, and again, and another, and another. The world turns sideways—no, she is on the floor. Blood fills her mouth. Arm dislocates—no, he is pulling her upwards, the world rights itself, and then—jolt, bump, smash—she is in the lab again, with him there, a flurry of paperwork, her careful files brushed aside like street refuse before a flood—the thud of her back against the wall, a sickening impact against her abdomen—

Wham.

She hits the coffee table on the way down. She is on the floor, splayed amid a sea of paper and splintered wood.

"You stupid bitch," he says. "You stupid, *stupid* little *bitch*." And, as if from an immense distance: "those are commercial secrets, Alex. Proprietary. Tell any more, and, well... you're a *scientist*, Alex. *You* work it out." When the sound of his shoes down the corridor has faded into nothingness, she starts to pick herself up.

Fitch pushes the trolley round the supermarket like a ballerina. The children are at school. She has an hour or so of cool, evenly air-conditioned calm, all to herself. Bliss! Love is all around, croons Marty Pellow over the distant public-address system. It's so wonderful she could pirouette, right there (mop heads, cleaning fluids).

Things are going well at work (fish fingers, frozen cod steaks). Alex's lead has been fruitful. She's tracked down seven Solstice Sea Bathers. All men, as Alex had said. Three now dead: symptoms the same as Bland and Franks (tomato soup, canned spaghetti). They hadn't been local, so she had had no reason to have heard of them before. But three out of seven starts to look suspicious.

Not poor old Bob, though. He wasn't a Bather, so Pickled Lily still remains in the frame for him. But thank goodness (novelty cakes) he hadn't got around to spiking the drinks at the Dazed Haddock with the preserving fluid (beers, wines, spirits). That was a close one!

But then, she asks herself, why all *men*? (Sausages, minced beef). Do women (milk, eggs, soft cheese) ever get contaminated—poisoned—with these carnostomid things?

Round the corner of the last aisle, fruit and veg on one side, stacks of milk on the other, and a clear run down the middle to the checkout. Dead ahead, two full trolleys, and two women, talking. They are both heavily pregnant. Can't be more than three weeks to go, between them. And still hauling trollies around, poor loves. Perhaps they've just come in to keep cool. She remembers (ginseng, Omega-3 supplements) how she was at that stage. So hot! And so *huge*! Almost like a whale! The worst thing was not being able to get behind the wheel of a car and flooring it.

And there was all that other stuff. Funny! She'd really only remembered the nice parts before, of blooming like a rose, and how proud she was when Jase stroked her inflated form when she was pregnant with Dean, and saying he thought pregnant women were really, *really* sexy. But, God, for some reason (why now?) she remembers the discomfort (headache tablets, sanitary towels). Not being able to bend over far enough to hitch up her underwear. How her boobs, now all the wrong shape for her bra, were too sore to even touch (Jase hadn't liked that part much, but he'd understood, bless him). How they felt like explosions about to go off. And—oh yes! -- not being able to cough without peeing herself (loo rolls, bleach). That was the worst part. Credit card, PIN, loading bags back into the trolley, up and out, into the alien heat of the car park.

Her car!

You could fry an egg on it!

Behind the wheel again. The car is an oven. She opens the window. The leatherette of the seat sticks and pulls at the backs of her legs in rhythm as she winds the handle. God, it *would* be nice to go to the beach, *right now* - sod the shopping, sod the Station—and just *run* into those cooling waves. Waves. Surf. Beach. She *was* the only female Solstice Sea Bather. She said so herself. And Fitch would swear blind she's pregnant.

Is *that* what happens to women who get infected with carnostomids? Her purse is on the passenger seat, picked out in a white-hot shaft of Sun, as if God's finger were pointing right at it. She rummages for her mobile.

"I think you're right, Fitch."

The Sun is above and to the westward; the burnished waves lap consolingly about her ears. Lying on her back in the gentle swell, she brings her feet up so they break the surface. Playfully, she makes them into a v-shaped gunsight, aiming at the beach, picking out families. Families with children. Abruptly, she swings her feet down and resumes treading water. Looking down, she sees the slightly puckered flesh on her abdomen.

"Hmm?" Fitch—treading water nearby, in a functional black one-piece, concealing her maternal curves.

"Swim. Lunchtime. Good idea." Somehow the Sun seems more benign when you're swimming in the sea. As if terrestrial harshness were a goad, a whip to drive you shorewards.

"Oh, yes—but that's not quite what you meant, was it?"

A laugh. "No, not quite. I meant what you said, about Alex Beach being pregnant. It explains a lot about her behaviour, poor girl. I don't think she's enjoying it, though." She had not enjoyed her own, either. The end product had been worth it, though. The dear, sweet—"and what you said, too, that there's something about pregnancy and carnostomid infection. Though I can't really see how …"

Sheepwool stands up sharply, her toes burying themselves in the sand.

"Ma'am?" Fitch comes to rest beside her, hands and sea-glossed arms above her, as she adjusts her bathing cap.

"Bloody hell, Fitch." Under her feet, the sea surges and rips.

Fitch, concerned. But Sheepwool's eyes are focussed at infinity, dead ahead.

"They get *infected*," she says. "And then they get *pregnant*. And then … then …" she turns her head to stare straight at Fitch's worried, pale, freckled young face. The face of a young girl, a young woman, yet one who had been pregnant three times and whose children now bounce happily around Deringland. Three to her one, and that only a memory, fading fast. Too fast. "And then they throw themselves into the sea and drown."

"That's ... *horrible.*"

"Yes. It is. But let's think about it. Remember Garrison Williams, and what happened to his wife?"

"Bev? Didn't he say how she ... of course..." Fitch looks down, brow furrowed, as if she might see tiny things as motes swarming in the water around her. She looks up again — "and there were all those stories about Lady Fred, remember, I told you?"

"Yes, Fitch, you did. When we first went to the Institute together." A bacon-faced woman on the sidewalk, berating the urchin who had nearly fallen beneath their wheels.

And Sheepwool recalls a third case, but it is too speculative even for this wild line of argument. What's more, it would have been a serious breach of protocol even to have floated it as a hypothesis with Fitch. Even when the two of them were in civvies, having a lunch-time bathe. They are, as Alex, Bland and Franks were before them, Solstice Sea Bathers.

It is the twenty-first of June.

"I still don't get the mermaid part. Where Pickled Lily fits in to all this," says Fitch, towelling her hair.

"Neither do I, not really. Whenever I've talked with Alex about it, I just can't follow her. Either she's incoherent, or I'm a bit dim, but more likely she hasn't worked it all out herself. " Sheepwool looks at her feet again. This time her feet are playing with each other, making sand angels, as if she has no volition at all in the matter.

"But she must fit in somewhere, mustn't she?" asks Fitch.

"Who? Alex? Or Pickled Lily?"

"Alex, of course!" Fitch laughs.

"I'm worried about Alex, you know. With Morrison around. Ever since she told me what she thought they were up to."

"But you said it yourself ... she has to be in place else Morrison might twig what we're doing ..."

"Yes, I know, and you're right, Fitch, as usual. But I do wonder whether it's right to expose her to such danger, especially if she's pregnant. The risks. The repercussions if not just she but her baby gets hurt."

It is then that Fitch realizes that this is the first time she has seen her superior substantially disrobed, her stick-thin form, in a rather unflattering green bikini. The laddered ribs, the slight distension in her lower abdomen, and she has a C-section scar, only partially concealed by the bikini line. And, well, it could just be the sunshine's glare, or the salt, but she's almost sure that there are tears in her superior officer's eyes. Sheepwool notices Fitch's inquiring gaze, then, and looks away: supposition swells to a certainty. Who'd have thought it?

7: Blinded By The Rain

It is difficult for me to write the words I must write. But write them I must, and in great haste—and then, no more.

Alex, holed up in a crevice of the library, a refuge she is confident no-one knows, reads the last page of a journal. It is cheap, octavo, with primitively thick laid paper in scuffed black leather bindings. The crabbed writing often fades out into stellate blotches, as if drops of water had smudged them. The edges of the pages, too, though once sharp, dissolve into pastel chromatograms of age-separated ink.

I had revered him. He was, and still is, a genius. But one must ask oneself how far one must follow a visionary in the […] of genius, in the cause of Art? How deep one must sink so that the rise will be higher still?

Alex scratches the back of her neck, wonders—again—at the tightness of her clothes in this musty claustrophobia, with the dust of ages falling around her in slow, invisible cascades, mingling with her body's sweat, slowly petrifying her.

It is with regret, and […] beloved rejected my suit. She […] could not consent to be my wife. *Could* not. For shame, I admit now that I pressed her, I asked […]. Her response in her eyes should have been eloquence enough, and when I pressed her further, she replied that she was already wed, to Art. To my Art, and his, and that her mind was quite […] Her agitation was plain […] swooned […] up, like a little child asleep, I perceived her lightness: and that when I had scaled the stairs to the house, that my left hand—which had been supporting her knees—was slick with her blood, which had issued from her body in thick,

massy gouts and had soaked her red [...]. It was red, I now
own, so that she could advertise what she felt was her shame —
and, at the same time, conceal it. I brought her to [...] she was
still alive, breathing [...] gasps, like a small bird in distress. My
master's reaction sent a chill through me — his eyes, glinting
with knowingness, with mal[...] scales began to peel from mine
own, to see, now, how I had been [...] devil.

The sun, barely filtered by the sashes and grime in the skylight,
burns imperious white squares on the text.

I could only watch with apprehension at the episodes of [...]
days. How [...] was deemed too far indisposed for my presence
to be welcomed. How my master kept me away through one
pretext or another. And how the delay was prolonged, when I
heard that he had been working many long hours at a specimen, greater and [...] he had earlier assayed — and yet, and yet,
he forbade my presence, which had always been so essential
aforetime. I forget where I had [...] Honeypott [...] loathly Cali-
bans now forever in his service, and I [...] as mockery at my ex-
clusion from the Sanctum, where they were now freely admitted. It was when I heard of the reaction of Lady F[...] with grief
and fear at the loss[...] whom I had thought indisposed that I
could not in all conscience steer her from my master's private
rooms. So, following her, to ensure that she should not come to
harm, we came to the threshold and saw that which I cannot
[...]

Alex's eyes are gripped to the fragments between the crumpled,
water-stained patches. Her heart strains against blood that seems to
have clotted in this heat.

Then it was that the final scales fell. But I could not, now,
leave, for a man accustomed to such depravity as I knew he was
would hardly allow me [...] his sight. I had seen the fates of
those who [...] worse — I had [...] slow disaggregation. I can say
no more, and I hope the Lord [...] to forgive me. That I am
doomed to follow [...] will, I hope, [...] balance of my punishment against that certainty of [...] in the world to come.

A chill closes. Goosebumps rise on her forearms, and, were one
close enough to hear, the rising hairs on her arms and the back of her

neck would make the tiny noises of cracks propagating through layers of sweat-mortared dust.

Clouds obscure the sun through the skylight, and in the last ray before the light is shut off, she reads the signature, making out the words and letters through a florid, uneven scrawl that had once worn the confidence of youth, but which now petered out into illegibility:

Ra[...] W[...]ou[...]

She puts down the diary, with great care, and in chill of the fast-closing dark, she is seized by an immense jolt as the life inside her kicks. She sits down, startled, new sweat beading her brow with cold, and a long-neglected memory now unfurls, opens up, like an egg, hatching.

You can play in the field and down the lane...

Daddy reads *The Tale of Peter Rabbit* to five-year-old Alex, curled up in her night-dress with her mass of toys. She remembers how Daddy lingered over the fate of those who stray into Mr McGregor's Garden.

Only in later years did she recall why — that after their one and only beach holiday, his wife, her mother, had fallen pregnant with her baby sister. Six months gone, Alex's mother had been seized with a red-eyed compulsion to leave so strong that none could resist her. The Police, when they were called, said that they could hardly restrain a grown woman from leaving, even in such distressing circumstances. Her car was found on the very edge of a lonely cliff-top, but of its driver there was no trace.

Alex, like all children, blamed herself, and, as she grew up, her father did rather little — she now thinks — to disabuse her of that notion. And to assuage her guilt, she thought, in her father's eyes, she would never go to the sea, or near it — a view reinforced and internalized to become one of loathing and hatred.

There were no more seaside holidays for Alex. No buckets and spades, no funfairs on the pier: Alex grew up, never again having felt the warm grit of sand between her toes, the sun on her back as it glinted on tidal pools.

Things changed in her teens, when, as all teenagers will, she taunted her father with the things she knew he most feared: held them up before his eyes, mocking. The long weekends when she would disappear seawards, leaving her father walking tiny, fretful circles as dawn rose. The boys she hung out with. Surfers. Divers.

Daddy had died, broken, less than a year ago. His emaciated, cancer-wracked body held together just long enough to see her awarded her doctorate. He lasted just two more days, and immediately after the funeral she had flown to that conference in Atlanta, when... well, Daddy was right.

Peter Rabbit's father had been put in a pie by Mrs McGregor.

Alex has now grown to full womanhood, her white skin now scarred, her rosy flesh now bruised like a ripe fruit, her flayed soul now screaming with the pain of betrayal -- first her own, of her father, and then of herself. She looks up into the darkness of the library. She knows, now, that the circle is complete. She must defy the sea, spurn it, run from it as far and as fast as possible.

And she must do it *right now*.

Beyond the Institute, way out to sea, clouds collide. A rent of lightning hits water, harbinger of the first summer thunder.

She has not stopped even to grab her things. Her attic room, the lab, both are closed to her now. As the dark snaps shut, so those parts of her mind are pinched off, discarded, so she can see them only as if reflections in tiny soap bubbles, fading, drifting away on the wind to expand and expire in the distance.

There is only *now*.

The need, above all else, to escape, squaring up against the relentless pull of the sea. She grabs her bike from the shed just behind Reception. Janice Squearn is there, but her weak attempts to attract her attention are enfeebled further by a crack of thunder so deep and so close that the ground heaves, and her ears ring in response. In the corner of her eye she sees Mrs Squearn look up at what appears to be a crack in the wall, and, as if in tableau, the receptionist grabs her bag, fumbles a mobile from its spilled contents, and starts tapping a text, furiously. Alex does not pause ask why, or to whom.

As she leaves, the lights of the Institute flicker, flash, and die.

Dizzy, almost deafened by the thunder, Alex wrenches her bike free and lurches from a side-door, out, to the car park. She feels rather than sees the gravel as it scrunches beneath her feet as they find the pedals, and she pushes away, free. She has gone no more than twenty yards before the dark above, and all around her, disgorges its load.

Wham.

The rain—more than rain—smacks into her like fists, a fusillade of blows.

Wham. Wham. WhamWhamWhamWhamWham.

She is drenched within a second, and can now feel the chill of water sluicing down the back of her neck, into her eyes. But she must keep pedalling. Away. Away from this place and all it means. Away from all this encircling, enticing sea.

But it is all so *heavy*. The sudden weight of the water; the increased bulk of her body; the accumulation of too many wired, febrile nights; the sheer weariness of fighting what seems no more than a long defeat; her knife-edge closeness to its acceptance—all conspire to drag her back. She feels that were she only to turn, to look at the Institute and the sea beyond, that tiny spark of her soul still weakly glowing in this endless dark would simply wink out.

She toils on, her sneakers now full of water, the wet denim of her jeans scraping and snagging at her inner thighs, impeding movement. She is now at that nodal point on the great prairie between the Institute and the main road where all that can be seen, in any direction, is grass, whirling in the gale, lit now only by lightning and the dimly livid glare from the belly of the thunderhead. Blinded by the rain, panting and hot from the effort, she puts her faith in what she imagines is the right direction.

Her faith, as it always has been, is misplaced. She careers from the path and hits a rut. The speed is not great, but the rain, and the wind, and the weight of her body and her sodden clothes, tip her over the handlebars and she lands, face-first, in a puddle. She loses consciousness for an instant, but then wakes, sits up, feeling a new wetness on her lips, her chin. She thinks she has cut her tongue. Crawling through gray, chalky mud and grass, she makes contact with her bike. The front tire has burst, the wheel bent out of shape.

She tries to stand. Her left leg wobbles, as if something has gone wrong with her knee. She turns, unsteadily, and sees two things.

The first is the sea. It is much closer than she thought it was. Indeed, she feels that she is on a warm beach under a fluorescent blue sky, with emerald palms, swaying on the shore of a wide jade lagoon, straight out of a holiday brochure. More compartments in her mind

close, denying access. Snap. She picks herself up and starts to walk
back the way she has come. Snap. The mote of light in her mind wa-
vers. Look at your Baby, Alex. *Look* at it. It's all your fault.

The second thing she sees is two points of halogen-white light, approaching. She stands, warmed by the glare. The lights get larger and
draw apart. They are headlights, the raindrops caught in its twin
beams like the uncountable tiny flecks of plankton in the ocean, the
Great Mother Ocean, who will grant her absolution in her healing
surf, would she but let her. But as the car pulls to a stop beside her
uncomprehending form, opening a door towards her, she can feel her
bloodied mouth open and frame just one word, almost too faint to
hear amid the rumble of the thunder, the splash of rain and the roar of
the engine.

"Daddy ..."

"What? Get in." She obeys.

It is Morrison.

"Christ, Alex, you stupid girl. Out here? In the rain? I'll have to
clean you up." She can make him out only in those pieces of him that
are picked out in the dashboard lights. The end of his nose. His
wristwatch. Cufflinks. She has not quite realized that he is anything
more than a loose collective of fireflies—his voice appears to come
from the centre of a green-golden cloud, but from a great distance. He
drives on, and sliding down the last incline to the main road in a
wash of water, turns right, into Deringland.

Swish, swish. The wipers battle against the sheeting water, clearing
intermittent patches in the windshield like strobes. Morrison has now
turned away from her, concentrating on the road ahead. He appears
to forget she is there, and, therefore, she is not. The wipers counterpoint a long speech he is making to himself. Of judgement. Of resolution. And, above all, of self-justification.

Swish, swish.

"It's all over for us here. But no matter, I believe with confidence
that our work here is done. It's time to re-strategize our priorities.
With the results we have we can rebuild capacity elsewhere, we can
..."

Swish, swish.

"The subject I can present now is currently in an advanced state of
development, rolling out a new research line, unfolding."

Swish, swish.

"Yes, it's just the one at the moment—and, yes, I admit, I have a major stake in its timely delivery. You could say it's personal."

Swish, swish.

"Of course, my role was only supervisory. Facilitatory. Sowing the seeds."

Swish, swish. He slows at the lights, and, with great care, turns left, headed for Norwich, and, beyond that, the rest of the world.

"My collaborator, Dr Beach, is much closer to this … uh … research than I am. She's onto it, twenty-four seven. It's taken her over completely, really got—how can I put it?—under her skin. So she was of some fucking use after all. If only as an incubator."

He turns to her then. All she can see are his teeth. His smile is disproportionately wide, as if it might unzip itself all the way round to the back of his head. It looks like he might eat her alive. Consume her. Consumables. And when consumed, discarded.

Internal fertilization.

Water, and more than water, pools on the seat below and between her thighs.

"Janice?"

Torchlight in the darkened corridor, the foyer of the Institute.

"Dr Williams! Is that you? I was just trying to text Frankie—Miss Honiton—but all the lights went out …"

"It's Alex, isn't it?" He leans against the Reception counter. The thunder grinds and cracks its way round the horizon. The rain hurls itself against the Institute with the faceless fury of a zombie army: the wind screams across the roof, ripping tiles, wrenching gutters from decayed walls. Janice Squearn stands: lit from below by the glare from her computer screen, her face is thrown into grotesque Hitchcockian shadows that finger their way to the high cornicing.

The computers have their own generators, at least. Uninterruptible Power Supply. He'd insisted on that, when he'd come here.

"Alex? Alex—yes, I just saw her go. She went to get her bike, and … oh my. In this weather!"

"Yeah. And I saw Morrison in his car. Leaving. In this weather. Perhaps he'll pick her up."

Janice sits down again, casting her face around the desk, looking for something. "Oh, do you think so?"

"Sure I do. And it'll be bad news for Alex if he does."

"Will it? That poor girl. Driven. Do you know, I think she's pregnant? Can't imagine who the father is. But a girl in that condition, she should rest, she should…"

"She should do a lot of things. And above all, she should stay away from Morrison. I know more about that man than you'd *want* to know."

Janice stands up again, quite straight, her face ashy white in Williams' flashlight beam. "Do you…? I… I forgot… I should have…. Oh my!" She looks down, and starts scrabbling once more among notes and papers and telephone books like a squirrel after the last of its hoard, muttering. Then she stares straight at him as if she had just spotted the severed head of John the Baptist hovering in the air, behind him. He wonders why she is so agitated, hopping around like spit on a griddle. Does he always have this effect on people?

Anyway, he has the distinct feeling that she's not listening when he tells her of how Morrison had been banned forever from lab work. After he, Professor Garrison Williams, had uncovered those so-called accidents. Those girl graduate students, those ditzy lab techs he'd knocked up.

And then sliced up.

Careless, though. One of them had been alive — only just — to finger him to the police, just as they raided his lab through the front, while he vamoosed out back.

He can still remember that girl. Haunts his dreams. On a gurney, awash with blood like you'd never seen, sliced like a bad C-section. Whatever was in there, though, had been ripped loose. *Ripped*. She died, that girl, right before his eyes — died right there, on the gurney, in all that blood.

It was hushed up, of course, as these things are. Drug money can do *so-o-o* much. He'd been under a cloak of anonymity, on the Board of Inquiry. But Morrison had been anonymous, kind of. Back then he was called John Wayne. God knows what he'll call himself now, after his latest flit.

With Alex. And what she's carrying.

And Williams remembers, and remembers, that girl on the gurney. How much she looked like Bev. He didn't do so much work after that. His research took a nosedive. The drugs helped, though, for a spell, until they took over from work, sort of, and, well, here he is, in the same place of banishment as the man he'd helped exile. Ironic. And with a girl who, if he didn't do something about it, would end up as his latest experiment. The voice of Janice Squearn knocks on the closing doors of his mind.

"Yes, that's all very well, Dr Williams. But we can do something about this. You see, Miss Honiton has found something I think you should see. Look—I found it!" She holds up a big, steel key. It shines and sparkles in the torchlight. "I had meant to do something—call Elaine Fitch—when we found out, but then Bob Honeypott, well, you know..."

"I liked Bob," he says, following Janice Squearn down the hall, pointing the way with a high beam between the lugubrious shadow-shifting shapes of the display cabinets, to Morrison's office. "He was always very good to me."

The door is not locked but ajar, the office abandoned. The desk has been stripped of papers—a few scraps lie untidily on the floor. Same old, same old.

"Bob Honeypott?" says Squearn, edging behind the desk to the concealed panel. "He had some redeeming features, then." The panel yawns open to worlds beyond. "When I taught him at school he was a little shit."

Ralph Willoughby is packing a case as fast as he can. A footman—one he knows shares his fear of Sir Frideric and the Honeypotts—is ready with a horse to speed him away before they notice his absence. He will run, he will hide, he knows not where. England will be too small a compass for their vengeful search. He will try America, perhaps. Or Hindustan. Or the South Seas. Anywhere but here.

But his last memory of this place will not be of Sir Frideric and their work together, but of eyes. The maddened, bulging eyes in the face of Lady Felicity as she hurled herself over the cliff, right before him, paralyzed as he was with incredulity at what they had together witnessed, and unable to stop her. They were the same eyes—the same sweet, blue eyes - that his beloved Rebecca had once worn, before Sir Frideric had desecrated her, had done to her what even he, so close to the mind and the ways of the great Artist, would have thought beyond speech, beyond imagining.

The same eyes, before Sir Frideric had scooped them from her dead skull and replaced them with perfect, unseeing glass.

8: Gestation

"You were right all the time, Sheepwool." Methwold's eyes seem even larger than usual, refracted through the thick lenses in a face that looks pinched and tired rather than calmly authoritative. "Can you sum up for us, then, Fitch?"

"Yes, Sir. Dr Williams' tip-off led us to a Board of Inquiry at Dr Morrison's old University, when he was a scientist there — this goes back fifteen years, and Morrison was working under an alias..."

"Do scientists do that sort of thing?" asks Methwold. Sheepwool smiles — all the world, it seems, is a stage, and even scientists are merely players.

"Apparently so, Sir", continues Fitch, "and Morrison was suspected of gross misconduct. Morrison — or John Wayne as he then was..." — Methwold suppresses a snort — "was implicated in several deaths. Junior colleagues, all female, all romantically involved with him at some time or another, which is why ..."

"... which is why Alex Beach is in terrible danger, Sir." This from Sheepwool, an urgency in her voice. "And Morrison seems to have disappeared, with Alex in tow."

"Hostage?"

"Hard to say, Sir." Sheepwool reflects on her view — a view she's held throughout the whole Insitute business — that Morrison and Beach are in it together. And so, perhaps, they are. But togetherness is rarely symmetrical, and there are as many species of togetherness as there are people — people, *squared*. And some people need to be protected from themselves. Especially if they're out in filthy weather like this. *Threatening Weather*, as Magritte had it, but that's a translation, and Sheepwool now idly wonders about its accuracy, given the ambiguity of the word 'threatening'. For who (whom?) is being threatened, here? The weather, or those who endure it? If Alex Beach is a hostage, how far is she complicit? Then, Sheepwool reflects, there may be a third force at work here. A force from the Sea. Ah, yes. Alex Beach may be a hostage—but is Morrison really the abductor?

"But just in case, Sir—given the evidence…" says Fitch, "now that we know—from what Janice Squearn said—that Morrison had a secret lab, in direct contravention, Sir, of the …"

"Oh, all right then," Methwold concedes. "Given the evidence. Do the usual ports-and-airports thing, would you, Fitch? Warrants? I'll call the Chief Constable. And we'll need a press conference. Morrison needs to be found." Methwold starts to rise from his desk, coughs pointedly to indicate that the interview is now at an end.

The phone rings—Methwold cradles the receiver in a single, easy movement.

"Bloody hell …"

The conversation is over in less than twenty seconds. Receiver down, he looks at the two detectives, now standing, poised like statues, purses and coats in hand.

"That was the coastguard", says Methwold. His face is drained of all colour. "It's the Institute. It's falling into the Sea."

Morrison had cleaned her up in the hotel as well as he could, but she is still filthy and dishevelled, and makes a sad contrast with the others seated at the table. They are all men in suits. The table is of a fine, dark wood, but the room, which is slightly too small for it, is furnished in the dull beiges and greens of cheap rented offices, a décor almost offensive in its sincere effort to be unobtrusive. Behind the vertical slats of the porridge-coloured window-blinds she can see the asphalt surface of a car park, slick and dark in the all-enfolding gloom. How sad. This really isn't where she wants to be, for her mind is full of blue.

There is no 'blue' *here*. Where is the blue? She wants it. She wants it, badly.

She looks at the men. They are all faceless. Literally, without faces. As hard as she tries—squinting with the effort—there is nothing to be seen beneath hairline and collar of any of them. Except teeth. Always, there are teeth.

"The potential of your research into carnostomids is great, Dr Morrison," one of the faceless men explains. "But you have not met your projected targets. The forecast was quite specific."

"Yes, of course. But as you see, the project took an unexpected new turn." This from Morrison, seated to her left. She can smell his sweat, now, rank and pungent, not entirely masked by the deception of his cologne. He turns to Alex, then, as if his faceless face is in a spotlight. The other faceless men turn towards her, in choreographed unison. Morrison continues, directing his words to Alex not as a person, but as if she were a business presentation. Or an exhibit. As if she's not really meant to be there. And so, therefore, she is not: she hears Morrison's words as no more than a collection of syllables hung on the gristle of presentational syntax. They seem to be taking a very long time. Another faceless man intervenes.

"This is all very well, Dr Morrison. It also fits your conjectures."

"Thank you". But Morrison's smugness is premature.

"They are, however, only conjectures", says another faceless face.

"Not even hypotheses," adds a third, "Let alone anything we might develop into anything we might possibly take to market in any reasonably projectable time-frame."

"Targets, Morrison, targets," says the second faceless face. "Science costs money. Blue-skies research is fine, but not on our ticket."

"But the effects of carnostomids—TubeWave—on pregnancy… the differential effects on males and females… think what it could …" Alex detects a pleading note in Morrison's voice.

"Conjecture, as we said." This from the first faceless face. Or is it the third? It's so hard to tell. And what is that about pregnancy? I think they must be referring to me, she thinks to herself, idly, as if she were one of *Les Tricoteuses* watching the guillotine's scrape, drop and crack, scrape, drop and crack—and not the victim, at center stage.

"Morrison."

This a faceless face at the far end of the table. It must be a senior example, for the room falls silent, all except for the lusty hum of the aircon, the only other sound in a room which might be anywhere. Cambridge? London? She'd lost track, somewhere on the way down, when the speeding scenery was enveloped in black cloud, the blueness she desired somewhere in the distance, receding.

"Sir?"

"Morrison, you have spent a great deal of our money for no discernible benefit. And now we see that your researcher has turned into your experimental subject."

"It was…"

"Don't interrupt, Morrison. Remember, your record is known to us. We are well aware of your tendencies. We are not prepared to underwrite them any more than we have to. There is only one way to test your conjectures, and that's by investigation. We're prepared to go that far, at least."

"Thank you, Sir."

"Don't mention it. Bring the subject here tomorrow for operative procedures."

"Operative … procedures…? Yes, Sir, of course."

"If you fail us, Morrison—if you don't show up—details of your past proclivities will find their way to the authorities. Our shareholders would demand nothing less."

There is general laughter around the table. Morrison's smell grows more insistently acrid: Alex detects a note of -- what is it—*fear*? She has never smelled that in Morrison before. She rather likes it, she thinks. It's a turn-on. She'd like to smell it some more. She feels suddenly conscious of the existence of her own physical body in a way that she hasn't felt for a very long time.

"But that was all cleared up, a long time ago." Morrison is on the defensive.

"Oh *really*? You really *think* so, do you? You were given a second chance, then. But you just couldn't keep away. We funded you, Morrison, when no-one else would. But there are many other—how can I put it?—fish in the sea. Well, there are no third chances. No sense throwing good money after bad. You fail us now, Morrison, and we'll bury you in shit and claim we never saw you before in our lives."

Morrison is in the tiny bathroom of the motel, trying to loosen his tie. His collar is sticky with sweat, darkening and crumpling the silk of tie and shirt alike, degrading the neatness of his neckwear into a mess like cold, wet spaghetti. He snags a nail on the recalcitrant knot. Oh, fuck it. And fuck *them*. Oh, I *wish*, he thinks. There's nothing for it now but to turn up tomorrow with Alex for the great carve-up. He doesn't know what they think they'll find inside except a fetus.

Well, they can analyze *that*, I suppose.

Oh, come *on*, Morrison, don't be such a dickhead. You know their suspicions. If carnostomids are the source of TubeWave, as they all seem to think, then they need to know the effects on the unborn. Why? Because, the Board has told him, the social experiment of

TubeWave on the streets has backfired. Pregnant women on Surf-D have had stillbirths, teratologies. Phocomelia. And scales. And fins. The shareholders are skittish: MagusPharm will have to withdraw TubeWave... and cover its tracks. Find out what's going on, at least — knowledge is power. Which is why he'll *have* to bring Alex in tomorrow. Alex — *pregnant* Alex - is the only reason MagusPharm is still supporting him at all. Oh, yes - they made that *abundantly* clear. Alex has bought him a little more time. A day or two, at least.

But what *then*?

Oh, he's sure he'll think of *something*. He always has.

Wham.

The kick hits him in the small of the back — pain erupts. Before he has had time to react, his tie is grabbed and yanked violently backwards. He chokes, and sees spots before his eyes. Bending down, forwards, he attempts to turn and head-butt the assailant in the stomach.

Bad move.

A knee comes up and smashes into his chin. He feels teeth shatter and hot blood spurt from his tongue. Then something hard crashes into his skull, shattering. Ah, must be that bottle of champagne. Or Cava, anyway. Nice touch, really, for a motel, muses the part of his mind curiously detached from the current doo-doo in which he finds himself. What a waste of perfectly good bubbly.

Resigned, he crumples backwards onto the hard, tiled bathroom floor, smacking the back of his head on the lip of the shower cubicle as he descends, and slumps into a puddle of blood and sparkling wine, still fizzing. After a second — or an hour — his vision clears. Oh, my fucking head. He looks up, through phosphorescent stabs of pain, and sees her towering above him.

Alex.

She's magnificent. Especially from this angle. She'd finally taken off her muddied jeans and underwear, and, well, those legs ... and, Christ, he can see *all* the way up. His eyes are drawn further upwards, though, over the swell of her abdomen, and what he sees then is *not* so nice. Oh yes, of course, she's aroused, all right. Taut and hot. But the general picture is *red*. Her whole skin is pulsing with crimson excitement.

Her hands are the reddest, both clenched, knuckles starting into bone-white knots round the neck of the broken bottle which she is brandishing like a club. The edges are sharp and menacing. Her eyes are red, too—huge, wild and scarlet, framed by hair that's standing out in all directions, like she's plugged herself into the mains. Oh, God, this is just too fucking Boadicea to take in. And so, so *sexy*. About time too, after all that passive humping, when, time after time, she's just lain there like a corpse, legs akimbo, while he made all the moves.

He hardens in an instant.

"Alex," he manages to say through the swollen wreck of his mouth: "nice to see you, too. Pull me up, and let's finish this in bed, shall we?"

Her expression does not soften. She just stands there like some Gothic Statue of Liberty as he kneels, painfully, slithering around on floor wet with wine and blood, grinding his knees and palms in the fragments of broken glass. No sooner than he's righted himself on the washbasin, unfolding himself ever so gently to dodge the knives of pain in his head, his back, his knees, his hands, his neck—than she hits him again with the broken bottle. Again, again, and again, until he staggers, his jacket and trousers blood-soaked rags, and falls backwards onto the bed.

She jumps on him then. He is powerless to resist. She mounts him, shoving his hardness inside her and pounding and grinding on top of him, and if he makes any sign of moving, she gouges the bottle's edges into his neck, his chest, his face. His left eye goes dark in a spasm of agony. He comes, and so does she, and as she does so she howls like a vixen at bay, arches over him, all distended belly and breasts and teeth and arms waving that bottle like a banner, and spits in his face.

"Take me back to the *sea*, you *bastard*," she growls: "take me *home*. Do it *now*."

"But … we … tomorrow… Alex…" He can hardly get the words out. It's not just that his mouth is a battlefield—it's that fantastic, endorphin rush of sex. He can't remember feeling so high, ever. If there was ever a time to lie back with a cigarette, this is it. He goes numb, smooth planes of pleasure taking the edge off his wounds; relaxes, his eyes heavy-lidded. Alex, however, has other plans.

"I said *now*", she shrieks, plunging the dagger-like shards so deeply into the side of his face that he feels the blades pass right through to the other side.

She has been careful not to damage so much of Morrison that he cannot drive. The blueness in her mind has guided her hand well. The rainy, night-time road is a white-lined, white-lit tunnel before them, leading outwards into the blue. She does not recognize the road — she does not care, so long as she can keep her target in view. She keeps her right hand hard round the bottle, in case Morrison tries to deviate from the ordained path.

Gradually, the blue ahead is softened by a lightness to the right, as the Sun rises and ascends into a low ceiling of cloud.

"Oh, no — that's all we need," mumbles Morrison, looking into the rear-view mirror: the only thing he's said since she'd ordered him into the car, threatening to cut his balls off if he didn't bow to the commands of Great Mother Ocean. He had looked at her with a mixture of disbelief and fear, from his one good eye.

Blue is all around. The much desired goal, full ahead; the emerging, faltering day; and the racing pulses of blue astern, gaining fast, sirens wailing. Morrison floors it hard — kickdown spurs the convertible into renewed life. He grimaces, and new blood emerges through a warped and broken smile, joining the congealed runnels already running down his chin, the rents in his cheeks. First light exposes Morrison's face as a mass of hideous, open wounds. Alex shifts, slightly, whispers into the heaving carnage, her lips and his almost meeting:

"If you stop now, I'll kill you." She jabs the jagged shards into his groin. Just enough to spur him on. Morrison takes the hint.

They race into the dawn.

Fitch is amazing. She's been up all night, helping to coordinate the emergency response, as well as keeping tabs on the manhunt. At 2 a.m. she had urged Sheepwool to go home and get some sleep, that she'd collect her at dawn, or if anything happened. All Sheepwool can now remember is wafting through the rain-dark streets, the wind still gusting after the storm, as if she were no more than thistledown.

It seems no more than a moment before she hears Fitch's voice, tetchy at the entry phone. Sheepwool is, frankly, amazed to find herself face down on the bed, still fully dressed. She can't even remember coming home. She rights herself in the gray north light of early morning and makes her way to the hall. Her clothes feel like they have been worn for far too long, and by someone else.

"Fitch?" She is pleased Fitch can't see her rearranging her disordered skirt and blouse.

"Ma'am? Get down here as quick as you can. They are coming."

The car leaves the last of the dilapidated fencing behind. Once more she and Fitch are in that great prairie void, after the last of the outlying barns of Deringland disappears over the southern horizon, but just before the Deringland Light appears to the north, the mass of the Institute behind it. The Sun, behind them and to their right, speaks through ragged clouds, barring Fitch's face with light as she surges through the gears.

But — that's odd. There are two Suns in the dawn, not one. The second comes from the north.

"Fitch…"

"Ma'am?"

"Look…"

And as they crest the ridge, the virginal whiteness of the Deringland Light rises against a backdrop of sudden flame.

They cannot get as far as the Institute. The track to the Institute and the car park is crowded with ambulances, fire tenders, paramedics, policemen and people wandering lost, confused and in their nightclothes, carrying anything they could pick up. Others had arrived from elsewhere — to help, to see what they could salvage, or just to watch. Fitch pulls the car to a halt in a mass of people, and immediately disappears into the throng to coordinate the rescue, shepherding people from danger. Sheepwool is slower to get out of the car, but as she does so, and stands tall, she peers over the crowd to see Maureen Boynton in a pink quilted dressing gown, being comforted by Lars Johansson in a trench coat, pyjamas and slippers; Janice Squearn and Frankie Honiton, obviously just arrived, with blankets and provisions; Garrison Williams, looking lost and alone.

All are dwarfed by the shattered hulk behind. The storm has, finally undermined the cliff on which the Institute was built. The roof collapsed sometime during the night, smashing through three floors, splintering rafters, cases of specimens. When a severed gas main and a mass of loose, live wires plunged through the spirit store, the building went up like a torch. It is not yet known if anyone has died — the building is now well alight and too dangerous to approach. The scene is punctuated by burning refuse, loose tiles, broken glass, a snowstorm of charred paper. It looks like a battlefield.

Even now, as she watches, enormous slabs of wall shear away from the great edifice like slices of a great cake, tumbling seawards, breaking up as they go—peeling back layer upon layer of the vast building, each one applied in a vain attempt to cover up the architectural sins of the previous generation, yet succeeding only in magnifying them.

The fires within illuminate the great Georgian windows bored so carelessly into the Jacobean folly. Great sloughs of Edwardian plasterwork crumble away from the walls, exposing timbers which take up the spreading flames.

Holding on to the car, Sheepwool imagines all that is going down with the building. The ranks upon ranks of stuffed heads; the strange idols; the cases of preserved marine life; the priceless library; the irreplaceable collections of HMS *Spaniel*; the statue of Sir Frideric.

But most of all, Pickled Lily. Yes, her, most of all.

And then a cry goes out. "Stand back! Everybody back! Clear the road!"

No sooner have the last of the stragglers scurried to safety in the long grass, or in the lighthouse compound, than the roar is heard of an engine in extremis, and shooting into view comes a bright red convertible, top down, trailed by two Police Range Rovers, blaring alarum and flooding the blasted landscape with blue and orange light.

The red car is spattered with mud, exhaust-pipe trailing gray smoke, and at the wheel a man with a face out of a nightmare.

Policemen whisper urgently into radio sets. "It's them—stop them!" But they cannot. No-one can.

Morrison is close to exhaustion. His one good eye is bloodied so that all he can see is stained with red. His muscles ache. He has lost so much blood in this last, frenetic chase that he thinks he is probably stuck to the seat and wouldn't be able to get out, even had he wanted to. The wind stings his broken face. It's painful, but he's convinced that it's the only thing keeping him awake and alive. The Police are behind him—they've trailed him, practically all the way from Thetford.

But he's beaten them.

The Board of MagusPharm is probably not far behind the Boys in

Blue. But they don't want him. And he doesn't want them. Not really. Ain't gonna work for MagusPharm no more.

He's beaten them, too.

If he could grin, he would. But it hurts even to think of trying.

But what's this? A welcome-home committee? People are too kind. And, fuck me, look at the Institute. Morrison, old son, you got out just in time. He was always the great expert at the time-honoured rat-deserts-sinking-ship routine.

For the first time in more than fifty miles he takes his foot off the accelerator and the car starts to slow down. The orange and blue lights in the rear view mirror come closer.

And then he remembers why he is driving so fast, and must drive still faster. All it takes is the stab of a broken bottle in the groin and the ferocious whisper in his ear—"*Drive*, you *filth*. By the Great Mother Ocean—*drive!*"

Morrison floors it. What the hell.

Sheepwool is rooted to the spot as the drama unfolds. The car—bearing Morrison and Alex, she is sure—first slows down. And then Alex, her hair blowing like pennants in the breeze, says something to Morrison, who looks in a very bad way indeed, and the car speeds up again, heading straight into the ruined building at what must be at least seventy or eighty miles an hour. It jounces and jolts through the gaps in the front wall where the gravel of the car park gives almost directly into the scorched parquet of the exhibition hall, and hits an obstacle—no, it can't be—it's Pickled Lily's case, going off like a bomb with all that alcohol. Tipping forwards and over the case, the car catches fire and explodes.

The two bodies are thrown clear.

One careens through the air, and—oh no—it comes closer and closer—to her—blotting out the Sun, blotting out the sky—and lands with a sickening crunch about ten yards from where she is standing. Paramedics rush up. Pierced with many wounds, clothes in tatters, face ruined, Morrison lies dead, with one eye open, and the remains of a smile that seems to go all the way round his head.

The other body is launched over the sea like a bloody comet.

The host who was once a woman named Alex Beach comes home. Her body falls into the healing waves from far above, and dives far beneath, clothed in a mass of bubbles. The sea is rich and blue. It is where she belongs.

Out of a still deeper blue they rush up to welcome her, to pull her to greater and more wonderful depths. Far out to sea, the host who was once a woman named Alex Beach looks down to see her body unfurl like the petals of the most beautiful flower. Her red juice, her red nectar, gushes out like a cloud, and with it, her baby.

Look at your baby, Alex. Look at it.

The little thing has the loveliest face, with blue-gray eyes and dark hair. Her tail is blue and shines in the faint sparkles of Sun from far above. One flick of it, and she has gone, without once looking back, vanished into the indigo dark.

The host who was once a woman named Alex Beach looks at her baby, and smiles. One last time.

Evening falls. Detective Sergeant Elaine Fitch comes home. She locks the car and trudges up the garden path. But the door is open wide and a welcoming light floods out—or it would do, were her husband not standing in the way. Warm arms surround her, tightly. A big, rough hand cradles the back of her head, running through her curls. She buries her face in his big chest and sobs: "what a day", she says, "what a *day*."

Jason Fitch, Builder, says nothing. He doesn't have to. Elaine (here she's just 'Elaine', or 'Pet', or 'Mum', but never 'Fitch') knows that the kids will all be in bed (except Dean, who's probably playing on his computer). And she can smell something good from the kitchen.

Winter falls once again on Deringland, but the residents take it with a degree of stoicism, for they know that Spring will follow, eventually. And things are valued here which take their time.

Looking towards the cliffs from the French windows of his bungalow, Superintendant Methwold muses on his future. He muses largely to himself, even though he has company, in the form of Detective Inspector Sheepwool. Percy. He hopes (and this is something he really *does* keep to himself) that she might stay the night.

Maybe. One day.

But Percy has wounds that are slow to heal. He knows that as well as anyone. That's why she came up here in the first place. And he has wounds, too. Slow to heal. Those cliffs. Maybe he'll move. That nice barn conversion in Tribenham is still for sale, knockdown price. He wonders why it hasn't shifted.

Bit big for him though, on his own.

Anyway, she's told him she doesn't really like pink chrysanthemums very much. That's a habit he'll have to break. And, oh yes, talking to himself. That's another one. Perhaps, he thinks more positively, he should seek to reacquire an old habit he thought was once lost, without hope of rescue.

He might be able to forgive the sea, but he will never be able to forget.

Author's Note

After I'd drafted what eventually became *The Sigil*, my agent, Jill Grinberg tactfully suggested I try something else instead. "A puzzle book," she suggested. "Like Dan Brown, only better." So germinated *By The Sea*.

To help plot and pacing, I wrote it in weekly parts. This worked for Dickens and Trollope, I thought, so it might work for me. My friend Jenny Rohn agreed to serialise it on her website LabLit.com, where it appeared in 2007. Having episodes published before you've finished a story — or even before you're halfway through — is a marvelous spur to writing. The book was written almost entirely on trains, between Norwich and London, in the Spring and Summer of 2007.

After it was finished, Jill Grinberg allowed me to self-publish it as a way of testing the market. I thank Jill for her forbearance; Jenny for agreeing to do this; for her expert editing; and for featuring the book in her occasional LabLit book club at the Royal Institution in London.

Much later, Andrew Burt at ReAnimus Press kindly took on a much-edited version of *The Sigil*, as well as picking up the lapsed paperback rights of *The Science of Middle-earth* and now *By The Sea*. After seven years in the Looking-Glass World of self-publishing, *By The Sea* has finally reached the shore.

In the writing, apart from the people above mentioned, I thank Jeff Crook — purveyor of Southern Gothic — for publishing a vignette of what became the chapter 'Pickled Lily' in his flash-fiction series *Postcards From Hell*; Karl Ziemelis, for thinking up the mermaid's name; and my daughter Phoebe, whose penchant for unusual names produced 'Sheepwool' and 'The Dazed Haddock'.

I'd also like to thank the small but select group of readers who took a chance on *By The Sea* in its self-published guise, were kind enough to tell their friends, and post favorable notices on Amazon and

Goodreads. Brian Clegg, John Gribbin, Jessica Goldfinch and Sarah Potter are perhaps the first among equals here—there are quite a few more among the Drunken Beagles, an online literary circle, from whose warm encouragement I have benefited. Thank you all.

The town of Deringland is very loosely based on Cromer, the small town in Norfolk which I have called home since 2006. Cromer is very much nicer than Deringland, and much less spooky. Needless to say none of the characters in the book are intended to resemble any persons living, dead, undead, fossilized, pickled, embalmed, dismembered, reanimated or merely asleep. Except for the mermaids, of course. They're entirely real.

An Interview with the Author

Mermaids, museums and murder are just some of the ingredients in Henry Gee's gothic horror crime novel *By The Sea* — a book that has earned him a decent number of five-star ratings on Amazon and Goodreads. He really knows how to paint a vivid canvas with words and, personally, I loved everything about his novel: its characters, setting, fast-paced plot, mystery, and suspense. Henry and I chatted about his book and how he came to write it. His answers to my questions make fascinating reading, which is why this post is longer than my usual…

Sarah Potter: In five sentences or less, how would you describe your novel *By the Sea*?

Henry Gee: Following horrific bereavement, Detective Inspector Persephone Sheepwool of the Met flees London for the quiet seaside town of Deringland, on the remote North Norfolk coast. But when the bodies start falling at the shadowy Lowdley-Purslane Institute, whose inhabitants are dedicated to finding the secrets of the Sea, Sheepwool finds that horror has a way of catching up with her. Even with the practically minded Detective Constable Elaine Fitch to help, Sheepwool finds that some secrets just don't stay unburied. That's three!

SP: For any reader of *By the Sea*, it is obvious that you have a scientific background. Do you agree with the conventional wisdom that fiction authors should write about what they know?

HG: Up to a point. I think it's important to get details right, inasmuch as one can, especially where they are important to the story. If you can't have the details, you have to employ a judicious vagueness.

For example, the novel is set up as a detective story, at least to start with, but I know nothing at all about how the police do their jobs. And although I am a scientist by training, I know rather little about the details of molecular biology—I was a palaeontologist, a botherer of bones. This aspect, though, allowed me to get a good feel for museums. I've always been fond of the more old-fashioned kind of museum, the kind that grew out of the 'cabinet of curiosities' of eccentric Regency or Victorian gentlemen. Museums whose collections are haphazard, with all kinds of objects of uncertain provenance mixed up together, to create unusual, almost surreal juxtapositions. I've haunted such museums since my childhood—the first museum I ever visited, as a very small child, was the Horniman in South London, which is still very much like that. During my years as a graduate student I visited strange and wonderful museums up and down the country in which you might find all kinds of things in odd corners, casually stuffed onto shelves or propping the doors open. Efforts to modernise such museums, make them more 'relevant', almost never work. Parts of the Lowdley-Purslane Institute are modelled after at least one real museum. No, I'm not telling you which one. But most of it was dreamed up anew, presumably from a multitude of influences each too small to isolate. I have recurring dreams about large, labyrinthine and rather spooky buildings.

SP: As a paleontologist, evolutionary biologist, senior editor of the scientific journal, Nature, and author of numerous science books that sometimes challenge the status quo, do you feel that when writing fiction the onus is upon you to be extra meticulous about facts, as well as maintaining an internal logic to your story?

HG: Yes. And then again, no. What I have found about science is that the more you find out, the less you know. Everything I've written, whether fiction or nonfiction, seems infused with the idea that science is not about knowledge and facts, but ignorance and doubt. If this sounds surprising, consider the day-to-day routine of my day job as an editor at Nature, which is to read scientific papers sent from all over the globe describing new knowledge, some of it surprising, bizarre, even horrifying. And because Nature is one of the most visible and highly read journals in the world, scientists want to send their best and most surprising research there. So, every day, I am forced to confront the very edge of the clifftop of knowledge and look over the edge. I am very lucky. Very few people get to do this. I reject nine out of ten scientific manuscripts that hit my desk. As a consequence I probably know more surprising secrets than the average spy. A very small amount of this ends up as public knowledge, written about in newspapers, even less gets discussed on TV. So, where most people see what seem to be irrefutable facts, I see a thin varnish covering an abyss of doubt, ignorance … and possibility.

As for internal logic — yes, that has to be maintained, not so much as a matter of scientific credibility but for the necessary suspension of disbelief all readers require. Even if many elements in the story are fantastic, they still have to hang together. For example, I spent quite a lot of time working out the complex semi-parasitic life-cycle of mermaids, making sure that it remained consistent despite the twists and turns of the plot.

SP: By the Sea crosses the genres of mystery, crime, horror, fantasy, and gothic fiction. Is this why you chose to self-publish this novel rather than submit to traditional publishers, who are forever mindful of books fitting neatly into a category? Do you believe that traditional publishers might one day force themselves out of business by sticking to such narrow criteria?

HG: As with all such things, the novel grew out of a rather disparate set of circumstances. I'd been a professional writer for about 15 years when I realised that I could hardly call myself a writer unless I had at least tried some fiction. So I sat down and wrote a huge SF novel. I wrote 125,000 words in three months. During this adrenaline rush I'd be up until 3 some nights and still go to work on a high. Finishing it was exhilarating. Of course, I thought it was wonderful, but like most novice novelists, I failed to realise that it was just the first draft, and would take a lot of hard work before it could be let out of doors on its own.

My agent tactfully suggested I shelve it and instead try what she called a 'puzzle' book, using my scientific knowledge and love of arcane riddles. "Like Dan Brown, only better," she said. That's when *By The Sea* was born. The experience of writing my embryonic SF novel showed that I was fine at characterisation, action and dialogue, but needed to work on pace and plotting. So I asked my friend Jennifer L.

Rohn—a working scientist and published novelist—if I could write it for her LabLit website (www.lablit.com) as a weekly serial. After all, I said to myself, if it worked for novelists such as Dickens and Trollope, it might work for me. It would help me keep the pacing even and the plot tight. Jenny kindly agreed, and I delivered the book to her chapter by chapter. Although I was usually a few chapters ahead of publication, the beginning of the novel was appearing online before I had finished writing it. It helps that Jenny is a terrific editor as well as a writer, so the book got tighter still before it hit the screens. If that wasn't enough, Jenny runs an occasional science-in-literature book group at the Royal Institution and By The Sea was the featured book for one of the meetings.

After the serial finished, I delivered it to my agent, but I think she found it a bit weird—as you say, somewhat of a genre-bender. So she agreed that I could self-publish it. You can get it as a print-on-demand paperback (on Lulu) as well as for Kindle. To be fair it hasn't sold many copies—I've given many more away than I have sold—but that's fine. Obviously, I'd love it to be a bestseller, but the people who've read it seem to like it, on the whole, and if it weren't for self-publication it wouldn't have seen the light of day.

There was a happy ending for my SF novel, too. Every so often I'd take it out of the bottom drawer and play with it. It turned from a single long novel into a trilogy, and after some years it was in a pretty decent state. Andrew Burt, a fan who'd seen and liked the draft when I'd loaded it up on his free fiction website, turned up years later as a small-press publisher in his own right. Andrew asked me if it was still available, so that's published too, as *The Sigil*. Like *By The Sea*, there's a lot of science (archaeology this time) and its confrontation with the unknown. Also, like *By The Sea*, the main protagonist is female.

SP: Pickled Lily, the mermaid, is of pivotal importance in your novel, as are some of the hybrid Victorian curiosities housed at the Institute. In amuses me, that in your work as a scientist, you have openly rejected the "aquatic ape theory of evolution", and yet choose to write about marine-animal/human hybrids in your fiction. Are you just letting down your hair here and having a bit of fun, or do you think that something genuinely scientific lies behind the legend of mermaids?

HG: The mermaids are there purely for fun — they are not meant to be taken seriously in the 'real' world outside the novel. However, as you'll have guessed, there's a certain ambiguity about all the stuffed mermaids we meet. Some are obviously very bad fakes. Others look disarmingly real. I don't want to give anything away, but that ambiguity is a key part of the big reveal — an ambiguity that acts as a focus, for me, for the whole novel, and for the pursuit of science as a whole. Scientists can only ever look at one tiny piece of reality, and even then under very carefully controlled conditions. What they think they have found, as a result of their experiments, might not say anything much at all about the vastness of the unknown.

SP: Your central bad guy, Morrison, who's in charge of the Institute, is obnoxious and driven to the point of derangement. He selects the beautiful Dr Alex Beach as his researcher, to then use as a sex toy with which to satiate his lust. His chauvinism, control freakery, and violence towards her is something to behold. Often, authors construct their fictional characters from people they've come across in real life: they get away with this by constructing a composite character based on several people rather than one. Does chauvinism still exist in the scientific establishment, and is Morrison purely a creature of your imagination, or an extreme pastiche of people you've met? (No names requested, of course.)

HG: After I drafted the novel which eventually became *The Sigil*, one of the comments I got was that all my characters were too 'nice'. That's why, when I started to plot *By The Sea*, I decided to create an out-and-out villain, and Morrison was the result. Yes, he is a creature of my imagination, but based, to begin with, on the 'suits' — the kinds of the people you only ever see in boardrooms, or on trains speaking far too loudly on their mobile phones and reeking of cologne, and who talk entirely in bullshit bingo — forever running things up the flagpole, thinking outside the box, pushing the envelope and so on. I have resolved never to use the word 'hate' about anyone or anything, because real life rarely admits of such absolutes, but I really, really, detest people like that. So, yes, Morrison is, as you put it, an extreme pastiche of people like that.

However, I'm sorry to say that such chauvinism is very much alive and well in the scientific establishment. The tales female scientists, colleagues and friends have told me about the behaviour of some people, especially at conferences, beggars belief. Morrison takes that behaviour to a violent extreme—but the more I learn, perhaps his behaviour isn't as extreme as one might imagine. Morrison's internal monologue, for example, is relentlessly sexist.

But even Morrison has a crumb of goodness and reasonableness. He is indeed charged with the impossible job of saving the collections in the Institute. And one might imagine that when he started his scientific career, his principles were as idealistic as those of any young scientist. I do not wish to exonerate him, but he's a prisoner of his circumstances as much as Alex Beach or Inspector Sheepwool.

SP: It's almost a tradition in thrillers to have an evil corporation or company behind the scenes controlling events for the worse. In *By the Sea*, you have Magus Pharm who are out to trawl the sea for new drug discoveries. And Dr Beach is at the Institute to investigate a "small and utterly obscure group of microscopic marine worms called carnostomids". As a scientist, do you believe that our oceans contain all manner of yet undiscovered cures for our illnesses? What are your views on marine conservation versus technological and scientific progress?

HG: The Earth has far more ocean than land, and there are parts of the ocean floor we know less well than the surface of Mars. There are sea creatures that can do amazing things, such as distil the metals nickel and vanadium from seawater. It's a fair bet that there'll be some that contain useful natural products. And if history is any guide, there'll be people sufficiently unscrupulous to exploit such things for profit and damn the consequences. Carnostomids, though, are precisely as fictional as mermaids.

SP: You've expressed an interest in resurrecting your female detectives, DI Sheepwool and DS Fitch for a possible sequel to *By the Sea*. Would you say these are your two favourite characters in the novel? If so, as you were writing, did you feel as though you were primarily writing a detective story?

HG: Elaine Fitch is definitely my favourite character—she's the only one who's normal. The name 'Sheepwool' came from my elder daughter, who has a knack for coming up with bizarre names. She expressed a desire for a story featuring an Inspector Sheepwool, so the character was born. She also came up with the name of the pub, the Dazed Haddock—complete with the pub sign. I haven't allowed my daughters to read *By The Sea* though, for obvious reasons.

I modelled Sheepwool explicitly on Colin Dexter's Inspector Morse and Sergeant Lewis. Like Morse, Sheepwool has a troubled past, and she's knowledgeable about an aspect of the arts. For Morse it's opera, with Sheepwool it's surrealist art. Like Lewis, Fitch is the down-to-earth one, the one who likes to drive, and have egg and chips for tea. With that in mind, I wanted to write a detective novel. It didn't quite turn out like that, though. Whatever By The Sea is, it's not a conventional police procedural. I don't think my mind is sufficiently tidy, disciplined or devious for the kind of plotting that such things require. I'm not at all sure that Sheepwool and Fitch actually solve the case, or even if there is a case to solve. They think they are, but they are dancing in the thin skin of what they think is knowledge that's stretched thin across an abyss of the unknown. So it's less a detective story than a gothic novel that happens to have detectives in it.

SP: For me, your attention to detail and setting are first-rate. Your writing is evocative, lyrical, and vivid. As I read *By the Sea*, I could almost smell the Norfolk air, feel the mist creeping around me, taste the salt, hear the waves, and see the greyness punctuated only occasionally by specks of sunlight. Many modern novels shy away from too much description or use of rich language. Do you see this insistence upon simple language as a dumbing down to suit lazy readers?

HG: Thank you—you are very kind. I wanted to do for Cromer, the place I call home, what Stephen King did for Maine. It's very easy for me to overdo the flowery language, but I felt that was an essential part of the gothic feel of the novel. I remember going to see Kenneth Branagh's *Frankenstein* at the cinema. Apart from one scene, it was a very faithful evocation of Mary Shelley's novel, but almost everyone I knew who'd seen it complained that it was over the top, and far too long. But that's the whole point, I'd say—it's gothic. It's supposed to be over the top and far too long. They just didn't get it. Now, writing concisely is a virtue, and when I advise scientists on how to write well, I always point them to Jane Austen, who was a master of subtlety and economy. Perhaps because Austen detested the gothic—witness the literary tastes of nice-but-dim Harriet Smith in Emma, and the gothic send-up that is *Northanger Abbey*—the literati have been conditioned ever since to equate gothic with trash. It's still easier to write at length than with brevity, but the trick with gothic is to keep it away from becoming either self-parody or camp.

SP: I know that you are a huge fan of JRR Tolkien, or you wouldn't be editor of *Mallorn*, the official Journal of the Tolkien Society. In what way has this great author, and others, influenced your writing? Do you read widely across all genres, or tend to stick to one or two?

HG: I admit it—I like Tolkien, though I have just stepped down from the editorship of *Mallorn* after eight years. I'm not sure how much Tolkien has influenced my writing, though. Neither am I convinced that it's always a simple thing to detect one's influences. If I'm influenced by anyone, it's the Argentine essayist Jorge Luis Borges. He had a few things to say about influence-spotting—which is the kind of nice irony Borges would have appreciated.

Interview with Sarah Potter
http://sarahpotterwrites.com/2013/11/15/interview-with-henry-gee/
Reproduced by kind permission.

About the Author

Author Photo by John Gilbey

Henry Gee was born in London in 1962. He received his B.Sc. in Zoology and Genetics from the University of Leeds, and his Ph.D. in Zoology from the University of Cambridge. Since 1987 he has been on the editorial staff of Nature, the international weekly science magazine, where he is now Senior Editor of Biological Sciences, and was the founding editor of Futures, Nature's award-winning SF column. He is the author of several works of nonfiction including The Science of Middle-earth, In Search of Deep Time and Jacob's Ladder; and two novels, The Sigil Trilogy and By The Sea. He lives in Cromer, Norfolk, England, with his family and numerous pets.

More books from Henry Gee are available at
www.ReAnimus.com/authors/henrygee

ReAnimus Press

Breathing Life into Great Books

If you enjoyed this book we hope you'll tell others or write a review! We also invite you to subscribe to our newsletter to learn about our new releases and join our affiliate program (where you earn 12% of sales you recommend) at www.ReAnimus.com.

Here are more ebooks you'll enjoy from ReAnimus Press, available from ReAnimus Press's web site, Amazon.com, bn.com, etc.:

The Sigil Trilogy (Omnibus vol.1-3), by Henry Gee

"Great stuff... everything you yearn to find in a very good contemporary SF novel. Really enjoyed it!"
--SFWA Grandmaster **Michael Moorcock**

"Brisk, funny, triumphant--and utterly compelling."
--Greg Bear

The Science of Middle Earth, by Henry Gee

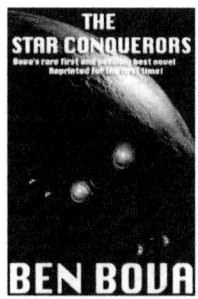

The Star Conquerors, by Ben Bova
(Standard Edition and
Special Collector's Edition)

Test of Fire, by Ben Bova

The Kinsman Saga, by Ben Bova

Shadrach in the Furnace, by Robert Silverberg

The Transcendent Man, by Jerry Sohl

Night Slaves, by Jerry Sohl

Bloom, by Wil McCarthy

The Craft of Writing Science Fiction that Sells, by Ben
Bova

Staying Alive - A Writer's Guide,
by Norman Spinrad

Space Travel — A Guide for Writers,
by Ben Bova

Side Effects, by Harvey Jacobs

American Goliath, by Harvey Jacobs

"An inspired novel" – *TIME Magazine*
"A masterpiece... year's best novel" – *Kirkus Reviews*

Check out these and many more great titles from ReAnimus Press!

Printed in Great Britain
by Amazon

86999096R00174